MW00575514

Tangled
LIKE US

KRISTA & BECCA
RITCHIE

CHARACTER LIST

Not all characters in this list will make an appearance in the book, but most will be mentioned. Ages represent the age of the character at the beginning of the book. Some characters will be older when they're introduced, depending on their birthday.

The Cobalts

Richard Connor Cobalt & Rose Calloway

Jane - 23

Charlie – 21

Beckett – 21

Eliot – 19

Tom – 18

Ben – 16

Audrey – 13

The Hales

Loren Hale & Lily Calloway

Maximoff - 23

Luna – 18

Xander – 15

Kinney – 13

The Meadows

Ryke Meadows & Daisy Calloway

Sullivan - 20

Winona – 14

The Security Team

These are the bodyguards that protect the Hales, Cobalts, and Meadows.

SECURITY FORCE OMEGA

Akara Kitsuwon (lead) - 26

Thatcher Moretti - 28

Banks Moretti - 28

Farrow Keene – 28

Oscar Oliveira - 31

Paul Donnelly – 27

Quinn Oliveira– 21

SECURITY FORCE EPSILON

Jon Sinclair (lead) - 40s

Tony Ramella - 28

O'Malley - 27

Ian Wreath - 30s

…and more

SECURITY FORCE ALPHA

Price Kepler (lead) – 40s

Bruno Bandoni - 50s

…and more

"I'm living to see a new world."

In loving memory of our beloved Grandma Lou

A NOTE FROM THE AUTHORS

The Italian used in this book is an Italian-American language developed by Italian immigrants. It is an incomplete language and uses Italian, English, or both. Different Italians speak different dialects in certain areas, and what is used in the Like Us series is prominent on the East Coast. Words may vary in pronunciation and spelling in different communities. A glossary with pronunciations for Tangled Like Us is included at the end of the book.

Tangled Like Us is the fourth book in the Like Us Series. Even though the series changes POVs throughout, to understand events that take place in the previous novels, the series should be read in its order of publication.

Tangled Like Us should be read after Alphas Like Us.

LIKE US SERIES READING ORDER

THATCHER MORETTI

First thing people know about me, I'm tall.

Second thing, I'm a twin.

Third thing, I'm a pain in your fucking ass. If you're not giving a hundred shits at rest or in high water, I will hammer you.

One further, I'll volunteer to be the bad guy if it means protecting lives and keeping minds right on the team.

But I didn't imagine I'd lose her in the process.

I stare straight ahead and breathe hot breath out of my fucking nose. *Can't think about that now.* I have a job to do.

She is my job.

And I need to unfuck this shit. I take full responsibility, and I'm going to shovel us out of the hellhole I've thrown ourselves in.

I have to.

A roaring beach bonfire lights up the sparkling night sky. The Aegean Sea calm and dark behind me, my boots sunk in damp sand on the shoreline. I stand still. Watchful.

Attentive.

Prepared for any hellfire.

This isn't my first time in Greece, and that fact sits with me for an extra beat. I grew up in a one-bedroom South Philly apartment and shared a pullout couch with my brother. In my head, there weren't many ways I'd see the world.

Eventually, Xander Hale happened. Becoming that kid's bodyguard was a bright spot in my life. Not because I could see more of the world, but because I still had a hand in protecting someone else's.

It's what fuels me.

I'm strong to protect the soft.

I've felt that, even as a fucking teenager. I read *The Iliad* in high school. Men fighting on an ancient battlefield. Facing challenges that'd test their strength of will. Embarking on harrowing adventures while serving their country.

I wanted to be a Spartan warrior.

And I grew to look like one. Broad-chested and shouldered, muscled and toned, towering and relentless at six-foot-seven. Severity within hard lines of my body and face.

No matter where my boots land, I'm meant to fight for something.

And at twenty-two, I began protecting these three famous families. Cut to six years later, and this is still where I need to be. Where I want to be. I'd put my life on the fucking line for them. It's more than a nine-to-five job, more than a career—this is a lifestyle meant for the men who aren't going to quit and take the easy fucking out.

I've kicked exits open for bodyguards who thought private security would be a straight shot to luxury. This is about keeping people safe 24-hours a day, and we're not entitled to anything. We fulfill our purpose. If we expect more, we've failed at our promise to these generous, loving families who just want to live in peace.

We should be humbled to be in Greece or wherever protecting them leads us.

Stay focused.

On her.

Jane Eleanor Cobalt.

She's sitting about twenty meters away, feet buried in the sand. Light-hearted blue eyes concentrated on one of her many brothers.

Eliot Cobalt stands near the bonfire and rehashes a story or some play. Flames lick the air, and as he gesticulates theatrically, the famous families laugh and clap.

She taps her beer bottle in applause.

I catch myself about to skim her up and down. *Don't.*

I remain stationary. I'm not supposed to be an active participant, but some surrounding bodyguards clap for Eliot. They're the ones who've grown closer to the Cobalts throughout the years.

I wouldn't place myself on that shelf.

Before transferring to Jane's detail, I was attached to the Hale family. Xander Hale had been my only other client, and even if I were better acquainted with the Cobalt Empire, I'm not interested in joking around while on-duty. If I wouldn't do it during an op, I'm not doing it on her detail.

Her safety comes first.

Jane sips a beer on the private beach, and she stays quiet while her brother quotes Shakespeare, or some other tragedy. I wouldn't know which.

I keep a close eye on Jane and her surroundings.

It's my job.

It's also my job to know her well. Like how she's been unusually quiet this summer trip, and it's my job to know that I'm to blame.

Can't worry about that now.

But I am.

Jane lets a beach blanket fall off her sunburnt shoulders, warmed near the bonfire. A pale blue tankini hugs her body.

I want to think some things I shouldn't be fucking thinking. Put in some adjectives that I shouldn't be using. All good things—*don't go there.*

Don't fucking do it.

I'm not overstepping the solid boundary.

I scan the beach with crossed arms, but eventually, my dark narrowed eyes return to Jane.

Long brunette hair frizzes around her freckled cheeks, and she smiles brightly at her brother. Applauding him again before she sticks two fingers in her mouth and whistles loudly. She's only twenty-three.

She's only twenty-three. And she's dealt with more harassment than any girl her age should—than any *person* should.

I've heard sacks of horseshit spew hatred and try to degrade her, and they actually believe they're entitled to her body and time like she's some fucking doll they can rip apart with no consequence.

`They're targets.

Men that I will fucking take out before they breathe on Jane. And after what happened with her recent friends-with-benefits, my duty to Jane is unquantifiable.

On the beach, I end up glancing back at her.

She leans some of her weight into Maximoff Hale, her best friend. He's been scanning the beaches almost as much as security. Preparing for threats like he's another bodyguard. Truth is, I'd welcome Maximoff on the team. But he can't be on it.

Not when he's a part of the famous families that we protect.

I try to scan the water, but my strict gaze drifts back to Jane, just as Maximoff wraps a strong arm around her shoulders. She whispers in his ear, a smile attached to her words.

He laughs back.

My stomach drops a bit.

For one second, I wish I could be in earshot. *Don't fucking wish that.*

Her smile seems to fade faster than usual, and slowly, her gaze begins to wander across the beach.

To the dark sea.

And then, her big blue eyes land right on me.

I blow out another rough breath through my nose. Never breaking eye contact.

Call her over.

Point-blank, I'm not sure how. This feels personal on some level, and it's against my fucking job to make a personal move. I can't interrupt her time with her family.

There are rules in security. Rules that help her just as much as they help the team, and I won't disobey them.

My jaw hardens, tendons in my arms and neck pulling taut. Muscles burning. I cement to the shoreline like the rest of the 24/7 bodyguards. Water rushes against the heels of my boots. I never shift out of my position.

Call her over, I'm still thinking.

But I'm immobile.

I can't move.

Can't disobey.

Jane quickly diverts her gaze, her neck reddened, frustration in her next hot sip of beer.

I breathe in another coarse breath.

We used to have a better working dynamic. She'd talk my ear off, and I'd listen. Now she says nothing, and I still say next-to-nothing.

Eight months.

I've been Jane's bodyguard for eight months, and I've been put on a silent treatment for almost two of those. Any other client and it wouldn't bother me, but I've grown used to Jane rambling to herself and filling the quiet.

I'm with her close to 24-hours a day. Replacing her light-as-air voice with silence has been fucking unbearable. It doesn't feel good knowing that I fucked it recently. I blew a short fuse even shorter and I made a mistake that I've never made before. *I shouldn't have punched Farrow.*

My fault.

It's all my fault.

I suddenly spot movement on my three. I glance at the shoreline.

Banks nods his chin to me.

Good timing.

Focusing on the team has always kept my mind right and off things I shouldn't be fucking contemplating.

Banks treks over to my position, boots sinking in wet sand. Carrying nothing more than a radio and a gun, both clipped to the waistband of his slacks. Sweat stains the abs and armpits of his white button-down.

I'm dressed in a black button-down. *Professional.* I'm not representing these billion-dollar families in fucking flannel. Not unless I'm off-duty. Or away from the parents.

Banks sidles next to me. He's gnawing on a toothpick like a damn llama.

My hard gaze narrows on him before I continue hawk-eyeing the beach. *Something's wrong with my brother.*

He's been trying to quit smoking for years, and the only time it looks like he's about to bite a toothpick in five halves is when he's craving nicotine.

He glances at me briefly, and then scans the darkened sea behind us. "You have any ibuprofen on you?"

My brows pull together while I survey the families. "You have a migraine?" I dig into my pocket.

"No, fortunately." He threads his arms over his chest. "This is just the kind of pain associated with me being a dumbass." His eyes flash to me. "I think I threw my back out."

I'm rigid, and concern grips my muscles. "When?" I pass him a packet of ibuprofen behind my back, as covertly as possible.

Without looking at me, he slips the medicine in his back pocket. Banks doesn't like the team knowing he's dealing with any kind of pain.

"Earlier today," he answers. "During the whole celebration." He cocks his head back to the sea. Referring to when Omega was horsing around. Shoving and tackling guys in the water. Because Farrow Keene was reinstated to the security team.

My eyes drill into pinpoints, just thinking about Farrow.

Again, shouldn't have punched him.

Can't shake that fucking truth.

I take a constricting breath, my nostrils flaring.

Banks notices, and he opens his mouth to speak—we both suddenly look to our eleven. At the sand dunes.

Three temp bodyguards are gawking directly at us. They're fresh blood. Newly-hired, just for this vacation.

Which is why their eyeballs are popping out of their faces. Staring at us like we're six-foot-seven woolly mammoths. It's not because we're tall or attractive or unshaven—or an extinct prehistoric fucking species.

It's because we're identical.

We glare head-on until they divert their gazes.

"Another day, another shitbag stares away," Banks says, sounding indifferent.

After twenty-eight years, we're both used to it.

Most of the time I forget that Banks and I look identical until someone eagle-eyes us to death, and then I remember I'm a twin.

Same DNA.

Same imposing height, large hands and feet. We've kept our hair the same for most of our time in security. Thick brown strands reach our necks, pieces tucked behind our ears. Same scruff along our jaws, same hard brown eyes.

Sturdy builds, intimidating demeanors—we share *a lot* in common, more than just physical features. We have the same interests. It's why we're both here.

But our personalities are *vastly* different. It just takes people actual effort to see that, and for some reason, most people would rather be told who's the "quiet one" and the "loud one" and the "funny one" instead of taking time to get to know us.

I don't go up to people I first meet and ask, "Are you funny?"

So after a while, I just stopped listing out our personalities, but now that we're older, we've become easier to tell apart from our features.

Banks has a fraction less muscle mass because I lift more, and my jaw is subtly more square to his narrow.

On the beach, I look at my brother, and I'm less tense. He's familiarity and comfort during rough days. No matter how bad I fuck it, he'll always be here.

I check over my shoulder, a routine sweep. "Which men need to rack out?" I ask him.

The past few days have been long and drawn out for the team with little to no sleep. Bodyguards will attempt to stay with their clients past exhaustion.

"Epsilon should be good," Banks says. "For SFO, Oscar is probably pushing twenty-hours. Farrow could be going into thirty."

Gut reaction, I glance down the shoreline and spot the bleach-white haired bodyguard, covered in skull and dagger tattoos. Farrow Redford

Keene looks between a swashbuckling pirate and a fucking guitarist in a rock band.

He's neither.

In actuality, he's a *doctor.* Now a bodyguard again. Assigned to both the med team and security team, and he's out of earshot while talking to Akara. The Omega lead is catching Farrow up on what he's missed in security.

Farrow turns his head slightly.

I scout the other side of the beach to avoid our eyes meeting. Muscles flexed, I suck in a strained breath.

Banks plants his gaze on me. "I thought you said you were snapped to?"

We always say that to one another: *you need to snap to. Can't live in the past.* He's referring to Farrow. My past mistake. My fuck-up.

What I haven't been able to mentally drop.

What I need to fix.

These men on the team are my responsibility.

My client is my life.

It's what I live by.

And you fucked it, Thatcher.

I rake my hand across my jaw. "I shouldn't have punched Farrow." I haven't said it out loud to my brother. Not until now. He's just known I've been neck-deep in regret.

He's been seeing and feeling my fucking torment the same way I can tell he's in physical pain. It's not some "psychic" connection. You just live with someone for twenty-eight years, and they're a part of you like that.

"Yeah," Banks agrees in a deep whisper. "But you're not the first guy to hit someone else on the team, and you've already paid a three-fucking-grand fine."

Doesn't matter. I rub my mouth roughly and then drop my hand.

I knew Banks would try to release me from my sins, but I don't deserve that kind of absolution.

Jane runs on loyalty and trust—like I do—and in one instant, I broke both. I compromised my ability to effectively communicate with her. Because I fucking *punched* Farrow: her best friend's boyfriend.

And it goes far beyond ruining the good thing I had working with Jane. I would've never wanted my men to do what I did.

I'm ashamed.

I don't care if I'm the third or fourth or hundredth fucking bodyguard to hit another bodyguard. I let my anger and frustration get the best of me.

I should've cooled off and kept my mouth shut.

But I was fucking fuming that day. Farrow told Omega that he decided to quit security—so he could finish his residency and become a concierge doctor—and I lost it.

I've always wanted him to choose this team first, and hearing him pick the hospital felt like a betrayal that I feared come to fruition. A betrayal not only to security but to his client.

And I reached a point where I wanted to sock Farrow hard. To provoke him, I took a personal shot and implied something about Maximoff Hale that I knew would set him off. Something I don't even *fucking* believe.

I insinuated Maximoff would sleep with any bodyguard that joined his detail.

Farrow charged. I swung.

"Thatcher." Banks bites his toothpick and sends a hard look at me that says, *don't do this to yourself.* My brother can't stare at me for more than half a second.

We're on-duty.

We need to scout our AO, and our area of operations tonight happens to be one of the most beautiful places on Earth.

I study the darkened sand fifty meters away.

Silence passes.

Until I break it.

"What I said—I can never take back," I tell my brother.

He cocks his head slightly. "Everyone knows the straight shot to Farrow is to go after his boyfriend."

I glare at the horizon. "And I'm the shitbag who took it, Banks."

He looks right at me, but I'm not turning my head. My narrowed eyes are in a vice that I can't loosen, and I don't like glaring at my brother.

That one moment has haunted me for months. I personally attacked Farrow, caused friction in SFO, and I disrespected Maximoff. A guy who's only shown a high-level of respect for every bodyguard.

Maximoff also just so happens to be Xander Hale's older brother. Xander is a kid that Banks and I spent over five years protecting together. And what Xander means to me—means to *us*…there are no words that can even encapsulate how much I feel for that kid.

I swallow a jagged rock in my raw throat. Hurting these families is gut-wrenching. And it contradicts my whole purpose.

I should've been fired.

I did try to quit.

Just as I started signing the termination papers, Akara grabbed the pen out of my fucking hand and Banks locked me in a room until I promised I'd stay on. The main reason why I'm still here is… Jane.

I didn't want to give up on her. I didn't want to quit on her.

I care too much about her well-being and safety, and she needs real stability. Placing her in the hands of a new bodyguard felt like ripping the rug from underneath her feet.

I couldn't do it.

And I know, well and fucking good, that dwelling on the past isn't going to help Jane.

"What happened, *happened*," Banks whispers, still staring at me. "But we've all got to push forward together."

I nod a few times, taking a deeper breath. "Watch the sea. I'm not the objective." We've had issues with paparazzi boating to shore this summer.

He fixes his earpiece. "You're such a fucking gabbadost'." *You're such a fucking hardhead*. His Philly lilt overpowers the Italian-American word.

I almost smile. After another quiet moment, I tell him, "I'm snapped to."

His lips slowly rise. "Right on, right on."

I instinctively pin my sights on my client.

Jane looks up from her spot near the fire, and her blue eyes crash against my brown.

My chest lifts, but I hardly fucking budge.

She tears our gazes apart and checks over her shoulder like the lights to the neighboring town are suddenly of interest.

Goddammit.

Banks scans the bonfires and then briefly glances at Jane. "She's still not talking to you?"

Affirmative. "I'm fixing it," I say stiffly.

A beat passes.

"Like now," Banks says. "You gotta stop tormenting yourself and just go."

"She's with her family, Banks." I raise the volume on my radio, but comms chatter has been nearly silent tonight. Everyone is in the same space. Not much happening.

"She's always with her family. If you don't move out, I'll push your ass in the fucking sand."

I give him a hard look. "You threw your fucking back out and you want to push me in the sand?"

He makes a move toward me, and I grab his bicep so he doesn't do anything stupid. Just then, in my peripheral, I spot Maximoff heading towards Farrow.

Leaving Jane alone. She wedges her empty bottle in the sand.

I release my hold on my brother's bicep. "I got this," I tell Banks.

He smacks the back of his hand against my chest. "Don't nuke it, man."

I nod and hike up the beach.

That phrase keeps rushing past me. Our dad would toss a football back and forth, and when Banks fumbled, our dad would just pat his shoulder and say, *Don't nuke it, kid.* It was his way of telling us to not overthink it.

Jane doesn't see me coming yet. She rises to her feet, brushes sand off her ass, and then goes to retrieve another beer. Aimed for the blue cooler near the dunes.

My stride is stringent. I pass the bonfires, heat stinging the back of my neck, and in seconds, I close in on her position.

Jane spots me, just as she crouches at the cooler and collects a beer from the melted ice. She hesitates. Frozen in place. I watch her beautiful blue eyes dart to the bonfire where her whole family congregates.

Don't use the word "beautiful".

I'm breathing hard through my nose, and I stop right in front of my client. Towering over Jane while she's squatting. She stares more curiously at me and then untwists the cap of her beer.

"Jane," I greet.

She straightens up. "Thatcher." The top of her head barely reaches my shoulders, but she lifts her chin and looks me right in the eye.

She replied to me.

Which is a good sign.

"Can we talk?" I ask, my voice gutturally deep. All the time.

She considers, silently.

I glance at her cold beer bottle. My joints lock. It strikes me that she's been drinking, and I should've factored in alcohol. *Fucking unprofessional.* "We should wait until you're sober—"

"I've only had one beer. I'm not even buzzed." Her cheeks are rosy, and she tentatively checks on the families again. Maybe even glancing at Farrow and Maximoff.

I don't follow her gaze to confirm. I'm only looking at her and the empty beach on my nine. "If now's a bad time, you can tell me, Jane." It's my job to alleviate pressure in her life. Not add to it.

Jane thinks for a moment. "We can go for a short walk, you and I." She must really want to hear what I have to say.

The private beach has been secure all day and night, so I don't need to lead the way like I would if there were crowds.

Jane is able to journey ahead, but I keep pace and flank her left side. I click my mic at my collar. "Thatcher to security, I'm Oscar Mike. Jane is going for a walk on the beach."

Jane glances curiously at me after I release my hand on the mic, but she thinks against speaking and turns her head forward.

Yeah, I need to unfuck this.

It's driving me insane.

Akara sounds in my ear. "Copy."

Keeping the team informed of changes in positions is important. Only a couple bodyguards have consistent problems with this rule.

Like Farrow. Figuring out where he's fucking off at during regular days is like playing Where's Waldo.

The more distance we add from the firelight, the more darkness descends over us. I turn my head to Jane.

She looks over at me.

We say nothing.

I'm trying not to think *anything* I shouldn't.

She focuses ahead again, and my flexed muscles contract. I keep the pace she sets. We're several meters away from her family. Tension snaking around us in thickening silence. But the rush of the sea grows louder as we leave behind the chatter.

We're alone together, but in my line of work, it's not uncommon at all that I'm alone with Jane. But it's not usually under the pretext of "can we talk?"—and I need to fucking talk.

My jaw feels wired shut.

Jane appears the furthest thing from annoyed when I'm quiet, and that *stuns* me. She just looks me over with that mounting curiosity, and she scuffs sand with her bare foot. Humidity expands the volume of her hair, and wind carries the strands.

"Can you hold this?" Jane lifts the beer up to me.

I take the bottle, and she ties her frizzing brunette hair into a low pony. We drift closer to the water. Making boot-prints and footprints in the damp sand.

I glance strongly back at Jane.

Being assertive is my natural state, and I just say it, "I want to make this right."

Finished tying her hair, her arms drop.

I hand the bottle back.

"Merci," she says, her features harder to read in the dark. "After you apologized to Farrow and Maximoff, they forgave you."

I could believe Farrow and Maximoff would give me another chance when I didn't deserve one because they're both good men. It didn't shock me, and it doesn't surprise me that Jane is still conflicted.

Her loyalties are to them. As they should be, and I hate that I've put her in a position where she felt like she had to cold-shoulder her own bodyguard.

I fix my earpiece and tuck a few strands of hair behind my ear. "I meant I want to make this right with you."

Her eyes slowly widen, and we come to a stop. "In what way?" Her shoulders curve forward, goosebumps pricking her skin. We're far from the fire now, and she didn't bring a jacket or blanket.

I unbutton my shirt.

"Oh—" Her lips part. "I can't take your shirt, Thatcher...you'll be terribly cold." Her breezy voice and distinctive way of speaking is like honey dripping down my throat.

It's my job to make her life safe.

It's *not* my job to imagine tasting her words against my tongue while I push deep inside—*don't*.

Don't.

My muscles sear as each tendon contracts.

Before I became her bodyguard, Banks warned me that being around Jane would be hard on my end. Figuratively.

And physically.

I didn't believe him. Not at the time.

I don't look away from her, and I keep unbuttoning. "I'm not cold, Jane."

A shiver snakes through her body. "Are you positive?"

"I'm positive." I reach the bottom button, a gust of air sweeping my hot skin.

She watches me take off the shirt, her gaze stroking the ridges of my abs and carved waist. Blood pumps through the veins in my cock.

Fuck.

Jane.

Not in that order. *Not in that fucking way.*

It's *not* my job to think about her in any setting outside of client-bodyguard relations.

It's *not* my job to think about what she'd taste like if I spread her legs. I have pictured it, and I'll do a hundred deadlifts as punishment for even thinking about her pussy.

Unprofessional.

Un-*fucking*-professional.

It's *not* my job to feel a fucking thing other than duty. Responsibility. Devotion—workplace devotion.

Not even as intrigue lights up her eyes.

I stay rigid.

"Before you worked in security," Jane says, "did you always gravitate towards button-downs?"

I thought she was about to say, *did you always gravitate towards me?*

That wouldn't make sense. I met Jane when I first became a bodyguard at twenty-two. She never knew me before security.

This is an easy question to answer. "Button-downs, no." I pull my arms out of the sleeves. "Before this job, I only wore them for formal events like mass, weddings, and funerals." I pass Jane my black shirt, and I take her beer, our hands brushing for a second too long.

Her neck tightens with a shallower breath, and she speaks quickly. "But security has no uniforms, except for some events. Correct?" She fits her arm through one hole.

I nod firmly. "The Tri-Force encourages bodyguards to dress professionally." *For the families.*

Jane pulls one more arm through. Stretched-out sleeves are baggy on her limbs, and my shirt hangs to her thighs. She clears her throat. "So...how are we making this right?"

We?

"Me," I correct. "I fucked this, not you."

She tilts her head like I'm revealing more of myself. Something beneath the hard exterior.

I try not to wear my guilt. That's for me to bear. "First," I say. "You should be able to speak openly with me. If you want to know how I feel about Farrow or the whole situation or anything about me, I'll tell you. I'm going to give you more transparency."

She deserves that.

"Starting when?" she wonders.

"Now."

A brighter smile pulls her freckled cheeks. "You're opening Pandora's box by giving me free reign to all questions, you know?"

I nod.

I'm not even close to afraid. But that lack of fear almost stokes *fear*. Because I must want Jane to know more about me. Under the circumstances and the rules of being her bodyguard, being too personal is wrong and feels fucking impossible.

Jane wraps her arms up in my shirt, and she puts her nose to the collar and breathes in.

I stiffen. *Don't think about her like that.*

She notices that I just noticed her sniffing my button-down. "Um… you smell wonderfully."

My dick strains against my slacks. I'm a brick wall. "Thank you."

Jane reaches for her beer that I'd been holding, and she lands on a question. "How do you feel about Farrow rejoining security? Are you upset?"

I shake my head, almost instantly. "I've always wanted him to be on the team. I voted for him to stay last December."

Back when I was a lead and the team found out Farrow had been sleeping with his client, Akara and I voted for him to keep his job.

We were two votes out of three in the Tri-Force, and majority wins.

"I remember. I thought…perhaps your feelings had changed since then, and now you wished you'd voted for him to be fired."

"No, I stand by my decision." I notice how she's straining her neck to keep eye contact with me. "You can look away if it's hurting your neck."

Jane smooths her lips together. "Um…" She blinks for a long second. "I'm quite fine…"

I can't discern much else in the dark, but I'm trying.

"Is there a second?" she asks me.

I frown. "What?"

Jane holds my gaze. "You said, 'first, you should be able to speak openly...' I wondered if you wanted to make things right some other way too."

She's perceptive. Especially when her whole attention is on you. It's like you're the center of the fucking universe.

Like now.

I'm undeservingly the focal point in her blue irises.

"Second," I tell her, "I want to make an oath with you."

Surprise catches her breath. "What kind of oath?" Her lips start to inch upward.

What I've learned about the Cobalt Empire: the family of nine loves pacts, oaths, soul-binding agreements that put loyalty and trust to the test.

"I want to make you an unbreakable promise," I tell her. "Do you do blood oaths?"

"Oh no, no blood." She smiles. "These days, we Cobalts shake on spit."

I would've even shaken on blood. *Good to go.* "I'm going to start unless you don't want me to."

She waves me forward, her face more cheerful towards me than I've seen in months. "I'm all ears."

I've never declared something like this to a woman, and it's the closest I've come to feeling like I need to drop to a fucking knee.

I grip her glittering eyes. "I'll never break your trust again," I promise, "and if I ever hurt Farrow or Maximoff, I'll quit security."

Seriousness draws her lips down. "You understand...that if you break this pact and you don't quit security, it reflects truly badly on your character and you will *never* be in my good graces again?"

The stakes have to be high for this to be meaningful, and I can't fathom hurting them or disappointing her. I won't fucking break this.

"I understand."

She tenses but then nods. "I accept the oath." Jane cups her hand below her mouth and spits on her palm, no hesitation.

I watch her for a second before I spit on my hand.

She ropes you in, Thatcher, Banks said.

I didn't believe him.

Whenever you hear about a heckler railing on Jane, you look like you want to pop them between the eyes, Banks told me. *And she's not even your client. What do you think'll happen if you actually join her detail?*

I extend my arm to Jane first.

Eight months later, I know I'm in deep, but I can control myself and my nine-inch cock.

Hell, I've held her hand before where security is concerned. To draw her away from paparazzi. To protect her from crowds.

And now to solidify a promise of trust and devotion.

It's for her safety. *Parameters still intact.*

"Bound to this oath, we shake," Jane declares, and she clasps my hand and with one strong shake, we should let go.

She holds a beat longer

I hold an extra beat longer. *Longer than I should.*

My chest tightens with a hot breath, and we both loosen our grip.

2

JANE COBALT

"*If you're just tuning in, this is 97.2 The Fix* with Cathy and Jackie, bringing you the latest trending hits and news during your morning commute."

I raise the volume of my car radio. Drowning out the honking paparazzi who are in a money-fueled cock-fight with each other behind my baby blue Volkswagen Beetle. Both sedans want to ride my bumper and snap pictures through my rear window, but only one can occupy the prime spot.

Pink cat pompoms hang from my rearview mirror and sway back and forth.

I take a quick peek at the mirror. "And the winner is a gray Toyota. Well done, sir, you have won a fabulous view of my scratched bumper."

One paparazzi cock-fight—at the very minimum—is a constant variable in the fickle equation of my life.

My clammy palms dampen the steering wheel. I'm remarkably *nervous*. Today, my great and terrible life takes a drastic turn, and I'm trying my best not to be late.

I wipe my hand on the thigh of my pastel purple jeans, and then I grab my giant 32-oz thermos in the cup holder. "Stay on Juniper and take Morris to 13th?" I ask the twenty-eight-year-old stringent, scruffy bodyguard in the passenger seat.

"You'll find more cover if you take Morris to 12th and McKean." His deep, husky voice is like wood smoke after a fire is extinguished.

I risk a glance.

Six-feet-seven-inches of raw masculinity engulfs my car. Thatcher Moretti is stoic.

Stern.

The sort of professional broodiness one would expect from a man who dedicates his whole existence to serving and protecting others. Those others just happen to be the people I love most: my only sister, my five brothers, my many cousins—all of my notoriously famous family.

He's shifted closer to the middle console for more room.

A swelter prickles my skin. There's only one inch of tense space between his bulging bicep and my arm. He feels closer, even, and he makes my Beetle look absurdly tiny.

When he was assigned to my detail, I wanted to exchange my Volkswagen to accommodate his…size, and he adamantly opposed the idea.

Thatcher surveys the Toyota behind us. Warmth from his strong build radiates against the nape of my neck. Flush ascends my chest, and he's not even touching me.

Because that'd be oh-so-inappropriate, Jane.

The oath intact, we're at a much better place than we were before Greece, but all we'll ever be is bodyguard-and-client.

Yet, it couldn't hurt to just imagine.

I sip my coffee and take another peek.

Bulked muscles stretch the sleeves of his gray button-down, fabric rolled to his forearms, and a few popped buttons show off his firm chest and natural hair.

Heat gathers between my legs.

I pulse as I picture his big arms and chest swathing me. In another life, I'd wrap myself up in the powerful heavenliness of Thatcher Moretti, like he's my warrior archangel prepared to blanket me with his twelve-foot wingspan. All before he hoists me up around—

Thatcher turns slightly. And he catches my ogling gaze.

Flush reaches my cheeks. *Merde.* "Thatcher." I've greeted him five times today already.

He crosses his arms. "Jane." His deep tone is never scolding towards me.

"You look…impressively big in my car," I confess, confronting embarrassment like blasting a slingshot at my own forehead.

I possess the unfortunate *inability* to run away from my own mortification.

Thatcher stays mostly stoic. His gaze is unflinchingly fixed on my eyes.

The way he's staring—with bold hardness—just lights my curiosity ablaze. I should definitely shut up now, but I've never been good at that. "Truly." I set my thermos in the cup holder and glance from him to the road. "You have nice muscles. Really quite nice."

I think I can live with that endnote. Treading the line carefully.

It could be much, much worse. I could've said, *Oh God, Thatcher, I'm dripping wet right now. You've soaked me like Niagara Falls. Please, please plunge your sinful tongue inside of me.*

Let me come out of this unscathed.

I look over.

Thatcher seizes my gaze. "I worked out yesterday." His nose flares some, his muscles tightening, and he uncrosses his arms, just to adjust the seat. Sliding further back so he's not crowding me.

The air strains with a hundred-and-twenty degree scorch.

I clear an aroused knot in my throat. "12ᵗʰ and McKean?"

"12ᵗʰ and McKean," he confirms, chest taut, and he rolls his sleeves higher.

I reroute my attention to the road and drive the speed limit. My approach to wild cameramen on Philly streets differs greatly from my best friend.

I avoid heavily trafficked roads. One-ways are my greatest allies, and the narrower the street, the better.

Maximoff's license will be reinstated in October. Just next month, and I'm hoping Farrow can convince him to not exceed ninety or maybe take the passenger seat. I worry about Moffy trying to outrun paparazzi, especially after the crash.

I turn onto 12th. "Merde," I curse aloud, suddenly noticing the coffee stain on my frilly white sleeve.

On this very important morning, I chose to wear a laced long-sleeve blouse, a faux fur cheetah vest, pastel jeans, ballet flats and an acorn squash-shaped purse, and the probability that I already made *Celebrity Crush's* Worst Dressed List is inevitably high.

And it's only 6 a.m.

Sometimes I believe the media relishes in putting me on blast. I could sneeze and tabloids and internet trolls would say I'm doing it wrong.

Normally, I wouldn't care about the coffee splotch, but I also don't want my appearance to read as disrespect.

I keep a hand on the wheel and lift my arm to my mouth. I bite the sleeve and try to tear the fabric off with my teeth.

Thatcher glances over with the same bold toughness.

I mumble, "This is more difficult…than it appears." *This is not working.* In my head, I succeeded gloriously all over this idea, but reality likes to slap me with failures left and right. I spit the sleeve off my tongue.

His mounting silence is like a heater in a blizzard. Comforting. And irresistible.

I look from my coffee stain to him and back to the road, spinning my wheel and turning on to McKean. I sigh. "I suppose there are worse stains like blood or jizz."

Jizz.

I talked about cum on my sleeve in front of my bodyguard.

My eyes gradually widen and widen. *So what if I did?* I tap the steering wheel, wondering what he's thinking.

I look right at him for the countless time.

He stares unblinkingly at me, and in one quick flash, he reaches over to the steering wheel and takes my wrist in his large hand. "Can I?"

"Can you…do what?" I squint at Thatcher, my pulse speeding. I have to watch the street, but as his fingers brush my sleeve, I understand. "Yes." I inhale. "Yes, you can."

Thatcher suddenly rips the frilly lace right off its seams. In one motion, it's gone.

My ovaries just exploded.

And my lips rise in a small smile. I give him my other arm. "Again, please." Our eyes meet for the shortest, most exhilarating second.

He gently cradles my other wrist, and in one strong tug, he tears off more lace.

I haven't exhaled yet.

Laughter from the radio hosts cuts the tension in two. "Cathy, that's so wrong. No one will ever be a better lead for Wolverine than Hugh Jackman. He's the OG."

"I'm going to have to disagree with you, Jackie..."

I tune out the radio. "How much time do we have?" I bang my dashboard to jostle my frozen clock. Fixing anything I break is always low priority.

Thatcher checks his wristwatch. "Seventeen minutes."

"We're dreadfully close to being late." I barely press the gas any harder. *Slow and steady, Jane.*

Thatcher straightens up. "Don't take Passyunk. Go to 19th." His Philly lilt is thicker on the street name, and I trust his advice.

I'm driving through South Philly where he grew up.

Brick row houses dart past us, along with the occasional market and deli. Hundreds of personal questions nip at me, but even with his promise of transparency, I've been very particular about what I ask my bodyguard.

Thatcher is like a sacred text. I'm tempted to rush through the pages, but something has compelled me to draw out each line, each word. Reading so slowly and carefully so as to never miss a syllable. So a single book, a single person, could last me forever.

I look over at him and settle on a question. "Do your parents still live here?"

He runs a hand across the firm line of his unshaven jaw. "Our—*my* mom." He blows out a heavy breath. "Sorry, it's a habit, always being with Banks."

I smile at the mention of his twin brother. He speaks more about Banks than anyone else in his life.

It reminds me of Charlie and Beckett. My twin brothers are extraordinarily close, but they're not identical and they didn't choose the same career path like Thatcher and Banks did.

"It's sweet," I tell him.

His brows pull hard together. One would think he's never heard that word before.

I flick my blinker and take 19th. "Does your mom live alone?" Last month, I asked if he was close to his parents. We didn't have long to chat at the time, and all he could get out was that his parents divorced when he was twelve.

Thatcher studies the traffic ahead of us. "My grandma still lives with her."

Reading into his voice is difficult. Everything sounds cut and dry and simple, and possibly that's just how it is for Thatcher. I'm used to a family that speaks in riddles and confounding subtext. If a Cobalt is blunt, usually we're blunt with added flair.

He adjusts his seat again. "My mom remarried, so her wife is with her too." He hawk-eyes the paparazzi behind us. "She's openly bi. Been that way since she was a teenager. She dated girls before she met my dad—take a right on Porter up ahead."

I nod, and my eyes flit to him. "Your dad isn't still here then?"

"No." Thatcher shakes his head. "He hasn't been in Philly for a while. He trains SEAL recruits in Coronado."

I do remember Thatcher said his dad isn't an active Navy SEAL at the moment, but he used to be.

I crane my neck to check the rearview mirror. The Toyota is encroaching my bumper. "I have to go a little faster." I press the gas and then rotate the wheel. Turning a sharp corner onto Porter.

I watch the Toyota mimic me and then slink right on up to my exhaust pipes. "Really?" I crinkle my nose at the mirror. "You're still going to ride my ass?"

Paparazzi are either about to force me to push twenty-over the speed limit or to endure a minor collision with their car.

Thatcher is already rolling down the passenger window. He sticks his head and muscular arm a little bit outside, and the more he leans, the more he lifts his ass off the seat.

My eyes dart down to his black slacks that mold his butt like perfectly rounded fruit.

"Oh my God," I breathe underneath my breath. I just checked out my bodyguard's ass. *It wouldn't be the first time.* "You're most surely going to hell, Jane," I whisper more softly to myself.

Two out of my five brothers will certainly be there, so at least I won't be alone. But knowing Tom and Eliot, those two menaces will destroy all eternal pits of fiery damnation the second they enter.

There will be no hell left for me to even occupy.

"Back up!" Thatcher waves for the car to move.

The Toyota hardly budges, and I tighten my grip on the wheel.

"BACK THE FUCK UP!" Thatcher yells in a deep, threatening voice that I've heard before. Life-or-death seriousness coats each word, and I can only imagine his features are as caustic.

The car drifts back from my Beetle, paparazzi finally granting me some breathing room.

Precisely why I prefer having a bodyguard as a co-pilot. And Thatcher, in particular. He intimidates cameramen far easier than me. Most of the paparazzi in Philly have seen me in diapers.

"You follow Jane Cobalt on Instagram, don't you, Cathy?"

My ears perk up at my name on the radio. At the same moment, Thatcher rests his ass on the seat and begins to roll up the window.

I should switch stations, but my curiosity outweighs rationality sometimes.

"You bet I do," Cathy answers. "*Jane Cobalt.* Oldest daughter of Rose and Connor Cobalt."

My lips rise. My mom is a brilliant, ball-busting woman who takes no shit from anyone, especially not from her husband. My dad acts like her rival, but they're equals in every way, shape, and form.

I love them dearly.

"Get this, Cath," Jackie says on air. "Just last night, Jane Cobalt posted on Instagram. Did you see it?"

"Let me pop it up."

Thatcher crosses his arms. Eyes narrowed on the street before veering to me. "You want me to change the channel?"

"It's okay." I frown a little. I'm perplexed, really. "I posted nothing terrible last night. Just a picture of my mom and me and a book…" *Jane Eyre*, my namesake. My voice fades as the radio host, Jackie, describes the photo.

"…and listen to this caption. Jane wrote, *spending time with these beauties.*"

I gape at the car speakers. "And what's so wrong with that?"

Jackie continues, "Jane Cobalt clearly isn't spending *enough* time with her mother because she's nowhere near the same caliber of woman as Rose Calloway."

My jaw drops further.

Thatcher is glaring at the row houses that pass us by.

"Oh, for sure," Cathy agrees. "Jane Cobalt is so ditzy in comparison. Rose Calloway is fierce and dominant. It's hard to believe Jane Cobalt is even her daughter."

My eyes flash hot at the radio. "Wow. Stomping on me just to uplift my mom." It happens too often, but when other women try to pit me against her, it hurts a little more.

The media will run bogus stories about how I'm jealous of mom's success. Celebrity news loves to define most of my female relationships in my family as catty, competitive, and *jealous.* Perpetuating an ugly stigma that we cannot work together or support one another.

I would much rather cheer in the stands and watch Sulli win an Olympic gold than *ever* hope she loses. I can't imagine rooting against people I love. It must be a lackluster truth since it's never graced a tabloid.

But the more the media compares me to my mom—just to point out my shortcomings—it does become harder to ignore my failures.

"Now that I think about it, Jackie," Cath continues on the radio, "what has Jane Cobalt even accomplished in comparison to her mom?"

Here we go.

I press my lips together. What have I done? *Not much, really.*

Jackie laughs. "She *bought* her way to Princeton with her last name and notoriety."

"I did do that," I admit aloud. Because I will never truly know if I would've been accepted to Princeton based on academics and merit alone. I'm very conscious of how much of a leg up I have in life.

"Such a shame," Cathy says. "Jane Cobalt was so intelligent in math. She could've been an engineer."

Jackie makes a disappointed noise. "Instead, she just rode the coattails of Maximoff Hale and helped his charity."

"Which Maximoff Hale was kicked out of!" Cathy exclaims with a laugh of disbelief.

"But you have to remember, Cath, his parents are addicts. The fact that Maximoff Hale has stayed sober is a real feat—"

"It is," I interject in agreement.

"—and Jane hasn't even come close to him. What is she doing with her time now? She's living off Mommy and Daddy."

Thatcher grumbles an Italian word that sounds like a curse, but I can't be certain.

Cathy snorts. "And she probably *actually* believes she's as successful as her mom."

My shoulders sink.

Of course I haven't achieved anywhere near what my mom has in her lifetime. My family is full of overachievers and goal-oriented prodigies, and as the eldest of the brood, I am pressured to live up to the Rose Calloway Cobalt ideal every day.

My mom started her fashion company when she was only fifteen. Ladies and gentlemen, let all of that sink in.

Fifteen.

I'm twenty-three and I can hardly decide which brand of toothpaste to use.

It's becoming shamefully easier to say, *I am not worthy to be a Cobalt.*

Confidence should be engrained in my DNA, but to reach into the well, I have to constantly remind myself that I am good enough.

I won't devalue her achievements just to find value in myself.

My mom is brilliant and beautiful.

And so am I. Just in my own way.

"It comes down to this. Jane Cobalt is nothing more than a conceited heiress to a billion-dollar fortune," Jackie tells the listeners. "She continues to be a disappo—"

Thatcher turns the radio off. "Fucking horseshit—sorry," he apologies quickly to me, his muscles flexed and jaw tensed.

"Are you apologizing for swearing or for cutting off the radio?" I wonder, eyeing the road.

"The radio, but if swearing offended you—"

"It doesn't offend me," I say quickly. I want him to feel comfortable being himself with me.

Thatcher holds my gaze for an extra beat and then checks his watch. "You have three minutes."

I scoot closer to the wheel. "We're on the right street," I say aloud, and I circle the block a few times just to find an open space. "Parking is horrendous."

"Up ahead," Thatcher says. "It's too small of a space. Jump the curb and park half on the sidewalk."

I don't ask if I'm allowed. I've already spotted *four* cars parked on the sidewalks here.

Zeroing in on the tight space between a hybrid and a Jeep, I reverse to parallel-park, and then I maneuver my Beetle up the curb in a diagonal. The car bounces, and I squeeze in tight. Front tire perches on the sidewalk, and my back bumper is nowhere near incoming traffic.

Looks good to me.

I park and move more quickly.

Two minutes remaining.

Thatcher and I both open our doors. Just as I gather my purse and my keys, I shuffle out of the Beetle—*no*, my ballet flat slips off and plummets to the pavement.

I hurry and shut the door, stepping barefoot on loose chunks of gravel. Crouching to retrieve my shoe. "Come here, shoe." I peer under the Beetle. "Please, *please* don't betray me."

Thatcher has already rounded my car. I sense his towering presence behind me.

Beeeeep!!

My head swerves to the road, and between Thatcher's legs, I spot a few cars honking at the Toyota which blocks traffic, unable to find a parking spot. A cameraman jumps out of the passenger seat, and the Toyota drives away.

"Jane, look here!" the cameraman shouts.

"I'm a little busy," I mutter and tune out paparazzi. I just now locate the sequined ballet flat behind the tire.

I snatch the shoe. And then I teeter to a stance and try to brush gravel off my foot. I wobble and instinctively reach for something to balance myself.

I grab on to Thatcher.

His muscular waist, specifically.

I look up at him while I slip on my shoe, and his hand hovers perilously close to my wide hips. He stares down at me, but his hard brown eyes never descend lower than my chin.

Shoe securely on, I set my foot on the ground, and I release my grip off Thatcher. "…thank you." I pat his firm chest, not just once, but *thrice*.

Before flush ascends, I spin on my heels. *I can't be late.* I walk hurriedly down the sidewalk and try to forget about patting my bodyguard.

"Jane," Thatcher calls as I take off without him.

I glance back, and Thatcher sprints towards me.

He clicks his mic at his collar and mutters something into the speaker. Instead of stopping at my side like a friend would, he passes me right on by.

Thatcher slows down a few inches out in front and walks ahead. Per the rules of being a bodyguard. He must lead his client (i.e. me) and clear a path. So I'm not too surprised.

I keep up from behind.

His rigorous commanding stride is so familiar by now. I'm terribly used to this view of Thatcher's peach-perfect ass, and I deeply, *deeply* wish I could regret how much I've stared at his butt.

I check the time on my phone.

Thirty seconds.

One block away, and we'll reach the destination. We pass more brick row houses.

A young twenty-something guy smokes on the steps of one, a skateboard on his lap. We're rapidly approaching his location.

I avoid direct eye contact, but I feel his penetrating gaze poke into me and into the trailing cameraman who snaps pictures.

"Hey!" Skateboard Smoker stands. "You're Jane Cobalt, aren't you?!"

My pulse spikes, more cautious.

Thatcher nails a warning glare at the pedestrian.

I attempt to mind my own business and keep pace.

Thatcher falls back and walks beside me, all six-feet seven-inches shielding my body completely from the onlooker. I'm a whole foot shorter than my bodyguard, and I find myself leaning closer to him than further away.

My heart rate eases, and I breathe normally.

"HEY!" Skateboard Smoker shouts while we trek past him. "HEY! Why are you walking away!! You fucking bitch! I hope your whole dumb fucking family dies!!"

From zero to one-hundred.

As expected.

I hardly flinch. Too used to these jeers and threats to take any stock in them.

Thatcher cements a narrowed eye on the Skateboard Smoker.

I'd rather not peek back and feed into the guy's hand, but I'd like to know... "Is he following us?" I whisper to Thatcher.

That will unnerve me, and I start to unzip my purse. Thatcher gifted me a new bottle of pepper spray for my 23rd birthday when he read the expired date on my last one. I also have a switchblade.

"No," Thatcher answers. "He hasn't moved from his position." He rotates a knob on his radio. "I can stay next to you until we reach the store." He adds, "If you'd feel safer."

A smile pulls at my cheeks. "I would." I nod. "Merci."

Having Thatcher this close brings a powerful comfort. A snaking tension. Even more temptation, and the greatest, most overwhelming curiosity.

My cross-body purse thunks my thigh as we round a corner, and I risk the umpteenth glance in his direction.

He simultaneously keeps track of our surroundings and looks down at me. As we drift nearer, his hand shifts towards the small of my back.

But his palm never makes contact, never touches or crosses that boundary unless safety decrees *he must*.

I wonder what his protective hands would feel like on my skin. Climbing up the slopes of my body.

Heat sears the nape of my neck again.

Come on, Jane.

No distractions. Not even of the panty-soaking hot bodyguard variety.

I have a bigger purpose today—and really, a purpose from now until forever.

Jackie and Cathy from 97.Kiss-My-Ass can delight in the fact that I am no longer aimless. I am floundering *no more*.

But I am two minutes late.

3

JANE COBALT

The cozy Philadelphia fabric shop is hidden behind an old bookstore. It seems as though only a couple shoppers are here perusing the disorderly store.

A bell dings when the door shuts softly behind Thatcher, and I peek down the sole three aisles for Vanessa.

Each shelf overflows with fabric rolls stacked upon more fabric rolls with no sense of color or texture coordination. Rolls that can't fit are propped up against the shelves, crowding the narrow aisles.

At the end of the second aisle, a Molly Ringwald lookalike speaks hastily on the phone and taps the musty carpet with her nude heel. "It shouldn't be that difficult. *Look again.*"

I recognize Vanessa instantly. We've met before, but not under the circumstance of me working for her.

"It's not there? Are you certain?" Her grip tightens on her phone.

I worry about interrupting her call. September Fashion Week has descended upon the *fashion enthusiasts* of the world. Causing stress and mayhem, and it's also why my mom is in London right now.

Hopefully Vanessa won't realize I'm late for my first day on the job.

I head down the aisle. One ballet flat in front of the other.

Confidence.

I lift my chin.

Vanessa turns her head. Catching sight of me. "Hold on, Lance." She struts quickly over to me. "Jane, *Jane*. I'm glad you've arrived." She air-kisses both of my cheeks in a perfunctory rush. "I have to leave for the offices. Just pick out four fabrics for the new Calloway Couture line. Think everyday girl, functional and classic."

Confusion parts my lips. "I was under the impression that I'd be running errands for you." Vanessa is an Assistant Designer, and I'm supposed to be *her* assistant. "If you need to fax and file or a magnificent café au lait or macchiato, I'm your girl—"

"No, no." Vanessa cups her hand over her phone's speakers. "Rose specifically said if you want to work for Calloway Couture, you're being placed above an entry-level position."

I try to smile, my cheeks tightening with false confidence.

My mom has thrown me into shark-infested waters on purpose. This is not nepotism. She's not trying to hand me a better job.

This is a slaughter. She's hoping I'll be chewed to pieces and quit when I can't hack it.

It's a clever move on her part, and I'd applaud if she were in the store.

My mom has always wanted me to choose a job that I'll enjoy. I'm aware it's far from a problem. I suspect not very many parents would push their children in the direction of "passion" over practicality, and even fewer have the billon-dollar cushion to fall back on.

I am grateful for them, for this life, and I'm trying not to take a moment for granted. And so I have to be realistic.

At the last Wednesday family dinner, I vehemently expressed that I have no one-true-passion in life. I've searched while I could, and my self-indulgent hunt is now *over*.

I'm committed to using my time wisely, and helping my family seems like the most sensible avenue. I used to work as a temporary CFO for H.M.C. Philanthropies, but ever since Moffy was ousted from the charity he built, I've refused to step through those doors.

Starting at the bottom of the fashion ladder at Calloway Couture— wherever my mom needs me—that was the plan. Instead, she's pole-vaulted me to a position I am so drastically unqualified for and one that I do *not* deserve.

I push a frizzed strand of hair out of my eyes. "Are you positive you wouldn't rather have me run errands? I could spend the day helping you—"

"No, four fabrics, cut enough for a maxi dress." She speeds through more directions and terminology that's only vaguely familiar.

Oh God.

In a brief pause, I cut in, "Vanessa—"

"Fashion is in your blood, Jane. As your mom always says, *do or die.*" She struts past me like a strong gust of wind and puts the phone back to her ear. "Lance, look again." The doorbell dings and she's gone.

In this scenario, my mom would like me to die.

To perish an ugly death on the musty carpet and then revive into the version of myself that is so hopelessly *me.*

I know who I am, but sometimes, I just don't know what I'm supposed to do.

On instinct, I unzip my acorn-squash purse. Itching to call Maximoff and ask him for advice. Two brains are better than one.

But I hesitate…

He's teaching a swim class at the aquatic center, and then he has a lunch date with Farrow. Moffy was beyond giddy about the date this morning. Even as he said Farrow was "fucking aggravating" him, he couldn't restrain a smile.

I catch myself smiling up at the fabrics. His happiness makes me extraordinarily happy.

Maximoff and Farrow have been on numerous dates before, but we all endure so many interruptions. If I can help it, I'd rather not interrupt them at all.

My best friend will be a last-resort phone call.

Do or die.

"My mom wants me to quit," I say aloud, more so to my bodyguard.

His domineering presence is my shadow. Always with me. Usually silent.

Longish hair tucked behind his ears, Thatcher is uncapping a water bottle while he blocks the entrance of the aisle. He hydrates often, and until Thatcher, I never knew the act of drinking water could look that unbelievably sexy.

His unwavering gaze stays fixed on me, and I watch him take a strong swig of water.

Ask him something.

But unearthing a question among the *thousands* of questions I have for my bodyguard will just heighten this sort of all-consuming pull. Just being alone with Thatcher is a perfect breeding ground for tension. I don't even need to plant a seed for attraction to sprout.

Ask him, Jane.

No.

I shouldn't torture myself. Not today.

So I take a breath, about to face the copious fabric rolls. Back to the task at hand. Just as I begin to turn, he speaks.

"If your mom wants you to quit, why hire you in the first place?" He slowly screws the cap onto the water bottle.

He's asking me a question. Surprise inches up my brows.

Hard lines crease his forehead, and he sets the water on a shelf. "I didn't mean to overstep—"

"You're not at all," I interject. A much larger smile tugs at the corners of my mouth. "This is the Cobalt way," I answer with pride. "It's what I know. We're given choices. Every choice has costs and benefits, and it's up to us to choose accordingly. She's made the cost of working here much higher so that I'll quit on my own terms." I tie my hair back into a low pony. "It's a mental chess game."

His gaze drops down me for one of the first times.

Ever.

As though I've just bared a new layer of myself.

Hairs prick on my arms, his roaming gaze like static electricity. Nearly compelling me forward in a dream, and I want to ask more, so many questions crowding me at once.

If you could be anywhere, would you still choose to be here?

What were you like as a teenager?

What made you join security?

What's your dirtiest, wildest fantasy?

When did you lose your virginity? Did you enjoy your first time?

Do you ever think about me? ...of course he does.

I shift my purse to my other shoulder.

He's my bodyguard. He has to think about me and my personal safety.

Perhaps he feels the same bottled-up sexual tension that writhes around, aching to be unleashed, but I wouldn't dare ask. To use his word, I'm not *overstepping*.

Thatcher suddenly diverts his gaze, his fingers to his earpiece before speaking hushed into the mic on his collar.

So I steeple my hands to my lips and stare down the disastrously enormous shelf of silks and sheer fabrics. "It's not checkmate yet," I say to myself. I'm not a sad little cub about to be eaten.

I'm a motherfucking lion.

Thatcher finishes with comms, arms crossing like usual. "You're sticking this out then?" he asks, his tone not disclosing an opinion of his own.

"I think so." I eye the fabrics. "I just hope I can figure out what fabric would work so I don't completely destroy my mom's new line. She'd do anything for me, and she'll include whatever ugly dress I construct in her collection." I take a breath. "This most definitely isn't my passion, but I don't know what I want." And I'm curious, of course, so my eyes drift to my towering bodyguard. "What do you think?"

Thatcher stands with commanding stillness. On-duty. But when I've seen him off-duty, he's just as stern. "I think you're twenty-three," he tells me. "You don't have to know exactly what you want."

I tip my head, my gaze falling in thought. Did he not know what he wanted at twenty-three? Or does he just think I'm young? But he's been going strong as a bodyguard for six years. It seems he knew what he wanted when he was my age.

"You think I'm young," I say aloud.

He hardly blinks. "I think you're twenty-three."

My pulse hops a measure. God, I'm too fond of how cut-and-dry he speaks. I say *too fond* because I shouldn't be drawn to him when he's not divulging much at all, you see. Yet, I nearly sway forward. "That, I am." I nod. "...good ole twenty-three."

Thatcher pins his gaze right onto my eyes.

I smooth my lips together, face heating as I recall the first time I met Thatcher Moretti. It was long ago, back on his official first day as a bodyguard. His client was Xander Hale, and I'd serendipitously been at the Hale house during their first interaction.

Thatcher was only twenty-two.

Good ole twenty-two.

And after he greeted me, these were the first words I ever uttered to him:

"I'm seventeen—I mean, I'm Jane.*"*

Six years later and he's still one of the few people who tongue-tie me.

But before that encounter, I have no idea what he was doing. Where he was living. What his life looked like, and this isn't the first time I've contemplated this cumbersome space of unknown time.

I can't bolt my tongue down fast enough. "What did you do before you became a bodyguard? Were you in college?"

He gives me a protective look like I'm about to step on a landmine. "No. I didn't go to college." His squared shoulders never budge out of their readiness state of being.

I nod.

Tread carefully.

"I don't mean to pry—that's a lie, I do mean to pry." I smile more at him.

I swear to all that is holy, his lips almost twitch into a tiny, fragment of a smile.

It causes me to carry onward. Like I live in a word vomitorium. "I don't know where you were between high school and joining security, and if you want me to stop talking, just tell me, because I can—"

"Jane." He breaks our eye contact, which worries me. He runs a rougher hand across his jaw and dips his head, causing a piece of brown hair to fall in his face. The strand lightly caresses his jaw before he tucks it back behind his ear.

I touch my hot cheek with a few fingers. "Really, you don't have to answer." I'm about to transition topics, but I'm stuck watching Thatcher.

He drops his arm to his side with a sort of decisiveness. As though he's certain about his next action.

I'm feverishly trying to read and understand him from four feet away.

Thatcher nods to me. "You really want to know?"

"Of course I do." I inhale a sharper breath and then lean my hip on the shelf, a lilac fabric roll poking my side.

Skin between his brows pleats, his confusion like cracking cement. "Why?"

You've always fascinated me. I open my mouth, those words trapped for a full second. I end up saying, "…I suppose those years, eighteen to twenty-two, make up who you are, and I'd like to know you better."

He seizes my gaze in a vice that I'd rather not escape. "Most people don't get this far. When I tell them I haven't gone to college, that's it. Hold on." He clicks his mic and speaks louder. "Thatcher to Omega, I don't copy. You're coming in weak." He scans the fabric store for threats while he listens.

Sometimes I envy bodyguards and their radios. To be a fly on the wall within the team. Farrow has let Moffy and me listen to comms chatter before. I thought it'd weaken my interest in security, namely Thatcher, but hearing how assertive he is just drastically increased his appeal.

He detaches the radio off his waistband, and his eyes dart to me. "Sorry, I've got to unfuck the comms."

I wave him onward. "Go ahead." While he handles security, I flag down the storeowner who passes the aisle. She's elderly and sweet enough to answer several questions I have about fabrics. After which I let her be, and now I've gained a morsel more knowledge.

More prepared. I'm veering towards sheer black fabric. Very Calloway Couture. Very *not* me.

Thatcher clips the radio back to his slacks and adjusts his earpiece.

I peek more over my shoulder. "Finished?"

Without tearing his gaze off me, he checks his holstered gun on his waistband.

In the silence, the word *finished* lingers oddly. "With comms," I add, facing him fully. "Not any other sort of finishing."

Oh my God. I'm on six months without sex, and I wonder if this is a symptom of dick starvation. It better not be because I've sworn to *never* let a man inside of me. Never again. Not after the last time.

Thatcher doesn't blink. "I know what you meant, Jane."

"Bien." I nod.

Good.

Good.

He sweeps the other end of the aisle. "About what you asked me…" His stern eyes return to my face. "If I tell you, you can't tell anyone else, not Maximoff or your brothers or sister."

Moffy is the hardest to keep a secret from. After coming home from Greece, I gushed to him about Thatcher's oath with me. I felt immensely better when Thatcher confessed that he told Banks about the oath too.

Out of everyone in my family, I'm closest to Moffy. Thinking of losing him, thinking of life without him by my side clenches my stomach and wells my eyes—because him and me, it's all I've known. Moffy is a part of me. We've shared so many experiences together. We grew older together. Only one-month apart in age.

But what Thatcher is willing to share now has nothing to do with me. It's personal and private information regarding himself, so it'll be easier to hold this secret hostage from Maximoff.

"I won't tell anyone," I promise. "Do you want to spit on it?"

Light almost reaches his eyes, but his seriousness never fissures. He shakes his head once. "I trust you." He takes a long pause and brushes his hand over his mouth. "You're going to need to tell me how you think I came into security."

He wants to see what I know first, I assume. I think back. "I heard that another bodyguard referred you and Banks to the Tri-Force, but I'm unsure who you knew from security. Ninety percent of bodyguards are hired off referrals, aren't they?"

"Most are," Thatcher says, voice deep.

"I've only just started learning more about the team this past year," I admit. "Not because I haven't been interested." I ramble on. "Security has been a fundamental part of my life since birth, but Moffy and I were always told not to worry about the details. Our parents didn't want us to stress about who's coming in and out. They'd rather we just trust in the team—and we do," I say quickly. "I still do. That hasn't changed."

Thatcher's palm pauses over his mouth. Letting very little emotion pass through his stoic features.

I'm much older now and some of the bodyguards around our age have become as close as friends. Farrow is about to become family now that he's newly-engaged to Moffy.

It's natural that I'd want to understand their world in security as much as they understand the famous parts of mine.

I keep talking. "Most bodyguards have martial arts backgrounds, from what I've seen." I motion to his chest. "Like how you're trained in boxing, and then you all met bodyguards at Akara's gym who then referred you to security."

Studio 9 Boxing & MMA Gym has even become a sort of headquarters for the security team.

Thatcher lowers his hand from his mouth. "That's only the recent wave of bodyguards."

The recent wave. "How recent?" I prop my elbow on a fabric roll, enthralled in the clearer picture. "How many waves are there?" I'm not even sure who *referred* him yet, and I already have a million more inquiries.

I wonder if he can tell how badly I want to explore all of him.

Thatcher touches his earpiece. "It's—sorry." He expels a rougher breath, apologizing for having to deal with malfunctioning comms. While he fiddles with the radio, he continues talking. "Guys come in and out if it's not the right fit, but I'd say there've only been about three waves. First, when you and your siblings and cousins were born." His eyes flit up to me. "Hold on."

I watch him click his mic.

"Thatcher to SFO, am I coming in clear?" He pauses for a full two seconds. "Is no one rogering up on the fucking comms?" Another pause. He spies movement down the aisle and turns his head an inch.

A stocky gray-haired man peeks sheepishly at us and then drifts toward the register.

With my elbow perched on a fabric roll, I rest my chin on my knuckles. "I'm guessing the second wave of bodyguards were the ones who spent my preteen and teenage years with me?"

Thatcher nods. "Back then, all the new hires were military, so the background of security became nearly one-hundred percent *military*."

My lips part. "No martial arts at all?" I thought there'd be *some* at least. It seems like most bodyguards are martial arts now.

"Not until Akara." Thatcher studies our surroundings before eyeing me. "The makeup of security today is about half military, half martial arts." He messes with a knob on his radio but keeps sight of everything, even me. "Akara drew in the most recent wave of men. Boxers, MMA fighters. You've been around a lot of them just on SFO. There's the Oliveira brothers, Farrow, Donnelly."

"You?" I question because he hasn't lumped himself in that category.

He's quiet.

"I'm confused." I tilt my head and frown. "I thought Akara joined the security team before you and Banks. So he'd have to usher you two in like the other boxers. I assume…" *I'm wrong.* I can see clearly that I'm wrong.

His brown eyes are narrowed at me like he's staring straight at the blazing sun and refuses to look away from the scorching heat. "Akara did join security first. About a year and a half before Banks and me. But he didn't give us a referral. No one at the gym did."

My mind races, and I make sense of his words quickly. "You must've known an older bodyguard. From the first or second wave?"

"Second," he says. "Bruno Bandoni recommended us to the Tri-Force."

Uncle Loren's current bodyguard. Moffy even had Bruno on his detail for a short period this year.

"We'd known Bruno since we were kids," Thatcher explains. "He served with our dad."

Of course. "Bruno was in the Navy too."

Thatcher leaves his radio alone to focus entirely on me. "All the current military bodyguards are Navy…" He rakes a hand through his hair. "Except two bodyguards. But no one has a fucking clue that we served."

My mouth keeps dropping. "Wait…are you saying you and Banks are…" I frown deeper. "Your background isn't in martial arts?"

"I box." He nods to me. "But Banks and I learned to box in the military. You asked what I was doing when I was eighteen to twenty-two. I was in the Marines, Jane."

I shift my weight in shock and *whack* a fabric roll with my elbow. "Fuck," I curse and hold my throbbing funny bone.

I freeze as the old wooden shelf lets out a long, threatening creak and sways unnaturally. "Do not fall." I brace my hands at the shelf.

Thatcher is suddenly a foot away. Right beside me.

I look up as he stabilizes the shelf high above my head, his large hand on top of the dusty surface. Just like that, the creaking wood goes silent, and now we're much, *much* closer.

His arm nearly brushes my shoulder, and his utility boot is only six or so inches from my ballet flat. He's a size 15 shoe. An unhelpful fact that I learned after my big mouth asked.

Thatcher stares down at me, and I can hear my shallow breath in the quiet.

He's a Marine.

I sweep him like I'm seeing more. "Why...?" I breathe. "Why keep your military service a secret from other bodyguards?"

Thatcher rubs his tense jawline. "If we told the whole team, they'd start asking why we chose the Marine Corps over the fucking Navy when our dad is a SEAL." He pauses. "And I can't get into it." His jaw muscle contracts, his eyes brutally narrowed like he's seared them looking into the sun. He turns his head from me, more so to fix his radio again.

I understand the rawness of painful moments that, without realizing, soon become painful pasts. Most of the time too sore to touch or talk about.

In the last year, I've barely been able to speak about the HaleCocest rumor or Nate, my horrible friends-with-benefits who is a fuck-buddy no more.

"I won't pry further," I tell him.

His eyes dart to mine and stay on me for a longer beat. I wish I knew what he was thinking.

"I promise you," I say wholeheartedly. "I'm honored that you gave me this much. Truly." It's more than he's even given other bodyguards. I ask Thatcher who in the entire team knows about their military background, and he only says three names.

Bruno, Akara, and Price, the Alpha lead.

Apparently, Price found out during Thatcher's initial background check for the position, but Price agreed to keep the information private.

That's it.

Those are the only people Thatcher and Banks ever told.

He inhales stronger, and we're somehow even closer, his boot touching the tip of my shoe, my chin a breath from his chest.

"Jane," he starts, but his mouth snaps shut as my phone rings.

I rarely desert a call. I'm about to apologize, but his attention is wrenched to comms. His hand flies to his ear and his other touches the mic at his collar.

"Say again?" He speaks through comms.

I find the blue zebra-print phone case in the pit of my purse, and as soon as I look at the Caller ID, my stomach falls out of my butt.

Something horrible is happening. Because Moffy is not supposed to call me.

This morning, he made me a cup of coffee for my first day at work, and he specifically said, "I'm not texting you. I'm not calling you. Not until five p.m. when you clock out. Today is about *you*, and you'll kickass as long as you stay focused on yourself. Alright? No family distractions."

I wavered, cup of coffee between my palms. "What if someone is in trouble—"

"You'll be my first call," he assured me. "But it won't happen."

It won't happen.

I waste no time. Phone to my ear. "Moffy? What's happened?"

4

JANE COBALT

"Janie...are..." Maximoff's voice crackles with static.

My heart thrashes in my chest. "Moffy? I can't hear you."

"...I...bad."

Bad.

I cage breath and pull my phone down to check the signal. I barely even have a single bar. Back to my ear, I speak quickly. "*Moffy,* who's in trouble? Are you okay?" I wander down the aisle for better reception, and Thatcher keeps pace beside me, speaking harshly in comms.

Which can't be a coincidence.

When shit hits the proverbial fan, the security team and my family will hurtle into action in swift harmony.

"Moffy, are you still there?" I hear absolutely nothing, and then faint static. "Who's in trouble? What's happened?"

"...Janie..."

"Moffy!"

"...okay...I—" His voice cuts out.

Silence.

I inspect the phone screen. The call just dropped. "No, it's not okay," I mutter, prepared to redial, but then someone else is calling me.

My brother.

A photo of Eliot from Greece pops up on the screen: windswept brown hair, a squared jaw, and eyes that cajole and ask *do you dare?* Moffy often says that Eliot looks like Clark Kent, to which I'd agree. But my nineteen-year-old brother has always possessed the devilish charm of a comic book villain, not of Superman.

Eliot just moved to New York with our eighteen-year-old brother Tom, and both fire-obsessed menaces are now living with Charlie and Beckett in Hell's Kitchen. Moffy and I have a bet on how long until they burn down the apartment.

I said four months. He said two.

But we're both hoping for *never.*

What if they've put themselves in real trouble? But I can't think of a situation where they'd be hurt or in danger this morning. They're incredibly busy these days. Eliot just joined a new theatre company, and Tom is a lead singer in an emo-punk band. Beckett is a principal dancer of an elite ballet company, and Charlie's daily whereabouts are a mystery, even to me.

I answer, phone to my ear. "Eliot, what's happening?"

"Sister…" His deep smooth voice breaks to pieces with the spotty signal. "…fucking fiend."

Eliot is often dramatic and hyperbolic, as we all can be, but hearing him call someone a "fiend" does not alleviate any sort of panic.

"I can't hear you, Eliot," I tell him. "What was that?"

Call dropped.

My sisterly dread has now shot to the moon.

I lower my phone as it rings again.

Audrey is calling, but my little sister should be in class right now. 8th grade.

I try to accept the call—*call dropped.*

"No," I breathe, clutching my phone like it's my lifeline to my family.

The name *Pippy* shows up on the screen. My youngest brother is calling me. Ben *Pirrip* Cobalt—he should be in school too. 10th grade.

Call dropped.

Charlie is suddenly ringing. My nonconformist brother is often hard to reach, but it's not uncommon for him to call during pandemonium.

My thumb taps the button. *Call dropped.*

A new name pops up on the Caller ID. *Tom.* He's typically dead asleep this early in the morning. I tap—*call dropped.*

Now Beckett is dialing.

I stare wide-eyed at the phone. Beckett is usually the last of my brothers to reach out due to his rigorous ballet schedule. The fact that he's calling now means this is a real catastrophe.

Who's in trouble?

His call drops like all the others. Every single one of my siblings just called me. Sullivan Meadows and Luna Hale, my closest female cousins, are the next two calls that drop.

I have no new texts, and I can only assume none are going through.

I have to find better reception. *Outside.* Go outside, Jane. I start to sprint down the aisle. Thatcher is already ahead of me. Leading the way.

He knows where I want to go without any doubt. He always seems to understand where I crave to be and what I need.

As I sprint, my ballet flat slips off my heel.

I stumble a little and then tear my flats off my feet. Cramming them into my purse while I rush after my bodyguard, his stride long and strict.

Thatcher glances back at me, his expression grave as he clicks his mic. "No, you're still coming in weak." We round the narrow aisle, in sight of the glass door to exit, and mayhem erupts outside.

I screech to a halt, phone ringing incessantly in my frozen fist.

Thatcher stops and checks on me again.

"JANE! JANE!" paparazzi scream over each other.

At least twelve men swarm the store's door. Lenses pressed to the glass since they're not allowed inside. Flashes ignite in furious succession.

I can't be surprised they're here. I've exited buildings with more, but these cameramen seem particularly hostile.

This won't be an easy getaway. I can't simply step outside and take a call. I'll have to rush to my car and possibly drive away first or else they'll bang on my windows. It'll be twenty minutes.

At the minimum.

Thatcher suddenly takes my hand in his, and with no hesitation or confusion, he's leading me towards the messy register. Piles of plastic binders, papers, and receipt books are strewn across an antique desk. Ms. Ramella, the wispy gray-haired storeowner, stares thunderstruck at the gathering media outside.

Thatcher shifts his grip so we're naturally clasping hands, and I feel hard calluses on his large palm. Too many conflicting emotions tumble through me.

My bodyguard has never held my hand for this long, side-by-side, and I look up at him questioningly. Curiously.

But he's already drawing my body forward.

Oh.

He just wants me to walk in front of him. So he can block the paparazzi's view of me with his build.

Right.

Once I'm out in front, he lets go of our hands. My pulse is in my throat, but I keep course, my bare feet squishing on the humid carpet. In my quick sprint, my jeans slid down a little, and I pull the waistband back up over my love handles.

Much more comfortable.

Thatcher Moretti is an iron shield behind me, and I sense his palm hovering beside my hip.

I breathe harder and check my phone. Moffy is calling again, but like the others, it drops within seconds.

I peek back at Thatcher while I approach the register. "Should we find a rear exit?"

He nods once, but then his eyes form lethal pinpoints. He speaks into comms. "Say again?" He listens.

"Youse twos." Ms. Ramella is waving us over to the antique desk, her Philly lilt thick on top of a few Italian words.

I'm only fluent in English and French, but I've heard Thatcher speak some Italian, mostly words mixed with English, and I'm not so sure his dialect is formal or a language one would learn in Italy or through textbooks.

I reach the register with Thatcher. "I'm so sorry, Ms. Ramella," I apologize for the noise outside. "The cameras and all the men will be gone as soon as I am."

She's stabbing a glare above me.

At Thatcher.

I crane my neck over my shoulder, and his serious eyes meet mine for half a second, almost softening in an apology.

He knows her.

Thatcher lifts the mic to his lips, tendons strained in his rigid shoulders. "Solid copy."

I turn more into his chest and adjust my slipping purse strap, cross-body again. "You know what's happened?" I whisper.

"Bits and pieces." He hasn't acknowledged the storeowner yet. His hand brushes against my hip, and his muscles contract. *Accidental.* That was an accidental touch. "It has nothing to do with your family."

Yet, his squared shoulders never loosen, and his lethal glare grows darker.

"It's about me," I realize.

He barely nods, not too elated, but I'm relaxing for the first time.

"I can handle a *me* crisis," I say confidently. "This is good news."

His grip strengthens on my gaze, looking dreadfully more protective of me than before. "We need to find a magazine."

I must be in the tabloids.

What gossip column has spread rumors about me this time? Nothing can be worse than the HaleCocest rumor that is now buried and gone, but it rocked and rattled my friendship with Moffy more than anything ever had before.

Nearly a year later since that awful day, we're at a much better place.

"So it's just tabloid gossip?" I ask Thatcher.

"No. I don't think it is."

I frown.

What could it be then?

If he knew the details, I think he'd share them, but he said he's only receiving fragments over comms. He must be piecing the information together.

Maybe this mysterious news has reached the internet. We both check our phones for cell service.

None for me.

Thatcher shakes his head and slips his phone in his pocket.

"Ms. Ramella." I spin toward the cluttered desk. "You wouldn't happen to have an entertainment magazine with you? Like *Star, Us Weekly, Celebrity Crush?*"

"I don't read any of that." She's still drilling a ginormous crater into Thatcher's forehead.

Thatcher finally settles his gaze on Ms. Ramella. "Michelina—"

"You come into my store and you don't even say a hello?" She throws up her frail, age-spotted hands at Thatcher. "And then you bring all this…" She spouts off another Italian word, her pointer finger jabbing toward the glass entrance where cameramen scream my name. "What's wrong with youse? *Ha?*"

Thatcher hardly bats an eye. He stays behind me, but with his height, he's able to stretch over to the elderly storeowner. "I'll make sure they clear out when we leave. It's nice to see you." He cups her face tenderly and kisses her cheek in greeting. "You look good."

I glance keenly from her to him, him to her. I'm seeing much more of Thatcher today than I would've ever expected.

She huffs but simmers down a great deal, and then she taps his jaw twice in affection. "Don't be a…" The Italian word may as well be redacted for me.

I can't be sure what she called him.

Ms. Ramella tries to lower her voice, but she's still very audible. "You take care of that famous girl, you hear? What's her name?"

"Jane," Thatcher says, nearly cradling the one syllable like he's protecting all four letters from harm.

My lips ache to rise. *Why do I love that so much?*

Ms. Ramella seems to know more about Thatcher working in security than she knows about my famous family. Which is terribly sweet.

"Are you related?" I ask while she's eyeing me.

"No." She points to him. "I play pinochle and Canasta with his grandma on Thursdays, and my grandson is the boys' age."

The boys. She must be referring to Banks, too.

Thatcher talks more urgently to Ms. Ramella, and after a short exchange, she hands him this morning's paper.

He eagle-eyes the rowdy paparazzi and then looks down at me. "Let's go in the back. It'll be more private."

"Why the newspaper?" I ask before we move a foot.

"The team is now telling me it's in *The Philadelphia Chronicle.*"

I used to read that newspaper when I was a little girl. My mom would pass me the business and finance section whenever I asked for them.

But I'm at a loss now. Why would I be mentioned in a reputable newspaper that *rarely* prints salacious gossip about my family?

"You don't know what it is?" I ask my bodyguard.

He shakes his head. "Not yet."

5

 **THATCHER MORETTI**

Fucking comms.

Bad signal—it's frustrating, but after I get word that this situation revolves around Jane, most of my irritation goes up in flames. Leaving my purpose clear.

Focused.

Protecting her is all that fucking matters.

At the back of Michelina's store, I lead Jane to a small, enclosed area where fabric swatches are staple-gunned in chaotic array to the wall. Supplies like scissors and rulers are packed in cardboard boxes on utility shelves—*shelves* that Banks and I helped put together for Michelina years ago.

It's not every week or even every year that my childhood collides with work. On the ride here, I'd been hoping that Michelina would be absent. Home picking parsley from her pots or stuck watching morning game shows.

Not because I wouldn't want Jane to meet my grandma's friend (I shouldn't want that)—but because when I'm on-duty, I need to be *on-duty*.

Family and family friends—they'd rather I switch that off and act like I'm on a fucking weekend stroll sipping boxed Chardonnay.

But being vigilant is usually my default setting, no matter what, and Jane's life is too important to me to be anything less than what I know and who I am.

Muffled voices crack in my eardrum. Comms chatter is close to fully down, but I received enough intel to figure out the rest on our own.

After she skims our new surroundings, Jane perches her hands on her hips. Blue eyes fixed on me with a poised determination. Like she's ready to help a fighter pilot navigate air space in combat.

I love that—*don't fucking go there, Thatcher.* I have a job to do. My cock needs to stand the fuck down.

Neither of us shifts our gazes.

Jane asks, "Is there anything I can do?"

Protocol: *do not engage your client in a crisis.* It could inflict unnecessary stress on them. For Xander Hale, the protocol is applicable. But pushing Jane out of these conflicts has always made her more anxious.

I edge closer. "You know how to read these?"

"I do. There should be a table of contents in the front." She glances quickly at me. "Have you read a newspaper before?"

I stand right beside Jane. "I never read through one." I pause and decide to add, "My grandma reads them all the time and she'll line drawers with old newspapers. I just use them to clean grill grates."

She smiles at that image, for some reason. I think I'm a pretty plain person. Too quiet, too serious, I've been told. But she appreciates even the simplest things I say.

I lower the newspaper to her height. Careful not to touch my body to any part of her body, the space between us like a tense void, and I fan out the paper with strict hands.

She skims the inked words. "The entertainment section begins on page thirty."

"We're not looking for that section from what I heard." A sharp electronic frequency from the comms suddenly nails my ear. I breathe in. Angry bands of my muscles tighten, but I can't recoil. I stay fixed in place.

Fixed on this mission.

I hold her gaze. "We're looking for an ad."

Her brows jump. "An ad?"

"I don't know what kind," I explain. "All I could hear was that there's an ad in a newspaper. It might not even be in this one."

She nods and then peers closer, practically tucked to my side. My muscles tighten while I resist an impulse to place my hand on the small of her back.

Jane points a finger to the table of contents. "Ads should all be in this section. The classifieds."

Page 52.

Good to go. I flip pages while I hold the paper between us.

One more page.

I turn the last one—and the advertisement is impossible to miss.

Jane freezes, wide-eyed at the paper, and my harsh gaze narrows on the typed headline and full-page ad below.

MODERN DAY CINDERELLA: JANE ELEANOR COBALT IS LOOKING FOR HER PRINCE CHARMING.

Are you single and searching for love? Are you a gentleman ready to spend your life with a studious young woman? Jane Cobalt, daughter of Rose Calloway Cobalt & Richard Connor Cobalt, is seeking a man who is...

1. **Formally educated:** college degree required, masters or doctorate preferred, bonus points if Ivy League.

2. **Property owner:** a man who bought his own place is sexy.

3. **Businessman:** can be a hobby or profession, bonus points if finance is involved.

4. **Financially set:** a six-figure salary minimum, and don't leave her with the bill, even if she's worth more than you.

5. Must own a 2nd mode of transportation, other than a car: yacht, private jet, helicopter, etc. Motorcycle does not count, sorry boys!

If you meet these five requirements, please contact 215-555-4908 or janecobaltcinderella@gmail.com. A resume and photo are required before the selection process begins.

Whatever deluded jackass wrote this pile of shit—they just put Jane in real danger, and instantly, I want to shield her from all of it. This ad won't go unnoticed. I've been a bodyguard long enough to know this'll attract a certain kind of man.

My eyes flash hot like missile strikes at the newspaper, blood boiling. I'm not letting anyone near Jane.

She expels a breath. "The initial shock is starting to wear off." Leaning closer, she rereads the ad with a methodical expression.

I look her over in another critical sweep. She's my first concern.

First priority.

And she's been through enough hellfire to be numb to a ton of fucked-up things. More than imaginable. I'm not surprised she's taking an analytical approach right now.

I lower my voice. "The team and I will deal with this. The Tri-Force should already be involving lawyers." When I used to be the lead of Epsilon, I had to handle those details, and I would've already had legal on call.

"Thank you," she says, almost in a whisper. "The paparazzi's enthusiasm outside is making more sense now." Her brows bunch, confused about something.

The team actively tries to stay ahead of the media, but no one tipped us off about the ad. Now that it's in print, I home in on a bigger security issue: *who's behind this bullshit?*

"Is that phone number familiar to you?" I ask Jane.

"Not at all."

I study the number. "It's a Philly area code."

"It is," she agrees, and then takes a brief pause. "Thatcher, this is a full-page ad. It must've cost…a great amount of money." Her eyes flit to me with intel that I need. Jane Cobalt is smart as all hell, and the whole world knows that fact.

But I'm fortunate enough that I get to see all of who she is on a daily basis.

I process what she's telling me, and my jaw hardens. "Whoever made the ad has money to burn."

"Precisely." She squints at the paper. "That picture they printed is from my Instagram." Her fingertip brushes the photo. "They retouched my hair and face."

I grip the newspaper with two hands and lift it higher. Inspecting the headshot of Jane where she's smiling mid-laugh and wearing a turtleneck.

All the normally frizzed strands of her hair are erased, and her freckles are gone.

The fucking jackass who did this—they shrunk her nose and moved her eyes closer together. Naturally, one of her blue eyes is round, the other oval, and they're the same size in this picture. Her features more symmetrical and even.

I'm going to fucking kill him.

"It's so odd," Jane mutters. "You'd think if this were an elaborate prank—'make Jane Cobalt look like a snobby heiress with shallow taste'—that they'd choose an unflattering photo, not *Photoshop* me to look prettier."

"You're prettier without it," I say without thinking. *Goddammit.* It's too late, and I'm not about to retract what I believe and form a fucking lie. I glance down at her.

Shock slowly breaks apart her lips.

Because I rarely word vomit anything. Anger makes me say what I shouldn't say, and right now, I'm pissed at an unknown jackass who's fucking with Jane. *My client*, I remind myself.

Shouldn't be thinking about her as anything else.

My stance is stern. Hopefully this just blows in a more appropriate direction. *Hopefully it doesn't*—yeah, that devil on my shoulder can take a fucking hike to hell.

Jane presses her lips together, suppressing a bright smile. "If you're just trying to make me feel better, I'm okay, really. I don't need reassurance."

"I know you don't," I say seriously. She rarely ever looks for it. "I didn't say it with any motive." *It just slipped.*

Her smile dimples her cheeks, more flushed. She tries to focus on the ad. "Regardless of…that… these Photoshop alterations make me fit with media and societal standards of beauty, so whoever is behind the ad must've wanted me to look prettier to the public."

I drop the newspaper back down to her height. "Could be created by a fan who wants to see you fall in love." My harsh gaze scorches holes into those *five* requirements. This jackass wants Jane to be with someone in high society. A business mogul. A helicopter-riding, yacht-owning educated rich prick.

Someone so unlike me.

"It could be," she says with a nod. "That seems most likely. I could exhaustively tell the world a million times that I'm perfectly fine on my own and I'm closed for dating and sex *forever*, and they'd still pull a stunt like this."

I hear her emphasis on *forever*.

My bones are iron. I can't help but think about Nate. That fucking bastard. His name makes me want a boxing bag. Searing a red-hot aggression in my veins.

She's made a life-long vow of celibacy because of what happened with him. I'm aware. The entire security team is aware. It's a hot topic among some bodyguards that I'm trying to turn cold.

Every time I walk in on men shooting the shit about Jane and sex, I shut it down.

"Is there a back?" she asks.

I turn the page, and we both read small print at the bottom: *turn to page 23 for the accompanying article to the Cinderella ad.*

We both flip pages of the newspaper together. With a lot more urgency.

"Here it is," Jane breathes.

We stop on the article, the ink faded in some spots.

JANE COBALT IS READY FOR LOVE

A close source to America's most famous families—the Hales, Meadows, and Cobalts—has told the Chronicle that the 23-year-old American princess is "over" being single. Jane is seeking a Prince Charming to sweep her off her feet.

This comes after the announcement that her best friend & cousin, Maximoff Hale, is now engaged to his boyfriend & bodyguard, Farrow Keene. Their impending nuptials has sparked a desire in Jane to find a "special someone" to spend the rest of her life with.

It's been hard for Jane to find true companionship, and avoiding men who want her for fame or money has been difficult in the past. Our source, Jane's grandmother, confirms.

Now things are about to change as she searches for love the royal way. (See page 52 for the Cinderella ad.)

"Oh my God," Jane says in one breath, unblinking. "My grandmother has officially lost all sense of reality."

Her rich grandmother contacted the press, her rich grandmother paid for the ad, and I've been mentally calling her rich grandmother a fucking jackass.

Still applies. Maybe even more. She's about to cause her own grand-daughter bad publicity and a dangerous amount of unwanted attention.

I let go of the newspaper to touch my earpiece. Static cracking. But I'm only eyeing Jane and her surroundings.

She clutches the paper and drifts away from me while rereading the article. Hurt pinching her brows. This is a familial betrayal. It would've been better if this came from a stranger.

"Jane," I say, my voice deep. I want to do more for her, comfort her, but I'm fucking limited to the boundaries and rules of my job.

Jane meets my gaze and takes a seat on a cardboard box. "This was a calculated move on my grandmother's part." She splays the newspaper on her thighs.

"Why do you think that?" I step nearer to her spot. I've met Grandmother Calloway before, and family is family, but after Greece this summer, I think she's the worst part of the famous ones. SFO would agree.

What she said to Farrow and Maximoff on the yacht reached some ears in security. Which then reached me.

"The timing," Jane explains. "Moffy is newly engaged, and our grandmother is most likely hoping I'll marry a man before him. Just so I'll be the first down the aisle. It's a heinous power-move that deserves booing and tomato-throwing." She exhales a harsher breath, frustrated and upset. Her eyes are tightened in anger.

She almost buries her face in the newspaper.

Pained for Maximoff, mostly. I understand Jane well enough to know that this would hurt her the most. Their grandmother is stealing this once-in-a-lifetime moment from Maximoff. He's supposed to enjoy his engagement, and she's shining a spotlight on Jane instead.

I check some movement outside of this enclosure. An elderly man meanders around the aisles. *Not a threat.*

So I approach Jane in another step. I tower above my client, and then I squat down. Eye-level, I grip the paper. Gently pulling it off her face.

Her breath comes out deeper, and she searches my hard gaze.

Words aren't my strong suit, but I'm here.

Jane seems to find comfort in my eyes, her shoulders relaxing. "The scariest thing in all of this is that my grandmother *truly* believes she has the best intentions. Most everything she ever does is selfish, but she thinks she's altruistic. In her mind, this ad must be a way to help me open my heart."

My brows pull together. "That's dangerous." She didn't even ask her granddaughter for permission to run the *public* ad.

"Oui." Jane folds up the newspaper. "It's good that this is about me and not my brothers or sister. I don't have a life-long career that can be destroyed because of bad press. I don't have a passion at stake."

My expression darkens. I respect her longing to protect her family—I understand that soul-deep need. But Jane doesn't deserve to be a dartboard just because she has less going on in her life. Less to lose. She has to combat more horseshit than most already.

Her mind must be reeling. She blinks a few times. "The phone number—my grandmother must've had her assistant set up a new number and email for the ad." She frowns. "How many men do you think will respond?"

"I can't know for sure, but I'll take care of it." I straighten up to a towering stance. "I've got your six, always."

She begins to smile, inhaling a lung full, and then rises to her feet. The top of her head reaching my collarbones.

Radiating confidence, Jane pulls back her shoulders and ties her hair into a low pony. She adjusts her purse and prepares for the chaos outside of this quiet sanctuary.

I've seen her do it a million-and-one times. This isn't the first fallout. Probably won't be the last. She's living inside some type of modern age battlefield. Which is the only reason she needs a soldier.

The only reason she needs me.

"Ready?" I ask, fixing the settings on my radio.

Another breath, she nods. "Let's go."

6

 THATCHER MORETTI

Dawn.

Fog hangs low outside the two brick townhouses in Philly's Rittenhouse-Fitler Historic District, windows shrouded with mist. It's where Jane, Maximoff, and Luna live, and by extension, their bodyguards. Left is their house.

Right is ours.

Exception being Farrow Keene, who lives with his client. Security makes a lot of exceptions for Farrow, and back when I was a lead and a third of the Tri-Force, I even helped pave that path for him.

Probably more than he realizes.

I step out onto the curb of the old narrow street. Tying drawstring pants tighter on my muscular waist. I didn't have time to grab a fucking shirt.

Cover of darkness vanishes with daybreak, and the early-morning September chill bites my bare chest.

I used to always wake up at first light. Before the Marine Corps, before my parent's divorce—our dad would tell us to get our asses up and finish our chores, all before breakfast.

I didn't really mind it, and to let Banks sleep longer, I'd do some of his tasks. Folding his clothes for him. Placing shirts and pants neatly in one dresser drawer that we had to share.

Being on my feet at dawn is like any other day.

But what's congregating on the old street—it's not the type of shit that I deal with before I can even shower.

"Hey, man," a stocky redheaded temp bodyguard greets me, coming up to my side. "I can't see much, but they keep calling her name and paparazzi are waking up." I hear multiple car doors shut.

Through an eerie layer of fog, I make out maybe…three or four men leaving their respective vehicles.

One is already on the street.

"Jane! Are you home?!" a guy yells. His whining desperation sounds less like typical demands of paparazzi.

He's a fucking *suitor*.

It's a polite term that the Alpha lead wants us to use.

Ever since the Cinderella ad, a bunch of delusional fuckbags have been congregating outside the townhouse. Swarming the street, along with the media.

It's been one week since the ad's been in print, and this should've died down already. But it's gotten worse. More suitors keep coming in from out of state, staking claim to a girl that they cannot fucking have.

I fit in my earpiece. "Get eyes on the pap vans and keep watch of the left townhouse. I'll handle the other targets."

In the filmy haze, I see a line of paparazzi vehicles camped out on the street. Most are parked on the adjacent sidewalk to free the road. Some have been there long before the Cinderella ad, but the media attention has doubled. Cameramen are also waking up earlier than usual.

Several already spill out of their cars.

One cameraman is squatting on the sidewalk, positioning the lens towards misted windows of Maximoff's room. Blinds and curtains shut.

Another guy sets up a tripod.

I look to the temp guard as he hesitates. "Copy?" I ask.

He frowns. "Sir, what's protocol if these targets bring Jane gifts?"

I drop my voice another octave. "Do *not* touch whatever they try to hand you. Don't accept any packages. Just tell them to fuck off without antagonizing them." I let the cord to my mic hang on my bare chest, and I hawk-eye the most vocal suitor right now.

"Thanks, sir." He exhales. "My shift is usually inactive."

I nod. Understanding.

Temp guards are on a rotation right now. Around the time Maximoff and Farrow's relationship went public, we had to hire 24-hour stationary guards outside the townhouses. Usually one man is enough at dawn.

That's drastically changed this week. And I got called out of bed to help.

Of all the properties the famous ones own, this is the most unsecure location. No gates. Too easy access for the public. Fans constantly take selfies on the stoop, and we had to disable the doorbell.

Other than the 24-hour guards, there's nothing the team can do to make it any safer. I'd build a stone fortress around the whole structure if I could, but city codes, violations, and all of that shit.

It's red fucking tape.

I glance at the temp guard. "Stay alert, watch your sector." And then I aim for the vocal suitor.

"Jane!" he wails, nearing the curb. "Jane Eleanor Cobalt!"

I approach with authority and intent.

He's older. Most of the suitors are between early-thirties and late sixties. It's disturbing, and I don't want Jane to see their faces. I don't want them to occupy space in her brain.

Clear them out.

Quick visual assessment: mid-forties, plain face, thin silver-framed glasses, jeans and scuffed white sneakers. He has a laser focus on the front door and a bouquet of red roses in hand.

"Sir." I block his path.

He skids to a stop.

"You need to back up." I point to the car I saw him get out of. "Go home." Through the fog, I notice the Florida license plate.

He stands uneasily in the middle of the street, his eyes growing behind his glasses. Staring up at me like I'm a character from *Game of Thrones*. Ready to smite him down with an axe.

Intimidation is one of the first defenses in this job. We have to scare them off, not provoke them or beat them to a bloody fucking pulp. No matter how much they antagonize and ridicule these families, people we genuinely care about.

"I just want to see Jane," the man squeaks out.

"You wanna see her?" I glower. "You can't." I hear my Philly lilt break through. Banks jokes that my accent is stronger the more pissed I get.

I don't think that's true.

He wavers, like he's considering outrunning me.

I stake him with a harsher glare. "You touch her property, and I'll escort you to your car. I'm not going to be nice about it." A threat hardens my voice.

He scuttles back, tripping over his untied shoelace. He drops the roses. "Sorr-so-sorry," he stammers, abandoning the flowers in the street and jogging to his car.

One down. Many more to go.

Comms ring in my ear. "Akara to Thatcher, what's the level of the threats?"

I stare down a white guy whose jeans are unzipped, his cagey eyes darting left and right, an envelope and box of chocolates in hand, and I click my mic. "Same as yesterday—" I almost say *over* at the tail end, and I cut myself off before I do. Military comms are much different than security's radio protocols. It was a hard transition at first.

But so was civilian life, and I jumped straight into security after my four-year tour ended.

I pick up more SFO comms chatter, and I listen while I motion to other middle-aged suitors to get the fuck out.

What I hear:

"Buncha skeevy fucks," Donnelly says, South Philly lilt thicker than mine.

Oscar sounds in. "At this rate of motherfucking deception, we're gonna need eyes on Grandmother Calloway."

"I'm sure she'd love your eyes on her, Oliveira," Farrow says next, his voice naturally rough and amusement audible.

Oscar laughs. "Maybe we should send you, Redford. You'd probably kill her before she hits ninety."

I grit my molars, forcing down the urge to tell them to shut up over comms.

Before joining Omega, I was always an *Epsilon* bodyguard. Since SFE works with minors, the differences between the two forces are night and day. SFE has more rules to protect the kids, and Omega has more freedoms working with adults.

But my biggest irritation is the radio. Omega uses comms like a gossip network or complaint hotline. It was fucking painful during the FanCon. Banks and I say that it's 104.1 Call-In-Your-Bullshit channel.

And look, I've got complaints.

A list fucking ten feet high. I'm concerned, like Oscar is, that someone in the families was able to pull this stunt. It's why we weren't tipped about the ad *before* it went into print.

I'm concerned that these fuckbags aren't going to ever get the message. Responding to that ad in the first place takes some guts, and it's been unnerving Jane all week.

But I'm not airing this shit on comms, and right now—I can't worry about any of that.

I send *seven* more suitors packing, clearing out the small crowd. Except for paparazzi. Can't do anything about that.

"Excuse me!" a suitor shouts, closer to where paparazzi are setting up tripods. He keeps his shined loafers off the curb, an inch from where I'd yell at him.

Only two strides later, I block him and scrutinize his features. Quick assessment: slicked-back dirt-brown hair, tailored suit, angular face, maybe early-thirties.

He looks like he made a wrong turn and ended up here instead of PHLX.

"You're in the wrong area, sir," I tell him. "Walnut Street is that way." I point in the direction, further in Center City where the Philly Stock Exchange is located.

He opens his mouth, but then gets distracted. He takes out his phone, screen lit with an incoming call.

I keep an eye on him but also survey the area.

Where's my guy? I quickly scan for the temp bodyguard. He's one fucking block down. Chatting with a mom and a daughter, who are probably bartering, tempting, bribing him—doing something they shouldn't—just to see the famous ones.

Come on.

He shouldn't have left his sector.

I'll deal with that later. Hand-holding temp bodyguards is routine, but this early and with Jane at the crux, I wish that the temp were Farrow right now.

"Actually"—the clean-cut guy pockets his phone—"I need to talk to Jane." He says her name like he personally knows her.

He's not the first guy to try to pull this. He won't be the last.

Jane gave me an extensive list of her known acquaintances when I first joined her detail. I have pictures. Names. I've even combed through her yearbooks multiple times in the past ten months, just to refresh my memory.

This guy is no one.

I start, "You can't see Jane—"

He steps forward to combat me.

I put out a warning hand, and he stops.

"My name is Gavin Reece."

Not familiar. "You need to keep your feet off my fucking curb," I say like a grumpy old man.

He lets out a disbelieving noise. "It's not your curb. Sidewalks are a public right-of-way, so you're blocking my access—"

"You have access right there." I extend an arm *down* the street. The law is so gray that it allows paparazzi to plant their asses in front of the townhouses. Even though homeowners own the land up to the house and to the curb.

Gavin sighs. "Look, we're off on the wrong foot here."

"I'm not debating you. I'm not your fucking transport or access to see Jane. If you want to approach her house or stand here and disturb the peace, you're going to eat asphalt."

Akara is in my ear again. "Second batch of temps should be here soon." Which means I can go take a shower.

I'm still staring this guy down, but I feel for the wire on my chest and then click my mic. "Solid copy."

Gavin reaches into his suit jacket.

I'm rigid. *Could be a gun.* Disarming hecklers is also routine. I'm not armed right now. Didn't grab my gun, barely tied my pants. Six years on the job, and I haven't had to use it that often. There aren't many situations where a gun is necessary.

He pulls out an envelope. "Jane will want to hear this. So if you can't help me contact her, then please direct me to someone who can."

My gaze is stern. *I'm not your fucking friend.* "She did three months of meet and greets. You missed your chance."

"That was before the ad."

He means before he knew what she was looking for.

Confirmed suitor.

Which means he's looking to what...date her...coerce her...fuck her? Fuck him.

Jane isn't someone you can casually call up for a quick word. This year, she ranked in the Top 20 Most Instagram Followers in the *world.* Her mom ranked at 8. Her aunts ranked at 4 and 11.

This isn't a girl you can email or DM or even cannon blast. She has the tech team, three forces of bodyguards, along with temp guards, and a wall of assistants, publicists, and managers.

He wants to meet Jane. Good luck. She's an American princess. Take a fucking number and wait forever. Because I'm never letting it happen.

She's my responsibly.

My duty.

He can go shove his dick in an exhaust pipe.

"What's in the envelope?" a cameraman asks, swinging his Canon lens to Gavin.

This prick glares back at me. "My resume." He tries to hand it to me.

I don't move. "Leave or I'll drag you off the fucking property."

"I'm not on it—"

I take one strong step towards Gavin, and he shuffles back in a hurry. "Okayokay." He raises his hands. All fake bravado.

He walks backwards to his red Bugatti. "I'm supposed to be with Jane Cobalt." He speaks into the camera. "Everything she listed in that ad, I have. Every *single* thing."

Everything in that ad—I don't have.

What does any of that matter?

My body tenses, and I study the perimeter.

I've got a job to do.

7

THATCHER MORETTI

Steam rises in security's small townhouse bathroom. Hot water soaks my hair, beads of liquid dripping off my eyelashes, and I press a firm left hand against the tiled shower wall. My right hand grips and strokes my long, hard length.

Should be taking a cold shower, but denying myself a release is a worse idea. I'm used to long-stints without sex, even before I became a bodyguard. But I can't go that long without shooting a load. On deployments, jerking off in a quiet porta shitter was the highlight of some days.

Now I've upgraded to a shower. One tall enough where I don't need to hunch.

Eyes snapped shut, I fixate on the feeling that I crave. Nerves lit, muscles contracted in searing bands—I quicken my pace. Back-and-forth friction of my hand against my throbbing cock heats up every inch of my body.

Come.

Come, already.

An aroused grunt rakes my throat, straining my neck. Jaw aching as I grit my teeth down.

My mind is blank. Just in the present. Until an image pops up in my head. In strong waves, I'm thrusting my erection between her trembling thighs.

She's clung to me on a mattress. Her legs trying to find support while I feed into her pleasure. I rock deeper inside her soaked warmth that tightens around my cock. And I watch orgasm after orgasm ripple through her body.

I see her clearly.

Brown wavy hair, frizzed pieces caressing freckled cheeks.

Long lashes that shade glimmering, overcome blue eyes.

"*Thatcher,*" she gasps.

Fuck.

Instantly, my eyes break open and I freeze. My hand is immobile on my rock-hard dick, veins pulsing with one desire.

"Get it the fuck together," I growl under my breath and slam the side of my fist at the tiled wall.

Come on. Don't go there.

Un-fucking-professional doesn't even come close to what this is. Every time I jack off, I picture my *client.* And I don't have thirty minutes to fuck around. I need a quick release, and if I keep blue-balling myself when I'm on the edge, I'm going to leave myself pent-up and agitated all day.

I have to just ride whatever comes to mind. I'll do some deadlifts later. Say a few Hail Marys. Try not to feel like shit.

But right now, I go with the moment.

Deeper breath, I kick-start the friction of my hand to cock.

And I try again.

I'm back thrusting.

Into her.

She gasps like she's melting inside hot euphoria. High-pitched, pleasured noises jolt out of her parted lips. "*Thatcher, Thatcher!*" Sweat beads around her perked nipples.

Tears squeeze out of her eyes.

Jane.

I give Jane the sex she deserves. Her orgasm arches her body up into my chest. Practically levitating her off the bed. I hold Jane in a protective grip against my build while her toes curl. I stroke the soft flesh of her inner-thigh. Down to her swelling clit.

Her eyes roll.

I kiss the tender nape of her neck.

Her head lolls back.

I fill her pussy.

I thrust.

And thrust.

And feed this unkempt hunger that I've left for dead in reality. Watching and feeling Jane come and come and *come* and *pulse* around my hardened need.

In the shower, I hit that peak and jerk forward in a powerful release. Cum washes down the drain. I draw out the climax with a few more strokes, and then a knock bangs the bathroom door.

"Thatcher!" Banks calls.

Christ.

I clean off quickly and crank off the water. It should be around oh-nine-thirty. I've been up since dawn, but the famous ones are probably waking up now. Once they leave their townhouse, we automatically go on-duty.

My brother could need to use the bathroom. Or he could be telling me he's about to head out. *Or* that I need to go. My radio is on the ledge of the sink.

I step out of the shower, the cramped bathroom only big enough for a toilet, sink, and shower stall.

Banks raps the door more aggressively. "Thatcher!"

Concern kicks my ass into gear. Forgoing the towel, which fell behind the toilet, I trek across the bathroom in a few forceful steps. Wet footprints track the floor.

Buck-ass naked, I open the door, and I instantly sidestep.

Banks barrels into the bathroom.

I shut the door behind us, and my brother aims straight for the toilet. Dropping a knee, he grips the sides of the basin.

He's nauseous.

He waits and takes a few controlled breaths.

My brows knit together. "Second one in two weeks." He hasn't had a migraine all summer, and now it's a cluster-fucking short timespan.

Banks spits roughly in the toilet. "I must just be lucky like that." He takes another measured breath.

My wet hair is dripping on my squared shoulders. Beads skidding down the ridges of my muscles, and more water pools at my feet.

I go grab my towel from behind the toilet.

About the same time, my brother eases backwards. "False alarm." He lets out a heavier breath and slumps against the shower stall. Already dressed for work in a white button-down and black slacks with a radio attached.

His slacks soak in fucking puddles that I tracked, but he's too spent to give a shit. "I'm supposed to be Oscar Mike in an hour."

I dry my hair with the towel. "Take today off."

He rubs his temple and shuts one eye. "I'm the man who *fills-in* for the men who take off."

Yeah.

Every time Farrow has to take a med call, he needs a bodyguard to fill his spot protecting Maximoff, and Banks volunteered to be that bodyguard.

Which inadvertently made him a full-time floater on the team. Whenever a 24/7 guard has a family or health emergency, Banks takes over their spot. It's not a demotion. It's the hardest job in security. Every day he gets pulled in a dozen different directions.

He says he likes the spontaneity of the position.

But Banks took this role for me.

He said I was gasoline in a bottle. I made a massive mistake when I hit Farrow, and I couldn't get out of my head. My brother wanted to be under the same roof as me again. Just so I wouldn't light myself on fire with rage and fucking regret.

"You can still take off, Banks." I dry water off my chest.

There'd be some reshuffling among the men, but we'd work it out.

Banks rests the back of his head on the shower door. "That means slamming the team with a headache which pretty much matches my headache. I'm not doin' it."

I give him a hard look and tie my towel around my waist. "How the fuck do you plan to go on-duty if you can't even keep both eyes open?"

"Easy. I plan to have both eyes open and alert by then." He tucks his hair behind his left ear, then right ear and motions to me. "I could use all you've got."

He's not asking for drugs.

Instinctively, I touch two horn pendants that lie against my sternum, and I feel along my deltoid and unclip the thin gold chain around my neck. Most of the time, I forget that I'm wearing a *cornic'*. Because I rarely take it off.

"Where are you needed?" I ask since he's leaving in an hour and he didn't say who he's filling in for.

"I'm headed to New York. Tom needs a bodyguard until tonight because…" He lifts a shoulder. "I don't know what's up with Ian." *Tom Cobalt's bodyguard.* "I don't ask. I just go."

I near him.

He holds out his hand, and I drop the necklace in his palm. He used to have a *cornic'*. Until he lost it in the Middle East.

But there are *two* pendants on my chain. "I can get you a new chain and give you the other horn—"

"No." Banks shoots me a glare like I'm out of my fucking mind. "*His* cornic' stays on your chain."

We don't mention *him* a lot—but when he gets brought up, my chest tightens.

I just nod, and I watch my brother clasp the necklace around his neck.

He wants me to do the *maliocch'* too. It helped last time I did it. But I'll need to get oil from the kitchen first.

Before I go, I grab my radio off the sink. "Whose detail did you cover yesterday?"

"Audrey, then Kinney, then back to Audrey."

That's a lot. "Three transitions in one day."

He touches the horns at his sternum. "Semper Gumby, man."

I almost smile. It means *always flexible*. Something from the Marines. It's my brother to a fucking tee. Missions get fragged, and you've got to be ready for new orders. New direction.

Always flexible.

"Oorah," I say lightly.

But I solidify. More rigid. Remembering something that I meant to tell my brother. But with the Cinderella ad at the fucking forefront—it just sat in the back of my head.

Until now.

"What is it?" Banks asks, studying my posture.

I unwrap the cord around the radio. "I told Jane that we served in the Corps."

Banks laughs hard. "No you didn't."

I look him right in the eyes. Unflinching. "I did."

His mouth downturns in thought. Not in anger.

Bottom line, Banks and I have been prepared for the whole truth to come out. Not just within the security team or the famous ones.

But the whole world.

Back in February, Security Force Omega gained some fame through a viral Hot Santa video, and we expected the press and public to find out about us being Marines.

Really, all it takes is an online search. But you have to know what you're looking for.

What ended up happening: no media or fans cared that much about SFO to dig that deep. The most Banks and I get are autographs while we're on-duty and the occasional paparazzi question about our height and being twins.

We'd built ourselves up for that impact, packed on our Kevlar and waited for the firefight, and it never even hit. I should've been relieved, but I think we both landed somewhere between frustration and discontent.

Banks stares back at me. "Did she ask why we keep it a secret?"

"Yeah." I nod. "I told her the truth: the security team would ask us why we didn't choose the Navy, and we didn't want to get into it."

We didn't want to unload our pasts on the team and deal with it again, and the real answer to that question surfaces a lot of shit.

Easiest solution was to keep our military service a secret. We never hid who we are. We use military jargon all the time, but no one questions us. They just conclude that our knowledge comes from our dad. Because we were raised by a SEAL.

Which is also true.

Just not the full story.

He rubs his eyes. "So you told her that we served, but you didn't tell her *why*. Did you tell her we're combat vets?"

"No."

"Did you tell her you were a squad leader?"

"No."

Banks scratches the scruff on his jaw. "What you're telling me then is you've given her a millimeter, and you made an *oath* with Jane to be more transparent." He lifts his shoulders in a tight shrug. "Just go the full hundred yards, Thatcher."

I want to tell her everything. Banks sees that I want to.

But I compartmentalize a lot, and ripping open taped boxes isn't natural for me. I turn on my radio. "I'll think on it."

He massages his forehead. Above his right eye. Breathing harder through his nose.

"You still want me to do the maliocch'?" I make sure before I go grab oil and matches.

He nods stiffly. "Please."

8

THATCHER MORETTI

Radio in hand, I exit the bathroom on the second-floor landing.

Left and right bedrooms belong to me and Quinn Oliveira: currently the youngest guy on the team. He's done a good job his first year on-duty.

Sometimes he can get too worked up. Especially when the girls get antagonized—but hearing a bunch of assholes rail on Jane and not being able to snap back has even been hard for me.

Floorboards creak as I head downstairs; wooden staircase is so narrow I feel like I need to turn sideways to fit. Brick walls squeezing me in on either side.

I'm not complaining.

The three-bedroom, one-bath townhouse may barely be 900 square feet, but it has a washer-dryer, working plumbing, no leaky ceilings or musty odors. Compared to where I grew up, it's the fucking Ritz.

I reach the bottom stair in the snug living room: a brick fireplace, bare mantel, a leather couch, and a high-top table with some stools. No space for much else. Guys keep it pretty clean, especially since SFO holds some meetings here.

I hear the sound of squeaking floorboards coming from the cramped kitchen. Quinn is probably awake getting chow.

I walk through the archway, mentally listing out what I need: oil, a matchbook, small bowl, a shot glass—*unholy fucking shit.*

I halt to a dead stop, towel hung low on my waist.

Jane is in my kitchen.

As in Jane Eleanor Cobalt, as in my client, as in the girl I just fantasized fucking not even thirty minutes ago.

I'm going to hell.

She's immobile, her eyes widening on me. She rarely comes into security's townhouse; it's more likely I'd be in hers.

"I, um…" She struggles for words. Fridge is open, a half-gallon of milk in her hand. "I was just…" Intrigue drops her gaze to my unshaved chest and carved muscles, the ridges of my eight-pack, and she mutters a breathy, "Oh my God."

This isn't fucking good.

I'm trying not to run my eyes over any part of her body. I'm trying not to place a single adjective against her name. She's just Jane.

Just my client. Unique in every wa—*unfuck this before you fuck it.*

"Jane." My strict voice tenses the air more. It's my normal tone. "How are you doing?"

"I'm…" She shakes cobwebs out of her head. "I've been well, just next door—which you already know…because you're off-duty." She stares unblinkingly at me, cheeks beet-red.

I keep holding her gaze, the temperature cranking up. *Fuck.*

Being off-duty shifts our dynamic into gray territory.

I'm twenty-eight. Not in a co-ed dorm, but this awkward, tension-filled run-in feels made for college. And I need to keep this professional.

I'm in a fucking towel.

Yeah, I've also been in a jockstrap in front of her before, but that was different. That was on the tour bus with SFO. Boundaries weren't this personal. This is just *me* and *her.* In a small as fuck kitchen.

I open my mouth to speak, but Jane beats me to it.

"If I would've known you were here like this…I wouldn't have…" She's tongue-tied. "I'm so, *so* sorry."

I step forward.

She startles herself at my movement, and milk slips out of her grasp.

The plastic jug crashes at her feet, and milk spills all over the floorboards, the cap coming loose.

"Merde," she curses.

We both move into action.

Jane searches drawers for a *mapeen*, and I set my radio on a counter. Holding the knot of my towel—because I'm not about to flash my client—I crouch and pick up the gallon with my other hand.

She glances quickly towards the spill, then away. "Do you…have, um…?" She shakes her head again and looks back at me.

I catch her gaze.

And we're caging breath like the air is toxic. Laced with pheromones that try to lure her and me together. To never come up for oxygen again.

With flexed muscles, I point at the cupboard below the sink. "A mapeen is in there."

She clears her throat. "Right." Fixing cat-eye sunglasses on her wavy hair, she squats to the cupboard with curiosity twinkling her gaze. "What exactly is a mapeen?"

Now I'm shaking the fucking cobwebs out of my head. "A…" What's a mapeen in English called? It's not hitting me fast. I take another beat. "…dish…towel, dish rag."

Her lips lift. "It's Italian?" She seems genuinely excited to learn this.

I screw on the cap to the half-gallon. "The only kind I know." I watch Jane open the cupboard.

Tell her more.

I stand up and add, "You can't learn it in college. Can't really write it, can't read it. It's just how we're raised to talk." I explain how I didn't even know *mapeen* wasn't English until the eighth grade.

"Is it more like a dialect?" She pushes past dish soap to find a blue mapeen.

I place the half-gallon on the counter. "Like a broken dialect, mixed with incomplete Italian, and then passed on from Italian immigrants to their children and then their children. It's a clusterfuck of a language, but it's our clusterfuck."

Jane returns to the spill. Smiling bright. "That's beautiful." Sincerity floods her voice and those words. Speaking with so much heart—there's never any question how much she means what she says.

I rake my hand through my damp hair, and then I reach out to take the mapeen from Jane.

"I have this covered. It's my mess to clean." She rolls up the purple frilly sleeves of her 50s-style blouse. "We're out of milk next door. But I already gathered all my cats for a treat and I felt like I played a horrible trick on them with empty bowls. So I thought I'd borrow a cup here."

"You can take the rest. There's still some left."

Jane squats down in a mint-green tutu, leopard-print leggings underneath, and she mops up the spill. "That's really sweet of you, but I meant to only take a little and now I've left SFO with none—" Her cat-eye sunglasses suddenly fall off her head. Splashing in milk.

I crouch down and pick up her sunglasses.

Our eyes meet for a hot beat before I stand and move to the sink. Washing them off for her under the faucet.

She stares at me, entranced. Like my silent authority is a slow-burning fuck.

My blood heats, muscles on fucking fire.

Cut the tension, Thatcher.

Don't cut a thing.

My brain is splitting in two directions, and it's killing me. I hate indecision.

"Take it." I nod to the half-gallon. "I can get more later." It's either going to her six cats or a cereal bowl, and her cats are more important than one of the guys eating Frosted Flakes.

She smiles softly up at me. "Merci." While I dry her sunglasses on the bath towel I'm wearing, she rises to her feet.

I hold the glasses out to Jane.

Our fingers brush as she reclaims them, and breath knots in my chest. I take the milk-soaked mapeen from her hand, washing and wringing it out in the sink. Constantly glancing back at Jane.

Meeting her gaze is where I want to be, but also where I shouldn't be. Not while I'm off-duty.

She places the sunglasses back on her head and grabs the half-gallon. But she hesitates to leave. Questions sparkle her eyes.

I check the oven clock.

I haven't forgotten my brother. Couldn't forget Banks if my life depended on erasing him from existence. I've been here for a few minutes tops, but it feels longer. Each second stretched taut.

I rub my hands dry on my bath towel, and her attention follows the movement and drifts on its own course to my crotch.

I'm trying not to imagine *a lot*, and as soon as she notices that I just noticed she stared at my cock—she sends me an apologetic look.

"You're fine," I confirm. She shouldn't feel bad for that. I've pictured her in more carnal positions, and I must wear some of my guilt.

"You're fine too," Jane says quickly.

"Good," I nod.

"Bien," she agrees.

We're not exhaling like we should. But I loosen my joints and open a top cabinet, seizing a shot glass. "You want to ask me something?"

"You're missing your necklace," she says in a single breath.

I didn't expect that.

My brows furrow, and I look back at Jane. I'm not sure what emotion crosses my features. But she stumbles over her next words.

"Not that I stare at your chest...all the time. Because I don't..." She pauses. "Though, it's inevitable to look at your chest. Because, you see, your chest is connected to your neck which is connected to your face..." She touches her forehead like she's burning up. "And it's in my line of sight."

I'm so close to a smile, it fucking alarms me.

Usually only Banks makes me smile.

I put the shot glass on the counter. "I gave the necklace to Banks to wear for today." I find a matchbook in the junk drawer.

She's not going to ask why. Or pry further. Because she's respectful of how far she digs, but I want to say more. I need to fucking say more.

Jane deserves the full hundred yards from me.

Not just a fucking millimeter.

"You know the horns on the necklace?" I ask.

Surprise jumps her brows. Not by what I'm asking. Just that I'm reciprocating. She can't hide this cheerful smile, and seeing her this happy makes me feel good.

Really good.

"Oui," she answers. "The horns are quite pretty."

I nod once. "It's called a cornic'—at least, that's what I know it by." *Cornic'* rhymes with *unique*. I take out a small bowl. "I was never taught the proper Italian word for it."

"It has a special meaning?" she wonders.

"Yeah." I check the matchbook to make sure there are at least three. *Four left.* "The horn is said to ward off the evil eye. It's Italian superstition tied into tradition."

She brims with intrigue. "Why would Banks need to ward off the evil eye?"

I head to the pantry. "It's said if you have a headache or migraine, then someone has put the evil eye on you." I pick olive oil off the shelf and return to the kitchen counter.

She loosely crosses her arms. "So you wear the cornic' to ward off the evil eye and then your headache just...vanishes?"

"My grandma will tell you it helps." I uncap the olive oil. "Others will say it's just superstition."

"What do you say?" she wonders, watching me measure oil into the shot glass.

I stare off for a short second. I see my chain ensnared with another chain. And I blink that flash out. Like a breeze passing by. "I like to believe in family first," I tell Jane. "And there's something about a generational tradition that seems fucking powerful to me."

She nods. "Je suis d'accord." *I agree.*

I tried to learn some French when I transferred to Jane's detail. All of the Cobalts are fluent, and protecting her is easier if I can understand *her.*

Ten months later, only simple phrases make much sense to me. I'm not that great at picking up other languages.

Jane continues on. "But in my family, there's also a thrill in irritating my dad with superstitions. As you're probably aware, along with the rest of the world, he's solely logic-based, but my mom is very much *fate*-driven. I suppose I'm somewhere in the middle."

She has a lot of love for Rose and Connor. In the public eye, her parents might as well be gods. Impossible to live up to, and I've seen that immense pressure weigh on her shoulders.

Jane peers closely at the oil and matchbook. "Is all of this to ward off the evil eye as well?"

I nod. "I do the maliocch'…which actually means *evil eye,* but it'll take the evil eye away. Which should help with my brother's headache."

Probably more than the cornic'.

She leans in closer, her shoulder a breath away from my chest. "What do you do with the oil?"

Air strains again.

I run my hand over my jaw and glance down at Jane, who lifts her chin to meet my hardening gaze.

"I can't tell you, Jane."

She nods, understanding. "Because you're my bodyguard, and I'm your client, and that'd be too much information…" Her voice fades in a shallow breath as she sees me shake my head. We're too close. My hand skims her waist, and her arm brushes my chest before she rests her knuckles to her lips.

Blood scorches my veins, and my cock throbs.

I force myself to take a step back before our legs touch. "Because it's a secret. I can't even tell Banks how to do it." I hold the knot of my towel. Secured.

Boundary intact.

She tucks a flyaway hair behind her ear like we just fucked on the counter. "So…how come you know how to do the maliocch' but your brother doesn't?"

It takes me a minute to explain how in my family, you can only learn the maliocch' at midnight on Christmas Eve. *Superstition and tradition.* My grandma taught me. Banks used to fall asleep by that time as a kid. As an adult, he just forgets. Drinks too much spiked eggnog or is working on the holiday.

We talk for half a minute, and then we exit the kitchen into the living room, my supplies in hand. The half-gallon of milk in hers.

Jane drifts towards the adjoining door, next to the brick fireplace. Which leads to her townhouse. I walk back towards the narrow staircase. But we haven't broken our gazes. Not yet.

"I suppose I'll see you sometime later," she says in a soft breath.

She's only going one door away, but when Jane is at home in her townhouse—when that door shuts—we stay separated and I give her space.

Because at the end of the day, I'm not supposed to mean anything to Jane Cobalt. I shouldn't be a thought she goes to sleep to.

I'm just someone who protects her from volatile people and dangerous situations.

I expel a coarser breath through my nose. I can't move yet. "I'll be there when you call."

"Sounds perfect." She smooths her lips together.

We linger.

She motions to me. "I should let you return to your brother."

I nod.

We stay still.

"Jane." I hear deep, solid longing in my voice.

"Yes?" Her chest elevates in a bigger breath.

Goddammit. I grind my teeth. Hoping to saw-down this attraction. *She's my client.* It takes me a long second, but I get out, "Call me if you need me."

"I will." She nods, her collarbones tight.

One of us needs to move.

She's just twenty-three.

"I'll see you later," I say another goodbye.

"À la prochaine." *Until next time.*

And finally, I lift my cemented feet and move to the staircase.

9

JANE COBALT

Oh my...oh...my...oh my God.

We just shared an intimate moment in his kitchen, didn't we? Heat still ascends my breastbone to my neck to my cheeks, and my breath comes out like I've jogged five-miles around the block. In practicality, that's five-miles more than I would ever jog.

Or perhaps I'm just drawing conclusions and filling in blanks that I shouldn't.

I gently shut the adjoining door behind me, half-gallon of milk tucked to my chest.

If I remove some bias, then I'm left with facts, and those facts are that I don't need more from anyone. Not love, not sex, not anything in between, and Thatcher and I simply had a *normal*, polite conversation.

About his personal life, which he very rarely shares.

While he was in a towel—but towels are just ordinary fabrics a person uses after bathing. Towels don't have to be sensual. Not even when they're fastened to six-feet seven-inches of heaven and man.

He talked about his family traditions, then he washed my sunglasses without second thought, and did we both struggle to depart?

I touch my lips, my smile absolutely uncontrollable.

"Janie?"

"Hmm." I wake out of a Thatcher Moretti stupor much too

slowly. Just barely noticing Maximoff, who stands rigid beside the pink Victorian loveseat.

"Are you panting?"

"She's definitely breathing hard," Farrow states.

"What?" My mind snaps into clearer focus, and my face burns as I notice my audience of two men. Right where I left them.

I'd been in deep conversation with Maximoff and Farrow before I went to retrieve milk next door, and I knew they'd be here when I returned.

I just didn't expect to be *this* distracted by my bodyguard.

"No, no panting." I intake a normal breath and step away from the door. "This is my regular breathing pattern."

The living room décor is frilly and pastel due to my taste. But Moffy didn't mind that I decorated our townhouse. I brought in a rocking chair, a pink Victorian loveseat, mint-green rug, framed pictures on the fireplace mantel, and a small iron café table.

Our home smells of coffee, tea, and candles, so very unlike the cedar and musk of security's townhouse.

"You look *flushed*." Maximoff gestures to me with his Batman mug, full of steaming hot tea. He also grips a pack of pushpins.

"I am," I say in a shallow breath, "so very flushed."

I have no desire to skirt around the truth with my best friend and his fiancé when I want them involved in my life as much as I love being a part of theirs.

Really, I can't remember a time where I haven't been a part of Maximoff's life. As the firstborns of the Hales and Cobalts, we've faced the brunt of the media spotlight and harassment together since birth.

I remember a school field trip to the zoo. Paparazzi were waiting outside the gated entrance, swarming the ticket booths. Two middle-aged cameramen kept shouting at us, *"Jane! Maximoff! Have you started dating anyone yet?! Is there someone you like in school?!"*

We were only twelve.

It was our normal. One we had to accept fully or else we'd go mad with irritations.

So once we entered the zoo, Maximoff looked over at me with confidence and a smile.

I smiled brightly back, and for the very first time, I told him, "It's just you and me, old chap."

He squeezed my shoulders in a side hug.

We were one another's comfort and refuge. As teenagers, we'd deal with worse, but we had each other.

And we felt responsible for our siblings and cousins.

Maximoff very much enjoys responsibility. And I do, but to an extent. I don't prefer leading anyone anywhere. It's a terrible pressure to make decisions for large groups.

But I love holding the torch with him. Helping those behind us avoid falling into the dark underbelly of fame.

Because we knew whatever we experienced, our younger brothers, sisters, and cousins could soon experience after us. We tried to protect them from the cruelest parts of our reality. Blocking the numbers of porn producers off their phones, bartering with paparazzi so they'd leave them alone after school.

And then we'd take deep breaths. We'd hug and share secrets—late night in the Meadows treehouse, parked outside the school's football field, after his swim meets and my mathlete competitions.

It's just you and me, old chap.

And then it wasn't.

Not anymore, not entirely.

Farrow Redford Keene came into vivid focus. With a picturesque know-it-all smile, unflappable confidence, and cascade of pirate tattoos. He'd comb a hand through his dyed platinum hair, roll his eyes, wear a teasing grin, and send my best friend into a fit of agitation.

Agitation that roused attraction.

He truly had this magnetic exchange with Maximoff that no one else did, and I saw it more up-close when he became Moffy's bodyguard, and then closer, when they first dated and trusted me, out of everyone, to keep it secret.

I could've been bitter that I'd have to share Moffy, I suppose. Or

I could've been awfully afraid that Farrow would take my place in my best friend's life.

But I was cautiously optimistic instead.

Maximoff—my compassionate, stubborn, strong-willed best friend with a great aversion to big life changes—was willing to complicate his world by letting Farrow in.

I couldn't resent the person who made Maximoff laugh and groan and smile in ways I'd never seen, but I was afraid of not meshing well with Farrow.

What if we never become friends? What if we actually dislike each other over time?

At first, building a friendship together seemed so dreadfully complex, but like all things with Farrow, he made it simple. During the Camp-Away last December, he chose to sit next to me in the mess hall. I was eating alone, and he could've easily sat next to Maximoff.

He made me feel like a first thought.

He's never once made me feel like an unwanted third-wheel. He's never pushed me out. He's also gone out of his way to ensure I have plenty of time with Moffy.

Even the night of the car crash.

He's given my best friend more, and somehow, he's given me more, too. I feel as though I've gained another confidante, another ally, another defender and secret-keeper from the perils of our chaotic world.

I think Farrow is a beautiful person inside and out, and I will never desire to go backwards. To a time where he's not with us. To just me and Maximoff.

Our worlds are more full of life with him here.

And now that I've *fully* admitted to both of them that I'm indeed very, *very* flushed, I plan to clarify further. But I'm easily distracted.

This time, by my cats. Five out of six are pawing at my calves.

"I know you've been waiting, my loves. Look what I have for you." I rattle the half-gallon of milk. "Come follow." I guide them to bowls lined in front of the brick fireplace.

Toodles, a tuxedo short-hair, is far too lazy to bother and lounges apathetically on the stair.

"Janie," Maximoff says firmly. In a way that reminds me to *focus*.

I divide milk evenly between the bowls. Admittedly, I'll put myself last because I find other people far more interesting. Cats as well.

But I love how much Maximoff helps me try to concentrate on *me* for more than a fleeting moment.

"It's not a lengthy story." I cap the empty gallon while Ophelia, Carpenter, Walrus, Lady Macbeth, and Licorice eagerly lap up milk. A smile touches my lips.

I stand straighter and turn to face both men.

Maximoff has thick brown hair, forest-green eyes, and sharp features full of protectiveness and concern. We're no longer teenagers. He's twenty-three, but he often stands like he's carrying the world on his broad shoulders.

I'd be able to see the fresh puffy scar on his collarbone from his surgery—but he's dressed in a Third Eye Blind tee, one of his fiancé's shirts.

Both men already showered this morning. We all got an early start to the day after the commotion outside. Guys screaming my name at the top of their lungs. Every day it grows louder.

It's not endearing. Some of them are older than my dad.

Thank you, Grandmother.

I'm in a warped version of *Say Anything*, but without the boombox and without John Cusack as my love interest. And I may be famous, but I don't typically deal with fanatic admirers.

I have hecklers.

Men who are quick to criticize my physical appearance. I'm not pretty enough. Not busty enough. Not full-assed enough. And I have too wide of hips. Too big of a stomach.

But after much consideration, I've learned to love my body. Because it's mine and there is only one of me.

I don't have all the right curves in the right places. I am chubby. But I love my belly rolls, and I adore my love handles and my flat pancake-like ass that's dimpled with cellulite.

The more I love myself, the more I feel a warm, invisible hug wrap around my body.

Better.

I watch Farrow dip a spoon in oatmeal, but he's taken a pause. His focused brown eyes are on me.

He's dressed in his usual black V-neck tucked in black slacks with a black belt and security radio attached, and he's been sitting casually on the Victorian loveseat. One tattooed foot on the cushion, elbow to his bent knee, and he's holding an oatmeal bowl.

Farrow tilts his head. "You saw Moretti."

He's also observant and perceptive, exactly what I'd hope for in the bodyguard to my best friend.

"Wait, what?" Maximoff whips toward his one true love so quickly that he nearly sloshes hot tea on himself. "*Fuck.*"

"Careful." Farrow smiles into a bite of oatmeal.

Maximoff almost reddens, not in embarrassment.

We are all so very flushed these days.

I place the empty milk jug on the mantel and take a seat on the rocking chair. Shifting a fuzzy purple pillow out of the way.

Moffy tries to grimace and hide his attraction. "I'm always more careful than you, man."

Farrow lifts his brows at him. "Never said you weren't, wolf scout." He unravels my best friend in such small moments.

I can't help but watch with an infectious smile.

Maximoff nods a few times. "Rewind." He motions with his mug, and hot tea almost spills again.

My smile grows.

Farrow laughs hard.

"Shut up," Maximoff groans, nearing a smile. He looks over at me like *save me from my bodyguard.*

He most definitely does not want to be saved. I cross my ankles and lean forward on the rocking chair. "Tu es tellement amoureux." *You're so in love.* I grab my monstrously large mug off the coffee table.

Maximoff opens his mouth, but then takes a breath. Not protesting or denying, but his lips slowly downturn in deeper thought.

He's staring at me with greater concern. Maybe, possibly, remembering that I'm closed off and out-of-business to the sort of love he's found with Farrow.

Or perhaps he's just remembering all the suitors outside.

Or he could be recalling how last night I quit my assistant position in Calloway Couture, and I hadn't really even begun. I'm such bad publicity right now with the Cinderella ad, and I don't want my drama to negatively impact my family's companies.

So I can't work for my mom's fashion line or even Cobalt Inc.

It's official: I'm back to being jobless, as well as passionless. But I'll figure something out. One thing at a time.

Whatever is on Moffy's mind, it's troubling him. He looks like he wants to dive into deep waters and help me swim to shore.

"I'm fine," I assure him. "We've all been through much worse."

"I don't care how damn big or small this doomsday is—I don't like that you're experiencing one at all."

I'd feel the same if our positions were reversed right now. Maximoff and Farrow have both been really attentive to my well-being this past week and especially this morning.

"Jaaaaaaane!!"

Our heads turn to the front door. Thankfully the suitors can't breach the house.

I rest my chin on my knuckles and peek at the staircase. "Should we check on Luna?" My nearly nineteen-year-old cousin is a beautifully brazen, quirky oddball, and I love that she's been living with us.

Maximoff follows my gaze. "My sister could sleep through a stampede of rhinos. I don't think she's dead." He stiffens, brotherly concern sharpening his cheekbones. "We should go check—"

"You two," Farrow cuts in, "she's fine. You checked on her an hour ago."

"That, we did." I nod and wrap two palms around my mug.

She was sleeping peacefully. I'm almost positive she stayed up late last night FaceTiming Eliot and Tom, my brothers. Her best friends.

Our bedrooms are on the second-floor, and with both doors cracked, I could hear them talking passionately about my plight. Which includes all the suitors that have now parked their asses on our street.

My brothers think I should change the requirements of the ad. Make "twelve-inch dick" a prerequisite and weed out everyone, and while funny, it'd only cause more headaches and bad press.

Maximoff tries to roll out his stiff neck. "So you saw Thatcher?" He reroutes the topic back to me.

"Oui." I sip my lukewarm coffee. "We just naturally ran into each other, but he was…a little…well, he was slightly naked."

"Naked?" Farrow repeats, his brown brows spiking. "Moretti? The fucking hall monitor?"

Maximoff scrunches his face. "What the fuck is slightly naked?"

"Chest high. He was in a towel," I clarify. "I think I must've caught him after a shower."

Farrow stares up at the ceiling, then looks at me. "You sure you saw Thatcher and not Banks?"

My forehead crinkles in hurt. "Of course I'm sure it was Thatcher. I can tell them apart. Easily."

Maximoff turns to Farrow. "How'd you even know she ran into Thatcher?"

I'm curious about this too.

He drops his foot off the cushion. "Man, she's hot and bothered, and there's only one bodyguard who makes her turn that red."

Very true.

"But the towel is news to me," he adds.

Maximoff and Farrow are the only two people I ever told that I've been attracted to Thatcher in the past…and the present.

I scratch behind Ophelia's ears as the fluffy white cat prances by. "It's nothing, really. Thatcher lives next door, and I went next door, so the probability of an intersection was high."

I can't read the room that well at the moment.

So I keep talking, what I shouldn't do. "It's not as though I'd ever act on my hot-and-bothered feelings. I don't trust any dick near my vagina." *Not after Nate.* "…although, that's not completely true because I do trust Thatcher. Naturally. He's my bodyguard, but he's off-limits, unattainable, just a man who turns me on. That's all." I stop myself.

Thank God.

Maximoff and Farrow are staring at me with piercing concern.

Possibly because I'm speaking about someone they're not fond of, and I don't want any of what I just said to feel like betrayal. Like I'm not with them.

I'm with them.

Always.

"You both know my feelings, and they haven't changed." I meet their toughened gazes. "I spend so much time with Thatcher, and I want to believe that what he did back in May isn't who he is. He still shows deep remorse when he's not as guarded." I pause. "It's been four months since he hit you, Farrow, and I don't think he's even forgiven himself yet."

Maximoff and Farrow exchange a strong look together that I can't understand. Maybe they've discussed all-things Thatcher recently without me.

Farrow combs an inked hand through his hair. "I don't love spending this much energy on a guy that I really don't give a flying shit about."

"That's fair." I sip my coffee, now cold.

"But," Farrow says, running a thumb over his hoop lip piercing, "I'm not a petty fucker. He hasn't even glared at me since your birthday." *Back in June.* "And he's not on my ass while we're on-duty. Shit, he's been relatively easy to work with, so something's changed." He looks to Maximoff, as though handing the baton over.

Moffy is too rigid to even drink his tea. "Your bodyguard cares about you, Janie. And it's on a personal level."

My eyes bug, and shock parts my lips. Of course I notice how considerate Thatcher is. But that's me seeing my bodyguard hours and *hours* throughout a single day.

Maximoff and Farrow only witness moments, and I just never thought they'd see even a fraction of his kindness.

"How do you know it's on a personal level?" I wonder, sweeping both of them for the signs. For the hints and clues that they must've read.

Farrow counts off his fingers, beginning with his thumb. "One, Thatcher made an 'oath' with you." He also uses air quotes.

"Just to stay on your detail," Maximoff adds.

"Correct." I straighten up a little.

When I told them about the oath, they asked for details but never gave much of an opinion. Not until now, it seems.

"Two." Farrow raises his pointer finger. "Back in Greece, you weren't even on speaking terms. It would've been easier for that motherfucker to ask for a transfer and just protect someone else. Instead of doing that, he committed to you."

A smile tugs at my lips, remembering the bonfire. How we took a short walk. How I shivered and he gave me his button-down without a single hesitation.

Maximoff homes in on Farrow's inked fingers. "Pretty sure your second point is still the oath."

"Pretty sure I couldn't care less," Farrow says easily while taking in all of Maximoff.

He feigns surprise. "I totally forgot you can't count. I'm sorry, man."

Farrow rolls his eyes into a short laugh. "Okay, smartass." They eye each other a little longer, and I'm about to stand to reheat my coffee.

As soon as the rocking chair creaks, their heads swerve to me.

"This is about *you*," Maximoff emphasizes. "You time, not us time." He gestures from his chest to Farrow. "Alright, we're here for you."

Farrow rubs his strong jawline, his muscles tensed.

I freeze.

Farrow and I have been deeply concerned about Maximoff feeling guilty about splitting his attention between us. He overthinks about the wrong and right timing and whether he's being unfair.

In actuality, he's beyond fair, beyond present for both of us, and Farrow and I just want him to relax and breathe.

I nod confidently and stay seated on the rocking chair. "Let's hear it then, old chap." I slide a furtive glance to Farrow, and we share a look of understanding. *Protect and love Maximoff Hale.*

Maximoff sets down his Batman mug. "By staying on your detail, Thatcher chose the harder path."

"Right," I say softly. My cheeks hurt as I try to subdue another smile.

I'm more than appreciative that Thatcher stayed. It shows how much he wanted to be here for me, and I haven't had that devoted feeling from a bodyguard ever. My first, now-retired, bodyguard never really gave me any hints that he enjoyed my company.

Quinn Oliveira, my second bodyguard, was incredibly kind-hearted, but I was his first client, and so when he was transferred to Luna, he seemed more excited for the new possibilities. Ready to leave.

I love that Thatcher wanted to stay with me, despite all the risks and hardships. Plus, working through a new bodyguard relationship while dealing with the Cinderella ad would've been so stressful.

"Three." Farrow lifts his middle finger. "Bodyguard transfers happen all the time. Guys may have their preferences on who they want to protect, but we all love your family enough to not really give a shit at the end of the day. We're just happy to be on-duty. You don't do what Moretti did without *liking* a client, and I'd know because I'd do whatever it took to stay on Maximoff's detail."

I hear what he's telling me.

So they believe, through the oath, that Thatcher finally showed his cards, and now they know that he must like me on some personal level.

My pulse is on an ascent.

Beating and beating, and I'm not sure why I'm so nervous. "So he likes me on a personal level. I'm attracted to him. It's not like anything can happen."

Maximoff pops his knuckles, a bad habit.

Farrow lifts his brows. "Okay, here's the thing." He places his oatmeal bowl on the coffee table. "Whatever personal and professional shit that I have going on with Thatcher, that's between me and him. We're both twenty-eight, not eighteen. We'd put protecting you two above every fucking thing."

It's why Farrow has been okay with Thatcher staying on security, even after the dreaded *punch*, and why Maximoff was fine with Thatcher remaining on my detail during that time.

They see Thatcher as an experienced, expertly-skilled bodyguard, and they know he'll keep me safe. Regardless of any bad blood.

So they still trust him, but they don't like him.

Farrow splays his earpiece cord over his shoulder. "Putting all that shit aside, I'm going to be honest here: Thatcher won't do what I did. He won't break the rules for you like I broke them for Maximoff. I can't even see him breaking a rule for his own twin brother."

Maximoff brushes a hand through his thick hair. "If he's unwilling to break those rules, then it's just going to end badly. Whatever feelings you have for him, Janie, he's going to crush them."

I arch my shoulders, inhaling and not exhaling very well. "The only feeling I have is *attraction*. And I know you want to protect me from heartache, Moffy, but my heart isn't involved." I swig a bigger gulp of room temp coffee and lick my lips. "No hearts. No body parts. It's solely faraway attraction. Love is a two-way street that neither of us are driving down."

Maximoff stares faraway in thought.

"Famous ones." Farrow looks between the two of us with slowly rising brows. "Your inexperience is showing."

I lean forward. "How so?"

Maximoff is still staring off into space, cracking his knuckles.

Farrow has a hard time pulling his gaze off him, but he tells me, "Love can definitely be a one-way street, and trust me, you don't want to be the one who drives down it."

"Did you drive down it?" I wonder.

Maximoff tunes in. "Drive where?"

We laugh.

He blinks slowly into a glare. "I apparated to another dimension."

"Still in Philly, wolf scout." Farrow smiles wider and then stands up, just to take a seat on the armrest, but he's much closer to his fiancé.

Maximoff is a wooden board, but his joints reanimate and he wraps a strong arm around Farrow's shoulders.

Farrow holds Moffy's waist, his hand dipped beneath his shirt.

They draw closer.

"What were you saying?" Maximoff asks me.

"One-way streets of love," I explain. "Farrow said they exist, and I asked if he's driven down one before."

"Sure," Farrow answers. "I thought I was in love at thirteen, and that was not reciprocated in the way I wanted."

"And then Rowin," Maximoff says, unearthing a name that causes Farrow to roll his eyes into all seven circles of hell.

Farrow's ex is hated among all of my family and all of security. I was almost tempted to take a page out of my mom's retaliation handbook, but it'd be like digging up a buried corpse.

Revenge is pointless, my dad would say.

"That fucker was driving down that road all on his own," Farrow tells Maximoff. "I was nowhere near it." His palm encases Maximoff's sharp jaw, and Moffy runs his hand up to the base of Farrow's skull.

I can tell they're about to kiss.

Maximoff mutters something under his breath, and Farrow murmurs back, their lips drawing closer—and like he's injected with a shot of Best Friend Guilt, Maximoff abruptly tears out of the embrace. Stepping to the side, he winces at himself, his nose flaring.

And he plants his apologetic eyes on me.

I wince at Maximoff's wince. "Moffy—"

"I'm totally focused on you," he reminds me.

Farrow is nowhere near annoyed. He's staring more protectively at Maximoff like he just wants to shield him from all his hang-ups and worries.

"Of course you are," I say with all my heart. "And I don't mind if you take a minute or even an hour to kiss the man you love."

His neck reddens. "But what about you?"

"What about me?"

Farrow picks up his bowl, trying to stay out of our exchange.

Maximoff's concern is like a hot blanket. Draping over the whole room. "One-way streets of love—you know those are wrong turns. It's the do-not-enter street."

I inhale sharply and try to nod.

He's afraid I'll be hurt in this process, and from his vantage, this has to be painful. Here he was able to fall in love with a bodyguard who could reciprocate his feelings tenfold.

And in his mind, here I am—his other half—about to head down a one-way road.

Ten minutes later, a new pot of coffee is brewing and our plan has officially taken beautiful flight. Like a grasshopper springing off the lawn. "He looks promising." I pass Maximoff a photograph of a twenty-something athlete with auburn hair, butterscotch eyes, and a hooked nose. "He's a professional football player."

I printed out his picture from Instagram. He sent me a direct message last night, along with 4,593 other people.

Not all are suitors.

Reyroo3245 told me to shut up and die.

So unnecessary.

I haven't checked my DMs since 1 a.m., and I'm sure my inbox is severely bloated. But I'm more timid to sink back into that cesspool.

Maximoff examines the photo. "Yeah, what kind of twenty-something plays football instead of owning his own sports team. Can we say, underachiever?"

His impression of Grandmother Calloway is spot-on. Those would be her thoughts.

"And he's not even the *star* quarterback."

Maximoff grabs a pushpin. "She'd probably pale at the word *football*."

"Far too much tackling," I note.

He pins the photo onto a corkboard, which we hung on the brick wall. Next to the adjoining door.

I wonder what Thatcher is up to while he's over there and I'm here. Is he thinking about our run-in from earlier at all?

"Famous ones."

We look over at the kitchen.

Farrow rests a shoulder casually on the archway, a red apple between his fingers. "While this entire pseudo Criminal Minds episode is entertaining as fuck, what's the endgame here?"

I rifle through a stack of printed photographs. "Like I said earlier, if we pick a man who our grandmother would absolutely loathe and bring him to her house, she'll see that the Cinderella ad failed."

Maximoff studies the twelve photos on the corkboard. "Hopefully once she realizes the ad didn't work, she'll back off Janie and stop trying to play matchmaker."

Our grandmother can't slide by without understanding how deep this betrayal goes. I don't want her to *ever* pull a tactic like this on any of our siblings or cousins.

It ends here.

My mom can be a murderous blizzard, and the day of the ad, she offered to fly straight to Philly from London to chew out her own mother with cold wrath. But I prefer to fight my battles myself, so I'm handling this alone.

Well…with a slight assist from my best friend. And his fiancé. And very soon, I'll need my bodyguard.

So I'm technically not alone, but as my dad always says, *some battles are best fought with a sidekick.* These three men are mine.

Farrow rotates his apple in his hand. "Just send your grandmother videos of all the middle-aged dipshits outside trying to harass you, and she'll regret what she did."

"My brothers flooded her email and phone last night with clips and articles." I had my publicist release a statement denying involvement in the Cinderella ad, and most media outlets said I was trying to cowardly backtrack.

A recent tabloid headline:

VAIN HEIRESS SCURRIES TO SALVAGE REPUTATION AFTER ADVERTISEMENT BACKFIRES

"How'd your grandmother respond?" Farrow asks.

"She emailed, *bad press is good press*. And that was it."

Farrow shoots a caustic look at the wall and mutters, "Fucking hell."

Maximoff glowers at the ceiling. Pissed. "I'm guessing she only thinks *bad press is good press* when it's convenient for her." He's not as close to our grandmother, which is another reason why she most likely wants me to marry first.

They already know this.

I shuffle through a few more photos. "I think she's convinced herself of a lot of terrible things."

Farrow waits to take a bite of apple. I notice him staring at the titanium wedding band on his finger. He looks up at Maximoff. "There is something we could do, wolf scout."

"No," I cut in. "You're *not* eloping because of her." Emotion burns my eyes.

His lip quirks. "I didn't say anything about eloping, Cobalt, but nice try." He locks gazes with Maximoff. "We could tell your grandmother we're not planning on getting married for a few years, maybe four or five. That way she'll stop feeling pressure to wed Jane off this fast, and she won't pull another stunt like this."

They wanted a long engagement, but they didn't want *that* long.

Maximoff nods powerfully. He'd do anything for me.

They both would.

But I don't want them to outright lie about their wedding for my sake. I don't want to tarnish what's supposed to be beautiful. "No," I say again, capturing their gazes. "*No*. It's not worth it."

Farrow eyes the corkboard. "So you'd rather date one of these dipshits—"

"Date is a strong word," I interject. "I'm going to have *one* luncheon with one of these suitors she'd despise. Most likely Mr. Football Man." I pat the photo on the board of the auburn-haired athlete.

Farrow bites into the juicy apple. "Call Moretti."

"Already?" I'm surprised he's even *asking* to be in the same room with Thatcher a second longer than he needs to be.

Farrow just nods. He has the ability to radio my bodyguard on my behalf and call him here, but that would mean talking to Thatcher longer than he wants to talk to him.

Maximoff crosses his arms. "Your bodyguard should be here if we're serious about this."

We are.

I instantly procure my phone.

10

 THATCHER MORETTI

I'm not gonna fucking like whatever this is. I can already tell, and I'm just staring at a bunch of photos tacked up to the brick wall.

More specifically: photos of guys, mostly around Jane's age.

Targets?

No doubt, my mind blares.

My mouth sets in a harder line. Knowing that's not right. I need to dislodge whatever protective, defensive feelings I have for Jane for a fucking second, and I'm left with a reasonable response: *too soon to tell.*

I step back and glance over at the kitchen. Where Jane and Maximoff talk on speakerphone to Sullivan Meadows. Jane's cousin called them about the same time I entered their townhouse.

Interruptions from family are routine. Especially with Jane and Maximoff, who try to be easily accessible to anyone who needs them.

I spot Jane in short glimpses through the archway. She breezes around the kitchen. Heating up a mug of coffee while chatting.

"There's more than enough room in the garage, Sulli," Jane reassures, "I promise your Jeep will fit."

Maximoff speaks. "We shifted around the bikes, and I can park my Audi on the street if it's still too cramped."

That'll be a major security issue. But Maximoff's car isn't as recognizable to the public as Sulli's old Jeep. If they're willing to risk vandalism or theft for one vehicle, the Audi is the least likely to be targeted.

It's the right pick.

"You both are the fucking best," Sulli says on the phone.

I catch another glimpse of Jane. *If she looks at you a lot, it means she likes you.* Childhood advice, man. It pops into my head like a bullet piercing a tin can.

And now I'm staring at my client and thinking, *look back at me.*

Jane rests a hip against the counter in a momentary pause. She smiles brightly at something that I can't see. Maybe the phone in Maximoff's hand.

I shouldn't want to be that phone. I shouldn't want to be the receiver of Jane's vibrant energy or any fucking thing that belongs to her mind or body, but I keep thinking, *look at me.*

She turns her head.

And looks right at me.

I'm not shifting away. Our gazes latch for a solid beat, but I stand about four meters from her position. Roughly fifteen feet apart.

Her blue eyes slowly dance over the stoic lines of my face, then my clothes: gray crew-neck and red flannel.

As though remembering earlier. The kitchen.

My towel.

Her flushed neck and shortened breath.

Don't go there, Thatcher.

"Hey, do any of you need anything at the grocery?" Sulli asks them, her voice audible through the phone speakers.

"I'm alright," Maximoff says. "Jane?"

She misses the question. I'm distracting my client. *Fucking unprofessional.* I try to wrench my gaze off her.

"Jane?" Maximoff asks again.

"Hmm?" Blush stains her freckled cheeks, and she dashes further into the kitchen. Disappearing from my view. I hear her say, "Both houses need milk."

I sense another pair of eyes on me.

Not Jane

Not Maximoff.

But Farrow—he's been sitting and lacing up his black boots at the iron café table. He's less than two meters away from me, and his threatening glare feels even fucking closer.

I take another step back.

Intimidation is vital to be a bodyguard on the team. I'd be more concerned if he couldn't do it that fucking well.

I shouldn't have punched him.

My jaw tightens.

Regret surges, biting. It's hard every time I see Farrow. Because it's nearly impossible not to think about my mistake.

I could've handled so many things better than I fucking did.

I should've apologized earlier. But for weeks, I couldn't get the words out, not without feeling like I should've been fired.

Seeing him just reminds me how badly I blew it. How much hurt I caused, what I deserve in return, and all the debts I feel like I can never repay.

Farrow knots one of his laces. Our clients are still talking, but their chatter muffles now that they're deeper in the kitchen.

The sound of brewing coffee cuts the air in half.

Say something to him.

I'm not quiet because I can't think of what to talk about. We have a lot in common. We like a lot of the same shit. Same interest in martial arts, Philly sports teams. Same taste in music. How he jokes around—constant ribs and digs at his friends, I used to be around that a lot in the military.

I hate it over comms.

But in person, it brings back good memories.

We have more in common. Worse things, and sometimes I wonder if he's realized that I've known he's been experiencing some form of PTSD.

In Greece, I had to hand a bottle of water *to* Banks to give *to* Farrow. I didn't think Farrow would've accepted it from me, but I could tell he was mentally thrown back. He doesn't speak to the team about it that much.

I'm not one to talk. I can barely say the word out loud. Shouldn't be that way, but it is.

In the end, I'm quiet because I can't unlock my jaw. It's like I'm made of cinderblock, and almost no one possesses the right tools to chisel me open.

Not even me, at times.

And all that has ever divided Farrow and me is *me*. He's done nothing.

Comms crackle in my eardrum. *Good thing.* I zero in on work and listen to the Omega lead speak.

"Akara to Thatcher, Farrow, and Quinn—we're at the grocery. Is there anything specific you want?"

I touch my flannel collar and press my mic. "Check to see if they have a stop leak additive. Jane's Beetle is leaking oil again." Ophelia rubs up against my ankles and purrs. I reach down and scratch behind her ear, she tries to bump her head into my hand, enjoying it. I do a quick sweep of the room and locate the cats.

All but one is in sight. Licorice can be shy, and he's the most skittish. It's made me more concerned about him. But there are plenty of places he could be hiding.

"Copy," Akara responds.

Static buzzes, waiting for Quinn's response.

I look right at Farrow while he stands up—done tying his boots—and I'm positive he's silenced his radio.

Wouldn't be the first time.

I drop my arm to my side. "SFO is at the grocery. You need something?"

"No," he says with the casual shake of his head. "I'm good." He quickens his pace towards the fireplace.

I spot movement a fraction of a second after Farrow does. Because the fireplace had been at my back.

He snatches Walrus, a calico cat, off the mantel. Plus, he catches a picture frame that teeters off the ledge.

He's vigilant, always a skilled set of hands, and constantly on guard, even if he's cracking jokes, smiling, or lounging on furniture like the world isn't on fire when it's actually up in fucking flames.

Walrus tries to paw his nose, and Farrow jerks back with a smile.

"Not today, you little bastard." He lets Walrus go, and the cat scampers into the kitchen.

I adjust my earpiece, and we're suddenly facing one another. I nod to the empty milk jug on the mantel. What Walrus was interested in.

Farrow grabs the milk jug and then flicks a switch on his radio. "You haven't railed on me for comms in a while." He raises his brows. "Bored?"

He has no clue.

He wouldn't.

Since I used to be the Epsilon lead, I know how the security team functions to the exact center. All the ins-and-outs. Every decision, every reasoning. I'm not in the dark.

The whole team is aware that Farrow selectively uses comms, so his lack of response is expected and not an issue among the leads.

Akara is only waiting for Quinn to reply.

Have I hated his lack of comms use in the past? Yeah. Things would've been easier if he just followed the fucking rules, but I accepted a long time ago that he was gonna do shit his own way.

Farrow gets away with it because he's never made a real mistake.

Because he picks up slack. Without needing to be asked.

Because he's so calm and reliable under fire, and *that*…just can't be taught. When lives are at stake, not just these families but the safety of the team, we want the best bodyguards here.

And by *we*, I mean Akara Kitsuwon, me, and anyone else who's been in charge.

I can't say every new hire on the team sees the depth of Farrow's value. Not when they're slapped on the wrist or *fired* for the same moves he pulls.

I can't say that my men on Epsilon have felt anything more than bitter fucking hostility. To the point where I had one man taking personal shots at Donnelly just to piss off Farrow.

Being a lead means making hard calls.

Years back during breakfast, Akara, Banks, and I had a talk about how to prevent in-fighting. Mainly, my guys antagonizing Farrow. Their jealousy was escalating. Something bad was going to happen.

I could see it.

I could hear it.

SFE and Farrow don't get along to this day.

Over frying bacon, Akara told me, *"You'll need to dig into Farrow harder, so none of the guys think he's getting special treatment."*

Akara knew that I'd already been trying to grill him.

I nodded. *"You stay easy on Farrow. I've been a pain in his ass this long. You don't need to lose his respect."*

Akara would've been willing to be the bad guy, but he's better at balancing the friend and boss role than I am.

I still remember what my brother said that morning. With a toothpick in the corner of his mouth, Banks told us, *"You two doing the good-cop, bad-cop routine, and it's starting to make me look like the fucking cowboy."*

Epsilon cooled off once I chewed out Farrow for every minor infraction. Things that I wouldn't even rag them about. I was on his case all the fucking time, and I even had to dock his pay during the FanCon whenever he broke the rules.

Akara and I were dealing with soured feelings in SFE because we voted to keep Farrow on the team.

After he had sex with a client.

Multiple times.

It's ironic that I spent so long trying to control the situation, and I ended up being the one to lose my temper and punch him.

There's no excuse for it.

I take full responsibility for my mistakes.

After that, I promised myself that I'd back off Farrow for good.

Now he's facing me in a cluttered living room that smells like fresh flowers and spring—like *Jane*—and he's wondering why I'm not hounding him for comms.

My gaze is as soft as it can be. "I don't care how you do your job," I say truthfully. "Just that you do it."

He tips his head, running his tongue over his molars, and he skims me up and down, gauging my sincerity. "Honestly, at this point I couldn't care less why you've been a raging asshole towards me as long as you're not one anymore."

I nod once. I wish I could put the past behind me as well as Farrow can. Maybe then my life wouldn't consist of me pulling the pins off so many fucking grenades.

Farrow drops his voice to a low, rough whisper. "Just don't coddle me. Don't kiss my ass as penance. Don't fuck with my fiancé or Jane, and we won't have a problem."

Easy. I nod again, and comms sound off in my ear.

"Quinn, do you need something from the grocery?" Akara repeats.

Oscar chimes in, "Speak up, little bro."

The line hangs, waiting for a response. Farrow chucks the milk jug to Maximoff, who appears in the archway.

He catches it easily.

"Trash," Farrow tells him.

Maximoff is giving us a weird look. It's rare that we stand this fucking close while we're off-duty.

Akara speaks in my ear. "Thatcher, is Quinn still asleep?"

I crossed paths with Quinn Oliveira in the kitchen. We were both eating breakfast, and I'm not someone who will cover his ass for the Omega lead. Akara needs to know.

I click my mic. "No."

Akara enters the line with two curt words. "Not good."

It means Quinn is silencing his radio. Ever since the twenty-one-year-old joined security, Akara has been concerned that Quinn is copying Farrow's maverick style of guarding.

I am too.

He's a lot younger than Farrow, and realistically, he's more hotheaded.

I move back to the corkboard. Crossing my arms. Instinct says this is a *Wall of Suitors.* But that'd mean Jane is interested in her grandmother's ploy.

And I'm positive she's not.

"What is this?" I glance back at Farrow.

He rests an elbow casually on the mantel. "The worst idea of the month."

"Counter argument," Jane says.

Our heads turn as she appears and blows on a steaming mug.

She continues without missing a beat. "This month's worst idea goes to my grandmother who pimped me out in an ad."

My brows draw together, concerned about Jane. But also, I'm narrowing a glare into the fucking corkboard.

Farrow refutes, "Except sex was never mentioned in the ad."

"Romantic pimping," Jane clarifies, placing her hot mug on a cat-shaped coaster, and I watch her sidle right...next to me.

I uncross my arms.

I don't know why. *Can't touch her.*

My nose flares, and I end up kneading my deltoid.

She places her hands on her hips and stares up at the photos. Like she's mapped out her whole future and she's reviewing the layout.

And then she sucks in a measured breath.

She's stressed.

"What's going on, Jane?" I ask for the details.

She's quick to explain everything. I listen, breathing out coarser breaths further and further through. When she's done talking, she tears a photo of an athlete off the wall. I recognize him as a fullback for the Eagles.

I was right.

I don't fucking like this.

Maximoff stands nearby, cracking his knuckles. He seems on edge about the whole scenario, but the guy is always on edge.

Farrow leaves his spot on the loveseat to be beside his fiancé.

Jane passes me the photo and cranes her neck to meet my gaze. "He seems like the best so far."

I haven't even looked at the photo.

My steel gaze is on her. *Don't do this, Jane.*

She searches my eyes and puts a few fingers to her cheek. "So..." She clears her throat and shakes her head, more to herself. "What do you think?"

This feels like that one time where I told Jane I'd help her find another guy to provide her "oral assistance"—when I was right there and she would've been willing. That was like running a 99-yard touchdown for the wrong team. Knowing I had to score for someone else.

Wanting to turn around every inch gained on the field.

Pretty much hell.

I swallow a jagged rock and drop my eyes to the photo. "I'll need to vet him," I remind her.

She nods. "I know." Her voice is tighter than usual.

I've never had to vet a guy that she could potentially date or fuck or both. For the majority of my time on her detail, she's been shut off to every intimate thing with men.

Fuck Nate, that fucking bastard.

Imagining Jane falling in love with other men punctures something hot in me and I need to think of brighter things before I pop a blood vessel.

Puppies.

Rainbows.

Pussy.

God, Jane is right in front of me. Maybe not pussy.

I scrutinize the photo. "Are you pursuing him?" I ask outright.

She tilts her head. "What do you mean by *pursuing?*"

"Dating," I clarify. *Having sex.*

"No dating." She's practically whispering. "Nothing else. It's purely platonic."

My expression closes up. What she intends as being *platonic* could become something more.

And then what?

And then nothing. My feelings don't matter. I can't just break rank and say, *fuck it.*

But something in my mind is saying, *unfuck this.*

Get rid of the fullback and the Wall of Suitors. "What about just calling your grandmother?" I ask Jane.

Farrow chimes in, "That's what I said before these two started tacking dipshits up on the wall."

Maximoff blinks slowly. "Thank you for illustrating how great of a friend I am."

"The best," Jane says in a warm smile.

Maximoff smiles back.

Jane turns to me. "And I have called our grandmother. Twenty times. She has to be screening the calls because I'm sent to voicemail every time. Watch." She picks up her phone from the coffee table and dials a number. Hoisting it in the air, we wait.

It rings once before the line clicks.

Her eyes expand to saucers, and she brings the speaker to her lips. "Grandmother?"

"Jane, dear." Grandmother Calloway sounds like she's sucked on helium for half her fucking life. Uppity blue-blooded aristocrats were foreign territory to me until I became a bodyguard.

Her grandmother eats foie gras and Beluga caviar.

I grew up eating fried baloney three days a week.

Jane starts, "I—"

"I'm so glad you called," she cuts her off.

She's been calling.

I keep an eye on Jane more than anyone else. She's worried about her cousin.

Maximoff is glaring at the phone, and Jane backs away from him like she can protect him from their grandmother at a distance.

Farrow has his hand on the back of Maximoff's neck in comfort.

He's lucky.

What I'd give to be able to—*no, it can't happen*—for Jane. My thoughts are now a clusterfuck. I rake my hand across my jaw.

She starts again, "Grandmother—"

"I was disappointed that you put out a press release demeaning the advertisement. But I understand. Not everyone loves surprises."

Farrow rolls his eyes.

"Grandmother. It was—"

"Better news is coming, dear."

Jane sighs out in frustration from being cut off.

"I've scheduled an afternoon tea this Saturday," her grandmother says.

"But—"

"And I've picked out the three best men from the resumes. You'll find a winner in one of them."

She takes a breath. "Grandmo—"

"I'll send the details over. See you Saturday, and wear a dress."

The line clicks.

"Shit," Farrow curses.

Things are now fucking worse. I'll have to vet three suitors. She's gone from just entertaining the football player to now taking four men on a tea *date*.

Jane stares at the phone in a daze. "What just happened?"

Maximoff tries to unclench his fist. "You just got roped into afternoon tea."

"I don't even like tea and dresses," she mutters. "And now she's staging an episode of *The Bachelorette*."

I look down at her. "You don't have to do this," I remind Jane.

She shakes her head like she's disoriented. "No, I can just…I'll take the football player to afternoon tea. The plan is the same that way. He can just upstage whatever men my grandmother chooses—"

A fist bangs the door loudly.

Jane jolts.

I put a hand to the small of her back. "Hold on." I pass her and head to the locked door. Farrow is right behind me in seconds.

Temp guards should be securing the perimeter outside.

The next sound is a *whack*. Sounds like an object.

I speak into my mic and try to communicate with the temps while Farrow checks the security cams on his phone.

We figure out the issue in less than a minute.

"Are they throwing eggs?" Jane asks. She's not even surprised that people would.

I shake my head.

"It's a drone," Farrow explains.

"Goddamn drones," Maximoff growls under his breath.

"One more thing," Farrow adds. "The drone dropped off a package."

11

JANE COBALT

My curiosity about the package is only half-
full. Thatcher occupies the other half, and I catch myself looking
backwards for him.

He's not here.

He carried the luxury shoebox to security's townhouse a few minutes
ago, Farrow in tow. But only after they scanned the package for metal.

Our bodyguards have more tools to test the contents for anything
hazardous. I know Moffy would prefer to be involved, but I don't love
hearing about all the ball gags and leather that stalkers send me.

Maximoff has stayed behind to keep me company, and our twenty-
year-old cousin has finally arrived.

"It's a fucking madhouse outside, guys. Way worse than a few days
ago," Sulli tells us in the tiny kitchen while the three of us unpack
groceries from canvas tote bags.

At six beautiful feet tall with cascading brown hair, carved biceps,
and a squared jaw, Sulli looks like the athlete she was born to be. She
lingers in the walk-in pantry. Just so we can hand her paper towels and
other items to shelve.

"Akara had to do some kind of reverse-maneuver and a three-point
turn just to avoid running over some old dude with flowers," Sulli says.
"And there are literal fucking news vans. Like Channel 14 and Good
Morning Philadelphia."

I slowly take out a dozen eggs from a tote. I can imagine a morning news segment about the Cinderella ad. All the smiling anchors and their theories about who I'll choose to date. It's one thing to have my grandmother play matchmaker.

It's another to have the world laser-focused and invested in my love life.

I'm trying not to worry, but I'm starting to realize this may be less of a passing storm and more of a staple to my every day.

I look to Sulli. "Hopefully they'll disperse and we'll be back to our regularly scheduled programming."

Maximoff feigns confusion. "What is that again?"

"Glorious dumpster fires on Tuesdays," I say theatrically.

He nods strongly. "Shit storms every other Friday."

I smile at him. "And we can't forget the evening apocalypse."

Maximoff smiles back. "Jesus, we've survived the apocalypse. It's like we're pros at this already."

"That we are, old chap." I mime tipping a top hat to him.

He hooks an arm around my shoulders. "Que ferais-je sans toi, ma moitié?" *What would I do without you, my other half?* He kisses the top of my head.

I'm about to reply, but we notice Sulli deep in thought, a few fingers to her lips.

"Sulli," I call out. "Is something wrong?"

"Fuck…no, I just…I hope you two know that I'm a novice at this stuff compared to you guys." She means the media chaos outside.

Maximoff hands her a jar of jellybeans, a topping she puts on pancakes. "You won't even notice them after a while, Sul."

"And we're in this together," I chime in. "You don't have to face anyone or anything alone."

"Yeah." She nods, thinking. "It's such a strange time to be moving in with you two. You're like Philly's Bachelorette, Jane, and Moffy, you're getting *married*—"

"Not any time soon," he cuts in, his tone forceful like he's enacting a new law: no wedding talk.

He's been adamant this whole week about it too. While this crisis revolves around me, he doesn't want any wedding planning going on.

Sulli smiles. "Got it. No wedding bells yet."

Maximoff flips open a box of donuts that we bought for Sulli as a *welcome, this house is now yours* gift. He picked them up yesterday, so they may be stale. "Are you regretting moving in already?" he asks.

"No way." She shelves the jellybeans. "I'm excited. Just a little freaked out by the people on the fucking street, but I think the FanCon prepared me for a lot."

I'm happy the tour could help more than just my friendship with Moffy.

Sulli reaches for a Fruity Pebbles donut and bites into the dough. Cereal crumbs fall on her striped shirt. "And this place already feels like home." She speaks with a mouthful. "I know where everything goes. I've slept over so many times, and you're both here and so is Luna."

My heart mushrooms, and a smile tugs my cheeks. I squeeze past Maximoff and wrap my arms around my cousin.

We hug and sway playfully side-to-side.

"I love you so much," I tell her.

"I love you more."

We pull back and smile. This past year, we've grown closer than ever before. Since she's retired from competitive swimming, she's been able to join us for more outings and trips.

And now she's finally decided to leave the nest. She's flown the parental coup and landed in our cramped but loving home.

Sulli could have so easily chosen my brothers' flat in Hell's Kitchen, seeing as how she's best friends with Beckett. We've always had the open invitation extended to her, but I was even surprised when she finally accepted it.

I remember asking, "It's because Eliot and Tom moved up to New York, isn't it?" Living with two Cobalt boys is one thing. Living with *four* is hazardous. And I should know, I grew up with all five of them.

"Nope," Sulli replied. "Beckett is super fucking busy with the new ballet, and I just really wanted a roommate. Luna sold me. She said we were going to get the fucked-up college experience that we'll probably never really have." She nudged my shoulder. "Plus, you and Moffy are pretty fucking rad."

Our big life changes affect the lives of our bodyguards. Sulli's move means that Akara Kitsuwon is officially living in security's townhouse. Right now, most of SFO, plus Jack Highland, are helping him settle in next door. While also dealing with the mystery shoebox.

Later this weekend, the rest of our family is planning to help Sulli move furniture into Luna's room. They're transforming the space into a mini dorm. Complete with a bunk bed and beanbags. It almost makes me nostalgic for the whole three months I lived in Princeton dorms.

Almost.

Because those were also the loneliest, most miserable times of my life.

I don't wish to repeat that.

The door to the adjoining townhouses suddenly opens. All of security returning. I try and look for Thatcher first, but I catch sight of Maximoff's gaze. His powerful green eyes carry one urgent inquiry. As if silently asking: *what was in the box?*

12

JANE COBALT

Akara just shared the disturbing details of the shoebox with Sulli, Maximoff, and me in the tightly packed living room. Mainly to let us know this is a security matter.

Don't worry, they all say.

It's not about you, they all say.

It only affects us, they all say.

I think Security Force Omega has forgotten how much we deeply care about them and how much it hurts seeing them harassed while they shield us from harassment.

It's our job, they say.

I know.

I appreciate their sacrifice more than they can possibly understand.

Did I ever imagine one of our bodyguards would be sent roadkill? In a box? With a bow wrapped around the mangled squirrel's broken neck? No.

Gross acts are tragically normal for me, but mostly when my family and I are the recipients. I'm not used to *my* bodyguard being a target.

Thatcher is a soldier. Tremendously tall. He's physically a powerhouse, a supreme godly and angelic being who is built to protect and defend. I see so clearly that this is where he wants to be. I see how much of himself he's willing to give to keep my family safe.

I'd just like to be next to him.

To be a wingwoman.

His confidante.

His right-hand.

I want to slip into his back pocket.

Possibly even literally sliding my hand down south and squeezing his...*oh-so-inappropriate, Jane.*

I try not to pulse. Now is definitely not the time. But the air has lightened as chatter returns, cats scampering around everyone who's gathered here, which includes Farrow, Donnelly, Oscar, Quinn, Thatcher, and Jack.

I sit on a stair, nibbling on a chocolate turtle, and I find myself picking my bodyguard out of the small crowd.

Thatcher stands incredibly stoic at the front door. He's shrugged off his flannel, his plain gray crew-neck snug on his firm build. Features hardened, biceps chiseled, and shoulders braced in a vigilant stronghold.

His narrowed gaze slides along the room and lands on me.

I inhale a soft breath.

His chest rises.

I ache to talk to him. To ask how he's feeling. I ache to be closer, for his large hand to hover beside my arm or waist. I ache for so much between him and me that I shouldn't welcome or invite.

But we are allowed to converse. We *should* talk.

Reach out, Jane.

Just as I begin to stand, Thatcher detaches from his spot, and he crosses the room. His attentive gaze never leaves me.

My heart begins to race, and I lower back onto the old creaking stair.

My bodyguard halts at the banister. Towering above me, the staircase too narrow for more than one person to sit.

"Thatcher," I greet.

"Jane." He asks, "How are you doing?"

Chocolate melts between my fingers, and I lick my thumb. "I'm doing fine. I'm more concerned..." *about you.*

My voice fades completely. We both seem to tense in our silence, but the room is quite loud as SFO, Jack, and my cousins talk.

I break our quiet. "How are you feeling?"

Thatcher drops his voice another cavernous octave. "The same." He holds my gaze much more securely. "I feel a strong responsibility to you."

Dear God, let me breathe properly. "To protect me," I state for clarity.

He nods firmly, but another raw emotion almost surfaces through his tightened gaze. He blinks and deadbolts it shut.

To protect me.

I push my wavy hair off my shoulder, hot all of a sudden. I need to backtrack, and I'm curious, of course. "What you found in the box, it doesn't affect you? It's not every day that bodyguards are sent roadkill."

Security hasn't discovered who dropped the package via a drone, but the anonymous delivery included a mutilated squirrel and a note:

For the tall bodyguard.
Fuck you.

That was all.

Omega thinks it must be a vexed suitor from earlier this morning. Someone Thatcher must've accidentally angered.

His expression darkens. "I've seen a lot worse than a dead squirrel." He ends there. Cut and dry.

I hesitate to prod. "Can I ask you something more personal?"

He looks readied. "Go ahead."

I rest my elbows on my knees, my mint-green tulle skirt splayed over them. "Have you seen worse while you've been in security or before this job?"

"Both," he answers without pause. He checks over his shoulder for a millisecond, and I track his brief glimpse to the fireplace. To Farrow.

Farrow is holding Maximoff's cheek and whispering in the pit of his ear. Less serious, I think, since Farrow smiles wider and wider with each word he murmurs.

I frown. "It involves Farrow?"

He gives me a serious look.

Nate.

The realization strikes me cold. The night that Nate was apprehended, there were only two bodyguards on the scene: Farrow and Thatcher. And he's telling me that night was more horrific than a dead mutilated squirrel.

I want to express my guilt for trusting Nate, but it'll open a dam and I'm not ready to drown in those feelings.

"Turtle?" I offer, holding up the tin of caramel pecan chocolates.

Thatcher has never rejected one before, and he doesn't now. We eat turtles and face the room together.

I whisper to my bodyguard, "It seems Akara and Sulli are back on good terms." They had an awkward month or so after Greece, but their buddy-guard friendship is intact.

The Omega lead, a six-foot-two commanding Akara Kitsuwon is dressed in his usual Studio 9 muscle shirt and backwards baseball cap, and he shares the Victorian loveseat with Sulli. Fuzzy pillow on their laps, their hands are clasped together in an intense arm-wrestle match.

I missed their bet, but they look about tied right now.

Thatcher studies them a little longer, and then his attention drifts to the corkboard. Where Oscar and Donnelly are surveying the photographs of suitors while eating Sun Chips and a pudding cup. I think they must have temp bodyguards covering their clients for a short bit so they could help Akara move in.

Jack and I make eye contact from across the room, and he treks over to the staircase to greet me. "Jane," he says; his charming smile radiates a thousand feet in all directions.

The exec producer is very charismatic, affectionate, and a good friend to me and Maximoff after so many seasons filming *We Are Calloway*. We shed our armor and share our insecurities in the docuseries, usually with Jack first.

I instantly smile back.

He hugs me. "Looking gorgeous as ever."

"You as well."

Oscar looks back at us, his curly hair falling over a rolled blue bandana. "Where's my positive affirmation, Highland?"

Jack wears a softer grin. "What kind are you looking for?"

"What do you want to give me?" Oscar shakes a water bottle full of protein mix.

Jack is about to reply.

"Give it to him sloppy," Donnelly smirks.

"Ignore Donnelly," Oscar tells Jack. "You'll feel smarter."

Donnelly scoops pudding with his finger. "Ignoring Oscar makes your dick feel bigger."

Oscar ends up laughing, but he nods to Jack. "I'm still waiting, Highland."

Jack opens his mouth, and now Farrow chimes in, "Really digging deep for a compliment, Oliveira."

Oscar sets down his water bottle. "At least I know what they look like, Redford." And then he throws a potato chip at Maximoff, which my best friend dodges easily.

Farrow points at his friend. "Fuck you." It's very lighthearted.

Oscar grins, and Jack has already left my side to go referee Akara and Sulli's arm wrestling match. Jack has grown closest to Akara out of all the bodyguards.

Thatcher observes all of them without much of a reaction.

I truly adore being a fly on the wall among security. The FanCon tour was a pivotal turning point. I was able to peek further and further into the lives of our bodyguards in ways I never had before, and I could spot pre-established friendships of their own.

"Who bought a hundred banana cream pie pudding cups? Literally, a *hundred*." Quinn scrunches his face and hoists a plastic bag at the table.

Oscar tosses a chip in his mouth. "Who do you think? There's only one guy who's eating that shit."

Donnelly is crushing the cup, squeezing pudding in his mouth.

Quinn reads the nutrition label with furrowed brows. He's a very clean eater, something I noticed during the FanCon tour. "Damn, how come no one bought avocados or bread, but we have a hundred pudding cups?"

Thatcher stares more sternly. "If you had your radio on, you could've asked for that."

Donnelly nods. "You tell him, Thatch."

"It's Thatcher," he corrects. Often, actually.

I've wondered if it frustrates him when people try to shorten his name, but I haven't found the proper time to ask.

I'm not even sure now is. Especially since the stairs creak behind us. Our heads swerve as Luna descends with a long yawn.

Bodyguards glance at Luna, but they offer privacy and try not to plaster their gazes for more than a few seconds.

I smile at my cousin. "Good afternoon, sleepyhead."

Light-brown hair splays messily on her shoulders, faded green marker streaks her cheeks, and her lanky arms and body are hidden beneath an oversized *Thrashers* hoodie.

"Howdie." She yawns longer. "I heard something upstairs about a squirrel in a box."

I shift from the staircase to let her pass. "You heard right." I explain what Akara told us in depth.

Luna hardly flinches at the news. She was gifted poop in a bag by a bully in high school, so this isn't shocking for her either.

"People suck," Luna says under her breath while she skates past Thatcher and me, and then the adjoining door quietly opens.

Banks slips inside.

All of Security Force Omega is now here.

I thought Thatcher's brother would be in New York all day. I look to Thatcher, and he leans closer to me. Just to speak privately. *Do not elevate any dangerous hopes or wishes, Jane.*

I inhale his strong woody scent as he says, "Tom's bodyguard went on-duty earlier."

"Right," I breathe.

It means that Banks is now off-duty and floating to wherever anyone on the team must need him. Especially if Farrow has a med call.

It's sometimes strange how security is more attuned to the happenings of my family as a whole unit, more than I can ever possibly be.

Sulli groans. "Cumbuckets." She just lost the competitive arm-wrestle match.

"There's always next time, Sul." Akara pushes himself off the cushion to a stance and steals a Fruity Pebble off the donut she'd been eating. He makes his way over to Banks, who has screeched to a halt beside Oscar.

Banks stares at the photographs of suitors. "What's this?"

Akara starts explaining the plan that's already spread through the rest of Omega, and everyone quiets to listen.

I hold the banister with two hands. Apprehension rolling around my stomach. Just having Maximoff, Farrow, and Thatcher in my plans is much easier. Having the whole room is more intimidating, but I'm open to more ideas and input.

I do the math.

7 Omega Bodyguards + 3 Cousins + 1 Exec Producer = 11 Brains.

Eleven brains on top of mine could easily make the situation more dysfunctional, but the professional hierarchy in SFO makes them a *functional* team. Most of them are good about checking their egos.

And when they don't, it never bothers me. I was raised in a family with parents and siblings who love to be right. The ego of my dad alone could fill the entire Milky Way.

Donnelly rips a photo off the wall. "This one looks like a straight up prick."

"Man, they're not dating you," Farrow says easily.

He grins. "They wish they could have this ass."

Oscar turns his head to me. "It's not a bad idea, Cobalt." He stuffs his hand in the chip bag. "You openly dating a guy should calm down some of the aggressive men outside. They'll leave knowing they lost their chance."

I hadn't even considered that benefit.

Subduing hecklers is usually an impossible feat. I always try to keep my chin up and live inside the chaos instead of fight against the forceful current. So my focus has been on ensuring my grandmother won't try this tactic again on my siblings. Sending her a message that she failed.

TANGLED LIKE US *123*

"All those guys outside will leave?" Sulli asks hopefully. I'd love for my cousin to feel more comfortable here.

"Will they?" I ask Oscar too.

"Not the whole crowd." Oscar speaks to us both. "But at least the creeps on the street looking to…" He gestures to me, trying to be polite. "You know."

"Sleep with me," I finish for him. *I know.*

"Bingo," Oscar says.

The room tenses.

Thatcher and Banks are staring hard at one another. Practically talking through their eyes, and I think I'd have to live inside their twenty-eight years of existence to fully comprehend what it all means.

I replay Oscar's words in my head, and I realize I've missed something. "You said *openly* dating," I say to Oscar. "But I was just going to take the football player on *one* afternoon tea. I'm not dating him. I'm not dating anyone."

The air could snap, tension stretched at a maximum. Concern bores into me from so many pairs of narrowed eyes.

Merde.

These men are all naturally protective. For Omega, it's practically a job requirement, but I'm starting to feel my age. Just twenty-three. Not the oldest of anything since they're all so much older than me.

Except for Moffy. I will always have one month on my best friend.

I pull back my shoulders, how my mom taught me. To combat brewing heat under my frilly blouse, I tie my hair into a low pony. "I'm perfectly fine."

Luna bounces her head. "I see it. I feel it." She air high-fives me from across the room while licking a pudding cup.

My lips rise. I adore Luna Hale.

"Until you've officially chosen someone," Oscar says more seriously, "the men outside are likely to keep coming back around."

Well then…there goes that.

Sullivan's shoulders drop, more bummed. When she catches me staring, she says hurriedly, "No big deal, Jane. Don't worry about it. It's not even your fucking fault. Grandmother Calloway sucks."

I take a breath. And I say to everyone, "I was never doing this to deter the men outside anyway."

Maximoff is acting strange. He stiffens, staring off at the brick wall and cracking his knuckles.

"Moffy?" I ask.

His eyes pin to me with a mountain of concern, his cheekbones sharpened like blades ready for war, and he asks the room, "What's the likelihood those guys outside become stalkers?"

"High," many bodyguards say at the same time.

I know why it's a high likelihood. It already takes a certain sort of person to not only believe the advertisement but to spend energy screeching my name outside my townhouse.

Maximoff and I have never feared stalkers before. Not until Nate. Once he breached the safety of our townhouse, he punctured our trust bubble and made me, in particular, feel incredibly violated.

I don't want that to happen again.

I leave Thatcher's side and approach the photographs. I scrutinize the auburn-haired football player and below his picture, a firefighter. Maybe I could date one of them?

Just for a little while.

"The firefighter looks nice maybe..." I trail off. It feels like a step too far, doesn't it? Especially after all that's happened.

"You're not dating him, Janie," Maximoff says, shutting it down.

"Just date Moretti," Oscar suggests so suddenly, and the room *explodes* in two exclamations:

"What?!"

"Oscar?!"

My big eyes have just popped out of my flushed face and rolled across the hardwood toward the source of my heat, shock, and all other tragically startled things.

Thatcher.

Thatcher.

Thatcher.

His name is a heartbeat in my head.

I look directly at him. He's still beside the staircase, and I'm frozen on the other side of the room.

His forehead is creased, brows drawn together, and his strong gaze pierces me so deeply that I wonder...*is* he actually considering this?

My mouth falls little by little, and my head tilts sideways off my neck. *Does he want to do this?*

His eyes detour to Banks.

My pulse has jumped on a trampoline, soared, and splattered on hard grass.

"Everyone, take a breath," Akara says, then he turns to the most tactical bodyguard. "Explain, Oscar."

Oscar crumples the chip bag in his hand. "I meant *pretend* to date. As in, just do it long enough that the unstable men outside can take a hint that she's taken."

Farrow lifts his brows at his friend. "You want Jane to pretend to date her bodyguard. Do you even know the consequences of that?"

"Not more than you would," Oscar admits.

Jack slips a pen behind his ear. He always has one handy for note-taking. "From a public perception standpoint, you're looking at two different headlines." He picks up my black cat, old and wise Lady Macbeth. "It'll be Heiress is Dating Her Bodyguard versus Heiress Seeks Rich Husband."

Maximoff shakes his head, neck tensed. "Either way, there'll be crowds. Christ, there might actually be *more* if she dates a bodyguard."

We saw an exponential increase in fans outside the house after Maximoff and Farrow's relationship went public. What they've experienced is a good basis for what would happen publicly if I dated Thatcher.

I clear my throat. "So there'd be no point to go forward with this." I hope I don't sound disappointed.

Oh my God, I can't believe my stomach is sinking in actual *disappointment* right now.

Why do I even want to take this dramatic turn? Is it because I'm a Cobalt? I'm a part of the most tragically dramatic family.

Or maybe my curiosity has piqued and finally punctured the atmosphere. Dating my bodyguard would break down doors that have been cemented shut.

Pretend dating, of course.

"It'd help," Oscar tells us. "It won't clear out the crowds, but it'll change the temperament of whoever surrounds Jane and the townhouse."

"More hecklers," Donnelly pipes in.

"More obsessive fans," Banks adds, sticking a toothpick between his lips.

Farrow peels a piece of Winterfresh gum. "Not to mention drunk fucks screaming outside bedroom windows."

"None of that is good," Quinn says with furrowed brows.

"But it's better than these unstable motherfuckers, little bro," Oscar tells him. "The ad lit something in some strange bastards, and now they think they have a chance with Jane. We can rid about sixty-five percent of the could-be stalkers if we nip this early and they think Jane's taken."

Farrow pops a bubble in his mouth, and he wraps an arm around Maximoff's waist, territorial and protective. "Okay, but there are still some hostile fuckers who think they have a shot with Maximoff, and he's not just dating a bodyguard like Jane would be. He's a fucking step further and engaged."

"That's why it's not a hundred-percent, Redford. Can't rid them all."

"Sixty-five percent success rate," Akara says. "It's not bad."

I lift a finger. "Pardon, but where did that number come from?"

Oscar answers, "Seven years of experience handling a thousand different kinds of motherfuckers."

"Amen," Banks nods.

It reminds me that I wasn't always a part of these serious security meetings. Not until Maximoff and I became closer to SFO. I trust their knowledge and what they've been through and dealt with as bodyguards.

I can't assume that I know best when I actually know very little about what they've each experienced.

But I have witnessed the consequences through Maximoff and Farrow.

I lock eyes with Thatcher, his stern expression yet to change shape. To lessen the risk of another Nate situation—I wonder how far he'd be willing to go.

I think being thrown into a media and public wildfire is too great of a sacrifice. "You can't go through what Farrow has gone through just to protect me," I tell him. "You'll be doxxed, and your family in South Philly could be harassed."

He's one of the most private people I've ever met. More private than even Farrow, and by publicly dating me, he'd expose himself to so many probes from paparazzi, tabloids, and internet fiends without the ability to say *no* or *stop.*

They will dig up his military service.

They will dig up more than he could even think of or imagine.

Akara looks to Thatcher. "The tech team can try to wipe out web searches that pop up your mom's home address, phone number, all of that. They think it's how Reddit users found out where Farrow's stepsister lived."

Maximoff slides an arm over Farrow's shoulders.

So there's a slight ability to circumvent some negative attention to his family. Keeping them safer if we were theoretically publicly together.

It seems like such a dreadfully high risk, but now mostly it's just on his shoulders and Banks.

"Your life will be fodder for the public. I can't let you do this for me," I tell Thatcher. "If you're considering it at all, that is." I'm not even sure what he's leaning towards.

"I'd do anything to keep you safe, Jane," he says deeply and without falter.

I hear what he just told me: *I feel a strong responsibility to you.*

I inhale a sharper breath.

Can we do this?

Should we do this?

Am I in the strangest dream?

And do I even want to wake up?

No.

I'd rather see what happens next. *Selfishly.* This may be the most selfish thing I've ever craved.

"Will her parents care?" Oscar asks.

Every person turns to me for the answer.

The attention doesn't cause me to balk, but Thatcher's intensity heats me up from head to toe.

My parents.

That hasn't even crossed my mind yet. My parents. My brothers. My little sister. What will they say?

"My parents," I ponder quickly. "No, they won't think it's unprofessional if I fake-date a bodyguard." I smile in thought. "I'm sure they'll actually think it's a bit of fun strategy. Like chess."

SFO relaxes more at this news.

Banks rotates to Akara. "What about Alpha and Epsilon? They're already on Omega's ass about all of us being barely famous, and they've limited our ability to go on-duty during events. So having another bodyguard as famous as Farrow will...?"

"The other forces may try to tie our hands, guys," Akara says diplomatically to all of SFO. "But we already have less power on the team right now, regardless if we take a risk today or down the line." He snaps his fingers to his palm and then glances between Thatcher and me. "Whatever you both decide, we'll all back."

Every bodyguard nods in agreement.

Even Farrow, who easily rises above his dislike for Thatcher if the outcome means protecting me.

Thatcher steps away from the staircase. Eyes set on Banks, he motions to the adjoining door, and then he glances at me. "We'll be back."

I nod, understanding completely.

Whatever happens will affect Banks, and possibly, he's confirming with his brother that he's okay about their military backgrounds being exposed to the team and the world.

As they disappear, SFO whispers quietly to each other, and I head to the fireplace where Maximoff and Farrow stand.

I'm so confused, and my voice is a whisper as I ask, "Shouldn't you two be anti-this-plan? It involves me being closer to someone you both dislike." I don't blame them at all for not loving Thatcher.

Maximoff puts a hand on my shoulder. "I'm pro-Jane." His intense green eyes speak a thousand promises. To always stick by my side. Through every terrible and wonderful thing.

My eyes burn with emotion, and I feel a smile at my lips.

Very casually, Farrow tells me, "I'm also pro-Jane more than I'm anti-anything-else."

Maximoff smiles at Farrow like he beat him at something strenuous. "You just copied me."

Farrow chews gum while grinning at him.

They both love one-upping each other.

His smile vanishes, and he gestures to Farrow's chest. "You did copy me, man."

"Technically, I said a hell of a lot more than you."

Maximoff grimaces, trying to hide his affection for his fiancé in this moment. He does a very decent job. I give my best friend a solid 7.5 out of 10 for effort and execution. His arm is still around Farrow's shoulders or else he'd be a perfect 10.

He's about to speak, but the adjoining door swings open.

The Moretti brothers are back already from their quick chat.

Thatcher's intense gaze descends upon me. "I need to talk to Jane alone."

My eyes grow and I sweep him more inquiringly. Moments like these, I'd love to be able to predict the future.

13

THATCHER MORETTI

"Ignore the mess," Jane says as she snatches dirty clothes off a fuzzy rug and flings them in a narrow, stuffed closet.

I shut the door behind me.

Her room is drenched in pastel colors, sequins, and animal prints. Coming here is like jumping into some type of milkshake-drinking bubblegum-blowing pop era that dresses up as the fucking 80s. Banks says it gives him *agita*. Makes him want to chug three bottles of Pepto-Bismol, and if it weren't for Jane, I might feel the same.

But I step foot in here and I just see all the sides of Jane Cobalt. Bold and soft. Outlandish and unabashed. Feminine and eager.

Beautiful.

It makes me never want to leave.

Don't go there—but I'm already here, and truth is, I've been in her room plenty before. For security. After the Nate incident, she asked if I could make routine checks each night.

I have.

It's not a big space. Not many places for a target to hide. Not many entry-points for a break-in. Her four-poster bed is tucked up against the only window, and a pale blue vanity and cushioned stool hug a corner.

I've opened the mirrored closet door and peered behind her skirts and blouses before. I've lifted up the pink duvet, so I could inspect the dark area underneath her bed. Always littered with cat toys.

I've had to stretch over her mattress and push aside cheetah-patterned drapes. Just to secure the latch on the window and reset an alarm.

But I'm not here right now to assess and observe. I'm here to *talk* to Jane.

This is still about security, I remind myself.

This is still about her protection.

That's all it should be.

I stand at the door like I'm on patrol and shouldering eighty-pounds of gear on my back. Just routine. What I'm trained for.

Nothing out of the ordinary.

I fold my arms over my chest, and I watch Jane fling a stray pair of cotton panties into the closet before she whirls around. Almost tripping over her own feet. She brushes wavy brown strands out of her face, and then she settles a confident hand on her waist.

Goddamn.

My blood heats.

"Thatcher," she says, breathless. Her chest rises and falls and pushes out her breasts. Temperature ratchets up a hundred degrees, veins lit up on fire. *Get it together.*

There's no waffling with me. Indecisiveness can fuck up a whole team, an entire op, and my mission this time is her.

Her.

"Jane," I say, clear and cut and definitive, "I've already made a decision."

She never breaks eye contact. "You have…?"

"I want to do this with you."

Her voice catches, words stuck on her tongue.

I hold her gaze in a tighter grip. "I want to date you in public."

Jane presses her knuckles to her lips. "For my protection." She's laying out the parameters before I even can. We've been good about that.

"For your protection," I agree, and in a millisecond, my gaze slips down the nape of her neck. And she leans a hip on the bedpost like I'm fucking her sideways.

Christ. My abs tighten, and I rub my jaw with a tensed hand. I need to get my mind right.

"You've truly considered all the costs and benefits of being in a public relationship with me?" she asks. "I gain more than you. You'll lose privacy, normalcy—your life will be forever different."

She's concerned about me being doxxed and the public scrutiny, but I've weighed the risks. "I know what I'm stepping into," I say with severity. "No cost is greater than the cost of your life."

Jane inhales, and then speaks in a whisper. "Just once more and I won't ever ask again: are you sure?"

"I'm positive." I would take any shot if it meant scaring off another stalker like Nate. If it meant keeping her safe. "Do you want to do this?"

"If you're confident—"

"I am."

"Then yes." She straightens up. "I'd like to deter a stalker or two, possibly more, so I'd very much like to fake date you…" Blush shades her freckles. "Platonically, I'm guessing. How does one actually *fake* date?" Her eyes glimmer like we're headed into *curious* territory.

I soak up her excitement. It amplifies my readiness, and I crave nothing more than to push forward with Jane.

"We'll have a new set of boundaries," I explain. "The main goal is to make the media and public buy the fact that I'm your boyfriend."

I can't act like I've been set free to do whatever the fuck I want. This is a security operation and a publicity stunt. I have a team to think about, and I'm positive Alpha and Epsilon especially will want to pull strings and have a hand in what I do with Jane.

Whether I like it or not, I have to obey the rules.

I can't think about how her eyes dropped to my dick at the word *boyfriend.* I can't think about how, if she weren't a client, I would've already had her on the bed. Bare and wet and ready for me.

My muscles bind.

I'm rigid, and silence stretches. While we stand on either side of the room, invisible tension threads from her body to mine.

Jane fills the quiet. "What type of boundaries are we talking about?"

"We can't have sex." I say the unsaid words that have hung untouched between us for months.

Shock drops her jaw. Jane reaches behind her back with two hands. Clasping the bedpost, standing pin-straight. "Sex?" Her eyes are fucking huge.

There's no way I've read her incorrectly, not for this long.

"Jane..." I fix the mic on my gray T-shirt collar.

She processes slowly like she's asleep. Dreaming.

"I want to make this clear." I rub my mouth and then drop my arm. "This arrangement isn't a free pass to sleep together. No matter how..." Don't say the word *horny* in front of her like we're fourteen. I'm twenty-eight.

She's twenty-three.

I restart, "No matter how attracted we both are to each other."

Her mouth falls and wavers into a shocked smile. "You just said out loud that you're attracted to me."

She's more surprised that I said the words than that I actually *am* attracted to her. Which means I did a piss-poor job at hiding it, but I already knew that.

"Jane," I say, voice deep. "No sex."

"Oui." She tucks a strand of hair behind her ear. "Everything we do from here on out needs to be for the sake of fake-dating." She tips her head, a question crinkling her forehead. "If you know that I'm forever closed off to sex, then why do you think it's such a concern that we'll sleep together?"

"I'm not a stranger. You feel safe with me. Right?" I ask.

"Yes."

"You still trust me?"

"Immensely."

I nod once. "That's why."

Jane smiles softly. "Just for clarity between us, I've thought the same: that you'd be the exception if I were to ever touch a dick again—but I won't touch yours," she adds quickly. "We're strictly fake boyfriend and fake girlfriend. Sex should stay out of bounds, I wholeheartedly agree."

My expression hardens.

I can't think about how she'd allow me to get her off. Because I hate that she's been hurt in the past and that's part of why she'd need me. On top of that, I hate that I'm jealous at even the idea of her opening up to another guy. When she should heal those wounds. When it's not even *possible* for her and me to be together for real.

And I fucking hate Nate.

Oh and one more: buried beneath all these professional restrictions and complications, I want to bring her to the edge with orgasms so fucking intense they eke out her energy and sink her to sleep.

Inappropriate.

That's the circle of hell I've been having a picnic in.

Jane shifts around the wooden post and leans on her bed, hands flat beside her waist on the pink duvet. "When we say *no sex*, maybe we should be more specific."

I never flinch. "Specifically, my cock isn't going inside your pussy."

Jane crosses her ankles, her chest concaving in arousal. "I usually dislike when guys say *pussy*, but…that was good…very direct and assertive." She smooths her lips together. "Assertiveness suits you." She straightens up again and dusts her skirt, and our eyes meet in raw desire.

Fuck.

My muscles flame. Nerves scorched. I'm literally pinning myself to the fucking door. I can't talk about this with her right now.

Not in her bedroom.

Not when we're severing a shitload of rope that'll allow me to move in closer.

"Let's talk about something else," I tell Jane.

She's quick to change the subject like it's as easy as counting to three. "We have to convince the world we're madly in love." She drifts to the vanity and then gracefully lowers onto the stool until she wobbles on the uneven floorboards. Jane catches her balance and then her big blue eyes lift up to me. "Do you have any experience in this area? Love."

We're really doing this.

I've wanted to.

I almost can't believe I have the ability now.

"We should research," Jane says in my silence. "Shouldn't we?"

"We should," I confirm.

She snaps off a hair tie, letting her wavy hair loose. "Well, you already know I'm looking down the barrel of four previous friends-with-benefits and zero boyfriends."

"Why no boyfriends?" I ask.

Her eyes are on mine while she slips on a purple cat-ear headband. "Fame makes serious relationships utterly complicated, and it always seemed like too much stress. I'd rather put energy into my family."

I nod.

She easily reads my features. "You're not surprised."

"No." I've been around her every day for nearly a year. If any of that surprised me, then I'm not paying attention.

Jane likes her life structured and planned out. It gives her a sense of control that she's inherently lost as a celebrity.

Feeling protected and confident in this plan to fake-date is important to her, and so it's critical to me.

I watch Jane slowly rise to her feet, and I tell her, "I have two ex-girlfriends."

"Two." Her eyes drift along the rug before lifting up to me. "Did you experience love with them?"

A rough laugh catches in my lungs. "Hell no." I shake my head. "They weren't relationships I'd model anything after either." I pause. "Not unless you want to cheat on me."

Her lips break apart. "I'm so sorry."

"It's way back." I can see she's interested in more. So I push forward. "Through all of eleventh grade, my high school girlfriend was sleeping with a guy she knew I couldn't stand. I had no idea until graduation."

She softens her gaze. "Teenagers can be particularly cruel." She cups her hands in front of her. "I'd say we're both equally awful at relationships, but you will be my first. *Fake* relationship, that is, but first nonetheless." Red blemishes her neck.

I nod. "We'll pull it off, Jane." I breathe in a lung full of her fresh flower, spring scent. *Wrong move.*

My whole body reacts to the smell. It drives me fucking nuts, muscles contracting. Veins blistering. Cock straining against my slacks.

She wafts her blouse, clearly hot. "We will," she agrees. "So what... um, kind of relationship should we have in public?" She talks quickly. "Should we be inseparably cute? Piggyback rides and sharing snow cones. Or scandalously flirty? French kissing and ass squeezes."

My hand is clamped on my jaw and mouth. Trying not to think about my hand on her ass. Three Hail Marys is not enough to atone for what I'm feeling about her.

She hooks an arm around her bedpost. "I think being an inseparably cute couple would be easiest, but also not necessarily true to me."

I drop my hand. "Not true to me either."

A smile dimples her cheeks. "To us, then. We are highly...physical?" she asks tentatively.

"Affirmative," I say.

The confirmation cranks the heat another hundred degrees.

"Okay..." She motions to me. "So cute couple is out then. The media might pick up on the deception. The other option is scandalously flirty. But how do we kiss? Not like the mechanics of kissing, which we both, I'm sure, understand." She rambles on. "But the idea of kissing without screwing. Because usually I screw the people I kiss." She presses her lips together like she's forcing herself to stop talking, but our eyes stay glued on each other.

"We're both adults," I remind her. "I think we can kiss and stop ourselves from having sex."

"Normally, I would agree. But it's been six months."

I'm inferring she's talking about how long since she last got laid. I have her beat. "Ten months for me."

She sways back in surprise. "Really? You didn't hookup with anyone during the FanCon?"

"No. I wouldn't fool around with tour crew, and I was busy." I was

focused on protecting Jane. I nod to her. "Been used to long dry spells."
I hear my Philly lilt come out thicker. "It's not a big deal."

She's quick and smart and I'm not surprised when she connects the
dots. "When you were in the military?"

I nod again. "I was deployed to combat twice overseas during my
four-year tour."

It feels like another lifetime, and since we're talking about sex, I'm
thinking more about the drawn-out dry spell I had.

Say more. I try to chisel my jaw open. "Staying celibate wasn't an issue,"
I explain. "I have no problem pushing myself into hard situations. I
like testing my strength—but I couldn't convince my girlfriend that I
was faithful, not while I was on deployment."

I explain briefly how my second ex-girlfriend was adamant that
someone like me would attract a lot of other women, and she believed
I'd struggle to resist and then slip up and cheat. When I got back home,
I found out that she'd slept with her ex.

Now they're married and have two kids.

"I take a lot of fault for what happened," I say. "I'm hard to read,
and I could've done better to ease her insecurities."

She inhales a deeper breath that stretches a silent second into a
boiling minute. Both of us hardly blink. Nearing a visceral edge.

Jane swallows and waves to me. "You're very self-aware, you know."

I don't respond yet. Wanting to hear what else she has to say.

"And you're respectful," she lists, like she's constructing a PowerPoint
of my traits. "Very considerate, as well. All things I'm drawn towards—
which is perfect since you're my fake boyfriend."

I throb harder. There is only one of Jane, no other person can be
all of who she is, and anyone who harasses this girl might as well be
tearing the wings off an angel.

I'm honored that I get to be the one to keep her safe.

She's my duty.

I also shouldn't want to fuck an angel.

She's my client. Remember that.

Jane continues on. "And as evidenced by our history, we can clearly restrain ourselves. Which means we can be two consenting adults who casually kiss and not have sex afterwards."

Our eyes roam beyond our old restraints.

"That sounds right," I nod, and I study her flushed body, her ankles crossed like she's squeezing her thighs together. "We should practice."

"We should," she agrees. "Kissing?"

"Kissing," I confirm. "I'm a whole foot taller than you."

"Exactly," she notes. "If we just do it in public *without* proper preparation, it'll be obvious that we're fake dating."

"And that it's your first time."

Her intrigue piques. "My first time…"

"With me," I say strongly.

"Right." Jane smiles. "Should we start now then?" She hesitates, waiting for my answer. "It will be a good litmus test to see if this will even work."

It's going to work.

Because the alternative is doing nothing, and I'd rather mount up and frighten away a bunch of targets.

"I'm good to go," I tell Jane.

She steps away from her bed.

I pry myself off the door, and I do more than take a single step closer. I take several unwavering strides.

She goes still, seeing me approach, and her eyes glint with eagerness. I watch her savor my assured demeanor, and I stop a breath away.

The top of her head, along with her purple cat ears, just reaches my shoulders.

Jane cranes her neck to look up at me. Dark lashes shading beautiful, emotive blue eyes. Silence bands around us, the space shrunken. Air vacuumed.

"So…" Her voice is a breathy whisper. "I'll just stand on my tiptoes." She rises on her toes, but barefoot, she barely lifts herself past the broad length of my shoulders.

I could just lean my head down.

I could.

But I don't.

In a swift, natural move, I cup the back of her thighs, and I hoist Jane up against my body—we're eye-level, her legs instinctively spreading apart. Wrapping around my waist, gripping tight.

Her hands fly around the back of my neck and nestle in my hair.

"Oh," she breathes, lips parted in arousal. I can practically hear the *my God* that sticks to her throat.

Jane.

I eye her, my pulse pounding.

Heat brews and overflows—she feels too good against my body. This is dangerous. I feel her panting. I feel her thumping heartbeat. I feel her in ways I never fucking have, and I just keep drinking in her breathless state.

She's lapping up this position. Me holding her. Us welded together.

Her palm slides against the back of my neck, fingers threading up in my hair.

My cock stirs to life, and I restrain myself from carrying her to the bed. *Don't.* This close, her scent overpowers me. Fresh flowers.

Spring.

Intoxicating me, stimulating places in me I didn't think existed. Primal fucking need, and we stare straight into each other. Head-on.

No diversions. No glimpses away.

I head towards the task at hand, closing in. Our noses brush, heads turning, and this should be slow, should be gentle.

Our lips finally meet, and we combust.

I pull her harder against my body in an untamed, blistering kiss, and her arms and thighs tighten around me.

"Thatcher." A breath expels from her lips into my mouth, and her delicate hand slips along my jaw.

My biceps flex, muscles scalding a billion degrees. We ransack all the passion that has been vaulted shut. All the heat and the fire.

I hold her soft ass, and I shift my other to her freckled cheek, hot as all fucking hell. I slide my tongue against hers, and she grips my shoulders to hang on and then bucks into me for more. *Fuck.*

Jane.

My dick aches against the fabric of my slacks.

Do not bring her to the bed.

Do not bring her to the fucking bed.

Lip-locked, I walk towards the bed, still tucking Jane protectively against me, but I only go for the wooden bedpost.

Her back meets the beam. I keep her in my strong arms, and her hands dive underneath my shirt and trace the ridges of my abs while I deepen the kiss.

I taste her need and longing against my tongue, and when I suck on her bottom lip, a strangled noise is trapped in her throat like she's trying to suppress the high-pitched sound.

A grunt scratches against my lungs, and I hold her closer. She trembles against my body. Sweat building up on my skin.

I slow down with Jane, and our stroking eyes say more than they should.

"This is just practice," she reaffirms in a shallow pant, lips reddened from the force.

I nod. "Just practice."

"Practicing is very professional of us." Her palm warms my chest, and we kiss deeper.

Again, and again.

Speeding up the tempo each time she arches her waist into me. She's practically dry-humping me—*don't go there.*

Yeah, I'm so far over there at the moment.

We pull back for a half second. Catching breath.

"If I'm too heavy, you can set me down," she says conversationally. "I don't mind."

My chest tightens, and I narrow a stern look on Jane. "I could bench press you all night." *Did I make her feel...?* Concern draws my brows together. I clasp her face, my large hand enveloping her flushed cheek. "You're meant to be in my arms, Jane."

She pulses against me and sets her laced fingers along the back of my neck. "I...um." She shakes out her scrambled thoughts. "We'll be experts in the art of fake-dating in no time. Don't you think?"

I nod, not wanting to set her down yet. I'm on another point. She's clearly in need of a release—I am too—but guilt gnaws at me for bringing her here without setting her off.

Leaving her like this...

Either my features aren't padlocked or she's getting better at reading them because she asks, "How many people are downstairs?"

"All of SFO, Jack, and three of your cousins."

"That's quite a lot of ears that could hear...things." She lifts her chin and straightens her off-kilter headband. "Rain check? For other things besides your cock in my pussy."

My nose flares.

I fight against conflicting emotions. I want to set her down, kneel at her feet, hike her leg over my shoulder and eat her out until she hits a trembling peak. I want to take care of Jane and satiate her fucking needs, but also do it when there aren't ten people downstairs.

I want to obey my orders and the leads.

I have to obey the leads.

I want Jane.

In another beat, I exhale a tensed breath. Readied for my purpose here, and it's always to keep her safe. Anything less is un-fucking-acceptable.

I tell her, "We can work out more details later." She'll want more structure, and after I go through security meetings, there won't be gray areas concerning what we need to do in public to pull this off.

She nods. "Bien."

We stare at each other like we could kiss for another hour.

I haven't let her go.

Come on, Thatcher. I need to move the fuck out, but I notice how she eyes the cord to my mic and earpiece.

I'm her bodyguard. Kissing me is just part of a security op.

We're aware.

Slowly, gradually, I lower Jane, and her feet gently touch the floor.

I start heading to the door, but on instinct, I glance over my shoulder to check on her.

Curiosity bubbles up in her eyes. Her lips are more pink and swollen because of me, and she's hanging on the bedpost again.

Move to the fucking door.

My body wants to go back to her.

She's staring through me now.

Like she wants me to come back.

Door.

Door.

Go to the fucking door.

I'm there. Hand on the knob.

"Goodnight, Jane," I say stiffly.

I crack open the door.

"Goodnight, Thatcher."

I leave.

All the while, her voice stays inside my head.

14

JANE COBALT

"It was practice," I explain to my best friend. "A *practice* kiss."

Maximoff stares at me like I'm talking in a foreign language. Hair damp from a morning shower and towel tied around his waist, he rubs a fist against our bathroom's fogged mirror. I try not to bump him while I take out my basket of skincare products from the sink cabinet.

We went from sharing this townhouse with just each other to now having three extra roommates: Farrow, Luna, and Sulli.

It makes mornings difficult since we all share one bathroom. Later jumpstarts to my day just means more time to chat with Moffy. At least, that's the bright spot since we've both chosen to take the bathroom last.

I can't keep secrets from Moffy, and Thatcher can't keep them from Banks. And I need someone to know this happened.

I cannot take it to my grave.

"Say something," I tell him.

"You and Thatcher kissed."

"Say something that doesn't involve stating facts," I rephrase and squirt cleanser on my palm.

"Did you like it?" He reaches for his toothbrush.

"Oui."

He looks at me through the mirror. "Did you do anything else?"

"I wanted to, but we've just begun fake-dating. It seems…premature and out of bounds."

His brows furrow. "Did he want to?"

"Most surely." I smile, liking how Thatcher and I keep finding ourselves on the same page. I remember my leg brushing his bulge as he lowered me off his waist.

That night, I went to bed with a vibrating sex toy. Imagining that he'd just taken me right there. I understand why he didn't. I respect the boundaries of his job and the parameters that are set.

"He was hard," I explain to Moffy, but I quickly clarify that I didn't actually *see* anything. I pause in another realization. "Unless his bulge feels that big when he's soft. I suppose I wouldn't know. But he seemed hard to me."

Maximoff solidifies in thought. "Your bodyguard has a literal hard-on for you."

I lather cleanser on my cheeks. "And yours, you."

He reanimates, pushing aside razors and grabbing a tube of toothpaste. "Say that a little louder next time you see Farrow. He keeps thinking I'm the one who's obsessed with him." He lets out a dry laugh. "In his dreams."

I smile, but it fades as I see more concern swim in his forest-green eyes.

He's worried about this situation with Thatcher and me.

"He's very professional," I remind Moffy. "Even pretending to date me, he somehow found a way to make that professional."

I explain the boundaries and how Thatcher and I are not to do anything that doesn't involve practicing to fool the media.

Which means *no sex*.

"I just want you to be happy," he reminds me, "and what you two are doing sounds like edging with no climax." He squirts toothpaste on bristles. "Which is pretty much torture."

He's still cautious about me driving down one-way streets and facing heartbreak since Thatcher is too strict to break rules. But that's not what's happening here.

We're in the same car with the same plan with the same destination.

"It was far from torture," I say distantly as my phone buzzes on the toilet seat. All uninhibited thoughts about Thatcher Moretti vanish from my mind.

I wipe my palms quickly on a hand towel and then pick up my phone. Maximoff glances over while I read the Caller ID.

"It's Tom," I tell him.

Most of my siblings call me at least once a day, and if they don't, I usually seek them out.

I click into the call and put it on speaker.

"Salut, petit diable," I say brightly. *Hello, little devil.*

Tom shouts over loud bass and percussion, currently at band practice. "As-tu parlé à Charlie récemment?!" *Have you spoken to Charlie recently?*

Maximoff's brows knit together at the mention of my iconoclastic brother.

They're both at a better place ever since the FanCon, but I try not to have any expectations. It's best that way. Because if they start fighting again, I won't be shadowed in disappointment. And if they do rebuild their friendship, I can be pleasantly surprised.

No expectations.

It's the best solution.

"I spoke to Charlie yesterday," I tell Tom. "When he told me that I'm officially the most dramatic Cobalt."

I spent the majority of last night calling each of my siblings and mom and dad, letting them know my plan to fake date my twenty-eight-year-old bodyguard. It was a quick call to each, and they all voiced their approval in their own way.

We're a supportive clan but, more importantly, we all love grandiose displays of loyalty. And nothing screams loyalty like shielding a secret from the entire world.

Music fades over the line, so my brother must've found a quieter spot.

"Charlie said you're officially the most dramatic?" Tom scoffs. "Give it a day, Jane Eleanor. Tomorrow, Eliot and I will have you beat. And anyway, you haven't even announced that you're dating your bodyguard yet. Call me back when your fake boyfriend wears a shirt with your initials on it."

He's referencing a real event when a pop singer "allegedly" dated a famous actor for publicity. My little sister said they had true love, but I guess we'll never really know. I recognize very well that that must be how the world feels about my family.

Most people will never really know us or have all the facts, and they have to be satisfied with whatever we give them.

"Thatcher will not be wearing an *I heart J.E.C.* shirt," I tell Tom. "We're going to be a little more discreet than that."

"Boring," he tells me. "So I, uh, still can't get ahold of Charlie." Tom sounds distracted wherever he is. Possibly he's also texting. He often tries to do both at once. "He's not picking up his phone, per usual. Do you know where he's at?"

One sibling usually calls me each day asking about Charlie's whereabouts. I rarely have much information to share. They'd call Beckett, but he's usually at rehearsal and I'm the next closest to Charlie.

Maximoff brushes his teeth and listens.

"Last night he was in Brooklyn," I tell Tom. But we all know that doesn't mean much. He could be on a plane to Dubai by now.

"Eliot should put another tracker on him," Tom says, mischief in his voice. "See how that works out."

"Tom," I warn. "Charlie is not a dog."

Last time Eliot and Tom attached a tracker to Charlie's phone, we almost had a Cobalt Civil War.

"Hey, is Moffy with you?"

Maximoff pauses brushing. "Hey, Tom."

"Dude." Tom takes a longer beat. He has to be texting. "You know that guy I've been kind of casually seeing in private?"

I've heard everything about the casual hookup that's on Tom's speed dial. Emphasis on *casual*. It's just about fooling around, Tom has said.

He isn't in search of anything serious. He says it's not because of the media, but I've seen him a little freaked out from how aggressive the paparazzi and public are towards Maximoff and Farrow. The rabid attention has scared many of my siblings away from diving into a relationship.

I love, most of all, that my eighteen-year-old brother has Maximoff for advice.

"Yeah, I remember." Maximoff spits into the sink.

"We locked a day to do anal," Tom explains in a rush, "and I was planning on taking fiber supplements like you said Farrow does. But I'm too paranoid to just rely on that since it's my first time. And now I have to get this stuff to douche, and I mean, I have to figure out *how* to even douche."

"It's alright, don't stress." Maximoff looks back at my phone. "I'll text you what you need. It gets easier every time. Call me if you're having trouble."

He exhales in relief. "Will do." To me, he says, "Adieu, ma soeur."

Farewell, sister.

"Adieu."

Maximoff rinses toothpaste out of his mouth. "I can ask Farrow if he can get ahold of Oscar and see if he knows where Charlie is."

I shake my head. "No, if Charlie wants to be alone, he should be left alone." But if I can't reach my brother in 36 hours, I'll send in the cavalry to find him.

Our heads turn as floorboards squeak.

Farrow appears, beautiful wings and crossed swords inked on his neck and throat. He leans casually on the doorway, already dressed in black slacks, his radio clipped to the waistband. He had an early security meeting at Studio 9 with Omega and some of Epsilon and Alpha.

Thatcher and I were the main topic at hand, I'm sure, but instead of digging into that, I raise my voice. "Moffy, your bodyguard has a terribly big hard-on for you."

Maximoff tries to boast, but he ends up smiling too much at Farrow. "You heard Janie. She only speaks the truth."

"I do," I play along and close my bottle of cleanser.

Farrow skims Maximoff's bare chest and towel. "You told her to tell me that, wolf scout."

Maximoff scrunches his face, about to put the toothbrush back. "How could you know that, man?"

He arches his brows. "Because I know you." He looks to me. "And you." His gaze darkens a little more than usual. Protective.

It must've been an intense security meeting.

His gaze flits to Maximoff's hand, and his smile suddenly stretches from cheek to cheek. "That's also my toothbrush."

Oh no.

Maximoff goes rigid. "No it's not." He checks.

Oh it is.

Farrow laughs and pushes into the bathroom. They have this moment where he cups Maximoff's jaw and kisses his lips tenderly in greeting, and they murmur under their breath to one another. Their hands pulling each other closer. Chest to chest.

I never want to be jealous of their love. I want to be satisfied with what I have, but my stomach tumbles in strange patterns.

I'm not sure what I really feel right now.

I just know what I want to feel.

I train my focus elsewhere and start texting on my phone. "I'm asking Thatcher to come over."

Maximoff detaches slightly from Farrow. "Are you going out?"

"I'm making an announcement, and you all need to hear it."

Concern washes over his eyes. "What kind of an announcement?"

"You'll see."

15

THATCHER MORETTI

Banks slides out from underneath the
Volkswagen Beetle, oil staining his palms. Since we were teenagers, he
was always fixing friends' cars for an extra buck. He got a job at an old
mechanic shop down the street when he was fifteen.

I hand my brother a torque wrench. "That briefing was fucking
horseshit," I tell him rigidly, both of us in the garage.

We just got back from Studio 9. The Alpha lead and the new Epsilon
lead spent the majority of the team's time rephrasing the same fucking
point and hammering it to death.

Do not fuck Jane.

Do not have sex with a client.

Do not sleep or screw or push forward inside that girl in any
goddamn way. Direct quote from my superior.

Men yelling in my face to make me take it is just a fucking side salad.
Tastes like nothing, I chow down in silence, and I move on to the main
course: my purpose, my reason for being.

My responsibility.

My client.

Jane.

But the fact that two leads opened a crass can of worms—talking
about her and sex and me in graphic warning—it didn't taste like
nothing. I was chewing on a bag of rusted nails.

It hit a nerve.

She means something to me, something that I should release in the fucking wind, but I'm clutching tighter. Bringing her closer.

I'm walking the thinnest line with security, and even tempering my anger is becoming harder.

I left the briefing with Banks, both of us glaring, and I muttered to him what I held back from saying earlier, "Respectfully, sir, shut the fuck up."

Banks bounced his head, up and down. "Amen."

Back in the garage, Banks uses the torque wrench to scratch an itch on his neck. "Old guards are still clearly paranoid since Farrow slept with Maximoff and kept his job. They already promised the parents that it wouldn't happen again."

The team wants to maintain trust and respect with the parents.

I stare hard at my brother. "I was one of the men who promised the parents." *Back when I was a lead.* I had to douse the fire that Farrow lit.

Banks motions his hand to my chest. "And I told you that was a bad call."

I narrow my gaze. "You don't even like making one fucking call, and you wanna tell me that one was bad?"

Banks prefers not being in charge, but briefly, he'd been a lead right after I stepped down. And when he relinquished the role, he was so fucking happy he kissed the pavement in Studio 9's parking lot.

"Just because I don't like making them doesn't mean I can't see a bad one from a good one." Banks points toward the door to Jane's townhouse. "You set course for trouble the second you joined her detail." He tosses and catches the wrench. "Probably even before that."

I give him a hard look. "Don't go there."

I never thought of her as more than the oldest Cobalt daughter: a quick-witted girl with a big heart. Who was constantly berated by fuckbags in public. Who should be kept safe and shielded from that hatred.

Being her bodyguard strengthened a feeling of duty that existed, I'll give my brother that, but I wasn't thinking about breaking Jane's knees apart and sinking my cock into her—because that'd be fucking wrong. Unprofessional.

I only mentally booked a room for hell around the time we shared *tight* space on a tour bus. And she was admittedly sexually frustrated.

I was sexually fucking frustrated, and we kept looking at each other. I wouldn't cross that line to help her.

I couldn't. *I couldn't.*

I still can't.

Banks pats the torque wrench in his palm, thinking, and then he nods his chin to me. "Remember that time when you wanted to put *three* full-time bodyguards on her after the chokehold incident?"

My muscles tense.

Yeah.

I wasn't her bodyguard. But I was in charge of the team back then.

Banks leans against the Beetle's tire. "You care beyond your duty."

He always says that when he brings up Jane.

You care beyond your duty.

One other phrase rings shrilly in the pit of my ear: *the chokehold incident.* Lines crease my forehead, eyes searing.

Some entitled piece of shit thought Jane was into BDSM, and he tried to choke her when they were hooking up at the townhouse. Her bodyguard had to break down the door and pry the guy off Jane. He followed protocol, but knowing that happened to her…

I hate men who take advantage of these girls. Who try to screw with Jane. And I fucking hate when she's hurt.

I needed to protect her. It always feels bigger than a job, but that was my job too.

"I was a lead," I tell my brother.

"So was Akara." Banks lifts one shoulder. "But he didn't vote to put three full-time bodyguards on her detail." Neither did Price, the Alpha lead.

She ended up just keeping one 24/7 bodyguard on-duty. After that happened to her, I took time to ensure she was protected.

I thought it was because I was a lead. But Banks believed differently.

I just nod a couple times, and I scrutinize my brother for a second. He shaved closer this morning, making his jawline appear narrower. Which makes me look about two years older than him, but only six-minutes separate us in reality. Growing up, he'd tell our dad I was the "older brother" to shirk responsibility.

I didn't care that it wound up on me.

I am six-minutes older, but I'm constantly turning to him for advice.

My phone pings, and I read a text.

Do not rush if you're preoccupied, but I have an announcement that you should hear. You can find me in my bathroom. — Jane

It can't be an emergency if she's saying not to hurry. But I'm still on guard.

"Jane?" Banks guesses off my expression.

"I need to head over there." I read the text out to him.

The corner of his lip hikes up like I read a portion of her diary. "In her bathroom? First a kiss, then a—"

"We have boundaries set," I cut him off, pocketing my phone. "This is just to protect her."

"But you like her," Banks says.

"Doesn't matter." I have to follow the hierarchy. Breaking the rules will rip a bullet through security and plunge all of Omega headfirst in boiling water with Alpha and Epsilon.

Banks nods and starts to crawl back underneath the car. "Gomesegiam'...you're in over your head?" *How do you say...you're in over your head?*

I exhale through my nose. "Fuck."

16

 THATCHER MORETTI

I'm in Jane's bathroom, and she isn't the only one here.

"Just a fair warning: if you fuck with Jane during this fake-dating stunt, I won't come for you," Maximoff says firmly, spearing a territorial glare into me. "Because I'll go after your brother instead, and I'll break both of his kneecaps and stake his head on a fucking pitchfork."

Gut reaction, I almost glare.

I'd die for Banks, no hesitation; the idea of living without him is eviscerating—but I get Maximoff's protectiveness of Jane. Fully.

"He's being hyperbolic," Jane says to me, her eyes widened. Cautious. Like all four of us are on the edge of a cliff together.

I steal another brief glance at her. She's in a purple bathrobe, hair twisted in a nest, and zit cream dotted on her chin and forehead.

Her ability to be comfortable in her own skin—it's gorgeous. Flat-out, and for once, I allow myself to think it without reprimand.

"Pretty sure I'm being honest," Maximoff says, pulling my attention back. He never shifts his intense green eyes off me. A straight razor is in his hand. He was shaving short stubble on his jaw.

The second that I ducked beneath the doorway and straightened up—only a foot inside the bathroom—Jane, Maximoff, and Farrow rotated towards me. And Maximoff got the first word out.

Sorry—the first *threat* out, and I don't blame him. Hell, I've been waiting for something like this from Maximoff. Being around the Hale family for a long time, I've heard their sharp-tongued threats. His dad is more brutal, but on some deep level, I know Maximoff is just as serious right now.

I open my mouth to reply.

He cuts back in, "And by *fuck with her*, I mean hurting her even a fraction of an inch."

I nod, just as serious. "Understood."

Because I'm complete shit at showing emotion, I force myself to add more. Just in case it's not clear.

I look him in the eyes. "I'll never hurt Jane. I wouldn't."

Jane steeples her fingertips to her lips. Eyes darting back and forth to everyone. Even to Farrow who leans casually on the shower door and smiles while chewing gum. I can't tell if he's entertained by his fiancé or just by me getting threatened.

"Glad we have that covered," Maximoff says strongly. "Especially since you kissed her already."

The air deadens.

I'm motionless.

Can't be surprised she told them. Not when I already told Banks.

"Yeah," I say out loud. "I kissed Jane." I'm assured that this is where I need to be, and I'm not someone who fucking cowers. But there are plenty of times I wish I would've taken a step back rather than barrel forward and rip myself up in barbed wire.

But this isn't even close to a regret.

Maximoff thinks hard for a second, and more silence weighs the room down.

"For practice," Jane reminds them.

Farrow pops a bubble in his mouth. "Is that what Cobalts call it?"

Jane knots her robe tighter. "We call everything what it should be. An orange is an orange. Your eyes are brown, and a practice kiss is simply a practice kiss."

I sweep her with more concern.

She's getting stressed, and they should be able to tell as much as I can. I've never seen Maximoff or Farrow actively be a roadblock in her life. Only support. And even now, they quickly back off.

"Fair enough," Farrow says easily.

Worry infiltrates her big blue eyes, and she looks between Maximoff and Farrow. "You're both supposed to help us with fake dating, not be a wedge—"

"I'm not *wedging*," Maximoff interjects, hurt in his voice at the idea of putting any distance between her and him. "I'm just letting Thatcher know that *we* know that *he* knows what's happening here."

I'm not sure what he's talking about other than the fact that they know I kissed Jane…and that I can't cross a boundary.

Farrow puts in his obsidian spear earring. "That could've used ten times more clarity, but D-minus for the effort."

Maximoff grimaces. "It's called *A* for effort."

"You're more like a D-minus, wolf scout."

His face falls blank. "Thank you for that inaccurate grading scale."

"Anytime."

Maximoff groans in the back of his throat, and Jane turns more to me, stepping nearer. Only a few feet away now.

She skims my black button-down and the gold horns that are back around my neck. And then we lock eyes for a hot beat.

"Thatcher," she says like we missed our routine greeting. "It's good to see you. Um…you look well." Confidence bleeds through her breezy voice, despite the pause.

Heat gathers in my fucking lungs.

Instantly, I remember yesterday—I remember her breathless noise against my mouth, my hands gripping her firmly against my strong build, and her soft thighs wrapped around my waist, clinging tighter and tighter.

Wanting more.

Aching.

And I couldn't satiate her full desire and my fucking hunger. *Good thing.* It's a good thing I didn't overstep, but for some reason, it's tearing me up.

Come on.

I put a hand to my radio and remember why the hell I exist here in the first place.

Her safety. "Jane…" I want to tell her she looks good too, but I should just get to the point. "You have an announcement."

"Right, yes." She arches her shoulders in preparation for the big reveal.

Maximoff and Farrow concentrate solely on her.

"So," she says, "you three are the most important people in my life right now. My best friend." She waves to Maximoff. "My best friend's fiancé." She waves to Farrow. "And my bodyguard—bold-hyphenation fake boyfriend." She smiles at me.

"Bold-hyphenation," Farrow repeats with raised brows. "Shit, what's next, eighteen point font and parentheses?"

Jane rocks on the tips of her toes. "Funny, but no, there is simply just bold-hyphenation happening." Her lips fall into a serious line, and all humor dies.

What's this about?

"My announcement," she continues, "is that I've chosen a career. I may be a passionless human being, but I will no longer be aimless."

This is a big deal.

Whether or not she likes this job, she'll throw herself into it with as much drive as she *thinks* she has to possess. Just in order to live up to the Cobalt name.

It's a lot of pressure.

Jane looks to Maximoff. "You remember how those publishers have been contacting me since college?"

Publishers. My mind immediately jumps to celebrity tell-alls. But I can't see her doing that, especially not as a *job.*

Maximoff is as rigid as a brick wall. Nothing out of the ordinary. "What publishers? There were tons, Janie."

"The ones with the fiction imprints," she answers, and then looks to me and Farrow. "They've requested that I narrate a few of their novels for audio. And I've finally accepted." She continues briskly like she's nervous about our reactions. "Celebrity narrators are very popular, and since my little sister *adores* romance, I figured that I'd kill two birds with one stone. Make her immensely happy by narrating her favorite genre and have a steady job." She claps her hands. "Any questions?"

Security issues: there aren't many. It's not a career that'll put her safety at risk. "Where will you record the audio?" I ask.

"There isn't enough space in the townhouse to set up any kind of recording booth, so I'll have to go into a studio."

Maximoff frowns. "I thought most celebrities narrate classics and children's books?"

"They do. But I was offered romance." To me, Jane adds, "And, when I'm not recording, we can do things that normal couples do or whatever security has planned for us."

Do not have sex with Jane Cobalt.

I nod, about to reply, but Maximoff interjects, "We need to talk alone." He's staring right at me.

I don't hesitate. "Alright."

"Right now." He's already putting away the straight razor.

"Moffy," Jane warns. "I thought we just said—"

"This isn't a wedge," Maximoff cuts in quickly, wiping off his jaw. "I just need to clear some things up with Thatcher."

I have no fucking idea what he's going to ask.

Farrow frowns, also confused, and Maximoff sends his fiancé a look that says, *I'll tell you later.*

He nods, accepting.

I back out of the bathroom. "Where do you want me?" I ask him but I check on Jane. Half a reflex, half a—*who am I fucking kidding*, it's mostly a desire. She's whispering with Farrow.

"My room."

We stand in the middle of his hot attic

bedroom. Warm lights wrapped around the ceiling rafters, and as he clenches his jaw, his cheekbones like knives.

I'm prepared for hell from Maximoff.

If he still wants to punch me because I punched Farrow—I'd open my arms and let him. Hundred times over. He can even throw kicks in.

But something in my gut says that's not where we're headed.

"I should've done this a long time ago." Maximoff carries himself like he's my age or older, even though he's five years younger. "But out of respect for Farrow, I didn't get into it with you. Now that you're about to become a *significant* part of Jane's life, I need you to tell me something."

I nod, not breaking eye contact.

"Farrow isn't going to ask because he'll tell you he doesn't care, but I care about him and Jane. And having a clearer picture about who you are makes a difference to me."

He's giving me one of the biggest privileges and letting me— *trusting me* to exist in the center of his world among people he loves.

I have to honor that the best I can. "What do you need to know?" A huge part of me is worried my answers won't be enough for Maximoff.

"Were you upset that Farrow was assigned to my mom?"

He's going that far back. I rub my tensed jaw, thinking. "At the time, I thought my brother was a better fit for Lily. Your mom is one of the hardest people to protect." *Because of the crowds*, which Maximoff knows. She's that popular in the media.

Farrow was fresh blood at the time. Brand new to security. I thought Lily needed someone with more experience.

Maximoff gestures to my chest. "So it upset you when Farrow got her detail and not Banks?"

I can't shake my head. Because he's not wrong. "If my brother is frustrated that he lost out on something he was preparing for, I'm going to be irritated and frustrated too. I'm on his side—I can't change that, but we try not to let our feelings affect the team."

He listens closely.

I push myself to add, "I thought Farrow was a good match for your mom. It didn't take long to see that."

Maximoff un-balls his fists to crack his knuckles. "Farrow's first day in security. You made him run a 19k in the Poconos Mountains in the *damn* dark. Alone." Anger flares in his green eyes. "Yet, that same day you gave Donnelly a pancake breakfast. Why single Farrow out?"

This, I should've expected. But it's a blip in my mind.

"I wasn't singling him out," I say, honest about this. About everything. "It'll take me longer than a second to explain."

"You're in luck. I have a millennium."

I've never had to draw this picture of the team for anyone. But I'm about to try. "When we're training new hires, we're trying to build them into a bodyguard. It's not about reading a textbook and doing a few jumping jacks. It's more than that."

Maximoff seems open to what I'm saying.

I pause for only a short beat. "The situations you and your family are in are so *abnormal*, and in training, we're preparing fresh blood for this new norm. To react quickly and efficiently when confronted by hecklers and amassing crowds. To be alert when mentally fatigued. To follow protocol and orders on instinct. And only the leads are aware that the first day on the job is actually the final day of training. It's a test."

"A test for what?" Maximoff asks.

"To see how well they can follow orders. And to make sure they're not here for fame and access to your family. If they complain or push back, we don't let them through."

Maximoff knows this isn't security at a music festival. It's 24/7, high-level close protection to American royalty. Some of us might be young, some of us might act like friends, but we're *on* more than we're *off*.

Vigilant, always.

"It's not for the weak-willed," I tell him.

His shoulders square. "That doesn't explain the 19k versus a pancake breakfast." He scrunches his face. "Were you just going easy on Donnelly?"

"No." I shake my head. "I observed some of Donnelly and Farrow's training, and it was clear to *all* the leads that those two were tight. To the point where Donnelly would probably slit his own fucking throat for his friend." I lift my shoulders. "But one was from my side of town and had no issues taking orders. The other was Farrow."

Maximoff thinks hard, brows cinched. Processing.

I keep going. "I knew if I asked Donnelly to run a 19k, he'd do it backwards, blindfolded, crawling on the fucking ground. The hardest thing for him isn't physical or mental exertion in harsh conditions—it's being told to sit down and eat celebratory pancakes knowing Farrow is about to go bust his ass in the pitch-black night."

We were seeing if Donnelly would complain. If he would ask or fight to be with Farrow. Spend two seconds back-talking, and that's two seconds you're not paying attention to what's important.

Their lives.

Our duty.

We could tell Donnelly hated it, but he did what he was told and never pushed back on the leads.

Farrow passed easily.

I rake my fingers through my hair, curling strands behind my ears. "Look, I can see how Farrow would think I was singling him out. A 19k in the dark, in the mountains, alone with no real path to follow—that was unlike anything we've ordered a bodyguard to do on their first day. But we had to make it hard on Donnelly to sit back."

Maximoff nods. "I get that. But why not just tell Farrow all of this later on?"

"Farrow and I don't talk, and like you said, he didn't care enough about it to ask." This might be the most I've ever said to Maximoff in one sitting.

Words start to pass out of my head. I don't know what else to say.

That's all I've got.

Everything else feels extraneous.

Maximoff takes a deeper breath, his shoulders loosening a fraction. "Why did you tase Farrow?"

This, I expected. "Farrow thinks it wasn't an accident," I state, already knowing. Farrow has told me as much. He couldn't believe that I'd fuck-up that badly and tase him.

But I did, and I've taken full ownership of that mistake.

I was assigned Jane's mom that day. Just for extra security. It was after a photo shoot for Forbes, and Farrow was leading Lily back to the car while Rose was being heckled.

The target wasn't backing down, and there were enough people pushing from behind that it created a major problem.

Protocol: *don't draw a weapon in crowds.*

I thought I had a clear shot. I broke the rule because it wasn't a gun. It was a taser. The range was shorter and not deadly.

I still remember my line of sight. Zeroed in on the target. As soon as I took the shot, Farrow came out of nowhere and cold-cocked him. The taser hit my guy instead.

It was one of the worst days of my career.

"I fucked it," I tell Maximoff. "I thought I had the shot."

"So it wasn't on purpose?" There's a lot of earnestness in his voice. Like he wants to believe this version of history.

"I'd *never* purposefully tase one of my men like that," I say sternly. The thought actually sickens me.

Silence blankets the room for a longer second.

Maximoff tries to read my features.

I'm not sure I'm anything but hard, strict lines. I push myself to add, "I've never hated Farrow, and I can't fault him if he's hated me."

He lets out a final breath. "Thanks," he says sincerely. "I needed to hear that." He also reminds me, "I'll tell Farrow what you told me, but it's not going to mean as much to him."

I nod.

Farrow believes in actions more than words, and he's already given me a pretty clean slate when he didn't have to. I've made Farrow repeatedly prove himself to the team. Now I have something to prove to him.

"About Jane." Maximoff changes the subject. "I just want you to know that I'm appreciative of what you're risking for her. It's not a small thing, losing your privacy."

She's worth it.

"She's my client," I tell him.

Just my client. *Gotta remember that.*

17

JANE COBALT

Our first order of business: announce our fledgling but oh-so-romantic relationship to the public.

The security team listed out the specifics to accentuate our role as boyfriend and girlfriend, and for this first task, we have to be calculated.

The Cinderella ad is still a hot topic on the web, and if I post a photo of us kissing online, it'll seem utterly suspicious. The media has to actually *believe* I'm dating my bodyguard and not trying to cover-up the ad.

For this to happen, we're tearing a page out of the good ole celebrity handbook. Get a gossipy-someone to tip off the paparazzi about my whereabouts—and that gossipy-someone is obviously being tipped off by my "team."

In LA, actresses, actors, celebrities and influencers do this all the time to stay relevant. I don't much care about relevancy.

But I do care about the public believing I'm dating Thatcher. Which means the run-around is terribly essential.

"Who's calling the paparazzi?" I ask Thatcher as I put my Volkswagen in park. We occupy a mid-row space outside a local grocery store. Pumpkins are already being sold in giant crates near the sliding glass entrances.

It's not too busy or crowded on this sunny afternoon. But it took two hours driving around the city just to lose the cars that followed us from the townhouse.

And not all were paparazzi. I noticed new vehicles. Strange men behind the wheels.

Suitors, most likely.

Thatcher scoots the passenger seat back from the dash, giving his long legs more room. "Banks called a friend and casually mentioned you'd be at the Acme on Passyunk." He pronounces *Acme* like Ack-a-me.

It makes me smile. I lift my blue retro sunglasses to my head. "How do we know he'll tip off the paparazzi?"

Thatcher unbuckles his seatbelt. "Because he's broke and his nickname was *Snitch* in high school."

"Does he realize he's called *Snitch*?"

"Yeah," Thatcher says, his brown eyes holding mine for a beat longer. "He didn't give a shit about it. Said it reminded him of *Harry Potter* or something like that." He shifts. Turning more towards me, and his strong arm slides across the back of the headrest.

His boldness and masculinity consumes my teeny car. And me.

I inhale without exhaling that often. It feels like hot air is blowing from my vents. I sweat underneath my checkered blouse and lilac, tulle skirt.

"How do we know when paparazzi have arrived?" I whisper.

He speaks just as quietly. "They pulled in a minute after us."

He'd know. Always alert. It's dreadfully attractive.

I try to subdue an overpowering smile, and I lift my chin. Rotating to face my bodyguard more, my elbow brushes the steering wheel.

Silence breeds more heat, and from a breath apart, we look one another over. We're allowed, you see.

I trace the chiseled edges of his scruffy jaw, the carve of his biceps that stretches against his black button-down, the way his muscles flex the more he sweeps me.

Thatcher studies my shallow breathing. "Ready?"

I eye his lips. "Yes please..." *Oh God, Jane.* "Just *yes.* Yes, I'm ready for you..." I have torched myself with flaming balls of desire and mortification.

There is no escape.

His large hand falls to the nape of my neck, and I place my palm on his firm chest.

Carefully, slowly…Thatcher leans forward until our lips meet. *Chastely*. It's what the security team decreed. He kisses me tenderly, a soft kiss that electrifies my senses.

Pulsates my veins, and I ache to touch my bundle of nerves.

I run my fingers up to his unshaven jaw and then thread my fingers through his tousled brown hair.

No tongue.

His muscles tighten.

The kiss lasts a few seconds—not nearly long enough—before we slowly draw our lips away, only putting a sliver of space between our mouths.

Our breath still melds as we look into one another.

I ache for even more. In places that shouldn't be aching. I think Thatcher can read my need too well.

"One more," Thatcher says huskily. Our hands are still on each other, and his other palm has found a home on my hip. Mine are woven in his hair.

"One more," I agree.

"Just in case they didn't catch the photo." His gaze already engulfs me.

"Yes."

Yes.

He closes the distance. Our lips crash together, our hands grasping—we pull into each other with piping hot desire. His tongue glides sensually along mine with such explosive skill. Both of our asses have risen off the seat for closer contact. Bodies meeting in the middle. His towering build nearly sheathing me.

His smell, his touch, drives me to carnal places that I haven't reached in forever with another man. But this is different than all those other times. It feels different.

Maybe because it's all pretend.

Maybe because I know I'm safe.

And I can't be certain when my hand went from his head to his peach-perfect ass or when he cupped my butt—but it happens. He sucks my bottom lip, and I pulse like a second heartbeat has dropped between my legs.

I moan against his mouth, and the soft noise catches both of our attention. He separates from me. I separate from him.

We drop our hands and lean back to our respective seats. Breathing heavily.

He fixes his earpiece cord that I must've accidentally pulled on. His jaw set more strictly, he scans the parking lot.

My fingers linger on my stinging lips. "That was very good? We did well?" I question. "Security said *chaste* and that was the virgin strawberry daiquiri of kisses, no? I could've easily straddled you—not that I would've, because *boundaries*." I flush but never divert from his tightened eyes.

"It was good," he confirms. "But it wasn't a virgin daiquiri."

I, so eagerly, want inside his head. "It was a dirty martini?"

I swear his lip tics upward in a momentary smile. "More like a Guinness."

It's his favorite beer. Which I shouldn't know, but I'm very aware he mostly orders Guinness when he's off-duty. A stout, full-bodied beer.

A stout, full-bodied kiss.

I can't help but smile, and then I lower my sunglasses over my eyes and slip my arms in a light sweater. We have to do a bit of shopping to make the grocery outing seem real.

He reaches into the back seat and grabs my zebra-patterned heels off the floor, and then he hands them to me.

"Merci." I slip them on my feet. "How upset will security be if the photos show roaming hands…and tongue?"

His firm expression is unreadable. "This should be believable to the public, and that's what'll matter most to the team."

I take note that he never said the team *wouldn't* be upset. He must not want me to fret about security's reactions. I trust Thatcher, and if he has that area handled, then I won't pry. Not until he needs an assist from me.

Delegation at its finest.

Thatcher touches his ear, security in communication, and then he looks to me. "Paparazzi have the photo."

Here we go.

18

THATCHER MORETTI

"Why is his hand halfway up her skirt?"

Price, the Alpha lead barks at Akara over speakerphone, volume soft.

I narrow my eyes at the phone in Akara's clutch.

Sir, my hand is not halfway up my client's fucking skirt.

It was planted on her ass.

The Tri-Force are on a three-way call, and after an hour of being chewed out, Akara is letting Banks and me listen in on the tail-end of their conversation. All while we make a pitcher of caipirinha in security's small kitchen.

Banks has to sit on the counter for all three of us to fit in here, limes and a bottle of cachaça next to him.

We've been friends with Akara since we joined security, clicking almost instantly, but I really grew closer to him when he became the Omega lead. I was the Epsilon lead at the time. We'd spend long hours in the same meetings. Volleying information back and forth, keeping intel safeguarded between us, and shooting the shit on dull days. And nine times out of ten, with major Tri-Force decisions, Akara and I voted the same way.

Excited commotion comes from the living room. Jane and her cousins are hanging out with us. Celebrating. Despite the disapproval from two leads, the photos have already circulated through major media outlets with rabid obsession.

Spreading like an unstoppable wildfire.

It's been two hours since Jane and I kissed in the Acme parking lot, and these are some of the most popular headlines:

Jane Cobalt Is Having a Secret Love Affair With Her Bodyguard!

Breaking News: Jane Cobalt Caught Kissing Her Bodyguard

Jane Cobalt Has Found Her Prince Charming After All

Akara leans on the counter, keeping his voice hushed so our clients don't hear. "You can clearly see Thatcher's hand in the photos, Price. It's not halfway up her skirt."

"Regardless, his hands *aren't* where they should be," Price retorts.

My nose flares, and I cross my arms over my chest.

I understand why they're up my ass, and if I were a lead, I might be doing the same thing. Karma—it's rolling in like a fucking tank, for all those times at the FanCon that I used to yell at Farrow. Telling him to *separate* from Maximoff.

I deserve the third-degree more than Akara. But that's not how security hierarchy works. And at the end of the day, the kiss was a success.

That's what matters.

"It's good that the photos show them clearly together," Akara reminds the Alpha lead. "We didn't need articles wondering if they even kissed." He lifts the speaker closer to his mouth. "You two don't need to be concerned about Thatcher. He's my guy. I'm keeping an eye on him."

I stand more on guard, and I nod to him in appreciation.

He nods back.

Akara is covering my ass. It feels fucking strange putting him in this position. Not long ago, we were two leads covering our men and helping each other.

"You do that," Jon Sinclair pipes up, the new Epsilon lead and current bodyguard to Audrey Cobalt. "And tell Thatcher to put his dick back in his pants and start using the right goddamn head."

Akara quickly decreases the volume on his phone.

Banks tries not to laugh—until Sinclair carries on, and then my brother glares at the phone.

"He's not a lead anymore. He needs to show respect to the men that've been here before him."

I rake a hand across my jaw.

That comment fucking bugs me. Because I feel like I have been respecting the leads.

I understand hierarchy. The Tri-Force is at the top of it in security, and each lead represents a different part of the team.

The Alpha lead, Price Kepler, represents the old guard. The first wave of guys that showed up when Jane and Maximoff were just babies. There's not many of the old guard left.

The Epsilon lead, Jon Sinclair, represents the military hires. The second wave of guys that all served in the Navy.

The Omega lead, Akara Kitsuwon, represents the mixed martial arts hires. The third wave. These are the ones who were mostly referred out of the gym.

Even though I came in with the third wave and most of the men thought my background was just boxing, I'm technically a military hire. I was referred by a Navy vet—not anyone at the gym. How I react. How I train. How I operate on a day-to-day basis lines up more with the guys like Sinclair.

He's Navy through and fucking through. Mid-forties and Korean-American, he's been in security for around a decade, spending most of his career protecting the Cobalts. He's crude in private, like right now, but he'll snap to a respectful disposition in an instant. He reminds me a lot of my dad—which is partly why nothing he says to me usually cuts deep.

We've gotten along fine until recently. Banks thinks he's going on a power trip. Akara thinks it just has to do with Sinclair disliking SFO.

When you've been a bodyguard this long, there's history, bad and good. He's had an axe to grind with Oscar Oliveira for years, and he's hated how Omega gained some fame through the Hot Santa Video.

Now he's in charge.

"Thatcher isn't stepping on your feet," Akara retorts, his tone more authoritative. "He's doing his job."

"Good," Sinclair says. "That's what I want to hear." Yeah, he sounds like my dad. Sternness wrapped in this quiet paternal concern.

Price chimes in, "This honeymoon phase will be over down the line, and when this all ends, we'll be going back to a more appropriate routine. Remind him of that. His face isn't going to be up against his client's face forever."

My muscles flex.

Loud and clear, sir.

I'm not thinking about a public breakup yet. Not when we've just started *dating*. It's too soon to go there.

Akara stares at me as he answers Price. "Thatcher knows this isn't forever."

My expression hardens.

Banks unscrews the bottle of cachaça. Looking me over like he's seeing how I feel. *I'm fine.* I know this is just an op.

I breathe out a hotter breath, and my phone buzzes in my back pocket. I take out my cell.

My brows pull together.

I called my mom a lot earlier. Right when I got back from the Acme, I told her about the photos that were about to leak. Told her to lock the fucking door and contact me if media contacted her.

Now she's calling me.

I lift my phone to Akara. Silently saying, *I have to take this.*

He instantly puts his call with the leads off speaker. "Thatcher understands," he tells them, phone to his ear.

I drift further towards the stove. Not worrying Banks yet. Rotating my back to my brother and Akara, I answer the call.

"Everything alright down there?" I ask first, my Philly accent making *down there* sound like *down'air.*

"Which headline is true? Should I be invitin' her down soon?" my mom asks, humor in her voice. "She's got Nicola's approval already, but you know Nic would bake the devil a pie. It's why I love her." Nicola is her wife, my stepmom. "And your grandma is already crocheting Jane a scarf for Christmas."

We're months out from December. "Ma," I say tightly, but I hear my grandma shout to be heard from the background.

"They're saying youse two are an item!"

Severity tightens my eyes. "Who's saying that?" I worry someone is at their house.

My mom answers, "We were reading the tabloids. Some think you've been with her for a while. Coulda told me about her sooner, but it must've been hard for you with work." I hear her warm, slightly teasing smile.

To kiss a client in public—she knows I'd never do it. So she thinks what's going on with Jane is serious.

I rub my mouth. "It just happened," I say, voice deep.

Banks and I agreed that our family shouldn't know that Jane and I are *fake* dating. To them, this is real. If the media were to contact our family or if their friends pry about Jane, it's too much to ask them to lie on my behalf.

"We wanna meet this girl!" my grandma says. "Bring her here! Nicola and I will cook up a big pot of braggiol'. Banks can come along too. It'll be real nice to see my boys again."

Lately, we haven't had as much time to stop by and see them. "I don't want the media hassling you three, grandma."

"Don't youse worry about us now," she says. "How's your brother doin'?"

"Menzamenz," I tell her. *Half and half.* Banks had a small migraine this morning. Didn't last long. "Has anyone been at the house?"

My mom cuts back in, "A journalist kept knocking on the door, but I shut the blinds. Your uncles already came over and scared him off."

Good.

One journalist is more than I'd want, but I'm aware of what Farrow's stepsister dealt with—and this is nothing in comparison. Banks and I have been expecting some media to find our mom's address and phone number.

We've been preparing for worse than that, and we're putting 24/7 security on their house tonight. Everything is set up to protect our family in South Philly.

After another short exchange, we say our goodbyes, and as I return to Akara, I notice he's off the phone too.

"How are they?" Banks asks me, tossing and catching a lime.

"Fine. One journalist so far."

He bobs his head. "They'll be alright."

I nod too.

I turn to Akara. "What's the word on Grandmother Calloway?" The last we've heard from her, she cancelled her afternoon tea. She didn't even call or text Jane. Just let her assistant email her. Letting her know that *under the circumstances* with the current headlines, an afternoon tea with potential suitors would be inappropriate.

Akara looks to me. "Not a sound." He pushes his black hair back, fitting on a baseball cap backwards.

Banks motions to the Omega lead. "I hear she's crawling back underneath the dirt from which she came."

Akara grabs the liquor bottle. "Hey, she even saw her shadow."

I check over at the archway on instinct, then look back to them. "Looks like we're due for a long winter, gents."

Akara smiles. "If only she were actually a groundhog, man."

We all know she'll be back at some point.

No one spends that much effort on a fucking ad without being invested in the cause. And in this case, it happens to be setting Jane up with some upper crust, gold-brick-shitting asshole.

"Do we have eyes on their grandmother?" I ask, opening the fridge.

"Twenty-four-seven," Akara confirms. "You can thank Jane's dad for that."

Connor Cobalt.

I don't interact with him often, and I'm not sure if this op will change that. Unlike my family, her parents know this is all for show.

I grab a couple beer bottles. "Do you two even know how to make caipirinha?"

Banks throws the lime at me. "I thought you did."

I catch the lime and chuck it back.

He grabs it easily.

"No," I answer.

Akara shakes his head and then calls, "Hey, Quinn!"

Quinn pops in the archway. He's rolling up the cuffs to his floral short-sleeve button-down. Recently he's been wearing a lot of florals shirts. Today: green palm leaves with yellow flowers.

His brother already gave him shit for being LA trendy. Whatever that means.

All I know is that when Akara moved in, he and Quinn refused to let me and my brother bunk up. Banks and I offered. Of course. We're twins. It's the easiest shuffle.

But Akara said we shared a room most of our lives, and they both didn't want us having to do it again. So like Luna and Sulli, Quinn and Akara now share a room.

It's a big deal to me and my brother. Not many people would choose to have a roommate and sleep on a bunk bed for us.

In the kitchen, Quinn notices the empty pitcher. "You need help?" He wanted to make the Brazilian drink today because Luna said she's never had one before.

Most of us in security have had them. Just never made them ourselves.

"Yes we do," Akara says smoothly and shifts to let him in, and I give Quinn space, squeezing past everyone and leaving the kitchen.

Instinctively I scope out the living room for Jane. Finding her in mere seconds. She lounges on a stool next to Maximoff and Farrow, chip bags spread out over the high tabletop.

She pops one in her mouth. Smiling at something Farrow says to Maximoff.

"Twitter is going nuts," Luna announces from the leather couch.

I see her in my peripheral. Laptop balancing on her knees, red marker underlines her eyes like she was in a flag football match. Knowing Luna, she probably just did it because she wanted to.

"Holy fuck." Sulli reads from over her shoulder. "It's trending. That's what that means, right?" She points to the screen.

"Yep yep, definitely trending," Luna says.

I shove off towards Jane.

Whispers and chatter from the table and couch seem to hush as I approach her. Until I'm right in front of Jane, and the room is awkwardly silent.

Here, among security and her family, we're back to being bodyguard and client. No dating. Her face can't be up against my face. Be professional.

I hand her the extra beer I grabbed.

Her lips rise. "Thank you."

Maximoff and Farrow aren't staking glares into me. They're just eyeing me closely.

I focus on Jane. She runs her thumb over the rim of the bottle, and her eyes search mine. "About you being more *in* the public," she says, "I wanted to let you know that whatever crops up on the internet about your life, I don't plan to read it. I'd rather hear whatever you're willing to share with me, but if you'd rather I just look, if that's easier for you—"

"You don't have to look," I interject. "I don't think the public will find much anyway."

There is one thing…*one thing* that I'd rather she never find out through a fucking online search engine or internet troll.

One thing that I can't figure out a good time to say. It's so far gone. Over fifteen years ago, but once I drop it, the air usually snaps and the mood darkens.

I hate going there.

Hell, I don't know *how* to go there most of the time.

"So it's a plan then," Jane notes.

I nod and remember what I needed to tell her. "The team wants us to wait to publicly confirm that we're together."

No posts.

No interviews.

No banners in the fucking sky.

Nothing.

We just have to appear like we're getting sloppier about hiding our "secret" relationship. Media will do the heavy lifting.

"Sounds brilliant." She sips her beer, then licks her lips. "Do we have our next objective as a couple?"

We do.

19

JANE COBALT

Security devises a plan that has tumbled my heart throughout my whole body like an erratic, too-eager-for-my-own-good pinball.

Thatcher and I are embarking on a weekend getaway at a local Bed & Breakfast. Our fake couple antics are starting strong. Just packing my travel suitcase, I felt like I was on an adrenaline high.

As I roll my luggage along the pretty floral carpet, I drink in the quaint Bed & Breakfast and cozy atmosphere, and I glance more than once at Thatcher.

He towers beside me like an archangel. His radio attached to his slacks, mic on the collar of his black long-sleeve tee, and I'm more aware this isn't a *real* romantic vacation.

He's still my bodyguard, and this is simply just a ruse. A strategy.

I have to keep my wits about me.

In the foyer, a brass chandelier hangs overhead and sunlight streams through stained-glass windows. A fifty-something innkeeper waits for us behind a polished mahogany desk.

I read her nametag as we approach. "Hi, Gretchen," I greet with a smile.

She returns the smile with a warm one. "Welcome to the Concord B&B."

"We have a reservation under..." I realize that I didn't book the reservation. I might be terribly messy, but I'm very organized and can juggle more than what meets the eye. I usually plan travel details myself. Never leaving them up to assistants or family members.

But this weekend trip was different.

Thatcher steps forward, his large hand hovering near my hip. "It's under Moretti."

Why was that so very sexy? *He put the reservation under his name.* Possibly the Tri-Force told him to do so. I try to read his stern features, but he's so vigilant at the moment. Constantly scanning the foyer, then glancing down at me.

Checking on me.

The back of my neck blazes, and I try to retrain my attention on the innkeeper.

"Let's see here." She plucks her reading glasses off her chest, a beaded chain linking them around her neck, and she perches them on her nose. Wispy blonde tendrils twist in a nest upon her head, and her honey brown eyes dart between me and the four bodyguards who flank my sides.

Thatcher, Banks, Oscar, and Donnelly.

This is a *team* mission, after all. Plus, SFO said there should be more security around, especially since a parade of paparazzi has been trailing our every move.

Now that Thatcher is gaining more fame, his job as a bodyguard is going to be harder, and Omega wants to protect him like they did Farrow.

I can still hear some of the fanatic shouting we left outside of the Bed & Breakfast.

"Jaaaaaane!"

"Thatcher!!"

I'm not sure how Oscar and Donnelly got off their details with my brothers. But I assume it might've been easiest to give Charlie and Beckett temp bodyguards this weekend.

Maximoff and Farrow would've come along. I wanted them here badly. There is a large absence that only they can fill in my life, and it's a strange feeling not having them with me on such a huge endeavor.

But Moffy and I knew if we stayed overnight together at a B&B, it could potentially unbury the HaleCocest rumor. Regardless if he's engaged to Farrow or not, it could happen, and that is the mother of all dumpster fires that we desperately do *not* want to reignite.

She types on a keyboard. "Breakfast starts at eight and ends at eleven." She squints at her computer screen. "Ah yes, you've requested the Metropolis, Blue Ridge, and Victorian rooms."

Skeleton keys are hung on wooden pegs behind the innkeeper, and there are only three out of six left. Meaning, strangers already occupy the other three rooms.

It's purposeful. Security is hoping the guests will spot Thatcher and me together. We need strangers passing pictures and information to the press.

Paparazzi will question anyone who leaves the Concord.

Gretchen gingerly picks the remaining three keys. "The Blue Ridge is on the first floor, two twin beds. The Metropolis and Victorian are a short distance up the stairs, second floor on the right. If you need anything, you can find me in the study. Third door down the main hall."

"Thank you," I say, and she passes the keys to Thatcher.

She darts off to the study.

Thatcher hands a skeleton key to Oscar. "You or Donnelly need to be on night watch. So rack out as soon as you can."

Donnelly surveys the ceiling, nooks, and corners of the old house.

"I'll be on during night," Oscar confirms.

Thatcher lowers his voice to a whisper. "I won't be on comms, so text if you can't hear us."

Hear us.

I smooth my lips together to keep from smiling. By *us*, he means me and him. Pretend fucking. That is precisely what we're doing here. Making sex noises in our room so other guests can hear from the thin walls.

I am terribly thrilled to fake sex with Thatcher. Maybe it's the Cobalt in me that thrives on strategic plans and deception. We're playing 3D chess, and my teammate happens to be serious and brooding and currently pinning his stern eyes onto me.

"Ready?" Thatcher asks, deep and husky.

I grip the handle to my weekend suitcase, my palms perspiring. "Yes, I am." I rub my clammy hand on the thigh of my pale yellow jeans.

The other bodyguards on SFO don't draw attention to my shallow breath. They're very mature about this whole ordeal.

Donnelly and Oscar say quick goodbyes to me.

"Stay frosty, boys," Banks tells them, and those two leave to locate their bedroom on the first floor.

Thatcher slings his backpack over his shoulder. "I can get that." He reaches for my suitcase, but he stops when he sees me shake my head.

"I can wheel it, really. I'd rather carry my fair share."

He nods, and as we make our way to the carpeted staircase, his hand falls to the small of my back, lightly brushing against my body. His fingers might as well carry static electricity, my nerves humming. Trembling.

We sneak glances at each other.

Banks follows behind us, duffel slung on his shoulder.

And we all ascend the creaky stairs. Before I try to drag my luggage, Thatcher reaches over and I let him take the handle. He hoists the suitcase up like it weighs no more than an inflatable beach ball.

He is impossibly attractive.

I skim him more openly and start to smile. I love that my terrible version of *Say Anything* with unnerving stalkers has now changed to something more enjoyable. More enthralling.

We reach the narrow hallway on the second-floor. Paintings hang off-kilter on dark wooden-paneled walls. I think we've been transported to a *Nancy Drew* novel, and so far, we haven't run into any other guests.

It's also possible that Gretchen could leak information. She hasn't signed an NDA, so there are no legal ramifications if she spills details about our stay here.

We all walk down the hall.

"What's the word on the Wi-Fi?" Banks asks his brother.

"None," Thatcher answers.

I glance back at Banks. "Is it a security problem?"

"Nope," Banks says.

Thatcher catches my gaze. "Queen of the Ring is on tonight."

Sounds unfamiliar. "Queen of the Ring?"

"It's a WPW pay-per-view match. World Pro Wrestling."

Realization washes over me. "I've heard of WPW before, but I wouldn't know the names of any big matches," I say aloud. "I've never seen one."

Thatcher is about to answer, but we reach our rooms.

Banks sticks his key in a door across from ours. The plaque reads: *Metropolis.* The Moretti brothers exchange a look that I can't decipher, and then Thatcher nods before Banks disappears.

Thatcher and I are officially alone.

It makes what we're about to do more real. Share a bed together for the night. Though, security reminded us to sleep on opposite ends. Bonus points if Thatcher takes the floor.

No cuddling produces zero temptations.

Or so they believe.

I think they're placing complete trust in Thatcher's professionalism. And I also think they've forgotten to add other variables. Like how I'm easily aroused by Thatcher, and all he has to do is be himself.

Assertive, considerate, stern and protective. And more, so much more—some layers I've only just glimpsed.

Thatcher uses the skeleton key and unlocks the door. I trail inside behind him, and he has me stop at the entrance. He checks the bathroom, and while he assesses the rest of the space, the interior catches me off guard.

Pretty pale green wallpaper lines the room, and a king-sized bed overpowers the space, a glittery champagne comforter tucked nicely in the iron frame. Three pink stained-glass windows above normal panes let in soft light, and a Victorian velvet chaise rests near the bathroom door.

It's eclectic and gorgeous and I'm immediately in love.

"This okay?" Thatcher asks, closing the door behind me.

"More than okay." I place my suitcase near the foot of the bed. "It's like someone dug around in my head and this exploded out of it."

"Hold on." He drops his backpack beside the chaise and then checks the latches on the windows. He tests the locks.

All seem to be secured, and then he snaps the blinds shut. The only source of light now comes from the stained glass above.

The sun has already begun to set, and I pull the tassel to a frilled lamp, a warm glow bathing the bed.

Quiet lingers, and nervous anticipation sizzles my skin and flip-flops my stomach. I eye him curiously, watching as he sits on the edge of the chaise and unties his boots.

If I don't fill the silence, I may boil to death—or in the very least, sweat through my long-sleeve fuzzy shirt.

"Who from security proposed this idea?" I ask, placing my beet-shaped purse on the nightstand.

He yanks off his boots. "I'm not sure. I came into the meeting and it was already the most popular option." He rolls up the sleeves of his black tee and then grabs his backpack.

He lifts his head, staring more strongly into me. His gaze is a thousand-watt bulb. Scorching me head to toe.

He asks, "Have you changed your mind about doing this?" His husky voice somehow contains deep concern and reassurance all at once.

"No, not at all." I push a frizzed strand of hair off my cheek. "Is it odd to say that I'm actually excited? I've never faked an orgasm before. Usually I just tell the guy that they didn't please me, and I'll provide pointers and then let them solve the rest. So this is a first—the faking orgasm part." I intake a short breath, my eyes widening at my unraveling thoughts that I'm purging out loud.

Does he even want to know about your orgasms, Jane?

He's stoic. Not breaking eye contact, but his hands have paused unzipping his backpack.

I speak faster. "Which just means that I'm not one-hundred percent positive I'll be the very best at faking an orgasm—but I am excited to try. Truly."

I can't blink.

My face is most definitely on fire.

"So…" I keep going. Why am I still going? "There's that."

Positive endnote. Let me survive this.

Thatcher is quiet, not unusual for him. His eyes are still on me. Still burning me alive. I shouldn't like that.

But in this moment, I don't want him to stare at anything or anyone but me.

His deep, husky voice fills the room. "So I'm the first guy you'll be faking an orgasm with."

He says it like it's a fact. Which I suppose it is. But I doubt that'd make anyone feel good.

I lean my hip on the nightstand. "Factually, yes—but if we were really having sex, there's a high probability that I'd orgasm." I'm unblinking. Unmoving.

Frozen.

His biceps seem to flex. "Not a high probability."

"No?" I hang on the edge of his words.

"If I put my cock in your pussy, there's a hundred-percent certainty you'd orgasm in my arms. More than twice."

Oh my God.

I cross my ankles. Somehow still standing, but I press my thighs harder together. Pulsating. "Good to know," I say as diplomatically as I can. "We're on the same page then."

It's all very professional here.

Thatcher nods, but his shoulders seem more bound. *He's on-duty, on guard, is all.* He pulls out a taser and water bottle from his backpack. When he stands, he feels even taller, or maybe I feel shorter.

With a confident stride, he heads nearer, and I shift out of the way so he can open the nightstand drawer. He stores the taser and then removes his holstered gun off his waistband. Sliding in the second weapon before closing the drawer.

I realize he has to sleep on this side of the bed. It's closest to the door.

Thatcher touches his earpiece, then clicks his mic. "Solid copy."

I've decided that watching him work is utterly captivating. And I have a front row seat each and every day.

He unscrews his water bottle. Veins in his arm muscles are more noticeable as he tips the bottle of water to his mouth.

I can't think…he is so…

My breath shallows. How am I going to survive? *Okay, you packed your favorite vibrator.* I can go into the bathroom tonight. All will work in my favor.

I take a measured breath.

Thatcher wipes his mouth with the back of his palm. He offers me his water, holding the bottle.

I press my lips together, a smile pulling my cheeks. I should decline. "Thank you," I say, my hand already reaching out to accept.

Oh, you are done for, Miss Jane Eleanor.

We never look away from one another, and I take a small sip. I am parched.

Just not for water.

When I finish, I pass the water bottle back to my bodyguard. "Should I test the bed?"

He nods and checks his watch. "We should start before the other guests fall asleep."

I peel off my chunky heels, and I notice the bed has a hefty iron-rung headboard. Without much hesitation, I climb up and stand on the mattress.

Box springs squeak, and the bed undulates beneath my feet. I bounce and watch him remove his earpiece and then unclip the mic wire from his collar. He detaches the radio from his waistband and places it on the nightstand.

A fan whirls only a few inches above my head, and I'm careful not to jump too high. "You can't stand on the bed with me," I realize. Clearly, he's too tall.

Thatcher nods, and stepping closer, he grips the headboard. "Jane," he says with the perfect mix of tenderness and force.

"Yes?" I balance on the creaking bed.

"You're gonna have to moan."

20

"Right," I say, *my chest rising and falling.*
I've never ached for someone to touch me as terribly as I ache for Thatcher. Desiring his large hands to run down every single plane and valley of my body. On this very bed.

He eyes my breasts for a short fleeting second. "Jane—"

"Mmm," I moan, starting softly.

Suppressing my orgasms has been a habit lately since I live in a townhouse with thin walls. It's going to be kind of fun trying to be louder.

Fake louder, Jane.

Thatcher shoves the iron headboard against the wall, the *thump* simulating aggressive sex perfectly.

"Ahh, yeah, *right there,*" I moan, bed squeaking beneath me. "Right there!"

We stare deep into one another, magnetized, the air heady and tense.

"Ohhh yeah!" I try to emulate the best porn I've seen.

He quickens the banging of the headboard. The intensity of his brown irises nearly steals my breath altogether.

"Oohhh!" I let out a long moan that sounds *nothing* like my actual sex noises. A lot is riding on the believability of this task.

And I might just be the reason we fail.

Thatcher suddenly stops rocking the headboard. Being around me so often, he can read my emotions very well. Like how my brows bunch in worry.

He shakes his head. "It wasn't that bad."

I think he's just being sweet. "My moans sound fake." I try to stay positive. "Maybe I should try a different tactic? More subtle, but then how will guests overhear?" I put my knuckles to my lips, almost lost in thought. "...I don't know how to make it sound more real than it being real." My mouth drops slightly. "I didn't mean—well, I did, but I'm not saying..."

What am I saying?

Our gazes draw to the mattress at the same exact time. We're thinking the same thing, most surely.

Our eyes catch again.

Thatcher releases his clutch off the headboard. "We don't have to take our clothes off."

I nod heartily. "Dry humping, I agree."

"Enough to make you come."

Holy... I nearly fall into his arms right there. Legs weak, body shuddering. "Yes," I whisper, slowly lowering to my knees so I don't face-plant into my bodyguard.

His muscles are tensed in arousal, but his eyes narrow in severity. "We only do this if you're okay with the guests hearing your real orgasm and not a fake one."

Because that's the whole point.

They're supposed to hear us intertwined and hot and heavy, and this does not change anything for me.

"I'm fine with this." I shift to my ass. The mattress lets out another squeak.

He's rigid with seriousness.

I continue on. "In all honesty, if people are going to talk about me, there's comfort knowing it's not all a fabrication." I waft my fuzzy shirt. I'm sweating.

"Then if you want to—"

"I do, do you?"

"Yeah," he says deeply, and he tears our gazes apart. Just to walk over and check the air conditioning panel on the wall. He pushes a few buttons. "It's broken."

The fan is whirling at maximum speed but circulates hot air. It was much cooler outside, but we won't risk cracking a window.

I lean against the headboard. "We don't have to leave all of our clothes on...possibly? We're two mature adults. You're twenty-eight. I'm...good ole twenty-three."

I did not mean to draw attention to our five-year age gap. But there I go.

Thatcher sweeps my entire body, and he wipes a trickle of sweat off his brow with the heel of his palm.

My pulse quickens.

"We are," he nods. He's decisive. There is no vacillation in his towering stance or his stern eyes. "You ready?"

"I am," I say, very assured.

I am so ready for him.

He reaches back and grabs the collar of his black shirt. He yanks the tee off over his head.

I've always been extraordinarily curious about why men do that— shed their shirts from the *back* instead of taking the bottom of the fabric and tugging it up and off. Their way is such an odd method, but it looks *extraordinarily* sexy. Like they just couldn't bother with the fabric of a shirt anyway.

Thatcher chucks his tee on the chaise.

His carved muscles in perfect view. I skim the cut of his biceps, his strong shoulders, ridges of his *eight* abs—and the natural hair that lines his chest and tracks downward. Tempting my gaze to his cock, hidden behind his slacks.

Now it seems so obvious that he was a soldier, a combat vet—his shoulders are often squared, his carriage raised in readiness like his instincts are always buzzing.

Thatcher walks to the bed, and as soon as he climbs on, the box springs let out a higher pitched creak.

My heart beats at a wild pace. I scoot down off the headboard, my back sinking into the soft mattress, but I prop myself up a little on my elbows.

He's knelt close.

We watch one another. I'm so mesmerized by Thatcher, by what his instincts tell him to do next. He may be quiet, but he's the furthest thing from shy or timid.

He weaves his arms underneath my thighs, and he clutches my hips, pulling me swiftly on his lap, my legs already broken apart for him.

I'm straddling my bodyguard.

Oh my God.

My hands fly to his neck, and his palm travels up my back and then encases my face. I touch his hand, feeling how much smaller mine is in comparison.

Our mouths are a breath apart.

I clench between my legs, aching for his hardness. "That was... nice." I swallow a shallower breath. "Really...very..." *nice.* Our lips naturally drift closer.

"Jane," he says, deeper and deeper. He is making love to all four letters of my name. Eight hard inches inside one syllable.

We kiss a soft, short kiss. Testing the waters.

I pant. "Kissing...and dry humping, they can pair well together." He's near my lips again, and I add, "Like peanut butter and jelly."

I swear he smiles, but words and thoughts are lost as his mouth meets mine for the second time tonight. A slow, scalding kiss suddenly explodes in a volcanic eruption.

He clutches me tighter. Pulling me into his chest, his hands diving down to my ass. I grind into his lap, and his muscles contract, a swelter brewing hotter.

And hotter.

Thatcher picks me up, just enough to bring my back gently down on the mattress.

My lips part in an overcome breath.

He's on top of me, his six-foot-seven stature swathing me, and my legs stay stretched around him.

Carnal emotions and sensations cocoon me at once. He's this protective force, and the way his body shields mine, I feel like I can come unraveled underneath him and he'd safeguard each and every moan. Each shudder.

Each small tremble of pleasure that ripples through my bones.

Thatcher reaches over and grips the rungs of the headboard with one hand.

Noise.

We must make noise.

He rocks against me and slams the headboard into the wall, perfectly timed with his movements.

Thump.

Thump.

Thump.

Each one blazes my nerves and wells an aching pressure, craving for harder entry. *Oh God.* Oh God. I'm so very wet, and we've only just begun.

Fully-clothed, my hips buck up into him and my shoulder blades dig into the mattress. "Thatcher," I say in want, raising my voice above a murmur.

He kisses me with deep, powerful tongue that vibrates my body, and then against my lips, he says, "Tell me how you want it." His voice is even louder than mine. *He's excelling at this.*

I hold on to his bare skin that beads with sweat while he rocks into me.

Thump.

"Harder," I beg.

Thump.

The noisy springs squeak as he picks up his pace.

"Oh God," I breathe.

My nerves prickle, and I'm suffocating beneath my fuzzy cotton shirt that I forgot to remove. His pants are still on. My jeans are still on.

I break from his lips and try to shimmy my top off. The long-sleeve shirt clings to me like a vice, and I fumble a little.

Thatcher assists, and together, we manage to free one of my elbows.

I'm absolutely stuck in this contraption.

My entire body thrums, just wanting more contact.

More thrusting.

Which will lead to the loudest, most mind-blistering orgasm this bedroom has ever heard or seen.

"Just rip it," I say, breathless.

Thatcher grabs at my collar with two hands and like the fabric is made of paper, he tears my shirt into two pieces.

Oh...

My...

I think my heart just came, if hearts could cum. Mine just did.

I'm exposed in a lacy, purple bra, and I stare at him like he just went down on me and delivered a gold-star performance.

"Better?" Thatcher asks, studying my body with desire and protectiveness.

"Yes, much better," I say with a nod. "Thank you."

He helps me pull off the sleeves, and he tosses the torn shirt on the floor. Back to me, we kiss with unbridled passion.

His firm hand finds my thigh and explores my body in hot, hungered trails. Dizzying me.

We're both insatiable, I realize.

I want to follow where he goes. To see his large, callused hand on my bare skin...on my clit—*I wish*. I ache.

He's not there. He can't be there.

I wish.

I run my hand across his hard, scruffy jaw, and then thread my fingers through his tousled brown hair. His lips reach the nape of my neck.

Sweat beads on my skin, his tongue and mouth more experienced than I even imagined. And I imagined quite...a lot. I gasp and tremble as he sucks on sensitive flesh.

I arch into Thatcher, a sound strangled in my throat. But it's not a moan.

It's a whimper.

"Louder," he grunts.

I watch how his muscles envelope me. Protect me. *"Thatcher,"* I moan.

His hardness bears against my heat. Pants, they're still on. I've never wanted to be naked so dreadfully and painfully before.

I'm about to touch myself. In front of him. *Is that out of bounds? Is that an overstep?* "I need…"

He unbuttons my jeans. He unzips me.

"Yes," I gasp. *"Yes,* please, *please."*

He kisses me like he's dying to taste my words and *need,* and then he whispers against my mouth, "Change of plans."

I nod in agreement. Our eyes say the same exact thing. *We need more. We want more.*

"What's…the new proposal?" I pant and watch him stand up at the foot of the bed.

Towering, he clasps my ankle and tugs me toward the edge of the mattress.

He yanks my pale yellow jeans down my thighs. "I'm eating out your pussy."

An irrepressible noise breaches my lips. "Yes," I gasp, nearly crying out in happiness. "Yes…*please."* Words jumble in my head as he continues without pause.

Thatcher pulls my jeans off each foot, revealing my cheetah-print panties, and his hand slopes down the length of my soft leg, stretching me wider, and another noise jettisons between my parted lips.

"Thatcher." I tremble.

His knee meets the floor, and he kisses my inner-thigh, his warm breath electrifying nerve-endings. His mouth ascends to my heat.

I sink back onto my shoulders, my body tightening with each breath, but I turn my head and feverishly try to watch this dream-like scenario unfold.

Our eyes meet in raw yearning, and he pushes aside my panties. His thumb teases my clit, and my back arches.

I inhale sharply.

He watches my pleasured spasms, and he replaces his thumb with his tongue—I can't catch my breath, I already cry out.

My legs already quiver.

"Thatcher."

His mouth knows exactly what parts of me crave touch and his skill—and a shockwave zips through my veins.

"Oh God," I cry, shaking in an orgasm. Oh so quickly.

I reach around my leg and clutch his broad shoulder for support. He hits another pleasure point—and my toes curl, eyes snapping shut.

Oh God. I try to keep them open. To watch in case this only ever happens once.

He kneads my breast before snapping off my bra.

I gasp, entirely overcome.

He stands up some, bracing his knee on the mattress, and he cups my heat with his large palm that clenches and thrums. His other hand pulls off my bra.

He returns to my exposed breasts, and his tongue teases my hardened nipple. He sucks the sensitive flesh, and the image is enough to make me come once more.

A soft, breathy moan escapes my quaking body. I'm soaked against his palm that still cups me. It's as though he's protecting my clit, knowing it's too swollen to toy with again just yet.

And I feel like I've been with *boys* in contrast. No one could satisfy me this quickly or without copious amount of direction. Which isn't bad, per se, just different. But I think I prefer *this*.

I prefer an experienced man.

I prefer him.

Trying to catch some breath, I manage to say, "You're very… knowledgeable…"

He holds my gaze in the hottest vice. "I love your pussy." Cut and dry. To the point.

I fight to speak and not just pant, but words…are…gone.

His fingers, the ones against my heat, slip between my folds. He pushes one finger inside of me, and I pulsate.

An overwhelmed, high-pitched moan comes with a sharp gasp. "*Yes.*"

He pumps his fingers, finding the perfect spot in seconds. His biceps flex.

I soar off another peak, my thighs shaking, drenched in sweat. I grip his wrist, keeping his finger inside of me.

He slips another in.

"Thatcher," I moan, trying to move and add friction against his hand. I prop up on an elbow, and he sits up slightly off me. Letting me see how his fingers are deep inside of me.

I lift my gaze to him. There is so much more that I desire. So much closer I wish and ache to be.

He wears a similar longing expression. We've ripped through restraints, but a giant one still remains intact.

"Jane." His chest is taut in need. "I want to put my cock in you."

I clench around his fingers. "I want you to."

Thatcher has a choice to make, and he does. "Fuck it." He eyes me strongly. "I'm fucking you."

Yes, God. I've never loved five words more than those. I release my clutch on his wrist.

He kisses me, gathering fire, and then gently pulls his fingers out.

While he shifts back, I drop my feet to the floor and sit on the edge of the mattress. Thatcher towers above me, but I'm at a perfect angle to give him head.

I also really, *really* want to grab his ass.

He unbuttons his slacks, and I tug them down. Dark gray boxer-briefs mold his hard length that is…impressive.

The longer I stare, the more my mouth slowly falls. I can feel him watching me like I just watched him.

My ankles hook around his legs, and I slip my palms down the back of his boxer-briefs. Squeezing his peach-perfect ass with two hands.

"I love your butt," I say as pointedly as he did.

Light reaches his brown eyes. He expels breath through his nose, pent-up. I can clearly see how badly.

He nods. "I love your voice."

My stomach flutters. Most people find my constant chatter grating after a while, but he makes me feel so very desired. And safe.

And terribly beautiful.

Thatcher pulls down his boxer-briefs, freeing his rock-hard erection. In stunning view.

He is huge. My jaw is now on the floor. I think my prior estimations were off. I think he may be more than eight-inches. *That is about to be inside of me.* I ache for more intense pressure.

Thatcher steps out of the boxer-briefs, buck-naked in front of me.

I stroke his length, my hand looking small around his shaft. His abs tighten, a heavier breath concaving his firm chest.

He brushes my sweaty hair off my cheeks, and we lock-eyes while I suck his tip.

A rough groan rumbles in his throat, and he grits down, his nose flaring.

I want to explore him too. Intrigue floods my eyes. I rub him up and down with a tight grip, and with my other hand I press two knuckles against his taint and knead gently.

His shoulders tighten, head almost tilting back. "Fuck." He cups the back of my head.

I'm about to shift my finger closer to his hole. He obviously *feels* where I'm going, and as Thatcher catches my eyes, he nods me onward. He even says, "Go ahead."

Have I found my perfect match?

In bed. I mean, *in bed.* I clarify to myself instantly, my cheeks roasting. It's not as though he heard my slip.

I'm fine.

"I have lube." I bend to my nearby suitcase that I left in reach. "I brought some...for my vibrator," I clarify, unzipping my suitcase and quickly procuring a lube packet in a pocket. I kick my suitcase closed, lube my finger, and continue onward.

One hand on his length, the other returns to his ass.

His palm is resting on top of my head now.

I tease outside of his hole, and I slip my finger inside of him. Using a *come hither* motion, I massage his prostate, and his muscles contract, breath heavies in a full-bodied manner.

He clutches my chin, and he guides his shaft between my lips.

Yes.

I suck his cock. Not able to take all of him, but a guttural noise tears through his lungs. His jaw tenses, and he blinks, his eyes aching to roll.

He pulls back, almost completely, and before I ask why, he tells me, "We have to be louder." He holds my gaze. "I need to be inside you, Jane."

I inhale. "Wholeheartedly…" *Agree.* He's already sliding my panties down my legs. Freeing us of the last article of clothing.

And then Thatcher goes to his backpack on the chaise.

I tie my sweaty hair in a low pony and watch him dig in the backpack.

In seconds, he returns to the bed with a condom. Standing in view, letting me see, he rips the package open, and he sheaths himself with one hand.

My eyes have grown. That will be a mental image engrained in my head for blissful eternity.

So swiftly, Thatcher hoists me up around his waist, my legs wrapped around him, and he climbs onto the bed with me tucked to his body.

He rests my back against the soft comforter. His build skimming my body, his palm pinned flat on the mattress way above my head.

I clutch his ass, and my hips instinctively rise up into him.

"*Fuck*, Jane," he groans; he has a hand on my thigh, and his other hand moves to the top of my head. He spreads my legs wider with his knees.

He's not in me yet, but while I'm lying on the bed, he sits up and tucks a pillow beneath my lower back. "I'm big, so I'm going to go slow at first. Try not to move that much when we start. I don't want to hurt you."

I feel his fingers brush against my swollen entry. I take a measured breath. "I'm curious. How do you know I haven't…taken something as big as you before?"

"The way you were staring at my cock said you haven't."

I smile softly. *He can read me so well.* But that is known.

"You heard what I said before?" he asks for confirmation.

"I did," I murmur. "I'll try to be still."

He leans down. Kissing me deeply, he finds my hand on the champagne comforter and laces our fingers. I feel him shift his other hand to our pelvises, and he slowly, *slowly* begins to fill me with his hardness.

The pressure is overwhelming at first, and my thighs quake, my whole body begging for another climax that he's been supplying.

"Thatcher," I moan.

"I have you." His words are firm. He concentrates on my features, my body, and he eases further inside of me.

I bow my hips, rocking forward on impulse—*oh no.* I intake a staggered breath at the pinch of pain, stars dancing in my vision. Too much too fast.

"Easy," Thatcher says, very serious, and he leans back down, kissing the outside of my lips. He studies me for another beat and rubs my clit.

I tremble. *Better.* And I blow out a controlled breath, relaxing.

He sits back up on his knees, and I fixate on how I'm lying on a beautiful bed, and my legs are spread around my handsome bodyguard, and his cock is sliding in me.

Arousal balls up in my throat.

I greedily and selfishly wish this could happen again. Possibly forever. *Jane.*

I push past those thoughts and enjoy this moment with Thatcher for all its worth, and to me, it's worth a lot. He is risking so much, and I don't take that for granted.

Thatcher lets go of my hand and clasps my wide hips. He drives deeper, *deeper* inside of me.

"Yes," I cry. "*Yesyesyes.*" I feel so full, and I reach a peak incredibly fast. He is just *in* me, and I contract around him. My head lolls back, my body arching. Sensations pummeling me like waves crashing to shore.

"God," Thatcher chokes on a husky groan, and he takes a pause. Letting me catch my breath. He puts his hand to my heart that speeds out of control.

After a minute, he starts to thrust in and out, in and out. His pace mounts a euphoric friction in my body. I angle my head and I watch his cock disappear in me—*oh my...*

Pleasure drives straight to my core. I shake.

"*Fuck*," he grunts.

My moan pitches the air like a cry of ecstasy, and I clench and come around him. My legs twitching. "ThatcherThatcher...*oh my God.*" Water wells the corners of my eyes, and I turn my head into the mattress, gasping.

"*Christ*, Jane," he groans, and finding my hand again, he threads our fingers. He leans down, and our mouths meet.

I'm sweaty and my heart is beating rapidly out of my body again, but still, I desperately want his lips against mine.

We kiss, his tongue urging my mouth apart so sensually, and he's rocking into me. Not having come yet, but he slows his tempo. Like he understands every inch of me is a tender hotspot. Gradually allowing me to build back up.

He deepens the kiss and then breaks away first. Just to ask, "Alright?" I'm nodding, but maybe he doesn't believe I understand what he's asking.

Possibly I look glazed and spent, but I'm not yet.

He reaches down between our bodies. His thumb skims my swollen clit. It's tender but touchable, and I instantly crave more friction. I grind forward into him.

Thatcher shifts us slightly. He hooks his arm under my knee, and he braces his forearm to the bed, spreading me more while he drives harder inside of me. *Oh God.* Missionary, but with Thatcher cloaking me...

I hold on to his toned back.

Every thrust is long and deep and makes a loud *screech* on the rickety, iron bed, and with each push forward inside of me, the headboard naturally knocks into the wall.

Thump.

Thump.

Thump.

Sweat glistening between us, we're intertwined. All restless limbs and unlocked passion.

He fucks me hard and so impossibly well, and I can't think—my back arches, my toes curl. "Thatcher," I cry, nearly blacking out in a realm I hardly ever reach. My heat contracts, and he groans my name, pounding deep.

He hits a strong climax, his muscles twitching. He empties himself in me, and with a few more pumps, he ekes out his pleasure. And then both of us start to come down with heavy breaths.

21

 THATCHER MORETTI

We shower together in the attached bathroom and have sex again.

It has nothing to do with this op.

Nothing to do with the task at hand. No one can hear her gasps and high-pitched moans or my deep groans with water *pouring*. That's fucking clear to me. It's *been* clear to me that we're kerosene together. And we've finally lit the match.

In my head, there's no going back.

I should be concerned about the un-crossable line that I just leapt over with two middle fingers—but I'm not.

I'm just concerned about Jane. Because she's spent. And if we were on the bed, she probably would've fallen asleep.

She assures me she can walk. Or else I'd carry her out of the bathroom. Her perseverance is something that I'm drawn towards. *Been aware of that for a while.*

When we return to the room, I rifle through my backpack and keep sweeping Jane.

She yawns into her palm, and then twists a towel around her wet hair, another around her body, and she's eyeing me just as intensely while I put on a pair of black boxer-briefs. Lifting the elastic band to my muscular waist.

She homes in on my gold necklace and then crouches to her suitcase. Barely having enough energy to sift through her clothes, she picks out a fuzzy blue robe and slips it on.

"Can I get you anything?" I ask Jane.

A small smile tugs her freckled cheeks. "Um…I'm okay, really." She takes out a notebook from her suitcase, and then heads to the bed.

My chest tightens, brows knitting together. It's not a diary. She'll scribble math equations on those pages, and I've noticed that she usually does this during high-stress situations. To stay focused and get her mind right.

I run a hand across my jaw. But she's also really forthcoming. If something were wrong, I think she'd tell me.

I hope she would.

Especially after we just had sex. *Multiple times.*

Jane rolls down the comforter and climbs onto the clean sheets, notebook in hand. Completely exhausted, she slumps against the headboard.

But she's not lying down. She checks any missed texts from her family and pulls a pen out of the spiral binding of her notebook. She's quiet, which puts me on edge, but I only spot fatigue and curiosity in her gaze.

Her big blue eyes also track my movements.

I go to the nightstand where I left my phone and water. Not breaking eye contact. "How do you feel?" I ask.

She contemplates this, pressing the pen to her lips.

I glance at my phone. *No new messages from security.* Which is good. I unscrew my water bottle and take a swig.

"I feel a little sore," she admits. "Like you're still inside of me."

I'm not choking on my water. Because I'm not that surprised. "You sure I can't get you anything?" I ask. "Ibuprofen?" She was tight, but soaked, and I'm not small.

"No, I don't mind the feeling."

I nod. Having sex with Jane for real—it obliterated any image I've ever had and blew the remnants out of the fucking atmosphere. Her constant, rippling orgasms will probably be seared in my head and body for life.

Seeing and feeling her that unraveled and lit up took me to a mind-splitting, earth-tilting un-fucking-believable level.

Jane tips her head in thought. "Did you go all the way in? You felt deep and I felt entirely full, but it wasn't that painful."

I swig my water. "I was trying not to hit your cervix." I cap the bottle and set it on the nightstand. "I pushed all the way in only a few times."

Realization causes her lips to rise, and she can't suppress the smile. "The nearly-blackout orgasm that I had, that was a posterior fornix orgasm." She knows sex and her body well, and it's flat-out attractive.

"Yeah." I hold her gaze. "I pushed my cock behind your cervix." My blood heats up as her breath comes out shallow. Either facts turn Jane on or me saying a bunch of facts does.

She clears her throat and untwists the towel around her hair. Damp wavy strands cascade down her bare shoulders. "I've never reached that orgasm with a man before. Always just myself. Same with the A-spot, which is…" Her voice tapers off as curiosity glimmers her eyes. "Do you know what it is?"

I do.

Intimately.

I reach over the bed and take the damp towel out of her hand. "It's where I push my cock towards your belly button." *In front of her cervix.*

She looks enamored. "Yes please…I mean, *yes.*" She tries to sit up straighter. "Yes, you're correct."

Temperature cranks up. My muscles flexed, I go hang up all the damp towels on the bathroom door. But I can't take my eyes off her.

Jane quickly fills the quiet. "These spots have always been terribly intense for me. In the best way." She peels a wet strand of hair off her cheek. "I usually either have frequent orgasms that feel like crashing waves one after the other or *intense* eye-rolling orgasms every few minutes—but rarely both of those types together." She takes a short pause. "Until today, which is to say that I enjoyed this immensely. Really, all of it."

I walk back to her. "I did too." I take a seat on the mattress, facing Jane. Bed creaking beneath me. I glimpse at the notebook still on her lap. *Don't nuke it, man.* "So you don't regret anything—"

"Not at all," she interjects, eyes widened. "Do you—?"

"No." I shake my head once. *Say more.* "Given the same choice, I'd do it all over again."

She smiles, one that reddens her cheeks. "Me, as well."

Good

This is good. We're on the same page. But I watch her smile fade... and that is—that's fucking bad.

My expression hardens. "Jane?" I glance to the notebook again. *Just say it.* "Something is wrong though. You usually don't write equations unless you're stressed."

She's about to answer, but my phone buzzes on the nightstand. Our heads turn towards the noise.

This is security, and her safety comes before everything. "Sorry." I grab my cell. "Hold on."

"No need to apologize," she says sincerely. "Just let me know if it's about my family."

I read the text. "It's not."

Don't open your blinds. A suitor is sitting in the B&B parking lot with a pair of binoculars directed at your window.
– Oscar

Ever since Jane and I had the public kiss at the Acme, a lot of suitors have packed up and left her vicinity. But there are still stragglers who haven't been deterred.

I'm concerned this is that rich gold-shitting prick. Sitting in his fucking Bugatti. Gavin Reece. I message Oscar back: target description?

And then I look back at Jane. "It's about the outside perimeter."

She eases more, not needing further details. Not unless there's an immediate crisis.

Truth is, I don't want to give her more detail on this fuckbag unless there's greater reason to.

"Was that Banks who texted you?" she wonders, taking interest in the team.

"Oscar," I correct, just as my phone buzzes in my fist.

Male mid-40s or 50s, a beat-up sedan with a Florida license plate. He just stepped out of his car, and he's wearing white sneakers and jeans and carrying a dozen red roses. — Oscar

He's someone I remember scaring off outside the townhouse. But it's clear he hasn't taken multiple hints. I text back: he's a familiar target and should be easy to tell off.

Jane rests her temple to the headboard, rotated more towards me. "What do you think of Oscar Oliveira?"

I glance at the window while my gaze tightens. Just thinking about all that I fucked to hell pulls out a caustic glare. And I'm not setting it on *her*. "You mean personally or professionally?"

"Both, but if you'd rather not share, I understand."

I'd rather talk about Jane, about what's wrong, but I can't backtrack. Because backtracking means not answering her, and I hate that.

I lower my eyes, then lift them to Jane when they're not lethal pinpoints. "Personally…Oscar and I aren't on that great of footing." My phone vibrates again. "Same with me and Donnelly. I punched their friend." I check the message.

Copy. I'll get Sneakers to leave the parking lot. — Oscar

"I haven't noticed," she says. "You all seem very cordial."

"Because on a professional level, we're all okay." *Oscar.* I've known the thirty-one-year-old bodyguard since I first came into security. He'd already been protecting her family for a whole year prior, and he's intelligent, reliable and thinks ahead before most bodyguards.

He's also more professional in front of the families. Which I used to be.

Until now.

I fucked my client.

Should regret that—I don't.

I push myself to add more while Jane is quiet. "Oscar isn't someone I'd want to lose on the team. He's one of the best we have."

Her brows jump. "Who else would you consider the best?"

This isn't ego-driven horseshit. When you're in charge of a team, you better know what your men can and cannot do well. I wouldn't put O'Malley, Kinney Hale's bodyguard, behind the wheel in a fucking blizzard when I have guys who can drive ten times better under duress.

I look to Jane. "The top three most vital bodyguards are currently all in Omega."

And I'm not naming my brother, even though I love Banks. Even though I believe he's necessary and skilled in so many areas that I'm not—there are three men that he'd agree with me are irreplaceable.

So I say, "Akara, Oscar, and Farrow."

Her lips part in a sudden, overwhelming realization. I understand why her eyes redden before she says the words. "They were all at the car crash."

I nod and cross my arms over my bare chest.

By dumb luck, the three best men on the team had been on site at the wreck. Hell, Farrow had been *in* the wreck and came out with only a scratch.

Alpha, Epsilon, and Omega have talked about what that night would've looked like if one of those three weren't on the scene, and we all know it would've been a different picture.

All of them had a hand in saving her family.

I explain one detail further to Jane. How security learned that Farrow asked Oscar for a needle decompression kit to help Maximoff. No one but Oscar would've known what Farrow was requesting, and time had been critical.

She takes a bigger breath. "I'm really grateful for all of you."

"I wasn't there—"

"You were with me that night, I remember. And Moffy needed the best to survive, but I needed you." She sits up straighter in a jolt. "*Professionally* speaking. On a professional level, I needed you—and I also...I also still need you, which is *also* to say that you're vital to me. Professionally." Her eyes are huge.

I nod a few times, my chest rising. "I didn't want to be anywhere else that night but next to you." I push myself to add, "As your bodyguard."

Jane taps her pen to her notebook. "So we're in agreement that you're the best bodyguard for me..." She trails off as I uncross my arms and climb further on the bed, leaning against the iron headboard. Right next to her.

I nod in response, and the air boils somehow—*I don't fucking know how.* We've already fucked. There should be no tension left, but we steal these glances that constrict my chest and scorch my veins.

And then my eyes land on her open notebook. At the math equations scribbled in nearly illegible handwriting on pastel purple paper. "Before security texted, I asked if something is stressing you?"

"Um." Jane shakes out her jumbled thoughts. "Yes..." She takes a breath in preparation. "I suppose the idea that this was a one-time occurrence is weighing on me. I'm not used to one-night stands." Her eyes drive into me, my chest burning.

Fuck.

"That's not what this was," I say and rub my lips. "That's not what I wanted it to be." I hate that what she thought we did here was something like a one-night stand. That didn't even cross my mind.

The notebook makes a hell of a lot more sense now.

Her lips part a little. "You want to sleep with me again," she realizes. "You want to take that risk...But if the Tri-Force finds out you're having sex with me, they'll fire you. Correct?"

"Correct." My voice is stricter, breath caged in my lungs. No one is covering my ass the way that Akara and I covered Farrow, and the leads are more protective of the girls in these families. "It would also do damage to the men on SFO."

She nods, understanding. "Because that's two Omega bodyguards who've slept with their clients, and from your bosses' vantage, that's two too many."

"Exactly." I nod. "But the fake dating op gives us more coverage to do what we want." We can do this again. I *want* to do this again. I'm settled with this fact. It feels right. No indecision. No backtracking.

Her eyes glimmer. "It gives us plausible deniability," she says into a warm smile. "So we use the fake dating ruse as a way to keep having sex." She closes her notebook and takes a lighter breath like something is rising off her shoulders. "I do think that this is the best thing to come out of the Cinderella ad. Wonderful, passionate sex. That no one can know about, of course." She frowns. "Including Maximoff. I wouldn't want him to have to keep a giant secret from all of security again."

"Then I won't tell Banks." It's only fair. "For the same reason."

We shift nearer, her blue robe parts between her soft thighs and slips further open at her chest, her small breasts peeking out. My cock strains in my boxer-briefs, and my hand warms her thigh. She places her palm atop mine.

Our eyes lock in an intense beat.

"It'll have to end eventually," she says. "We can't have sex, if we're not fake dating. The risk of getting caught would increase tenfold."

I nod, more tense. She's right. The end date has to be the breakup. A public breakup that security is choosing the date and time and details for. Then things return to the way they were.

No touching.

No kissing.

Definitely not my cock in her pussy.

These logistics aren't the kind with a happily ever after for us. But at this point, I think we're both willing to enjoy anything we can.

"Sounds right," I tell Jane.

This is the only way I can keep Jane safe, the team safe, remain her bodyguard and fulfill a knockout desire we've both restrained ourselves from and hungered after.

She begins to smile more brightly. "It seems we are dreadfully tangled, you and I."

Couldn't agree more.

22

JANE COBALT

"*That is so unnecessary and categorically* illegal," I say aloud and adjust my clutch on the steering wheel, watching paparazzi drive on the *shoulder* of the bumpy two-lane highway.

Reckless cars fight with each other to be closest to my blue Beetle and to Maximoff's red Audi, my best friend driving in front of me.

We stay in the right lane, and I concentrate and ride close to his bumper. Not letting anyone squeeze in between our cars.

Thatcher and I would've just taken back roads and split up from Maximoff and Farrow, but with the sheer aggression and swarms of cameramen who like to play chicken and bumper cars, we would've been trapped in Center City for a troublesome decade. We've chosen a troublesome *hour* on a highway instead.

As my brother Eliot would say, "Paparazzi are ravenous fiends out for flesh and blood." That has never been truer.

Especially since the Bed & Breakfast.

The ploy worked as well as security planned. When we were checking out, I caught Oscar telling Thatcher, "*Heard you almost all night. Incredibly believable.*"

I'd hope so.

At least Oscar, Donnelly, and Banks believe they just listened in on our pretend sex noises. We have *no* intention of ever telling them they overheard real grunts, real moans, real orgasms—I will most surely die with this secret.

But Oscar's predictions were right. The guests believed us. And so has the media and thusly, the world. Click-bait articles were trending for days.

JANE COBALT AND HER BODYGUARD CAUGHT LEAVING A BED & BREAKFAST TOGETHER!

And you're not going to believe what the other guests overheard!

I did swipe through some of the comments on posts.

Vera K: Jane is living the dream!

EarlyBird_4: Can't believe she's hooking up with her bodyguard. The crops are thriving.

PrincessPeachez16: If my bodyguard looked like that, you best believe I'd be dating him too.

HeyyyHey: Get it girl!!!

I glazed over most negativity and just basked in the positives for a while.

These scandalous rumors incited the media, but the tipping point that caused paparazzi to drive in emergency lanes and feverishly crowd us—it came just yesterday.

When I publicly confirmed the rumors.

That I, Jane Eleanor Cobalt, am dating my handsome and oh-so-stern bodyguard. I wanted it to be more personal than a press release. So we became official via a Live Story on Instagram.

Secretly overseen by security, of course. Their hand in everything reminds me this is a *fake* relationship.

Totally, undeniably *fake*...

I take a quick peek at Thatcher in the passenger seat. He's surveying the rabid paparazzi and our extra security vehicles in tow. He clicks his mic, attached to the collar of his black button-down. Sleeves rolled up to his carved biceps.

"You want to do a hand-off?" He's radioing Farrow in the Audi. "...Copy." When he drops his arm, his large hand just naturally rests on my thigh.

Beneath my purple tulle skirt.

I rub my lips together that rise. His touch sends electric jolts coursing through my veins. Reminding me that our sex has been over-whelmingly *real*.

Every night since the Bed & Breakfast, Thatcher has snuck out of security's townhouse and into my room. It feels illicit and clandestine, a covert mission that only we share, one that has scorched my bed with my eagerness and his strength and volcanic yearnings. Blazing strokes of skin to skin as we try to keep quiet, so no one overhears.

And I've never been held against a man's chest the way that he holds me.

I've never had a friends-with-benefits ask how I felt. I was fully aware that they wanted me for fifteen minutes of fame or notoriety—to say they hooked up with the daughter of Connor Cobalt and Rose Calloway. But all I wanted from them was sex. I felt like I was using them too, and I chose these guys purposefully knowing I'd never fall for them.

It was easier that way.

But how Thatcher treats me is so catastrophically new from what I've experienced. I've never felt so appreciated before, during, and after sex.

We're very careful about being caught, and we have a routine. He must *never* fall asleep in my bed. As soon as the clock strikes 3 a.m., he must go back to security's townhouse.

I check my side mirrors, not able to smile or daze off for long. I'm incredibly wedged into the right lane by two silver SUVs and a four-door truck, and our extra security vehicles trail far behind us.

The woes of not breaking the law when paparazzi do—they've lost an advantage. But as I check my rearview, I see our Range Rovers trying to catch up by driving in the emergency lanes.

I stay fixed on the street and do my best to stand my ground.

"I'm watching your left." Thatcher eagle-eyes the truck that tries to creep in my lane. "You're doing good, Jane."

I risk a glance his way, and our eyes catch for a sweltering beat. He looks deeper in me with a sort of powerful reassurance that makes me feel invincible. And safe.

"Thank you," I say, more breathless than I intend, and my cheeks heat while I crane my neck. My sight returning to the red Audi's bumper. *Stay with Moffy.*

Stay with Moffy.

Stay with my best friend.

I repeat my clear focus. Maximoff and I are en route to a costume shop. Since October is here, my best friend has a license again.

Despite his speeding habit, it's difficult to deny how skilled he is at offensive and defensive driving. He has maneuvered us through hoards of paparazzi since we left the townhouse, and if I didn't follow him so closely, I would've been stuck long ago.

I tap my brake a little, and an advance copy of *Wildfire Heart* slides on the dashboard of my car.

Thatcher takes his hand off my thigh and grabs the romance book, slipping it in the glove compartment.

I've already devoured the love story between a cocky firefighter and his best friend's spunky sister. My second read-through, I've started taking notes. Just so I'm more prepared before I go in the studio.

Thatcher adjusts his seat forward, bending his knees. "Are you okay with a hand-off in five?" He knows I've done them before, but not under these conditions. He adds, "It might be the only way to get off the highway."

Otherwise, the silver SUVs will continue to block us from the exits. I've realized this too. We could wait for police to pull them over, but that's assuming they will.

"Is a hand-off even possible at this speed?" I wonder.

It involves bodyguards rolling down car windows and paying paparazzi to move out of the way, and if the cameramen are nice, they'll even block other paparazzi vehicles for us.

Thatcher explains, "Farrow is getting Maximoff to slow down to twenty."

I take a breath. "Then yes, I'm okay with one." Sun crests the horizon, a harsh glare piercing the windshield, and I flip my car visor down, barely blocking the light.

Thatcher hands me my cat-eye sunglasses and speaks into comms. "Jane is good to go in five."

After slipping on my sunglasses, I edge closer to the wheel. The Audi slowly decelerates, and I follow suit.

I squint at another ray of light, and I shield my hand over my eyes. "How dangerously close am I to his bumper?"

"A few inches." He extends an arm over my seat and assesses our surroundings. "You're still good, honey."

My eyes bug and lips part—he called me *honey*. So innately and instinctively and with such tenderness. I inhale without exhaling, and I can't help but turn my head to Thatcher.

His attention is plastered to the street. "Jane, *brake*."

"Merde." I slam on my brake.

Thatcher plants a firm hand on the dashboard. I brake too late, and I crunch into Maximoff's bumper. Both of our cars jerk forward from the light impact.

My pulse has shot out of my butt, and I am a frozen chunk of ice. "Oh my God."

"It wasn't bad. It's alright, Jane," Thatcher says, very huskily and seriously and not at all alarmed. I have a soldier in my car. He speaks lowly into comms, then checks back on me.

"Oh my God," I keep unhelpfully repeating, and I try to peer at the damage of Maximoff's Audi. I use a phone voice-command. "*Call Moffy.* I can't believe I rear-ended my best friend—"

"It was my fault," Thatcher cuts me off, looking down at me, then eyeing the road.

"No, I should've been watching the street." I do now. My eyeballs are attached to the concrete and the Audi and my mistake.

Thatcher adds, "I distracted you."

I hear his voice in my head, *You're still good, honey.*

My heart skips. "Not on purpo—"

"Janie?" Maximoff's voice sounds through my car speakers. "Are you two okay?"

"We're fine," I say, sitting straighter. Face on fire. "How are you and Farrow? How's your collarbone?" Back in May, he broke the bone from the force of the seatbelt, and I feel sick at the thought of causing him any pain.

"Totally shattered like a regular Humpty Dumpty," Maximoff says with complete sarcasm. "I think I died back there."

I try not to smile. I need him to be serious about his injury. At least in this moment. Before I respond, I hear his fiancé.

"You're not dead; you're breathing right next to me, wolf scout."

"Or maybe we all just died, and we're in purgatory."

Farrow lets out a short laugh. "Or maybe you're just a dork who wants to spend purgatory with me."

"Or maybe—"

"Farrow," I interject and instantly feel badly about cutting off my best friend, but I must. "How is he?"

"He's not hurt," Farrow says very casually, as though we're leisurely having a four-course meal in the middle of nightmarish traffic. "You still want to do a hand-off?"

I glance at Thatcher since he's been watching the surrounding vehicles.

He nods to me like it's still possible.

"Yes," I answer.

"I'm going twenty," Maximoff tells me, his voice firm and more serious. "I can go slower if you need me to."

"This is perfect."

Thatcher takes out a few hundred-dollar bills from his wallet. "Three, Farrow."

"Eh, let's do four. I don't want to barter with these fuckers."

It sounds like code, but they've been doing this for years. Neither one needs to say three hundred dollars to understand they're referring to cash.

Thatcher instructs me to drift closer to the silver SUV, and the four of us work in unison, despite being in different cars.

Our bodyguards roll down their windows, and paparazzi begin to roll down theirs. Camera lenses directed at our cars. Arms reaching out of the windows on either side, a few loud words exchanged, along with nods.

The hand-off works, and the SUVs slow to clear a passage as we come upon our exit.

We have the costume shop to ourselves for a

few hours. Darkly lit with black-painted walls and stocked to the brim with Halloween decorations, fog machines smoke the concrete floor and spooky laughter echoes from speakers.

Maximoff and I rarely used to close down places, but lately, it's been more necessary. Right now, over a hundred excitable teenagers are outside the glassed entrance, screaming our names and banging on the windows.

If I do say so, I prefer this crowd to what the Cinderella ad initially roused.

Maximoff and I browse a rack of steampunk costumes, and our bodyguards are in sight but out of earshot, standing at the locked glassed entrance and ensuring no one breaches.

Just until the temp bodyguards, the ones trailing us in the Range Rovers, arrive here. When the temps take over door-duty, Thatcher and Farrow will flank our sides once again.

It's very systematic.

Which provides a great deal of calmness to my life.

I can't bite my tongue. "Thatcher called me *honey*," I confess in a whisper to Maximoff. It is a small, innocent confession, seeing as how the much greater one is under lock and key.

That Thatcher spends the night fucking me.

Maximoff's brows furrow. "In what way did he say it?"

I push aside a few leather corsets. "Caringly, and like it was the most natural thing in the world." I feel oddly giddy; my lungs might as well be inflated with helium, levitating inside my chest.

He scrutinizes me. "I've never seen you like a guy this much."

I send him a furtive look. "It's just physical attraction."

Maximoff gestures towards our bodyguards while he speaks. "Gawking at Thatcher, who looks like a six-foot-seven version of Jon Snow after he killed White Walkers and made friends with wildlings—that's physical attraction. Liking when a guy calls you *honey* is…" He scrunches his face. "I don't know what it is, but it's not *physical.*"

"It's verbal," I point out. "Verbal communication comes from the tongue, which is in fact a physical appendage."

He blinks and then stares off. "Tu as peut-être raison." *Maybe you're right.*

I smile. "Thatcher is also…" I catch myself before I blurt out, *Thatcher is also good with his tongue in more physical ways.*

I want to express how Thatcher's otherworldly talents in bed are by far the best I've had between my legs. But roping Maximoff into this secret will complicate his life when he just uncomplicated it.

Sheltering these moments in my life from Moffy is so difficult. I have a giant urge to gush forth what's happening. Just like he told me all about his first time sleeping with Farrow.

There are so few people I trust in the world, and since we learned to talk, Maximoff and I shared everything.

"Thatcher is also what?" Maximoff picks out a spiked brown leather jacket.

I try to recover. "He's also exceptionally sweet."

"Jesus, that is nowhere *near* physical attraction." He motions to me. "You're supposed to be light-years smarter than me." He gives me a look like I'm acting strange.

I'm sweating beneath my pale yellow faux-fur vest. I try to smile, but it feels a little forced.

Maximoff can tell. "Everything okay?" He sets the leather jacket back and focuses on me.

"Fake dating is just complex, but not in a bad way." I smile in thought. "It's more stimulating, actually."

Stimulating. Really, Jane? I suppose I could've chosen a more sexual word. At least I didn't say *erotic.* I tie my wavy hair back into a low pony, my neck flushed.

Maximoff is in deeper thought, and he cracks a few knuckles.

I pull back my shoulders. *Confidence.* I can survive tiptoeing around this secret. "And I'd rather talk about you, old chap."

He's about to speak, but Thatcher and Farrow approach us as temp guards claim their positions.

Teenagers shriek outside the windows as our 24/7 bodyguards walk over to us. Cellphones braced at the glass, along with paparazzi's professional cameras. Everyone takes such keen interest in Thatcher and Farrow, who do their best to ignore the extra attention.

I'm taking a very keen interest in Thatcher Moretti at the moment too.

As he nears, he's only staring at me.

"Thatcher," I greet, a smile playing at my lips.

"Jane," he says huskily, looking into me with open-booked desire. In public.

It's not only allowed, it's *encouraged.*

My heartbeat accelerates to unknown, unquantifiable speeds, and as soon as I take one step closer to Thatcher, he's already here.

His large hands clasp the back of my thighs, and my arms take flight around his broad shoulders. All in one seamless movement. He hoists me up and my legs wrap around him. Breath abandoning my body.

His hand travels in a boiling trail up my spine, and he pulls me into his muscular build with a deep, full kiss that I reciprocate in kind.

I run my fingers across his scruffy jaw, and as I catch my breath, my lips stinging, we both seem to register the onslaught of passionate squealing.

"JANE! THATCHER!!"

We're not glancing in that direction just yet, and I whisper, "We're selling this well." Another small smile tugs my cheeks. "It's like we're partners in crime, you and I."

Light touches his vigilant eyes, and his gaze drifts at the next wave of shrieking. More so to double-check the safety of the perimeter.

His attention returns to me, his seriousness never waning. He's safety, the forceful gravity that grounds me, that helps stop me from rattling sideways inside a world that tries and tries to shake me.

Thatcher drops his voice to a deep whisper. "The team will love this." He cups my cheek in affection before setting me on my feet, his hand pressed to the small of my back. "But not more than me."

I go to speak, but flush has overtaken my face and my tongue is tied.

My eyes glimmer with so many questions and curiosities. I want to know every miniscule detail about Thatcher. I feel as though we've just started this exploration. We've just pressed *play*, and we keep hitting *pause* to draw this out longer.

As we near Maximoff and Farrow, Thatcher's hand falls into mine like second-nature, having no hesitation at treating me like a real girlfriend for our fake relationship.

All of our heads turn as a girl outside shrieks bloody-murder, "MAKE LOVE TO ME, THATCHER MORETTI!"

It's not so humorous. She can't be older than a very young thirteen.

Thatcher is unflinching. He's used to these impassioned declarations, but not directed his way. Yet, this hardly seems to bother him.

I frown a little—there is guilt knowing that I've traded the suitors who were only interested in *me* for crowds that are now obsessed with *him* and *us*.

We all look back at each other, and they spot my unease.

"They're harmless." Farrow lifts his aviators to his head, pushing back his platinum hair. "That girl isn't going to force herself on Moretti. But the sick dipshits who think they have a shot with you…" He raises his brows.

"They're threats," Thatcher says curtly.

"True." I tip my head towards Thatcher.

"And those potential stalkers are *gone*," Maximoff emphasizes to me, his strong arm across Farrow's shoulders.

I want to mention that 35% still remain. Just to be more specific. None of these threats concern me because stalkers will always exist, and I trust our security team to handle them. But I can see that Maximoff wants me to feel safe. And I do, especially with Thatcher so close.

So I don't mention the statistics.

Thatcher looks down at me, and as added reassurance, he says, "It's better this way, Jane."

"Maybe not for you," I point out.

He shakes his head, his brows drawn together. "Eliminating anyone who wants to hurt you is the better path for me."

He sounds incredibly sincere. *I trust him.* And I'm fortunate to have him. "That's..." I grapple for words that tumble in my head. "You know, I..." I take a breath. "I like..."

You.

I clear my throat. "I like that you feel that way."

Thatcher starts to smile. Really and truly, and then he threads our fingers, his hand so much larger than mine.

My pulse speeds, and I glance back at Maximoff and Farrow. "Have you two decided on a couple's Halloween costume yet?" I know Moffy has been leaning towards a superhero pairing, but he's also wanted to see what Farrow would choose.

"No," Maximoff says. "Because Farrow is being an asshole and leaving this shit up to me."

Farrow rolls his eyes into a wider smile, staring at Maximoff with such pure love. "You want me to hold your hand and walk you through this shit because I will, but only for you."

Maximoff grimaces and smiles all at once. Trying to hide his affections. I give my best friend a weak 4 out of 10 this time, deductions for poor effort.

He's suddenly more rigid, his forest-green eyes on me. "You and Thatcher are picking out couple costumes too, right? You haven't said anything about it."

"I don't know if it's up to me," I say. "I'm assuming security will need to verify whatever we choose?" I look up at Thatcher for confirmation.

"I already asked," Thatcher tells me, more than he speaks to Moffy. "The team agreed on no couple costumes." His voice is strict, and his chest is tight like this isn't news he wanted. But he has to obey.

Maximoff growls, "What, why?"

"Is there a reason?" I ask too, not expecting this kind of finality from security.

Thatcher lowers his voice. "They said it's probable that our breakup will happen before Halloween." His gaze softens a fraction on me.

That soon? October just began. My eyes grow in shock. "Wow." I let go of his hand and tuck a flyaway frizzed hair behind my ear. "Well, I suppose this isn't terrible...we have a clearer timeline to work with now."

The bottom of my stomach has dropped, and I wish it'd float back to its proper anatomical position, please.

His chest concaves with a constricted breath, and he's about to speak—but Maximoff beats him to it. "Just tell the team that Jane wants this to go past October."

"I tried at the meeting," Thatcher explains. "Farrow did too."

My lungs swell, liking that they're both on my side. Even if the outcome isn't necessarily what I would've hoped for, and anyway, it was presumptuous to expect to spend Halloween with my fake boyfriend.

There was always going to be an end.

But we just started.

"They said *probable*, right?" Maximoff says, on edge. "So it's not set in stone, and if you and Farrow really hammer in the fact that Jane wants this—"

"What I want and she wants doesn't fucking matter," Thatcher says tightly. "Our feelings aren't important to security's op. That's just how it is."

I've understood this part, but Maximoff is like my heart fighting for something deeper inside me that I can't even unearth. I wonder if Banks were here, if he'd be fighting for something deeper inside Thatcher too.

Maximoff crosses his arms. "So security related: if this is a shotgun breakup, all the stalkers outside will just come back. Tell them that."

"We did," Thatcher says sternly. "The leads don't want to risk more exposure to SFO. They think me being with Jane longer than necessary will draw too much attention to the rest of the team."

SFO has already been in the public spotlight from the Hot Santa video, and some fans have paired us off and made creative ship names. Like Quinnivan is Quinn plus Sullivan.

But it's been contained to one fandom realm of the internet. As Farrow would say, *harmless.* I can see how security would be concerned if that one realm mushroomed into popular public opinion.

Maximoff thinks hard. "Then Jane and I will talk directly to the Tri-Force. We're the clients. They'll have to listen to us."

"Man, that's not how that works," Farrow says, his hand on the back of Maximoff's neck in comfort. "We can't have our clients running to our bosses because we want something."

Thatcher nods once. "We can't undermine the leads."

They'd both lose a great deal of respect among security. "You don't need to put pressure on the security team for this," I state. "I'm not searching for longer or more."

Thatcher tenses, looking me over in concern. He rakes his palm across his hardened jaw and then tries to hold my hand again. But I slip out of his fingers and browse through the costumes.

"We have a greater purpose. We're here for the girls," I remind all of them.

They know I'm referring to the Girl Squad: my sister Audrey, plus Winona Meadows, Kinney Hale, and Vada Abbey.

They each requested that their older sisters pick out their Halloween costumes this year, and since Vada is an only child, she asked Maximoff, her cousin, to do the honors.

The four girls said, *"Surprise us."*

Luna and Sullivan already ordered costumes online for their little sisters—Dorothy from *The Wizard of Oz* for Kinney and Harley Quinn for Winona. Even if I fail miserably at this and choose something my thirteen-year-old sister despises, I know Audrey will pretend to love it.

Big sister duties are truly my favorite.

And yet, I can't stop thinking about how abruptly this may all end between Thatcher and me. I have *so* many questions left to ask.

So much that I prolonged, and I wonder if our fake breakup will force us to return to a time where it's uncomfortable, where we're not speaking at all.

Timelines are necessary, I remind myself. *You like structure, Jane.*

I do, and I sift through more steampunk corsets and a few frocks.

I can feel all three sets of their eyes on my back.

And they're tall.

Towering behind me.

"Really, I'm fine," I say loudly.

Men. I love them dearly, but their concern comes so powerfully in my family and security. It could bowl you over, and while Luna, Sulli, and I are harassed more heavily and frequently, we were all raised by three extraordinary sisters who could summon hell and part seas together.

"Would vouching for you help?" Maximoff asks Thatcher behind me. "I won't persuade the Tri-Force, but I can just tell them you'd never cross a line with Jane—"

"No," I interject, spinning on my heels with wide eyes, a leather corset in my hands. Unbeknownst to Moffy, Thatcher has already erased that line and drawn a new circle around himself and me.

Thatcher's arms are ironbound over his chest. Difficult to read, but I think he's just on guard.

Maximoff looks between us.

I speak quickly. "I highly doubt an extra recommendation in Thatcher's resume will persuade the Tri-Force of anything." I hook the corset on the rack. "Let's just leave things as they should be and not cause more trouble for our bodyguards."

Maximoff reluctantly nods. "Alright." He cracks another knuckle. "You want to split up? Farrow and I will meet you back at the checkout?"

I clasp my hands. "Oui. Diviser et conquérir." *Yes. Divide and conquer.*

23

JANE COBALT

We hug before I go.

Farrow and Maximoff stay in the steampunk section for Vada's costume, and Thatcher and I walk into the darker depths of the shop, away from paparazzi and onlookers at the entrance.

His hand brushes along my back, and he scouts every inch of ground. He's on-duty. Regardless of fake-dating, he places my safety above all else, and so each glance we take still feels stolen.

Each touch still feels forbidden, and I've come to realize that this allure will never die with Thatcher Moretti. As long as he's my bodyguard, as long as he values protecting me and taking care of me first and foremost, our embraces in public will be drawn out slowly like flowing magma.

Until an eruption happens. Somewhere, sometime. At night.

Thatcher surveys the back area. "I meant to tell you in the car, about what the team decided." He stares down at me, then fixes on a fog machine that gurgles out smoke, whisking along his boots, my ballet flats. He adds a deep, "I'm sorry."

"No need to be." We trek further, and he pushes aside a fake spider web that almost catches in his hair. I take a breath. "I distracted you back in the car."

He lets out a soft laugh. "We both know I distracted you." He glances back at me, his eyes falling down my body. "Honey." He cradles those five letters.

I inhale, about to say more, but I'm trapped just watching him. Staying pinned to his hard features. Engraining all the stern creases around his eyes. As though he may vanish soon. It's terribly illogical.

He's still here.

And he'll still be my bodyguard no matter—Thatcher suddenly catches me around the waist, stopping me from bumping into a life-sized mummy.

He pulls me back against his muscular chest, my breath ejecting.

Heartbeat racing.

And while I'm in his protective, warm clutch, while we're alone, I feel safe to ask him anything. "I have so many questions," I say softly, thinking aloud. "I want to know all about you, but I can't ask fast enough—and when I think about you, I wonder what your hands have held. What your eyes have seen." My pulse has skyrocketed, but I keep speaking. "What your ears have heard and where your feet have landed."

He's quiet, and I ache to see him. So gradually, I unfreeze and turn to look up at Thatcher. I skim his stoic features, more entranced. But I also mentally replay what I just said and my eyes grow bigger. "If that sounds disturbing, I'm so sor—"

"No," he cuts me off, one of the few times he ever has. "You're an American princess. You being comfortable enough to say what's on your mind in front of me—and to me—is something I don't take for granted."

My lungs flood, knowing he's felt this way means more than I realize or thought it would.

His hands fall to his radio, and he hawk-eyes the rear exit that says *emergency only*. We're very close to the back of the store. Where neon wigs and animal masks are shelved on endless rows of mannequin heads, and I'm multitasking, perusing the nearest rack of gothic costumes, heavy lace and black veils.

Fog continuously rolls over the ground, hiding our feet.

He seems to be aware of every little thing.

Especially me.

Thatcher sweeps me head to toe. "And I want you to know all about me. So shoot."

I will most surely fire away. "How old were you when you lost your virginity?" I'm too intrigued, especially after how exceptional he is under the sheets...and on top of the sheets, on the floor and against the shower wall.

"Fifteen," he answers, unflinchingly. "What about you?"

My brows bunch, fingers paused on a veil. "Don't you know about me already?"

It's not public information. But the boy had to sign an NDA, and my bodyguard at the time was around to protect me.

Our bodyguards are privy to stories and secrets that they're supposed to safeguard. For most of my life, I had Mitchell, who's now retired. I always believed he shared more stories with the team about me, which is allowed. So I just assumed all of security knew this one.

"I do know how old you were." He holds my gaze tighter. "But I want to hear it from you."

My lips rise. The act of sharing personal stories feels intimate. I've never really done this with anyone beyond the docuseries producers and family.

"I was fifteen when I lost my virginity," I say aloud. "Same as you." I can't restrain a smile.

His carriage lifts in a headier breath.

"Did you enjoy your first time?" I ask.

"Hell yeah," he nods a few times. "Did you?"

"I did, immensely, and I really love that you enjoyed your first too." Feeling that there was happiness in his life makes me happy.

He checks slight movement on his right, orange streamers blowing as the air conditioning kicks on, and then he looks at me. "Your first time didn't hurt?"

I inspect a pair of black wings in a fallen angel costume. "A little bit in the beginning, but then it felt better." I turn more to him. "The overall experience was illuminating and exciting, and now sex is practically a favorite hobby."

He nods. "Sex feels different with you though."

We both tense at his admission. Treading carefully.

"Good different?" I pry a little deeper.

"Beyond fucking good, honey," he answers, inhaling strongly like my scent does him in and we're only a few feet apart.

Heat pricks my nerves, flush ascending my cheeks. *He's on-duty*, I remind myself, and I'm respecting his position as my bodyguard from now until forever.

He shifts around me, standing closer to the emergency exit as someone pounds on the door from the outside.

I flinch at the noise.

Thatcher's indomitable *I will annihilate anyone who tries to harm you* presence eases me considerably. Anyone who tries to hurt me will have to pass through his iron-will and brawn, and it won't be an easy feat.

I hear a muffled, masculine voice. "It's locked." And then footsteps drift further away.

Thatcher turns to me. "It's still safe here."

I relax more, and he watches me examine the black angel wings. I manage to land on another question. "What were you like as a teenager?"

He's a second from responding, but his phone rings. Security would communicate through comms, so I'm assuming this has to be his family in South Philly.

"Mannaggia," he curses under his breath in Italian and digs for his phone in his pocket.

I asked him what the Italian-American word meant not long ago, and he said, *Damn*.

Thatcher narrows his gaze onto the phone screen. "Xander is calling me." We share a look of confusion.

When Thatcher permanently transferred to my detail, I asked him repeatedly if he was positive, if he was comfortable, leaving Xander Hale: my fragile cousin, who Thatcher protected and saw grow up from nine-years-old to fourteen.

I love my cousins as if they were my sisters and brothers, and Xander needed Thatcher more than me. There was a giant place inside my heart that felt like I was stealing someone crucial and vital to Xander's mental well-being and life.

Thatcher told me, "I need to leave Xander, and Banks is going to have to leave at some point soon too. And it's going to be one of the hardest things we ever do."

I didn't understand at first, but he said, "It'll be good for all three of us." Thatcher explained that Xander relied on them to the point where he'd panic if they needed to take a day off and couldn't be on his detail. If they needed to switch with a temp for an hour, he'd be more anxious and upset.

I think Thatcher felt like they made a mistake for five years in not helping Xander be more comfortable with other bodyguards. Becoming so dependent on them that only they could be his safety net—when they needed Xander to trust the entire team.

And so they had to help him move on.

Now Xander is calling him, and it's a little out of the ordinary. Thatcher has been off his detail for almost a year, and if Xander calls anyone, it's most likely he'll dial his older brother's number. Possibly he couldn't reach Maximoff, but that'd mean something terrible is happening to my best friend.

Moffy is almost always reachable.

"Maximoff is still here?" I ask Thatcher before he answers the call.

"As far as I know," Thatcher says. "But Farrow doesn't always use comms if he changes locations."

I wait to text Moffy.

Because there are more possibilities for the call. Xander could be hurt knowing that Thatcher never told him he was a Marine. His military service leaked recently, and Banks and Thatcher have had to assuage confusion and some stronger feelings in the team. All without answering a probing question as to why they didn't enlist in the Navy and follow their father's footsteps.

No one knows.

And I wouldn't pry, but Farrow said the Navy guys were digging at the Moretti brothers during the meeting. Until Akara stepped in with harsher words.

Thatcher taps his phone screen.

"Thatcher?" Xander sounds a little out of breath.

"Hey, kid," Thatcher says, concern lining his forehead. "Jane is here; you're on speaker."

"Bonjour, Xander," I say brightly. "Is everything okay where you are?"

"Yeah…life's going, I guess." Xander pants some. "I'm at Uncle Ryke's gym…hitting this bag, or trying to." He pauses. "Thatcher, you know how I've been learning to box?"

He's been working out with Moffy and Farrow more recently, and he's taken more interest in boxing, so Farrow has been helping teach him.

"Yeah," Thatcher says, eyes on me and our surroundings.

I plant a hand on my hip, staring at the phone.

"I asked Farrow if he thought it'd be cool if maybe…you, him, and Banks could train me or something. To actually fight in a ring. And I get that you don't have a lot of off-duty time. It was just an idea I had…"

Thatcher is unblinking, thinking at rapid pace. I can practically see the gears shifting in his mind, and he cares about Xander. But he must be gauging how healthy it'll be to reconnect in this way.

To give Thatcher more time to consider, I chime in, "What'd Farrow say?"

Xander catches his breath. "He said he's up for it."

I'm not so sure I understand what Thatcher and Farrow are at the moment other than co-workers. But they've been far more willing to share space together.

"Okay, I'm up for this too," Thatcher suddenly agrees. "I'll help you in the ring, but with Farrow."

"Yeahyeah," he says, a joyful smile in his voice. It swells my heart. "Thanks, man. Just text me when you're free."

"Sounds good. Take care of yourself, kid."

Once they both hang up, Thatcher has a faraway look in his eye that he tries to extinguish. He blinks hard a few times, centering himself to the here and now. His muscles are taut, and he rubs his mouth with a rougher hand.

My curiosity has fallen to the wayside. Replaced by concern. "Can I do anything for you?" I whisper and hook the angel wings back onto the rack.

Skin wrinkles between his constricted eyes, staring at me like he's looking directly into the brightest light.

I keep going. "Maybe I can help with whatever you need. I fully recognize we're *fake* boyfriend-and-girlfriend, but I'm a terrific wingwoman. I can be your right-hand."

His lips almost tic upward. "I have no doubt you'd be great. But I'm *your* right-hand, honey. I'm your wingman."

I smile a very overwhelming smile. "And you've been a superb wingman, but maybe *my* wingman needs a wingwoman from time to time, and I'm at your service." I mime the tip of a top hat.

He's more lost in my eyes than before. "If you want to be my wingwoman, there's something I need to tell you."

I stare up at him more curiously and prepare for impact. "I'm all ears."

24

THATCHER MORETTI

I'm literally a half a second from telling Jane something I almost never talk about. To anyone. Barely even Banks.

Call it divine intervention or maybe the devil is laughing in my fucking face—but her phone rings and blows this one shot to hell.

Truth is, I'm not even close to upset. Because she's my purpose. I want to be here for Jane more than anything; it's my drive in life and I'm already squared away to push out.

"I'm so sorry," Jane says quickly, her face torn in a wince while she unzips her purse and grabs her phone. "I want to say this will only take a minute, but if it's my family, we'll need to leave."

I think she's forgetting I'm her bodyguard and that I've been around her for almost a year, a part of her daily routine. Nine times out of ten, her phone calls lead her in a new direction.

Always family.

Her big blue eyes lift up to me.

"I want you to take as long as you need," I tell her, not breaking our gazes. "I'll still be here beside you at the end of everything."

She breathes deeper and nods repeatedly, then reads the Caller ID. "It's Charlie."

Her twenty-one-year-old brother is hard to pin down. Literally and everything else in between. Hell, I spent months on a tour bus with the kid, and I can't say I fully understand him. I just assume he prefers being at arm's length.

Which makes protecting him a clusterfucking shit show. He's gone through the most 24/7 bodyguards of any client. It used to be a running issue on the team. Who can last on Charlie Cobalt's detail for more than two weeks?

Almost no one. We had brand new hires *quit* after being paired with Charlie, and then finally, we found his perfect match. Oscar Oliveira is the only bodyguard able to keep up with him.

Jane puts the call on speaker. "Charlie?"

"How far from New York are you?" His voice is smooth, but I hear some frustration.

"I'm a couple hours without traffic." She lifts the speaker to her lips. "What do you need?"

He speaks in French, and then hangs up.

Jane growls a little at the phone. "Charlie."

Oscar isn't speaking on comms. I switch frequencies to Epsilon. But no one is talking about Charlie or any of Jane's brothers in Hell's Kitchen. "How serious is it?" I ask Jane.

"I've no idea." She slips her phone in her purse, quickly plucking a deep, red lacy dress off the rack. A sticker on the fabric reads: **Gothic Queen of Hearts.**

By her urgency alone, I can tell we're moving out. I touch my mic, about to radio in the location change, but I home in on Jane, checking to see if she's okay.

She speaks faster. "Charlie has never been forthcoming with me, even before his feud with Moffy. He's always been closest to Beckett, which I respect entirely."

I nod. Beckett is Charlie's fraternal twin, and Jane can empathize with that close relationship better than most people. I think because she has a strong bond with Maximoff—a bond that always reminds me of what I have with Banks.

They've even dealt with the "incest" horseshit that we used to get all the fucking time in high school. Guys we barely knew would joke about us jerking each other off or me giving my brother a blowjob.

I'm not sensitive. You can earn the right to rib me like that and I won't bat an eye. Infantrymen did, bodyguards still do. But if I don't know you and you tell me to go suck off my brother, then you're just an asshole trying to piss me off.

And don't be surprised if I deck you.

Before I agreed to the fake dating op, I asked Banks if he'd be okay with "incest" shit exploding on a larger public scale.

Everything I do reflects on my brother. I'm never just thinking about myself. I'm constantly thinking about how my actions will affect him.

We're identical. People see *one* person. An entity. *The twins.* Growing up like that, we lose out on a lot. I wasn't an *I*. I was a *we* from birth, and I know who I am. I can differentiate myself from my brother.

The fight is having other people see *me*. And not just *us*.

To be treated more like a singular human being in the eyes of my peers, all I had to do was not be around my twin brother.

Seems easy.

Except that's the one person who I loved most growing up—so it's not that easy after all. A kid shouldn't have to make that fucking choice. To have people see you as a person or to be friends with your twin.

Letting go of what people think—it made us stronger. We have thick skin, and we can handle every kind of fucked situation. We're bred for days that are like ten-pounds of shit in a five-pound bag.

Still, I needed to confirm with Banks about the fake dating op.

He smacked my chest with the back of his hand. "Semper Gumby, man. I'm ready for it all."

In the costume shop, I stare down at Jane, my hand still on my mic. "Charlie didn't tell you anything then?"

"Just that he wants me to come over to his apartment—and he said there's an issue, but he wouldn't tell me what." She adjusts her purse. "He always says I'm smarter than most and can solve mysteries with less. But he's also aware that I really do prefer knowing who's in trouble. Charlie withholding this is…" She sighs. "…not very pleasant."

"We'll figure it out without him." I trust that my men are keeping their eyes peeled. I click my mic. "Thatcher to security, is there any word on issues in Hell's Kitchen?"

Jane is looking at me breathlessly, like I just fucked her for three hours straight. *We've done that.* I've been sneaking in and out of her room every night like we're in college and she's in a dorm with a 3 a.m. curfew.

Blood wants to pump through veins in my dick, but I stay ice-cold. Frosty. When I'm working, I'm thinking about protecting Jane.

When I'm not working, I'm thinking about having sex with Jane.

I listen to comms in my ear, bodyguards responding, and Jane and I already start heading to the checkout. I wrap an arm around her waist and hold the Queen of Hearts costume for her. She's busy texting and walking.

I click my mic. "Copy that. Jane is Oscar Mike in ten. We'll be at your AO in a couple hours." I glance down at Jane. "It's probably Eliot. His bodyguard said he's been day drinking and then bought a handle of bourbon. He's safe back at the apartment. But he was stumbling in."

She exhales, about to speak, but our heads swerve to Farrow and Maximoff who move to the checkout with matched urgency.

We all meet at the wooden counter. Where a college-aged girl with bright pink hair smacks gum and taps the keyboard to a computer. She's already signed an NDA. So Jane and Maximoff talk freely, catching up one another.

Farrow and I hang back, eyeing the gathering paparazzi outside. But I notice how Farrow puts in his earpiece and switches on his radio. He raises his brows at me. "What the fuck are you looking at?"

Yeah, we're still feeling things out. "You turned on your radio."

He tucks his black V-neck into the waistband of his black pants. "Don't get excited. I didn't do it for you."

I skip over that. "Did med call you?"

"No."

I nod. *Good.* It means no one is hurt.

"I can't go with you, Janie," Maximoff says, his body rigid and on guard. "I just got a call from Kinney. She was trying not to cry."

My chest tightens. I care about everyone in these families. Deeply. Kinney Hale is a girl I saw grow up for years, and now she's thirteen. I was with the Hale family day-in, day-out. Along with Farrow, who was protecting their mom.

As weird as that fucking sounds, we worked together. He may've been on Alpha while I was on Epsilon back then, but we still went on all the same Hale family trips.

"Oh no," Jane whispers. "What happened?"

I splay the costume over the counter. Farrow grabs the ones that Maximoff is buying while we check out for them.

I listen in.

Maximoff pockets his phone. "Her new girlfriend Holly is apparently moving to Nebraska next week, and she just found out."

Jane presses her knuckles to her lips. "Not again."

Maximoff nods tensely. We all know about Kinney's first girlfriend Viv, who moved to LA to be on some tween show so they broke-up.

"Go be with your sister," Jane says. "I'll take care of the debacle with my brothers."

I catch comms chatter in my ear while we pay for the costumes. "Thatcher, Farrow—we've got a problem outside." Temp guards are speaking. "Someone slashed the tires of the Beetle and Audi."

They should've been watching our clients' vehicles. But I'm not ripping into them. That's for the leads to do.

I make the next decision fast, and I speak into my mic. "Call a tow truck. Your job now is to babysit their cars at the repair shop. We're going to take security's Range Rovers."

"Roger."

Maximoff and Jane heard my end of the line.

"Some fucker slashed tires on both cars," Farrow informs them.

Maximoff crosses his arms. "Typical."

Jane nods. "Will we manage without extra security to block paparazzi? Or will we need to wait for more?"

"We should be fine," I tell her. "I'll drive to New York." I know she prefers not to drive security's vehicles.

Farrow turns to his fiancé. "You going to let me behind the wheel, wolf scout?"

"Maybe," Maximoff says firmly.

"Maybe," Farrow repeats, but comms suddenly reignite.

Oscar speaks. "I think you should come to Hell's Kitchen, Redford."

Goddammit.

Farrow and I exchange a serious look. This isn't news I like delivering to Jane.

"What's wrong?" Maximoff asks his future husband.

Farrow has to respond to the team first. He clicks his mic at the collar of his V-neck. "How critical?" To Maximoff and Jane, he says, "Something's going on at Charlie's place."

Jane unfreezes. "We need to hurry." She collects the shopping bags off the counter, says a quick thanks to the pink-haired girl, and then I hear more through comms.

"I'd say not too critical," Oscar says in my ear. "Charlie isn't letting me in the apartment, but I heard broken glass and groaning. Just to be safe, a doctor should come here with Jane."

Farrow relays this to our clients, and I radio my brother to come fill Farrow's position as Maximoff's bodyguard.

I speak to Banks in my mic. "I'll text you the address."

"Right on," Banks says. "I'll be there soon."

Maximoff sets his green eyes on Farrow. "You're not waiting around for Banks just for me. I can have one of the temps on my detail until he arrives. You need to go to New York now."

Farrow's jaw muscle tics. He sweeps our extra security standing at the entrance. He has to trust the temp guards, who are heavily vetted and trained for these situations. They have less direct access to our clients, but they're still our men. I'll defend them, and their mistakes in the end are my mistakes.

I'm about to reinforce this out loud, but Farrow already tells Maximoff, "Okay. I'll leave you here."

Jane is antsy. Ready to go, and she asks Farrow, "Are you riding with us?"

"No, I'm taking the other Range Rover." He clasps Maximoff's face in a loving hand. "Please wait here for Banks. Don't go outside. Don't do anything impatient as fuck."

"I'll wait." Maximoff cups the back of Farrow's head, and they kiss before they leave one another. Their love is palpable—and I'm not some Scrooge. They've found something rare in a profession where all the odds were against them.

It can't happen twice.

I hear the leads warning me in my fucking head. *Can't happen again.*

I take Jane's hand in mine, and as much as I love being able to hold her hand like this. I'm thinking about the best advantage to protect her.

So I draw her behind my back while we reach the door where screaming fans and paparazzi remain. "Stay behind me."

"If it's too hard to push through the masses, is the plan to go to the rear?" she wonders.

I assess the crowds. "Affirmative."

She inhales, preparing, and she clasps onto my waist for a second, her grip similar to someone bracing themselves for a free-fall. I reach back and keep hold of her hand again. Tighter.

You're safe with me, honey.

That's a lasting promise I'll always make.

25

 THATCHER MORETTI

Charlie isn't letting me inside his apartment.

I stand silently on guard in the wide hallway of the 21st floor. Walls painted deep red, industrial lights lining the stretch of hall.

I narrow my eyes on the dark wooden door with a gold number: *2166.*

About five minutes ago, Charlie cracked the door open but only for his older sister. Jane slipped in and slid me an apologetic look. Right before the door shut behind her.

Being next to Jane would've been the best option. What I prefer. What I want.

But setting aside personal feelings—which I shouldn't fucking have for my client—I also would've taken the second-best thing and been satisfied with *one* SFO bodyguard in there. Just to have eyes on the situation.

But Charlie shut out all of security.

Farrow drops his black trauma bag next to security's apartment, which is right across the hall from *2166.*

The luxury apartment complex in Hell's Kitchen is the best housing for a bodyguard. But most on the 24/7 roster would take the worst housing without a fucking complaint.

We're all here for the ugly, painful realities of what these families go through.

To carry them out of ditches. To unfuck whatever is fucked. Not being able to help clean up whatever the hell is going on is one of the hardest orders I have to obey.

And not just for me.

Oscar and Donnelly stand near the ajar door of their apartment. Waiting with Farrow and me to see if Jane or Charlie will call us in, but the air isn't that tense.

If this were life-or-death serious, Jane would've come back out in a second flat.

"See, this is why I try to stay out of Cobalt Empire drama," Farrow says, leaning a shoulder casually on the wall and looking from Oscar to Donnelly. "It leads me to an empty hallway with you two mother-fuckers."

Oscar grins, only wearing gray sweatpants. Inked script lines his golden-brown skin along his collarbone, and his curly dark-brown hair is disheveled like he just passed out for an hour. "You're just pissed because the Fiancé isn't here."

Farrow tilts his head. Not denying.

"Don't be sad, Redford." Oscar squeezes his shoulder. "I'm sure Maximoff will give you a pity blowjob later."

Farrow smiles. "You'll have to explain to me what a *pity* blowjob is, Oliveira. Never had one before."

"Donnelly can explain it to you. It's all he ever gets."

Donnelly laughs hard. He's eating a bowl of cereal at 10 p.m.—in nothing but black boxer-briefs, a sleeve of tattoos and pierced nipples in view.

I weave my arms over my chest. Stoic. Staying quiet. I'm not some-one who usually joins in with them, and Oscar and Donnelly won't be quick to include me, not after I punched Farrow.

It's my fault.

My mistake.

But I'm not cowering or shying away from them. I'm here. Quiet—but here.

"Pity blowjobs are better than fake fucking a girl." Donnelly shovels a spoonful of cereal in his mouth.

"Thatcher would know," Farrow says. It sounds too easygoing to be a real dig at me.

My brows knit, surprised and somewhat *confused* as to why they're including me all of a sudden. My expression hardens. *They could be fishing.* Just to see what's going on with me and Jane. I didn't think they would because they don't care about me personally.

But they do care about her.

I fix my gaze on the door across from us. "I'm not going to talk about my client and sex."

Farrow puts a piece of gum in his mouth. "I think you mean 'fake' sex."

My muscles burn, tendons straining in my neck, but I manage to nod in agreement. *Stoic.* Walled-off. Focused on the fucking door.

Donnelly wipes milk off his chin. "Why not talk 'bout it? We already know you've had sex outside a Walmart."

Because of drinking games. I don't care that they fucking know this. "That wasn't about Jane, who's my client."

"He doesn't fake-fuck and tell," Farrow quips. Unknowingly saving my ass.

Donnelly smirks. "What about *real*-fuck and tell?"

I shake my head.

Oscar fixes pieces of his ruffled hair. "If Moretti really fucked his client, there'd be consequences."

My pulse solidifies like cement in my veins. I'm not looking at them.

Farrow blows a bubble and pops it in his mouth. "Yeah, we'd have to get Donnelly to tattoo *hypocrite* on his ass."

If that's what it took to make things right with him, I'd fucking do it.

The elevator along the hallway *dings.* The three of them go quiet.

We all watch a few women in their late-twenties spill into the hall. Wearing business-casual dresses like they work for some upper crust law firm in New York.

They laugh loudly, and then the tall brunette asks, "What's Talia's apartment number?" *They're visiting someone.* Can't be residents then.

Slowly, they begin to walk past us and their chatter dies down. Most of the women are checking out Oscar.

The Oliveira brothers probably get the most ass of anyone on the team. I'm straight, but that doesn't mean I can't see that they're good-looking men.

They keep moving past, and their eyes start to dart between Farrow and me. Recognizing us.

Donnelly calls out to them through a mouthful of cereal, "Hey, wanna be my Valentine?"

The brunette glares. "Go fuck yourself."

Farrow sucks in a breath. "You're too late. He already did that last night."

Donnelly grins, then sticks his tongue out with half-chewed cereal to the women.

They all cringe.

"God, uh," a blonde grimaces.

"Wait a sec." The shortest girl with a red bob points to Farrow, then to me. "Aren't you two dating Maximoff Hale and Jane Cobalt?"

Protocol: *do not engage more than necessary.* I'm about to brush them off, but Farrow does it first.

He loosely crosses his arms. "Who's Maximoff Hale?"

"We're not idiots," the brunette snaps, coming to a full stop in front of us. "You're *clearly* Farrow Keene, and he's Thatcher Moretti."

"Why are you coming in so hot, Barbra?" Donnelly asks the brunette.

"Who the fuck is Barbra—and aren't you the bodyguard to Beckett Cobalt? Where is he?" She stares around the hall like Beckett will materialize out of thin fucking air.

What I've heard: Beckett is asleep in Donnelly's bedroom. He just got back from a ballet performance for *Cinderella*, and apparently Charlie told him not to enter their shared apartment yet.

Their place must be a mess, and Beckett likes things in order. It boils down to Charlie protecting his twin brother, who has OCD.

Donnelly shrugs. "Never heard of a Beckett Cobalt."

We need to shut this down. "We can't talk," I say, direct. "We're working."

"He's in his *underwear*." She points to Donnelly's boxer-briefs.

Oscar is about to rebut, but our attention swerves to *2166*. Something crashes in Charlie's apartment.

"What was that?" the brunette asks.

The door cracks open. Jane slips out, eyes wide on the group of women, but she's good at course correcting.

She smiles in greeting. "Hello."

"Jane motherfucking Cobalt," the brunette gapes. "We *love* your mom."

"She's our idol," the blonde says.

"Mine too," Jane smiles more, and her eyes subtly flit to me. I approach, my fingers brushing her hip, and she whispers rapidly in my ear, "Charlie doesn't want Oscar to clean this mess. I convinced him to let you and Farrow in."

Copy that. I wrap my arm around her waist and then motion with a nod to Farrow to enter Charlie's apartment. He kicks off the wall and grabs his trauma bag. Too nonchalant to cause attention.

Oscar and Donnelly retreat back into security's apartment. Shutting the door. Jane has an easy time excusing herself from the women.

We're right behind Farrow.

I lock the door when we're inside.

"Watch your step," Jane cautions, the four-bedroom apartment dimly lit.

I've been here plenty before. High ceilings, dark wooden floors, and leather furniture—it looks like an upscale bachelor pad, and I've never seen a fucking dish, a wine glass, or a pillow this out of place. Now, surveying the spacious apartment, I'd think a fistfight broke out or someone raided kitchen cabinets and smashed every dish and drinking glass for dramatic effect.

And knowing the Cobalts, either one could be likely.

Broken glass crunches under my boots. Further in the living room, bourbon stains a shag rug and leaks onto the floorboards.

I spot Eliot Cobalt.

Shirtless and slumped against the far wall, near a bookcase—red wine bleeds into his white pants.

"I thought it was blood at first," Jane admits. "Thankfully it's just wine. He's not hurt."

Farrow approaches to check on him. Eliot's groggy eyes fight to stay open.

Charlie comes out from a bedroom. He runs a hand through his hair. The strands stick up in a thousand different directions. Lean build beneath an opened button-down, spots of wine stain the white fabric. He glances at me. "He doesn't do this often, if that's what you're wondering."

"I wasn't." Honestly, it didn't even cross my mind. I just want to help where I can, and right now, I see sharp, broken glass on the floor. Jane is wearing thin ballet flats. The faster we can get this cleaned up, the faster we can avoid a deeper clusterfuck.

Jane looks to Charlie. "I already told Thatcher about Eliot's new play."

She did.

In the car on the way here, she explained how Eliot joined a new theatre company when he moved to New York. Jane said all her brothers were concerned when he was cast as an alcoholic in the upcoming play. Eliot throws himself head-first into his craft. Method acting, she told me.

Jane steeples her fingers to her mouth and watches as Farrow bends down to Eliot. Checking his pulse.

"He's going to hate himself in the morning," Jane says. "He promised he wouldn't get pass-out, sloppy wasted."

"You actually believed him?" Charlie looks at her like she's lost her mind.

"I wanted to," Jane breathes into a sigh.

Eliot squints like he's trying to open his eyes. They land on me first. "Is that my...fake brother-in-law?" He barely gets those words out before he heaves onto the floor, missing a bowl at his side. Farrow grabs it and puts it under his mouth.

Brother-in-law. This is Eliot's normal humor, and I know it's not just a drunken joke.

Jane edges nearer to me like she's called to be closer. "Eliot, I'm not fake married," she corrects him. "Thatcher is my fake *boyfriend*. He is of no fake relation to you."

Eliot wipes his mouth with the back of his wrist. "I'm losing track of your deception, dear sister."

"I'm losing track of my patience," Charlie says as he crosses the room to right a tilted painting on the wall. "I leave you for one extra second and you're smashing wine bottles now?"

"It was...an..." Eliot's eyes slowly close. "Accident." The word comes out breathy and soft. He leans over like he's going to slump down on a pillow.

There's no pillow. Just hard floor.

Farrow catches him by the shoulders before he thumps his head hard into the ground.

"Charlie, watch your feet," I call out as the other Cobalt brother almost steps onto a large broken shard. He's wearing a pair of fucking flip-flops.

He glares at the floor. "This is—"

"Fixable," Jane cuts in. "We're going to help." She motions from me to her. "We'll do the glass and stains. You do all the little things that we'd miss but Beckett would notice."

Charlie nods in agreement and then sets his gaze on me. "Fake boyfriend or not, you don't have to be here. But you are. So thanks." It's a curt *thanks*. To the point. But sincere. Before I can reply, he zeroes in on the mantle and crosses the room to collect an empty wine bottle on it.

At that, we split up. I take one last glance back at Farrow before Jane and I head to the kitchen. Farrow is rolling Eliot onto his side and asking Charlie for a washcloth. These are the days I'm glad he's on the med *and* security team. I have no reservations or concerns when I leave the living room.

Warm light from above the stove bathes the kitchen, and now alone with Jane again the air seems to still and thicken. There's a lot I haven't said. That I want to say, still. Especially the stuff that I almost told her at the costume shop. But I'm not sure if there's a right time. If there ever really will be.

Jane bends down to gather cleaning supplies. She's been tense since she got Charlie's phone call, but being here has eased her worry. She breathes easier. Less stressed.

Still, I ask, "Jane, you okay?"

"Oui," she says. "It's a situation that can be solved." She hands me a brush and dustpan set and then rises to her feet with a clear container. Bottles of cleaner, trash bags, scrubbers, and more all meticulously stashed away inside.

"It is," I agree.

Her lips lift, thinking of something. "I always wondered how Charlie would react if I introduced him to a boyfriend." She lowers her voice to a whisper. "He's the most unpredictable of my brothers." She sets the container on the counter and unclips the lid.

And all of her brothers never met any of her friends-with-benefits.

She pulls out a pair of elbow-length yellow rubber gloves. "He was *very* quick to let you in," she tells me. "That rarely ever happens."

"Probably because I'm on security."

She doesn't look convinced. "Probably."

I don't know another reason, and I can't worry about it.

We return to the living room with the supplies. She takes the hardwood while I focus on the rugs. Sweeping up the glass and removing the stains.

Five minutes later, Jane says, "Thatcher."

I glance over from my area, a few meters from hers. Jane still has on the gloves, the rubber wet with wine. But she forgot to put her hair up. A tendril sticks to her lip and her arms are outstretched, trying not to touch herself with the gloves.

She tries to blow the strand off. "I made a fatal error."

"Not fatal," I tell her and come to her side. She's kneeling on a clean patch of floor by the fireplace. We both avoid glancing to the window where her brothers and Farrow sit.

They can see us.

They can hear us.

They think we're *fake* dating. *Fake* fucking. It's so far from the truth that even being in this room feels like wading in a lie.

But I'm here. Beside her. And there's really nowhere else I want to be.

I squat down to be nearer to her height. *They're watching us.* Can't think about that now. I brush her hair from her lips. Natural. It looks natural.

I'm just her bodyguard.

"Thank you," she says, but her breath is heavy like I'm one second from taking her right here. I was inside her last night. And the night before that. And in a few hours, I'll be deep between her legs again.

That's also where I want to be.

She's about to return to the wet floorboards.

"Wait." I quickly roll a hairband off my wrist. My hair doesn't reach my shoulders, but it's just long enough that I can put it in a bun.

Her smile widens when she realizes what I'm doing. Our eyes never detour, not even as I start gathering her hair in my hands. It's messy.

Not even close to perfect.

But I'm able to tie her hair up into a knot at the top of her head. When I'm finished, her gloved hand hovers above her bun, and she scans the room for a mirror. None.

Her eyes hit mine. "How do I look?" she asks.

Beautiful.

But I feel the hot gazes of Charlie and Farrow. They're quiet, which means they're listening.

Fuck it.

"Beautiful," I tell her.

Surprise parts her lips, but her smile reaches her eyes. "Tom called you an honorary Cobalt this morning on the phone," she says. I didn't know that.

Charlie overhears and he calls out to us. "Until you two stop fake dating." His yellow-green eyes pierce me. "Then you turn back into a pumpkin."

We hold each other's gaze.

He's calling *me* the Cinderella in all of this.

And maybe he's right.

I am coming from nothing suddenly being welcomed into a world that I don't belong in. An uncomfortable tension winds between Jane and me. Security is holding the "end" of the fake dating op over our heads. I hate that it could come sooner than Halloween. I hate that I can't do shit about that.

Mostly, I hate when we have to breakup, I won't be able to call her beautiful. Not out loud. It'll stay in my head. Like it always has before.

26

 THATCHER MORETTI

Dear Jane,

I hope you're doing well. I realize now that my earlier intentions to set you up with a respectable man, while well-meaning, were misplaced since you have already found yourself a boyfriend. I'd love to meet him and have the chance to speak to you in person. Let me know if you'd be free for an afternoon tea this weekend.

Love,

Grandmother Calloway

That email still rips through my head. Jane showed it to me yesterday and stated plainly, "I have to put this whole ordeal to bed. And the only way to do that is to meet with my grandmother and tell her what's on my mind." I don't blame her. Grandmother Calloway has been too quiet, too silent, and she's always worse when she's lurking in the fucking shadows.

So Jane accepted the invitation.

And now we're sitting on a leather couch in the infamous Avondale Club. Cigar smoke wafts in the poorly lit parlor, and cocktail tables, couches and chairs are all filled with blue-blooded aristocrats.

Jane tucks her pastel-sequined purse closer to her stomach. We sit side-by-side but turned into each other. Knees knocking. Legs brushing.

My hand feels glued to the inside of her thigh, like that's where it was always meant to be.

Her eyes flit around the room before settling on me. "She's late."

I go to touch my mic, thinking I can radio to see her grandmother's whereabouts, but my fingers brush the fabric of my collar. No wire.

No mic.

No comms.

I'm off-duty. Here as Jane's boyfriend only.

I don't fucking hate it. But I do wish I at least had my taser. Not that I'd tase her grandmother. I'd tase one of these pricks that keep leering at her from across the room. Two targets are at a high-top table by the window, puffing on cigars, and eyeing her up and down like they're etching her body into their memories.

That, I hate.

I wrap an arm around Jane's waist, trying to ease her tension in a different way. "I can go ask Banks if he has any word on her ETA."

My brother sits with Akara on the first lounge, raised a couple steps above the parlor and separated by a mahogany half-wall.

The Avondale Club has been a topic among security since I first joined. Only a handful of the Hales, Meadows, and Cobalts attend. Even less do so regularly. Cell phones aren't allowed beyond the doors, and the country club's own security is so tight that our guys aren't even permitted past the first lounge.

But from that vantage, you can still clearly see the main parlor and do your job. Honest, most of the guys on the team just want to see the inside. To say they've been here. A place only the most affluent will ever gather.

For the most part, being stuck at the club all day on duty is considered dull work. And after the second time a bodyguard has to go, they'll start complaining real fucking fast.

I've always thought the longer I worked in security, one day I'd probably make it here.

I just never thought it would be as a boyfriend. *Fake* boyfriend.

Not a bodyguard.

Jane shakes her head. "No, I'd rather you stay here," she says and leans closer into me. "This place gives me the chills. My dad does business here sometimes, and growing up, when he'd come home after, he was always a little different." She tucks a strand of hair behind her ear. Her gaze sinks into me. "My dad says he has many *faces* and the one he puts on for this place is the coldest of them all."

Christ.

It reminds me.

This is her first time here, too.

"We're not staying long," I tell her. Talk to her grandmother. Get out. That's the op. No straying.

"Yes," she agrees. "No longer than we need to. And if my tardy grandmother would so kindly show up, we could move this along even quicker."

I slide the sleeve of my sports coat back and check my watch. Who the fuck is late to their own apology tour? It's horseshit.

Jane's knees start to bounce.

Fuck.

I make the call. "Five minutes and we're leaving."

Relief lowers her shoulder. "Oui."

She rests her palm on the inside of my thigh and scoots even nearer.

Soft chatter from guests drowns our own conversations. Each member of the club looks like they could be from the same Yale Secret Society.

I do a fine job at blending. I've been in even fancier black tie events for work.

Servers walk around the room, carrying silver trays with flutes of champagne. Jane motions for one. The server bends down for her to take a glass.

She doesn't reach. "Can we get two beers?"

He blinks. "This is Dom Pérignon."

"I'm aware," she says. "But I'm more of a beer drinker. Two pints of Guinness perhaps?"

The server nods and leaves quickly.

Jane knows my favorite beer. That simple fact sends blood rushing south. I return my hand to her thigh. Like a fucking magnet. She shifts to look at me head-on, and my palm slides a little higher up her baby-blue dress pants. I stop before it becomes inappropriate.

"Guinness," I say first.

She smiles. "The best kind of kisses."

Fuck. My free hand rises to the back of her head, prepared to remind her what those kind of kisses feel like. I'd do more if we weren't in public. She'd be on the table. Legs open. Ready for my tongue. Then my cock.

I tell her, "Also the best kind of sex."

Flush runs up her neck and shallow breath leaves her lips. "Have we had Guinness sex yet?"

I shake my head.

"We should rectify that. Most surely," she says and pats my chest like she doesn't know where else to put her hands. Her eyes drop to my crotch. I think she wants to put them there. She's sexy as all hell and right now, I get to call her my girlfriend. *Fake* girlfriend, but still, it's a good feeling.

I open my mouth to reply, but movement on my four catches my eye.

We both look up as her cousin approaches, wearing jeans and a T-shirt. A strict code violation for the club, but Sullivan Meadows was able to skate on by.

According to the owner, she's the first Olympic gold medalist to step foot on the premises.

"Just a heads up—there are no cupcakes or donuts here," Sulli says, but she carries a stack of pastries on a small plate. "Fucking waste of a good tea party."

She slumps down on the couch beside Jane.

"Thank you for coming," Jane says into a smile and squeezes her side.

"Fuck yeah, had to check this place out." Sulli pops a pastry in her mouth. "Still don't get it. It's kinda dark in here." She cranes her neck back to the first lounge where Akara and my brother chill out. On duty and not allowed down to this part of the parlor.

"Un-fucking-fair," Sulli curses.

I agree with her on that one.

Jane nods. "This would have been my last choice of venue, but I didn't want to argue with Grandmother."

Like she was summoned out of thin fucking air, her grandmother exits from two double doors that leads to a private dining area.

Gray hair spooled into a bun and pearls on her bony neck, she meanders over with a tight smile. Before anyone can say anything, she spots Sulli's attire. Her collarbones jut out like she sucked on helium. "Oh Sullivan, dear, did you not get the email about the dress code?"

"Got it, but I asked my dad and he told me it was fucking optional." Sulli smiles into her next bite of pastry. In reality, her dad told her to wear what she wanted and blame it on him.

Her grandmother sighs. "Of course he did." She swings her head to me. Jane and I rise to our feet, and I hold out my hand for her grandmother to shake.

She does. "Thatcher, so lovely to finally meet my granddaughter's boyfriend." She appraises me in quick once-over. "It's nice that you could follow the dress code...considering."

She leaves that word *considering* hanging in the air like a dead note.

Jane's eyes bug. "Considering *what*, Grandmother?"

I shake my head. I don't want to cause friction right now. Jane's here to grab an apology and a promise from her grandmother. That's it. Anything else is extraneous.

We don't need to be on good terms.

We don't need to be on *any* terms.

Grandmother Calloway snatches a flute of champagne off a server's tray. "Jane, dear, he's not from here," she says. "It's naïve to think everyone is aware of the customs of high society. That's all." Her eyes ping to a server carrying our two beers. "Those aren't for us." She waves him off with a hand.

Jane lets out an annoyed breath.

"You invited us to tea, ma'am," I remind her grandmother. *No straying*. We're in and out.

She purses her lips. "It's polite to chat first."

"Respectfully, ma'am, it's also polite not to be fifteen minutes late," I refute.

Her shoulders lock.

Sulli mumbles an *uh-oh* under her breath and sinks down to the leather couch, leaving the rest of us standing.

"You were late," Jane says like she's gearing up for battle by my side. "And you haven't apologized for that either."

Her grandmother narrows her eyes at Jane. They suddenly seem to soften. "You are so much like your mother."

"I'm not her," Jane says with a shake of her head. "If I were, I wouldn't be standing here. You would have received one *scathing* voicemail and then never hear from me for at least a year. And I've contemplated doing that, but instead, I'd truly love to sit down and speak with you."

"Now," I add. "She's busy, ma'am."

"Very busy." Jane smiles. "I have many more places to be." That aren't in a parlor with men three times her age staring at her like she's fucking meat. Preferably where I also have a taser.

And a gun.

And my comms.

Grandmother Calloway inhales sharply. "I only reserved a table for you and your new boyfriend and myself. I'd hoped we could get some private time to address our issues."

"Oh, fuck, no problem," Sulli says, dropping crumbs into her shirt. Jane and her share a smile. "I can just sit right here and eat some more of these non-cupcakes and non-donuts." She looks to Akara like she might go hang with him and Banks.

Grandmother Calloway touches Sulli's shoulder. "Another time, dear. Tell your mother to call. I haven't spoken with her in a while."

"I'll pass it along," Sulli says.

Grandmother Calloway looks from Jane to me. "Follow me."

Ten minutes. I clocked it. From the minute we sat down at the private table to the minute we stood up to leave. And all ten minutes felt like a brutal underhanded rag on me.

"I'm *so* sorry," Jane apologizes for the tenth time. She sits on the rung of a vintage wooden ladder. We've slipped into a small wine closet before we head back to the parlor. Shelves and racks of wine reaching at least ten feet high.

I cross my arms over my chest. My coat tight on my muscles. "Don't be sorry, honey."

She stares at me a second longer.

I continue, "It wasn't that bad."

Her eyes enlarge. "She brought out *escargot* just to see if you knew how to eat it. And don't get me started on quizzing you about your education."

Her grandmother asked if I went to Wharton.

When I said *no* she started listing a bunch of Ivy Leagues and asking about those.

It took a while before Jane could cut in and tell her what needed to be said. That she shouldn't have done something that involved Jane's personal life without Jane's permission. That if anything like this happens to her siblings or cousins, there will be hell to pay.

Jane was firm.

Resolute.

And she even got a half-hearted *I'm sorry* from her grandmother. I'd take all the fucking underhanded comments about where I'm from and how I don't fit into high society just to see and hear all of that over again.

But I also understand Jane feels like she didn't protect me in the process. I'm really the last person that needs shields or handrails. Grandmother Calloway can throw underhanded comments my way, all day long. As long as she's not pulling shit on Jane, I'm fine.

That's all there is to it.

My eyes sink into Jane's. "I can handle your grandmother." I was polite. I didn't raise my voice. Didn't wish for my taser but only *once*.

And that was in my head, so no fault there. "And," I continue. "I'm glad you did this. She needed to hear all of that shit as much as I think you needed to say it to her."

She nods. "I think so, too."

I hold out a hand. She stares at my opened palm and her lips upturn. "Merci." She takes my hand and rises off the ladder to her feet.

"So we're in agreement," she says into a stronger breath. "No regrets."

"None here."

She smiles brighter and adjusts her purse on her hip. "The best part is that she's already disinvited to Christmas, so I won't have to see her for a good while."

"Whose call was that?"

"My mom's," she says into a wider grin. "But that decision was actually made back during Greece. For what she said to Maximoff and Farrow."

Good. I think most of the family will be happier with a Grandmother Calloway free zone for the foreseeable future. It won't change anything with security. We'll still keep tabs on her in case she decides to go rogue again.

Jane and I shift nearer. I slide my hand along the small of her back, and her breath shallows as she tucks hers into my back pocket. We thread together.

This close in the small closet, I can smell her shampoo. Spring. Flowers.

It's intoxicating.

"We are just two people in a wine closet with zero regrets," Jane whispers. We stare at one another for a silent moment. Fuck it. I lean down and kiss her. Lips swelling beneath mine. She stands on her tiptoes, and then I pick her up to lessen the strain on both of us. More eyelevel. Lips lined up.

I suck on the bottom of hers.

Her breath catches in her throat, and her fingers tighten in my hair. But it's her thighs that squeeze around me that causes my cock to beg for her.

"Thatcher," she breathes my name in my ear like honey dripping down flesh.

I press my mouth to her neck. She moans a little.

Christ.

I pull back just to meet her eyes. I have to be direct. "I'm going to set you down," I tell her. "Because if we keep kissing, I'm going to put my cock in you."

Flush dots her cheeks. "That sounds pleasant…"

"Jane."

"I meant to say, pleasant *and* something we can do later at our scheduled hour." She smiles and pats my chest. "You may set me down." Our scheduled hour: *tonight.* Couldn't come fast enough.

It takes all my energy to drop her to her feet. But I'm aware that we tend to go overboard when we start making out like this. Too insatiable. Too hungry for each other's bodies.

Her ballet flats hit the floor and she lets out a deeper breath. I wait for her to adjust her clothes. She pulls up her pants that slipped below her love handles.

When she meets my eyes, I ask, "Good to go?"

"Oui."

I'm still careful when I open the door. I crack it first, just out of precaution.

Two voices filter in. Clear like they're standing right outside. It doesn't much matter if they see us. The public thinks we're dating. I'm about to open it wider, but I stop when I hear *her* name.

"*Jane Cobalt* is here," the woman says. Her voice is gravel like she's been smoking too many cigars.

"I saw," another woman says. "Can't believe she's narrating romance books when she went to *Princeton* for math. Girl is wasting her degree."

"Seriously, why did she even go to school?" The voices drift off until they're no longer audible.

I turn around to see Jane rolling her eyes.

"You okay?" I ask.

"Everyone has an opinion," she tells me. "Not all welcome and nice and they can think what they want but it won't change what I'm doing. So they can go to hell and find someone else to criticize there."

"Agreed," I say.

Her lips quirk up. "I like when you do that."

"Do what?" I open the door fully now. The hallway clear.

"Say only one or two words to get your point across. Like that's all it takes. And for you, it does." She holds my gaze for a strong beat. "I just really like that."

I can't name another person who said they like my brevity or quietness.

We make our way back. Both of us keep glancing more at each other than ahead. We stop by the opened archway that leads into the main parlor.

"I don't mean to interrupt, but are you a twin?" That question comes from a middle-aged man with a graying mustache. He motions toward the first lounge where I see Banks sitting and still chatting with Akara. "I could have sworn I was seeing double."

"Yes, sir, I'm a twin." I don't elaborate. Don't say anything else. Don't really feel like it. But I do try to smile so I don't make him feel bad for asking.

He laughs. "Thought so. You know my niece and nephew are twins. Six. Adorable."

I'm sure they're sweet, but what they'll never understand is having to have these unprompted conversations with complete strangers.

He's one second away from taking out his phone and showing me photographs.

"Oh this is interesting," Jane says, but her gaze isn't on the old man. It's pinned to the couch that we had left.

Sulli isn't alone anymore. Some preppy guy in his twenties is seated right next to her.

I assess: dishwater-blond hair that's combed back, a crisp gray suit jacket over a striped button-down like he stepped out of some J.Crew catalogue.

My first instinct is to look back at the first lounge. Where Sulli's body-guard sits. Akara and Banks are eagle-eyeing the fuck out of this guy.

But there's not much they can do. The club's security would throw a fit if they crossed into the parlor for no reason.

"Excuse us, sir," I tell the old man and follow Jane to a bookshelf, a few meters from the couch but far enough to give us some privacy.

Jane whispers, "I'm ninety-nine percent sure that's Wesley Rochester's older brother. I've never met him. I think his name is Will."

She's already told me about her first kiss. Kindergarten. Wesley Rochester. How she thought she was fated to be with him just because of his last name and her namesake—Jane Eyre. Wesley grew up to be a prick, according to Jane, but I've never met him. And his older brother Will is an unknown variable.

It's hard to detach my gaze from her, but I do.

I watch as Will passes Sulli a glazed donut wrapped in a napkin. Like Sulli mentioned earlier, there aren't any donuts in the club, which either means Will brought it for her or convinced the chef to make her one from scratch.

Sulli holds out her other hand and Will takes out a pen. He scrawls on her wrist. Has to be his number. She keeps smiling, her face turning red, and her gaze sweeps his body in a slow once-over.

I look to Akara. He is frozen. Marbleized. Banks is talking to him, almost rapidly, concern in my brother's eyes.

"I don't want to interrupt them," Jane whispers to me, referring to Sulli and Will. "Sulli says all guys see her as a best buddy, not a potential girlfriend or even hookup. So now I get to remind her of this moment." She smiles even wider.

I wrap my arm around her waist. "So this a good thing?"

"I think so," she says. She touches her lips that are still a little red from our kiss in the wine pantry. I wanted to do more, but that will have to happen later tonight. Her eyes drift to me and then down to my lips.

Thinking the same thing.

Tonight.

I feel a hot gaze to my four. Someone is staring at me. Quick check, and I meet my brother's eyes.

Akara is talking into his mic, concentrated elsewhere. Banks is the only one watching me with a newfound intensity. Can he tell I'm looking at Jane differently now that we've slept together? He'd be the only one able to figure it out.

My stomach knots.

Keeping a secret from him is out of my nature.

It's like running backwards up a fucking hill. And there's only so long I can keep running before I trip over my own goddamn feet.

27

JANE COBALT

"*I have more somewhere in here...*" I sink to my knees and open the bottom bathroom cabinet. Thatcher watches me. Shirtless. Chiseled body covered in a light layer of sweat.

I'm in nothing but a pair of panties and a fuzzy baby blue robe. Tied a little too tight. Heat brews everywhere, but I wasn't about to make the three foot trek from my doorway to the bathroom in *nothing*. Because I have roommates.

Who are thankfully gloriously asleep, but I'm quiet anyway as I shift products and hair irons out of the way. "It's in the back," I whisper more to myself. Ten seconds later my fingers wrap around a familiar slender bottle.

I grab the lube and carefully and *oh so* gently shut the cabinet closed.

When I turn back around, Thatcher is still watching me. Eyes planted like he can't look away. It's been that way all night. Wonderful, mind-altering sex that neither of us wants to end just yet. We aren't even close to three in the morning.

My gaze travels the length of his body. He's in drawstring pants. He had enough time to hop into those before we made it to the bathroom. No underwear. That is a very clear and well-defined...fact.

"You are very big," I say what's on my mind. Oh God. My eyes spring back up to catch his.

He's quiet and hard to read.

I continue on. "In a very pleasurable way. The best of ways. I love your dick." I'll leave it there. It's a fine endnote. He's already told me he loves my pussy, so there is no harm in mentioning the fact that his cock is also very appreciated.

His nose flares in arousal and his ab muscles tighten. "Thank you." His eyes don't leave mine, but he draws forward. His hands slowly untie my robe. In barely a whisper, he breathes, "I love your breasts."

Oh…I reach back for the lip of the sink. My nipples stiffen. I've officially decided I enjoy us so plainly and directly telling each other what we love.

His palm slips into my robe, sliding against my bare waist. I set aside the lube, and then curl my fingers over the hem of his drawstring pants, pulling him closer.

A noise gravels his throat. With his free hand, he reaches past my shoulder, his hardness pressing up against me, and he turns on the sink faucet. To drown our noises, most surely.

He's a very skilled multi-tasker. At the same time, his other hand is on its own mission to my breast. He cups me with a firm palm. His thumb brushes over my tender and aching nipple.

I'm already soaked from all we've done tonight. And so thankful that I at least put on a pair of panties before we left the bedroom.

I reach down in his pants to clutch him. "Fuck," he groans softly and thrusts forward on instinct. My ass digs into the cabinet, and I throb for a harder entry.

Quickly, he picks me up around the waist and sets me on the sink. Breath ejects from my mouth. Frizzed hair sticks to my lips.

My robe opens completely exposing my bare skin. But it doesn't feel any cooler. I'm burning alive underneath his heady gaze.

"Thatcher," I say his name like I'm pleading for him. I reach for the strings to his pants to tug him closer. My legs spread and he fits between them.

"We have to be quiet," he whispers so softly. It's barely audible even over the water gushing into the sink.

He bends down to kiss me. Lips on lips. His hands start to roam my body with an intensity that I thought we left in the bedroom.

Apparently, it's here. Everywhere. As long as we're together, I'm not sure it will disappear.

He slowly trails kisses down my neck. My breasts. Stopping to take my nipple into his mouth. I fist his hair and tremble.

Fingers digging into the soft flesh of my inner thighs, he releases my nipple and stands straighter. He takes all of me in for a moment. Back in the bedroom, I'd drink up the look he's giving me. Like he could devour each and every inch of my body.

But for some reason, here under the bright bathroom lights, I suddenly stiffen like a wooden board. Frozen up.

He notices almost immediately, his eyes jumping up and digging into mine with concern.

"Jane."

Don't close your robe. I command myself. My breathing comes out in a weird panicked wave. This has never happened. Not once in all the times I've been with a guy. And I know what's causing it. I do.

"Jane, please talk to me," Thatcher says, worry cinching his voice. He actually raises it above a whisper, risking it.

I take a measured breath. "So you may have noticed that I have stretch marks," I say briskly, trying to spit this out. "And I've never felt the need to explain them to any of my past friends-with-benefits. They didn't need to know why I have a freckle on my butt cheek any more than why I have stretch marks on my belly." I keep going, barely a pause. "But you're different. I actually care what you think of me." *Because I really, really like him.* More than I've ever liked anyone before.

I continue quickly, "And before you say anything, I just need to get this out." I take a deeper breath and straighten my shoulders. "When I was nineteen..." I stop there because suddenly my eyes begin to water. Pressure wells on my chest. The opening to this story is like digging up a painful insecurity I'd long ago buried.

Shitshitshit.

"Jane," he whispers. "You don't have to say a fucking word, if you don't want to. I like *all* of you. Every part." He frowns. "Goddammit."

He curses under his breath and then shakes his head. "I'm really fucking sorry, if I ever gave you the impression that I didn't."

"No." I balk. "You haven't. Not once. This is just a sudden, old insecurity come to wreak havoc on me. I thought I'd put it to bed. Honest. It's me."

He looks deeper into me and then *past* me and his eyes narrow into blazed pinpoints. "If it wasn't me—" He looks murderous.

I grab at the waistband to his pants. He nears again, his palms on my thighs. "You can't fight them," I say into a soft smile. His willingness to slay my enemies and any foe that has ever hurt me is so very attractive.

"I can. Physically, I can." His muscles are pulled into taut bands. I have no doubt, he could destroy most men.

"I wish you could," I rephrase. "But they're long gone, and others are just nameless, faceless humans sitting behind a computer." I take a breath and continue on, ready to explain. "When I was nineteen, I gained twenty pounds really quickly. Practically overnight it felt like. And out of the blue, these showed up. I lost some of the weight, but the marks are here to stay."

I touch my belly where the white stretch marks have been for years. Though, they started out puffy and red. My weight has always fluctuated between ten and twenty pounds, and anything I gain goes directly to my hips and belly. I'm not plus-sized or curvy in all the right places. I'm not skinny. I'm not fat. I'm an odd in-between, a size that the media hardly ever shows. In the end, I consider myself chubby.

"When I noticed them forming, I was at Princeton," I explain to Thatcher. "Alone. My best friend was miles away, and I had barely anyone to talk to. So I went to the internet. Which—was a *massive* oversight. Because all I could find were women talking about how they take pride in their mommy stretch marks. They're badges of honor. And they *are*. But the more and more I searched for people to make me feel better about *mine,* all I could find were horrible, demeaning blog posts and comments in forums. They called them *permanent, everlasting reminders of a mistake.* Then they continued on explaining how it should be a wake-up call to a lifestyle change." I shake my head. "Those were the last words I should have read at the time." All I wanted was for someone to reach out of the computer and give me a hug.

To tell me that I'm beautiful. And that I never made a mistake. That my body is mine. And it's unique. And it happened to say *you're going to get stretch marks* this month. But that's okay. Because it loves you. You love it.

And really that's all that matters.

And I did eventually hear all of those things.

When I went home and my mom hugged me and told them to me.

In the bathroom, Thatcher still looks like he could go *into* a computer and commit murder. "Please tell me you didn't take those shitbags' advice."

"I almost did," I say. "I started a diet and forced myself into a gym every day for two weeks. But I was so unhappy. I don't like working out to lose weight. Now I only exercise when I know it'll make me happy."

It's not every day. Sometimes I go for months without it. I do what feels right. It's how I've learned to love myself despite what other people think.

"I admire that about you," he says outright. I almost think I hear him wrong, or it was a slip up. That he was just thinking it in his head. But he keeps going. "You do things that make you happy. That's hard for some people."

"Is it hard for you?" I wonder.

He stares into me like he's thinking about something in particular. "Sometimes."

I'm about to ask for more details, but his hands rise back to my soft hips. "Jane." He looks at me with a level of seriousness that steals my breath. "I love your stretch marks."

He says as plainly and definitively as he said *I love your breasts* earlier. I smile.

"I love your lips," I tell him. "They are quite soft and kissable."

Light reaches his eyes. "I love your freckles."

"I love your ears." They're prominent when he tucks his hair behind them. They frame his face *very* well.

He leans in closer, our mouths a breath apart. "I love your thighs." His hands dip down between them. His lips on mine. Our tongues caress in a frenzied, hot kiss.

I only part to breath out, "I love your throat."

He's a heartbeat away from a laugh.

"It's very..." I run a finger down his Adam's apple, sending chills down my *own* arms. "I love it."

He nods like he's taking in this fact. "Well, I love your armpits." He lifts me up under them and sets me on the ground. We continue complimenting each other. Loving different things. Clothes are shed until I'm disrobed and bare and his pants are in a heap on the ground.

We're breath and limbs and I've found myself straddling him on the bathroom floor. His shoulders rest against the glass of the closed shower door.

Breathless and panting, I'm in between a kiss, when he whispers against my ear, "Christ, you're beautiful."

Those words sting my eyes for a second.

I usually don't need to hear those words to feel them. *Especially* from a man. But sometimes, it's so very nice to have it reaffirmed. It feels so wonderfully good to be called beautiful. *Especially* from him.

I return the kiss deeper and harder and then break away to reach for the condom package on the ground. He grabs the bottle of lube as I rip open the foil.

"I've been meaning to ask," I whisper. "You've had fingers or other things in your ass before? I wasn't your first?" He seems to be far too comfortable letting me back there. Unfortunately for someone who likes butts, like me, not many guys are.

He leans up to put a kiss on my lips and take the condom from me. "Fingers, yeah." He rolls the condom on his length. "Other things, yeah." He rubs lube along his erection and then holds out the bottle to me. Our eyes catch. I'm a little frozen.

"Other things," I repeat.

"Toys, very small," he says. "Here." He rubs lube on my fingers and then reaches for a towel so he can dry his off. Just so he can clutch the back of my head without getting it in my hair.

My brain is spinning with excitement and possibilities. "Do you have a prostate massager with you?" I ask.

"In my bedroom. Another night." He kisses outside my lips. "Was I your first? I couldn't tell."

"You couldn't?" I frown.

He shakes his head. "You're good with your fingers, but you were really curious." He looks me up and down, taking in my reaction. "I wasn't your first, then."

I nod and then his own fingers slide up between my legs. To check to see how aroused I am. He does that a lot. I realize because he's so big that he really doesn't want to hurt me. He's very well attuned to his body.

And he's been adeptly learning mine.

Our mouths meet again, and while we kiss, he slowly slides himself into me. His lips are beside my ear. "Remember go slow at first."

I learned that the hard way the first time I was on top with him. Overeager, I tried to take him completely in me way too fast, and he bottomed out. There was more pain than pleasure, and he spent most of the night concerned and going so slow it was like riding a torturous edge.

My knees dig into the fuzzy bath rug, and Thatcher grips the bottoms of my thighs as I start to move up and down on him. Everything throbs and aches for more and more and more. Like I'm finding the right switch on my body.

I move a little faster.

"Jane. *Fuck,*" he says almost under his breath. Still trying to be quiet.

He stifles a deeper groan, so much so, that I can feel the noise rumble through his body. Up against mine.

"*God,*" I say in a heavy breath and then lay a palm flat on his chest. It's slick with sweat. Still sitting against the shower door, he bucks up into me, his length sinking deeper.

Oh God.

I'm already clenching around him. Legs trembling. Earth splitting feelings pinching me with pleasure.

"Jesus," he breathes, still awed at how sensitive I am under his touch. It makes staying on top of him difficult because I get tender fast. But I try because I adore this position.

He quickens his pace, and I lean closer, our foreheads pressing together. Heat gathers and our lips find each other and break and find each other and break.

The rhythm fills my core. And the intensity builds around me. His fingers dip down between us and brush over my sensitive clit. Like a wave crashing ashore, I'm completely gone.

My hips stop moving.

My mouth parts from his and I bury my head into the crook of his neck.

He quickly raises his hand, fingers glistening and wet, and presses his palm to my mouth to stifle my noises. In the bathroom, we can't be too careful.

I shudder into him, orgasms rippling through me and he continues to pump up. His hips thrusting. His palm keeping my noises at bay.

We're practically silent except for the *thump* of our bodies colliding, but even that is drowned out by the sink faucet.

And then from the depths of my fuzzy bath robe, my phone rings.

28

JANE COBALT

It's FaceTime.

It's Beckett.

And it's almost two-thirty in the morning.

Those three variables add together like toxic chemicals. Highly combustible and only appearing when the situation has reached critical levels.

I am also *very* naked. Urgency speeding my pulse, I try to put my arms through the holes of my robe as quick as I can. Thatcher helps, and in my attempt to wrangle the fabric, I elbow him in the cheek.

"Merde." I reach to try and touch his cheekbone. "I'm so sorry."

"Jane," he says, still moving to put my other arm through the hole. Not even affected by my elbow punch. "Your phone." It's stopped ringing. We both stare at the blank screen, but Thatcher is also still dressing me. Two arms in the holes. Check. He tightens it around me by tying off the fuzzy belt.

"Maybe it was a butt dial," I say, hopefully.

Thatcher looks pissed.

"What?" I ask him.

"I don't have my radio."

It's in his room. He was off-duty tonight. There's no reason he would have needed it.

Seconds later, my phone lights up. Beckett's trying to FaceTime *again*. This is most surely *not* a butt dial.

Dread sinks into my stomach. I'm imagining catastrophic scenarios. There's not much that would cause Beckett to call me in the dead of night. He'd normally be resting up for early-morning rehearsals or out enjoying what little free time he has.

"I'm going to get my radio," Thatcher says as he rises to his feet. Buck-naked. He walks to the other side of the bathroom, shuts off the faucet and collects his pants.

"Will you come back?" I wonder. I want him here, I realize. If this is a disaster, he's someone I would choose to face it with.

He pulls his pants on, his eyes flitting around me like he's assessing the situation. "I'll be one minute." It sounds like a promise.

"Thank you," I say.

He nods and goes to the door. I make sure that the screen is pointed at *me* and not the opposite direction before I click into FaceTime.

Four of my brothers fill the screen. All the ones who are currently living together in Hell's Kitchen. Beckett and Charlie share the couch while Tom and Eliot sit on the floor. I can see all of their hands, like a wide shot, which just means that Beckett must have called me from his laptop.

All four of them wear solemn, serious expressions. Utterly tense, and less jovial than they usually are. I'd expect Eliot and Tom to be jumping on the couches in the very least. The pit in my stomach mushrooms.

"Hey, sis," Beckett says, cupping his hands in front of him. He leans forward a little. "Have you been online tonight?"

"No," I say. "What's going on?"

Pulse hammering, I scan them all quickly again, checking for any visible wounds.

Charlie rubs at his eyes and then rises off the couch, obscuring my view of him and then he disappears completely off screen.

Beckett watches him. "We said we'd do this together, Charlie."

"I'm coming back," Charlie says in the distance.

Eliot and Tom watch him leave. Beckett focuses on me.

"Who's this about?" I ask.

"Me," Beckett says just as my bathroom door opens again.

I glance up.

Thatcher walks in, adjusting the mic in his ear and clipping it to the collar of his T-shirt. He's dressed in clean flannel pajama pants, and he leans a shoulder against the frame, keeping the door open.

Officially on-duty.

He meets my eyes. Brows furrowed but not confused. If anything, I think he might be learning about what happened right this very moment through comms.

"Beckett," I say and look to my phone again. "Please tell me what's going on. I'm thinking the worst. Are you okay? Physically, mentally, emotionally. Did someone hurt you?"

He opens his mouth to speak, but he closes it and then cringes. "Physically, I'm fine."

That leaves mentally and emotionally hurt, and that's just as bad. "I'm coming to New York." I rise to my feet.

"No," Beckett says quickly. "You're not. You're wearing a robe."

"I can go to New York in a robe, thank you," I say and brush my fingers through my hair.

He smiles. His yellow-green eyes softening. "You don't even know what happened yet."

"I don't have to know," I say. "I'm your big sister."

He nods for a long moment and then pinches the bridge of his nose like he's trying to stop from crying. My heart nearly shatters.

"Shit," Eliot curses. "Charlie!"

Tom leaves the living room.

Eliot sits on the couch and puts an arm around Beckett's shoulders, but my thespian brother is staring at me. "One of Beckett's... hookups...took screenshots of their texts. They're all on the internet."

Oh my God.

Texts are beyond personal. Especially from someone who Beckett had a sexual relationship with. If one of my friends-with-benefits had ever posted my texts for the world to see...if Nate...

I feel ill.

Before I can say anything, Charlie and Tom both return to the living room and in my line of sight.

Charlie taps Eliot's shoulders. "Move."

Eliot slides from the couch cushion down to the floor in almost a single effortless movement, and Charlie hops onto the couch. He puts a hand to Beckett's knee and grabs his attention. They begin to whisper quietly to each other, not audible for me. Tom and Eliot half-listen, while I tell them my FaceTime screen is going to turn off for a quick second to read the texts.

"Do *not* hang up on me," I tell Tom.

He gives me a thumbs up and then I click into the internet on my phone. They can still hear me. I can still hear them. But both our screens say *connection lost.*

It doesn't take long to find the screenshots. It's trending on Twitter. My eyes breeze through them.

Can we do that thing we did last time? ;) — Kara

Sure, baby. Call me? I don't love texting. — Beckett

Can't call. I'm in a lecture. Do you think that I could bring my friend? Chelsea. She's super sweet. Open to threesomes. You'll love her. — Kara

As long as she signs the NDA. Sure. — Beckett

Won't be a problem. Are you going to the party? It's leather night. — Kara

Yeah — Beckett

That's the last text. But it's enough for the public to decide that Beckett is not only into threesomes, sex parties, and leather, but he's also a short *rude* texter to a girl he's supposedly sleeping with.

Maybe they missed the fact that he said he doesn't like to text.

Beckett has always been the most private of *all* my siblings. Of the seven of us, he's the only one who doesn't appear on *We Are Calloway*, and he refuses to do interviews unless the ballet company requires him.

Beckett may have suggested and participated in the FanCon, but he did so for me. And that was a great leap out of his norm.

He barely posts on social media, and if he could, he'd have chosen to grow up so far away from the spotlight.

It feels so utterly invasive to post texts, but for Beckett, this is a gross violation of his trust. I look to Thatcher before I click back into FaceTime.

"She broke her NDA," I say, eyes burning.

Thatcher nods. "Legal is on it."

Tom must hear Thatcher's voice because my brother asks, "Is that your fake boyfriend?"

I leave the internet and click back into FaceTime. All four are in the screen, but Charlie and Beckett are scrolling on their phones. Tom has a shit-eating grin on his face, and in the wake of true chaos, he'd of course find something else to light on fire.

"We're not discussing me," I remind Tom.

"Tell my fake brother-in-law I said *hi*," Eliot smiles like he's both clever and wicked.

God. *Don't look at Thatcher.*

"Jane, I don't hear you," Eliot says quickly, teasing me. "Why aren't you relaying my message?"

"Because he can hear you, Eliot," I say. "He's in the room."

Thatcher crosses his arms over his chest.

"Knew it," Tom says and taps a pair of drumsticks on the edge of the coffee table.

"Beckett." I catch my brother's attention. He glances up from his cell. "I'm so sorry this happened. It's terrible, awful luck."

"It's not luck. I fucked up," Beckett says. "I shouldn't have texted. I knew I shouldn't have—"

"Dude, we're in the twenty-first century, you can't *not* text," Tom says.

"Not about this shit," Beckett refutes and runs a hand over his head.

Charlie sets down his phone and glances at him in concern before looking to me. "Jane, we called to ask you a favor."

"Anything." I pull back my shoulders. And I suddenly hear footsteps and creaking stairs in the townhouse, coming from the attic. Thatcher looks over his shoulder, up the stairs, and then back to me. He mouths, *Farrow.* He holds up three fingers, and I take that as *three minutes.* He leaves the bathroom, and their voices are soft and muffled in the second-floor landing.

"Jane," Charlie calls my name.

I focus on him. "Yes. Anything," I repeat.

He holds up his phone. "We're all going on a Cobalt social media blackout," he says. "In solidarity."

A social media blackout.

He quickly explains that means deactivating our Twitter accounts. Deleting all Instagram photos. They hurt one of us. We're all going dark. *Yes.* This is a perfect plan.

"Done," I say without even hesitating. "Anything else? Beckett, I can come up there."

He shakes his head. "Really, I'm fine. And you doing this…it means more to me. But I don't want it to fuck with your fake dating ploy."

"It won't," I say. I actually have no clue how being off social media will affect it. Instagram is a big part of my life, and I've been using it to sell my fake relationship with Thatcher. But that doesn't matter right now.

"Thank you," Beckett says.

"Ensemble," I tell him. *Together.*

All four of my brothers repeat the word.

And then Eliot grins, mischievous twinkle in his eye, and he says something I've heard him recite a thousand-and-one times. But tonight, it's never felt truer.

"'Let me play the lion too…*I will roar.*'"

29

 THATCHER MORETTI

I speak into my mic. "Pull back the three guys at the door."

The temp bodyguard covering the entrance of the frozen yogurt shop, Sprinkle Your Life, replies, "Which three?"

My eyes blaze into narrowed pinpoints, but I don't move from the small café table. Jane watches me in interest and swirls her spoon in her strawberry frozen yogurt.

I click the mic at my collar. "They're on your seven o'clock," I say. "Noses pressed to the glass." I watch through the full-length glass windows for a second.

The temp on-duty doesn't move at first, and I'm seconds away from telling him to stop standing there with his foot on his dick. Which is usually something my brother says.

But he finally moves.

"Sorry," I say to Jane and look back to her. We agreed that I'd stay on-duty, even if we're officially on a date.

She said she'd feel safer. Which is good. Because my first instinct is to protect her and to be vigilant. And being "off-duty" while out in public with Jane would probably drive me nuts.

Me being on a date with a radio and a gun is fucking better for us both.

And this is our first fake public date. With Jane officially on a media blackout like the rest of her family, we're going to do more of these.

Security is choosing all of them. And it took hours just to come up with this first one. It was a massive debate that ended with Alpha and Epsilon siding together and outvoting Omega.

A frozen yogurt date.

Jane and I wanted to go to a brewery, but here we are.

She shakes her head. "No need to apologize. I love watching you do your job," she says. "It's dreadfully interesting. Like seeing more of who you are."

I rub my lips. Something strains my chest. *This is a fake date,* I remind myself. For the op. But what we've been talking about, it's been real. I don't want any of our interactions to be anything less than that. "Where were we?" I ask her and pick up the small plastic spoon.

"Veni qua," she says into a bright smile, saying the Italian words I'd just taught her almost perfectly. It means *come here.* "I like that one. I think I'm going to use it for Licorice when I can't find him." She picks a cookie dough piece out of her yogurt. "I tried putting a collar on him. One with bells. It was a pitiful sight. He's just not a collar kind of cat. Not like Carpenter who loves his bejeweled ones."

I love when she talks about her cats. She can do it for hours, and there's love and light in her entire being.

Out of my peripheral, I check the windows again but keep my eyes on Jane. "So Carpenter loves attention. Licorice hates it. Walrus is the rebel. Ophelia is the princess. Toodles is a sloth, and Lady Macbeth a wise, old owl. That about right?"

Her lips part, and she looks like I just agreed to eat her out at this table.

"Jane," I say.

Flush rises up her neck. "You know my cats very well," she says, recovering. "It's very attractive. But you already know that I'm attracted to you. So that's redundant. But important. An important redundancy."

My eyes sweep her for a second. "I don't think our attraction to each other has ever been a question, honey."

She smiles. "True."

"Gomesegiam'," I say in Italian. "That means *How do you say?*"

"Gomesegiam'," She repeats. "I like that one, too." She's liked every word I've said in Italian. I'm beginning to realize it's not just the language. She likes me. There aren't many people that get off on other people's happiness. Other people's interests. Jane is that rare kind of person.

"Ma che bell'," I say another phrase. Our eyes latch for a hot second. "*How beautiful.*"

Her lips part.

My muscles strain underneath my shirt, and she doesn't look away. It's an intense moment of silence, just drinking each other in.

Then she crumples her napkin and puts it in her empty cup. "So I've decided," she says softly, her eyes still on me. "That's my favorite."

"It's a good one," I agree and then look down to her cup. "Done?"

"Only if you are."

"We can push out," I say. "But the crowds are bad, so you're going to stay behind me. I'll have the temp bring up the rear."

She cranes her neck to the window. Fans and paparazzi line the sidewalk, snapping photos of us through the windows. She's blocked them from her mind thus far. It's easy for her to just forget they're there. Like background noise.

I can imagine that comes with twenty-three years of practice living in the spotlight.

Jane meets my gaze and secures her purse over her shoulder. "Let's do this."

Minutes later we're outside the frozen yogurt shop. Swarmed.

"Jane! Jane! Look here!"

"Thatcher! Thatcher!"

Jane is fisting my shirt, her fingers tightened on the fabric. I have one arm wrapped behind me, hand on her hip and pressing her chest up against my back. My other hand shoves a cameraman in front.

Create a path.

Clear the way.

Objective: her Beetle.

Distance: one block.

Targets: every shitbag in my vision.

A Canon is inches from smacking me in the eye. Pissed, I knock it back with my wrist. The cameraman looks like I assaulted his child.

I growl, "You take my eye out, I'm going to put you on the ground."

"Dude, back up!" Another pap yells at him. They do that a lot. Dissociate from the shitbags like they're not also here blocking our path.

"Jane! What flavor of fro-yo did you get?!" The question comes from my four. Can't see who.

"Strawberry," Jane answers like it's second nature. She doesn't sound rattled from the amount of people. Though this is twice the size of the crowds she normally gets.

"Thatcher! What about you?! What's your favorite flavor?!"

My instinct is to not reply. Ignore. But then I remember my security meeting, where my superiors basically said, *give the media what they want.* Be compliant. Answer their questions as long as they're respectful.

So to not be chewed out later, I say, "Vanilla." My voice is stringent. No-nonsense. Still on-duty.

"Is that also your kink preference?!" someone shouts.

"Highly rude!" Jane yells back.

I squeeze her hip. She doesn't need to defend me. Also, I don't want her in a fucking fight. I will kill anyone who tries to lay a hand on her.

"So your relationship is nothing like Rose and Connor Cobalt?! You don't do *any* bondage?" a pap asks.

I narrow my eyes. "That's inappropriate." I'm one second away from smashing his camera. I'm also one minute from the car. I can see it across the street. But we have to stop at a red light and wait for the pedestrian walk signal. Would have had a temp pull the car up to let us in at the curb, but the crowds are too amassed for that.

"Is that yes or a no?" the same pap asks.

"Shut up, man!" a young fan yells at him. "She already said it was rude!"

"Yeah!" a few people yell in agreement.

"Thatcher! Which of Jane's cats is your favorite?!"

Innocent. Respectful. *Engage.*

"I love them all," I reply.

I can't see it, but I can practically feel Jane's radiant smile.

The walk sign appears. We're on the move again.

"Ugly bitch!" That scream comes from the sidewalk we're approaching. A group of young teenage guys ride electric scooters and pop wheelies near her car.

"Spoiled cunt!"

That one tries to steal *all* of my attention. But I'm alert and focused and some mouthy teenager isn't going to distract me. I grit my molars down, holding back a harsh *fuck you.*

She tucks her head into my back, and I take out the keys to her car. The crowds grow louder, more aggressive. Some shouting at Jane. Others shouting at the scooter-riding teenagers. Adrenaline pumps into my veins, fueling me along with my purpose.

When I unlock the door, fingers tightening around the handle, the tempo of the crowds suddenly change.

"Jaaaane! Don't go!" someone screams.

"Jane! You didn't sign my photo!" an older guy yells angrily.

"Jane! JANE!!! I just want a selfie!!"

I know Jane wants to accommodate them, but I have to make the call. There are too many people here. Not enough temp guards. And by the time she finishes signing everything, it'll be well past dark. People will be pissed, no matter which way you spin it.

"Jaaaaaane! *Please!*" A girl holds out her phone.

"She's running late," I tell the girl. "Sorry everyone!" I wave them to back up and then carefully open the door for Jane. She squeezes past my waist and into the car. Our eyes lock briefly and she mouths *thanks.*

"Bitch!" someone yells at Jane as I walk to the other side of the door. The temps leave me for security's SUV parked behind the Beetle.

"You selfish brat!"

Her "fans" suddenly turn. Wave of angry tears and yells at the car. "We just wanted *one* photo!"

"You suuuck!" Someone throws a water bottle at the Beetle and it bounces off the tire. Realization hits me, that even though I was the one that told them she's running late, I'm the one that gave the excuse, they're all attacking her.

Farrow gets the brunt of the harassment while he's publicly dating Maximoff. They call him controlling. A shitty boyfriend and bad influence.

No one has said that about me.

They just blame her.

I open my door. The scooter-riding teenager yells at the windshield, "It's what you deserve, you spoiled cu—"

"Hey!" I yell at him. Hand on the top of my slightly ajar, driver-side door. His eyes hit mine, but I'm full of untapped rage. "Fuck off." I need a punching bag and three million hours to blow this steam.

I dip down into the car and shut the door. Locked. Closed. I turn to the only person that matters in this situation. All things considered, Jane looks unafflicted by the name calling. She gives me a tight smile. "From zero to one-hundred," she says. "First they love me and then I'm the very thing that exists on the bottom of their shoe."

I put the car in gear and head out, careful to avoid paparazzi. "Does that bother you? Especially because your brothers don't get that kind of shit."

"I wouldn't wish that on them." She takes a deeper breath. "Though, it is funny how my brothers can shirk off autographs and photos and not have an angry crowd chanting horrible things at them." Jane reaches for the air conditioning. Even though it's a chilly mid-October day, and we're both wearing light coats.

I look from her. To the road. Back to her.

"You didn't deserve that," I tell Jane.

Her eyes redden suddenly. "I know," she breathes. "And I usually don't need to hear that, but...that was nice. Really nice. Especially coming from you." *Good.* I slide my hand against her thigh. She places a palm on top of it. Silence bleeds into the car for a second.

It's so different on her detail than Xander's. He was idolized to the point where he could do no wrong. Jane makes one small decision that someone doesn't agree with and she's cancelled, condemned, hated.

If this were ancient Sparta, all her enemies would be dead right now. I'd kill them. No question. I felt this way for a long time, but something feels different.

Do I want more with her?

More than just sex inside a fake dating op?

Doesn't matter. It's never going to happen. She's not open to a relationship *or* love.

This is the part where I'd ask my brother for advice. He'd help me figure out if I should talk to her about it or just drop it. Never bring it up. Not being able to confide in Banks is a really strange position, and I'm not sure I love it.

I'm not sure how long it can last.

30

 THATCHER MORETTI

I watch a fifteen-year-old scrawny kid circle a boxing ring against an equal-sized opponent. Teaching Xander how to defend himself—it's an honor. One I didn't think he'd grant me or my brother. Not after we left him.

There are days where I miss checking up on Xander. Hearing him speak in Elvish and talk about whatever shitpost he found on Reddit.

But I needed to be with Jane—*as her bodyguard*. I transferred to her detail with her safety in mind, and Xander needs to trust the whole team.

Not just me. Not just Banks.

In the ring, Xander is bouncing on his feet like Farrow, Banks, and I taught him a few days ago. His shoulders are hunched from bad posture—from trying to hide most of his life. Shrinking in on himself.

Being six-foot-two hasn't helped his case. But despite that, he still has this photogenic, youthful face that conveys teen angst. Preteen girls are already waiting for him to exit Studio 9. Just to say they were close enough to breathe the same air as Xander Hale.

I wish Banks were here today, but he's filling in on Audrey Cobalt's detail.

"Keep your left hand up!" I call out to Xander.

He raises his red glove for half a second, and then his arm droops again.

My expression hardens. Out of all the bad habits…this is one that makes me want to pull him out of the ring. Boxing is a contact sport. If he doesn't guard his face, he will be hit in the fucking face.

Maximoff stands rigid. On alert. He's having trouble watching. I can tell more by Farrow constantly looking over at him and because Jane told me after the first training session.

I'm not the only one used to protecting Xander from heavy blows. His older brother acts like another bodyguard on-duty to his siblings.

Xander eyes his teenaged practice opponent, who's a member of Akara's gym. Garrett already signed an NDA with no problem.

Everyone else at Studio 9 right now is either a bodyguard or part of the famous families. Akara has started shutting down his gym early on Tuesdays. *Half-days*, he calls them. It allows the team to use the space for meetings and for some men to squeeze in gym time.

Farrow chews his gum more slowly. "Protect your face, Xander!"

He shields his cheek with his right glove and jabs at Garrett with his left. Catching the boy's jaw.

"Nice job, kid." I keep my arms crossed and narrow in on their movements.

Xander pants and barely slips out of a left hook.

"Hang in there," Farrow calls out.

The bathroom door opens nearby. Splitting my focus. Jane rubs her hands on her leopard-print leggings. She catches me staring. "Out of paper towels," she explains and kicks off her ballet flats, putting them in a wooden locker.

Not why I was staring, honey.

She smiles a little, cheeks flushed while I steal glances in her direction. She walks across the mats to me and tries to watch Xander too.

"How's he doing?" Jane whispers.

"Good. He just needs to keep his hands up." I glance back down at her, my muscles contracting.

Her fingers touch her freckled cheek. Jane radiates heat like she's remembering last night.

Our world-class sex.

I've remembered it too. More than a dozen times. I was deep inside her for three earth-shattering hours to the point where she was gone in my arms. Shuddering, eyes in the back of her head. Guttural groans throttled my chest, and I couldn't let any escape.

We have to fuck in near-silence to keep this massive secret, and the only bad part was that I had to leave.

Zero three hundred hours on the dot.

I respect her wishes, and I wouldn't stay a minute longer. But walking out that door is like walking on a bed of fucking nails.

"He'll learn," she says optimistically. "He has good coaches."

I'm just okay. The Oliveira brothers are better boxers, but they're both on-duty. I'm about to mention that, but Xander suddenly ducks beneath an incoming right hook.

"Go Xander!" Jane cheers. She made pompoms the last session, but Xander was embarrassed, so she hid them in a locker.

This girl is heaven-sent, and I'm fucking an angel. And gripping a one-way ticket to hell.

Stay frosty. I focus on the ring.

And her.

When Xander and Garrett take a water break, I face Jane fully and grab a set of purple hand-wraps that I brought over for her.

"Hold out your hand flat." I demonstrate palm-down with my fingers spread.

She copies me, and I start looping the soft fabric around her wrist and over her knuckles. With every brush of my skin to her skin, she takes a sharper inhale.

My veins pulse, and our eyes latch for a headier beat.

It feels different in this setting.

Studio 9.

Home to security. My work. The overseers of this fake dating op.

Rows of boxing bags line the other side of the gym, and in my peripheral, I sense bodyguards watching us. Wondering what it's like for me to "fake date" my client.

I'm not a buddy-guard. I've gone from being strictly professional with Jane to trekking across landmine-riddled territory. Guys have pried, and I shut down most questions.

My client is none of your business.

Focus on your work.

This isn't your objective.

But the heat of their gazes is different than camera flashes or ogling fans. Security can't find out that I broke the golden rule.

I wrap the purple fabric between her fingers.

Jane peeks over her shoulder. "Is it just me…or are we being stared at? Not that I'm *not* used to the staring—it's just that I know all the names of the people looking at us."

I fasten the Velcro at her wrist and narrow my eyes onto a younger SFE bodyguard. He sits up on a weight bench, not hiding the fact that he's observing us.

He catches sight of my glare and turns his head.

"They know better," I say huskily, looking back at Jane. "But they're still human."

"They're curious," she realizes. "About our relationship as body-guard and client."

I nod. "About us."

She tenses. "But not in a dangerous way?"

"No." I lower my voice. "We're fine." *No one knows.*

She exhales a little bit and nods. I wrap her other hand.

Jane isn't here just for this training session. The team wants Maximoff to take a fabricated "candid" video of me doing pad work with Jane. He'll upload it to his Instagram.

Showing the public that Jane is interested in me as more than just a *friends-with-benefits* is a top priority to the team. She doesn't go to the gym often. So if she posts that she's here for me, it means something more apparently.

Farrow ducks beneath the ropes and climbs into the ring. While he helps Xander with technique, he's giving me time to spend with Jane.

For the op.

I lead her to the corner of the gym. Where a worn boxing bag hangs from the ceiling and a mirrored wall catches our reflections.

"I've taken self-defense classes before with my brothers," Jane says, slipping on a white glove, "but Krav Maga is quite different from boxing, isn't it?"

I nod.

All of the Cobalts, Meadows, and Hales took Krav Maga when they were kids.

I watch Jane struggle to undo the Velcro of her second glove. Biting the end, she tries to pry it open with her teeth.

"Here." I take the glove from Jane.

"Thank you." She holds out her arm.

I tug the glove onto her wrist, and my eyes fix on hers. "What you learned is based on instinct and defense," I explain briefly. "If someone grabbed you from behind and you were alone and afraid—God fucking forbid." I attach the Velcro at her wrist. "Krav Maga teaches you to react confidently and efficiently. To turn, knee them in the groin, and run."

"Avoiding and preventing greater violence," she concludes with a nod. "Beckett was particularly good at the knee-to-the-groin move when we were little."

I stiffen at the mention of Beckett.

Banks recently told me something he saw while he was on-duty in New York. Something involving Beckett Cobalt, her twenty-one-year-old brother.

Something that's not good.

I shouldn't tell Jane. Ethically I should keep my mouth wired shut. It's not information that's pertinent to her life. So this should stay within the team.

It should stay buried.

But I'm looking at this glowing, freckle-cheeked angel with a honey-dripping, heart-exploding voice. A girl who loves her family like an extension of her fucking soul. And if our positions were reversed, I'd want to know about Banks.

Jane starts to frown. "Is something wrong?"

I make a choice.

While she leans a hip into the boxing bag, I edge close. Gripping the top of the bag, I dip my head towards her. Until it feels like we're the only two in the gym.

I just say it. "Banks told me he saw Beckett doing key bumps behind a dumpster."

She freezes. Her wide-eyed reaction is harder to read.

I drop my voice. "Do you know what key bumps are?"

"Oui." She rests her gloved hands on my chest. Chin on top of them.

I drape my arm around her shoulders. *I'm allowed.* She's safe here, and they all think this is for the video.

She further clarifies, "Your brother saw my brother snorting cocaine."

"You knew about his drug use?" I ask. She seems more surprised that Banks found out. That I found out.

"It just came to my attention this summer." In one breath, she quickly explains how Beckett has been using drugs because he believes he dances better on them. "Only Charlie, Moffy, Oscar, Donnelly, and Farrow know about this…now you and Banks do as well—you both can't tell anyone else. We're still trying to help Beckett, but it's a… delicate process."

I'm always thinking about the team too. And Beckett's bodyguard has a family history of drug abuse. Their pairing is now an instant red flag.

Donnelly won't supply drugs to his client. He passed his initial background check because he said he has *no* contact with suppliers. He said he hates hard drugs. He said he prefers not being around them.

I assume he loves Beckett enough that he doesn't want to leave his detail.

But for his well-being, he should be transferred. Akara is my good friend, and he's in charge of these men. If he finds out about this, he'll move Donnelly to a new client. He has to look out for everyone on SFO and make the hard calls that no one likes to make.

I hold her gaze tighter. "I planned to tell Akara."

"You don't need to," she says quickly. "Donnelly will go to Akara if he's having trouble. That's what Farrow has said."

I don't think Donnelly ever would, but I also recognize that Farrow knows him better than I do. And bottom line, I'm not in charge anymore.

I have to worry about Jane first. So I nod. Settled with this decision. "I won't tell anyone. I'll make sure Banks doesn't either."

Jane relaxes. "Thank you." Her eyes soften. "I do…very much appreciate it…and you—both it and you…" She clears her throat, blushing, and she leans most of her weight back into the boxing bag.

My muscles flex, and I take my arm off her shoulders. Her eyes flit to the cut of my biceps in my gray shirt.

If we were alone at night, I'd already be knelt at her feet.

She tries to elbow a piece of hair off her cheek, since her fingers are sheathed in the gloves.

I push closer, my chest brushing against her body, and I tuck the strand behind her ear.

Jane blushes more and crosses her ankles.

How wet is she? I breathe harder through my nose. Arousal fisting my cock.

She motions to me, thunking my chest with her glove. "Oh, I…"

I almost smile. Christ, it's a thousand degrees in here, and I glance back at Maximoff. He's busy talking to his brother and Farrow.

Not filming.

So I can't kiss her yet. I've already been pushing my luck with the *practicing* excuse.

Jane raises her chin. "Beckett…my brother, he should be more careful in public. With the you-know-what." *Key bumps.*

I nod once, both of us ignoring the heat. "No one on the team wants to see your brother's mug shot." It'd be slapped on the front page of *Celebrity Crush.*

She smiles up at me. "It's a good feeling knowing you all care about us so…deeply. Some deeper than…others." She traps a breath as though I'm nine-inches *deep* inside of her. Thrusting hard. Right here. Right now.

She murmurs, "Like Farrow to Maximoff."

I stare into Jane. "And me to you."

"Yes…please." She's melting against the boxing bag, and it takes all of my control not to lift her up in my fucking arms.

I inhale strongly. Her spring scent floods my senses. Trying to overpower the last restraint I have. "Jane," I say in the core of my chest.

I hear the *click* of a door shutting. My reflexes buzzing, and I see a familiar face sauntering out of the Studio 9 office like he's the number one draft pick in the NFL. I do a literal double-take.

To the point where Jane follows my boiling gaze.

He's not a football player. He has a self-important swagger, slicked-back, dark-brown hair, thick eyebrows, olive skin, and light stubble along a narrow jaw. He looks like he could be a soccer player for Italy. But he acts like the most expensive socket wrench in a fucking toolbox.

Tony shouldn't be here. He's not on the security team. He's not on the med team.

He's not a part of the famous families.

If I were a lead, I'd know what the fuck he's doing here. This lack of knowledge stabs my eardrums. A shrill ring in the pit of my ears.

I hardly blink.

"You recognize him?" Jane whispers to me.

"Yeah." My muscles are tensed.

He should be in LA. It's too early for him to be home for Christmas since it's still October. I'm about to clarify to Jane, but Tony catches sight of me.

"Moretti!" He grins and saunters over with outstretched arms. "I thought I might bump into you." He gestures to my chest. "Heard you're the talk of South Philly these days." South Philly sounds like *Sow-Philly*.

"What are you doing here?" I ask bluntly. I'm not shooting the shit or playing patty-fucking-cake with someone I can't stand

"Flew in from LA 'bout an hour ago. All anyone has been asking me is have you seen Thatcher and Jane?" He's still approaching us. Still talking a mile-a-minute. "Should've known you two were a fake couple. She's not anything close to your type."

Jane shifts uneasily beside me.

Goddammit.

Lethal agitation and hate tighten my eyes on Tony. *He just told Jane that she's not my type.* And on top of that, I'm concerned.

Because he shouldn't know I'm fake dating Jane.

He was told. By who?

Tony stops short of us, his gold cross thumping against his chest. He sticks his hands in his green aviator jacket.

I need to fill in Jane, so I introduce him first. "This is Tony Ramella."

Realization washes over her face. She's smart, and I don't need to add more for her to connect the pieces. "I see—"

"Moretti and I go way back," Tony cuts her off. Which is a fucking sin in my book. "We both went to Saint Joseph's High School, same grade. Same age. We used to ride our bikes down the street together."

"When we were eight," I clarify. "We're not friends." We haven't been since early childhood. We grew apart like most kids do.

Jane slides off her boxing gloves. "You're Michelina's grandson." She met Michelina Ramella in the fabric store last month and recognized his last name. "Your grandmas play cards together."

He looks her over with quirked, smug lips. "My grandma said she met you."

"She's a sweet woman." Jane sounds more guarded than usual, and she has to be feeding off my mistrust. She hasn't homed in on his *striking* light-blue eyes. What most people usually notice first about him.

Tony cocks his head at Jane. "Not sweeter than you—"

"You're not flirting with my client," I cut him off now.

"Is that how it—"

"Yeah, that's how it is," I growl. "I don't know why you're here or how you know about the fake dating op, but one thing's certain—you don't know me and you sure as *fucking* hell don't know my type. If you did, you'd realize it's the girl right next to me."

Jane presses her fingers to her lips.

My pulse is hammering my eardrums, and the gym—the gym has gone quiet. Bodyguards heard that minor declaration.

My jaw tenses, tendons pulled taut in my neck. I'm not backing down from Tony. I don't need to unfuck a thing. As long as I act like I didn't just profess eternal love and devotion to my *client*—she's fine.

We're fine.

Tony motions to me. "You've only been with girls over six feet."

I almost roll my eyes. "That's *Banks*." My brother has only been in serious relationships with tall girls.

"You're basically the same person." He's serious, and this isn't the first time I've heard that. Not just from him.

You're the same person.

You share one brain.

And Tony rarely uses his.

"Why would you say that?" Jane questions hotly, like she's putting him on trial.

Tony motions to me. "He's an identical twin."

"Yes, and clearly identical twins are not the same person. They're *two* people with two separate thoughts and feelings—"

"We don't know that for sure," Tony interjects.

She huffs. "It's scientific fact—"

"Is it?"

I'm going to kill him. "Don't cut her off again." It's a threat.

He gives me an aggravated look. "You're not on-duty, Moretti. Your client can defend herself."

"I quite like a right-hand," Jane says strongly. "And you're being positively rude to him."

"He can defend himself too," Tony shoots back.

I tell him point-blank, "I like a right-hand just as much as Jane."

She can't restrain a smile.

Tony bobs his head a few times, laughing under his breath. "Guess your type of girl must be the ones with your balls in their purse."

Her nose crinkles, pissed. "Excuse me?"

"No offense to you," Tony tells her but only looks at me and my caustic glare.

Jane and I are both alphas, and I'm attracted to that part of her. Anyone who thinks I'm less of a man because I'd rather uphold all of

who she is, including her dominance—they can go stand on their own
dick and spin around in twenty circles.

Their opinion will never fucking matter to me. I value *none* of the
horseshit out of his mouth.

So arguing with him, debating him, doesn't matter to me. "How do
you know about the op?" This is what's important.

Jane scrutinizes him more. Wondering this too.

He has no clearance for this kind of information.

Unless he's joining the team.

No.

It's not…

It is possible. Tony is a bodyguard in LA. He works in private security,
but he used to say he'd never "slum" it back in Philly.

"Got a call from your boss last week," Tony says.

"Which one?"

"Price, the Alpha lead. Apparently your team isn't up to par with
pro-level security services, and he wants someone to pick up the slack.
Someone who knows their shit, and that's where I come in. There's no
one better than me."

There is.

His name is Farrow Keene, and he's across the gym. Akara Kitsuwon
and Oscar Oliveira are also ten times better than he will ever be.

Hell, I would take every fucking bodyguard on the team over Tony
Ramella. I wouldn't trust him to have my six. I punched Farrow and I
still trust that he'll have my back at the end of the day. Because that's
who he is—but that's not Tony.

Jane tenses. "You're a bodyguard?"

I glance down at her. "Tony protects a boy band out in LA."

"The most popular boy band in the entire country," Tony amends
with outstretched arms. "Worked my ass off, and now I'm a hot
commodity."

It was a big deal among family and friends when Tony Ramella,
Banks, and I ended up in the same career field. Gossip, mostly. People
comparing and talking about who works for the most *famous* celebrity.

Like I give a fuck about that.

"Why leave the *most popular* boy band?" Jane wonders.

"It wasn't easy. I didn't want to leave LA," Tony admits. "Philly is a fucking armpit in comparison. But Price sounded desperate, and I like to think of this as my civil service."

I hate how he's talking about this team like he's doing *charity* work by being here. We're not fucked enough to where we'd ever need Tony. "The 24/7 roster is full," I tell him.

It's what I know. There are only openings for temp guards.

Tony grins and rocks forward on the balls of his feet. "Not true. I just signed-on for a full-time position, Moretti." He lowers his voice. "My training course starts tomorrow, but it's just for show. The Tri-Force doesn't want the other guys to think I'm getting special treatment."

I clamp an iron-stiff hand over my mouth. *Furious.*

Because Price is rolling out the red carpet for Tony and pushing him into the fold *fast*. And truth is, I have no idea why. He could be thunderstruck by Tony's experience working for Hollywood celebrities for all I know.

I'm not used to being in the complete dark. And I have no power to complain or overturn this hiring.

Neither does Akara, who's a part of the Tri-Force. He's one vote against two.

"Full-time?" Jane repeats. "Who exactly are you protecting?"

"Guy named Silvio is retiring," Tony says. "I'm taking his spot."

I unclamp my hand and rake my fingers through my hair. Silvio is Xander's current bodyguard. I hadn't heard about him retiring, and I doubt Xander knows. He would've mentioned something earlier today.

"You're going to be Xander's 24/7 bodyguard," Jane realizes out loud.

Tony rests his hands on the back of his neck. "The best he's ever had." He grins smugly at me. Knowing that I was on Xander's detail. "I always gotta come behind you, Moretti, and pick up your slack."

Don't sock him in the face.

It's the only thing I can think right now.

290 KRISTA & BECCA RITCHIE

Do not put your hands on him. My breath heavies in my burning lungs. I'm not hitting another bodyguard, and he's about to be on the team.

Even if I've knocked him out before.

In middle school.

In high school.

Right before I deployed.

He's tried to punch me, but he's never landed a single one.

"Why don't you go pick up my slack then?" I retort. "And stop talking to me."

He lets out a drier laugh. "Glad to see you haven't changed." He flashes a smile to Jane. "Nice to finally meet the one and only Jane Cobalt. I'll be seeing you around."

"I suppose so," she says cautiously.

We watch him leave the gym, and then Jane spins to me, her head tipped in deeper thought. "You two have greater history, don't you?"

She suspects something.

I'm just going to say it. "Tony slept with my high school girlfriend."

Her lips part. "You said she cheated on you with a guy you can't stand."

Yeah. "That's the guy I can't stand."

Her face falls. "Merde."

And now he's on the security team. Being trusted to keep a secret from the world. *Our* secret. That I'm fake-dating Jane.

31

"*Someone's coming for you, I'm sure of it.*" I scratch underneath a short-haired brown tabby's chin. She purrs and turns her head into my knuckles.

Pumpkin is the only cat remaining in the local shelter, and my heart aches thinking she won't be adopted today.

I've spent the last four hours here, trying my best to promote the shelter on social media. And since I'm still going dark on my socials, Maximoff let me log into his Instagram and do live stories on his account. I was able to find homes for the cats. Even some of the dogs were adopted too.

I'd like to think it's a success.

But Pumpkin curls up on my lap, kneads my leg for a second and then closes her eyes.

Merde.

I sit on the floor in the front room, the owner and manager doing a stack of paperwork at their desks. Far enough away that the only real company I have right now is the handsome man leaning against a shelf of cat food.

Thatcher meets my eyes and then looks to the cat. He doesn't say anything, but I'm sure he's thinking *Jane Cobalt, you have six cats already— seven is going over the edge.*

In actuality, I have zero clue what he's thinking.

But I'm having a hard time imagining leaving this tabby in the shelter. I'm not sure I physically can.

"How many cats is too many cats?" I ask Thatcher.

His brows knot the longer he looks at Pumpkin. "Before I met you," he says. "I'd have said three."

"And now?"

He shakes his head. "I don't really know." He looks me up and down and shifts his arms off the shelf and crosses them over his chest. "Are you thinking of bringing her home?"

"I don't know," I mutter. "I promised myself I'd stop at six because I live with Moffy and now Luna *and* Sulli. It feels selfish to bring another animal in the house, but it feels heartless leaving her here." Conflicted, I take a tighter breath and glance to the clock.

I've already been at the shelter *much* longer than I previously planned.

I was supposed to be home and working on reading *Wildfire Heart* two hours ago. I have zero experience narrating audiobooks, and so I have to research and do more vocal work before I even start recording. I've failed at so many things already, I don't want to add this on to the list.

But it's just so easy to toss aside my obligations for other things. My family. Cats.

I do love cats.

And I don't regret the amount of time I spend at the shelters and cat sanctuaries, dedicating one day a week to the local ones. I also try to donate as much money as I can to the shelters in other cities.

People often ask if cats are my passion.

I love them.

But I don't want to run my own shelter. It's a managerial headache, and charity work has always been a hobby but not something I crave to devote every waking minute to.

Like right now.

Holding Pumpkin is shattering my heart to a million pieces. I couldn't do this every day. Go to sleep with the faces of each and every animal in my head. Knowing they haven't found their forever home yet.

"Jane," Sasha, the owner, rounds the corner with a clipboard and beaming smile. "We're closing up in twenty. If there's anything else you need, just let us know. It was a great day today."

It was.

Truly great.

Except for this little one…

Sasha walks away, her sneakers squeaking on the tile.

Thatcher bends down closer and pets the sleeping tabby's tiny head, which seems even tinier against Thatcher's large palm. "I can take her and keep her in security's townhouse," he tells me. Our eyes meet, my mouth falling.

What…he'd do that?

"Is that even possible?" I ask, surprised. "There aren't rules against having animals in security?"

"Not specifically," Thatcher says. "It's not really recommended, but there's no rule against it either."

I shake my head. Even if there's a part of him that might want her himself. I know it's also *for* me. And I can't let him do that.

The door jingles open. We both perk up. The only people allowed in the shelter have been potential adopters. Otherwise, the curb is home to cameramen and fans waiting for Thatcher and me to exit.

A girl with French braids and burgundy overalls enters. "Hi, I'm looking to adopt a cat." I hear her say to the employee at the front. "Jane Cobalt, she…um had an Instagram video of her. Her name is Pumpkin. Is she still here?"

Relief wells inside me. Thatcher touches my shoulder, and I smile while he nods like *it worked out, Jane.* It did.

"Ready to push out?" he asks me. Already knowing I'm beyond behind schedule. I'm about to reply but he suddenly frowns deeply. I've come to recognize that look. Someone is talking to him in his comms. And it's not good news.

He touches his ear—his mic. Confirming this.

Something isn't right.

32

JANE COBALT

There was a break-in.

At *our* townhouse. The security alarms were triggered, and thank God no one was home at the time. It's the saving grace that I cling on to.

Police and our bodyguards have canvassed every inch of the townhouse.

Secure, they decreed.

Whoever broke in has fled. I'm not sure of the details yet. So many missing links unnerve me and unsettle my stomach.

How did they break in?

How many intruders were there?

Do we know the intruders or are they merely strangers?

How did they slip past security guards who watch the townhouse?

What did they even want?

At the moment, the police and our bodyguards are trying to answer those questions. They're reviewing security cam footage in the living room while Moffy and I head upstairs to take inventory of anything that may've been stolen or destroyed.

So we can file a police report.

I carry old and wise Lady Macbeth up the creaking staircase, my black cat snuggled against my chest. "What happened here, my love?" I whisper.

She meows contently. Not so frightened or skittish—she rarely is. Yet Lady Macbeth saw who crept into the empty house.

Only my six cats were here, and I've triple-checked each one and hugged them to death. They're all accounted for. None are hurt.

None escaped.

But an eerie feeling pricks my arms and the back of my neck. Just picturing an intruder *touching* my cats.

Imagining one or two or even three pairs of feet ascending these stairs without our permission. Entering our bedrooms. Hands skating over our belongings. Maybe with malicious intent.

Maybe with cruel hate.

I feel awfully gross.

Like I need to bathe and scrub every wall and floor and all of me. And I can't help but remember the last time I experienced this nauseating violation that sinks and churns the bottom of my stomach.

Nate.

I worry he had a hand in the break-in.

But there's no use in dwelling right now. I need to be on top of damage control. It's what Moffy and I are good at, and Sulli and Luna *have* to feel safe to return here. They're spending the night in Hell's Kitchen with my brothers while we sort through this mess.

"I can't make sense of what they were hoping to steal," I whisper to Moffy, only one stair ahead of me, climbing the narrow staircase. "We live in the least lavish house of all the properties." Mind spinning, I talk rapidly. "I hot-glued a bottle cap on my twelve-dollar vest the other day. My mom is the one who collects designer handbags and wears Chanel and Prada. And if I could guess, the most expensive item you own would be your car."

Thatcher and Farrow already checked the garage and every vehicle. *All clear*, they said. We were mostly worried about Sulli's Jeep, but it's completely intact.

Nothing stolen or damaged there.

"Maybe it's not the price tag they're after, Janie," Maximoff whispers back.

"They want something of sentimental value?" I wonder. "If that were the case, they would've taken Sulli's Jeep."

He steps over Toodles who sprawls sluggishly on an entire stair. "I bet it'd be harder to steal a car than things you can hold."

Good points. "Yes, the risk does seem higher."

His shoulders are squared, and once we reach the second-floor landing, I set Lady Macbeth down. Moffy and I work together to check Sulli and Luna's room. We do a deep-dive and ensure everything is in place.

Including Sulli's Olympic gold medals, climbing gear, framed family photos, and Luna's laptop, Wampa cap, and sweatshirts. For the most part, their room appears entirely *untouched*.

We check my perpetually messy room next.

I find my pink buckled sandals stuffed in my closet where I last left them. Ones that my mom gifted me after the FanCon tour, and I let out a sigh of relief.

I have other keepsakes. Like a Siamese cat bobble-head that Moffy and I won at a fair, my diploma from Princeton, a stack of birthday cards tied with ribbon from all my siblings each and every year.

That and more are here. Undisturbed.

We exit.

Maximoff stares off in deeper thought.

"What is it, old chap?"

His powerful forest-green eyes rise to me. "We aren't sure this was a burglary."

It sickens me a little. To think that maybe someone entered with other motives in mind.

To hurt one of us?

To take pictures of themselves? On our beds? I shift my weight. "Right, and if it's not a burglary then…perhaps they just wanted to tour our house."

"Because there's so much to see." He motions towards the third-floor attic. "Let me show you my awesome dresser and my even more awesome *bed* where I rest my awesome head on an earth-shattering, revolutionary *pillow*."

I nearly smile. "You sleep in that awesome bed with your future husband," I remind him. "It's what people care about."

He nods, knowing this too, and then he goes rigid in sudden thought. "Jesus fucking Christ—if they raided our hampers and took Farrow's underwear, someone is alligator bait, honest to God, Janie."

I put my hands on his stiff shoulders. "Farrow won't care. Just like you don't care about your underwear being stolen. Just like I think that's positively the *least* worst thing they could've taken."

Dirty underwear.

Hair from our brushes.

Both are much better than anything meaningful to us.

He nods, exhaling a tense breath.

And as we climb the stairs to the attic, Maximoff says, "I keep thinking the timing of the break-in is bad with Sulli and Luna living here, but there is one good thing." The stairs creak under our weight. "You're on a sex hiatus, and Farrow and I don't use condoms anymore. Which means no one could've stolen used condoms from the trash and taken sperm."

Oh God.

Thatcher and I have *protected* sex.

He came in multiple condoms just last night, but I did check my trash bins. I even counted. I'm thorough.

None were taken.

More so, I am sweating at the thought of lying to my best friend right now. Who is so assured that I'm not having sex with anyone. Because he trusts that I would've told him.

I try to maintain total composure. "Good observation." My heart is beating out of my chest.

He's about to turn around and look at me, but Walrus and Carpenter scamper past our heels. Distracting him enough that the topic is dropped.

The lie sits heavy on top of my unease from the intruder, and I'm not sure staying quiet is the right thing to do.

But tonight is hard enough on us. I'm not going to make it harder.

The police just left, and the four of us stand

tensely in the living room. I warm my hands around a mug of coffee.

Suspect: *one male, identity unconfirmed.*

He broke the kitchen window and crawled inside the house. He concealed his face with a baseball cap, and so his age and features are nondescript.

Apparently, he paid some teenagers to distract the security guards on-duty, so the police are tracking down the kids for a better suspect description. Plus, any footage paparazzi may've inadvertently caught.

The intruder was in the townhouse for about ten minutes. Our cameras showed him running away. Right before security entered.

Thatcher switches a knob on his radio. "We need to talk about this house." He looks at me with grave concern, then to Moffy.

Strangely enough, Farrow is beside *Thatcher.* Radios and guns holstered on their waistbands, earpieces likely still humming with chatter.

Both twenty-eight-year-old men are facing Maximoff and me. Like we're young and in need of guidance in this decision. I suppose this is a security issue and they are our bodyguards—but they're more, too.

"We're not moving out," Maximoff declares in finality.

Farrow combs a hand through his platinum hair. "Before you take that off the fucking table, how about we talk this through?"

"Alright." Moffy nods. "And so my brain isn't all over the place, I need to know. Are you here as my bodyguard or my husband—*future* husband." He rolls his neck back, glaring at the ceiling.

The air tenses with his slip. Mostly because Farrow isn't joking back like he normally would. This really is a serious matter to our bodyguards.

"Both," Farrow tells him. "But you need a bodyguard more right now to tell you you're being stubborn."

"Then I must be stubborn too," I interject quickly. "Because I agree with Moffy. I don't think we should move out."

Thatcher's jaw contracts. He's only looking at me.

I explain fast to him, gripping my mug tighter. "The townhouse is our home. We *shouldn't* run in fear."

Thatcher never drops his gaze. "It's the most unsecure location, Jane."

"That doesn't mean it's not secure," I note. "And I know that you *both*"—my eyes ping between Thatcher and Farrow—"think we'll be safer if we move, but I don't believe we really will be."

Maximoff nods strongly. "And we've been dealing with this shit for ages. It's nothing new."

"The Cobalt brothers don't have drones smacking into their doors," Farrow combats. "You know why? Because their front door is *inside* a hallway."

Maximoff crosses his arms over his green crew-neck. "So we move and some drones quit annoying us? But, man, that's not going to stop the possibility of a *break-in*." He uncrosses his arms just to motion to the door. "Celebrity homes are getting broken into in fucking Malibu and Calabasas left and right and they live behind gates and security force fields. If a burglar wants in, he's gonna get in. We can't be afraid of it."

"Burglar?" Farrow repeats, brows rising. "What did this fucker steal tonight, Maximoff? Tell me."

Silence deadens the air, but none of us look away from each other.

I stand tall. Like my mom taught me. Chin raised. Shoulders back. Whoever says the truth aloud will make the truth more real.

"He stole nothing," Thatcher says bluntly. "It's looking more likely that whoever broke into this house wanted one of you to be home."

The intruder wanted to put his hands on one of us. To touch us.

To hurt us. In some terrible way. A sickening feeling creeps down my body again, and my face twists in a cringe. But I look straight at Thatcher.

His strong, protective gaze is right on me. Such a source of comfort that I never want to leave.

I say softer, "How do we know that he's not after you or Farrow? You're both in the limelight as well, and Luna and Sulli live here too. They could be potential targets." That possibility worries me.

Seeing them afraid always hurts more.

Thatcher looks deeply into me. "The active stalkers on our radar right now are surrounding you."

Because of the Cinderella ad.

Farrow runs his thumb over his lip piercing. "And there's one fucker out there who we know for certain wants to torture Maximoff."

My stomach drops.

Nate.

I look from Thatcher to Farrow to Maximoff beside me. These are the three men that have been so inextricably affected by the bad apple that I brought into the house.

I clear a pained ball in my throat. "What's the probability that Nate is the one who broke in?" It hurts even saying his name.

Thatcher explains, "The team is still looking into where he was tonight." His eyes carry more security than anything I've met. As though to say, *you're safe in my arms no matter where he is.*

I want to be shielded within Thatcher Moretti's powerful embrace tonight, tomorrow, and next week and far beyond Halloween.

I've never met such a taunting dream. And this one is taunting me oh-so-very hard.

I take a tight breath. "I just want this to be out in the open. The threat of Nate is *not* enough to make me want to move out of the townhouse. In fact, it's exactly why I think moving will serve little purpose."

They all wait for me to explain. Their concern bearing down on me. This is the most I've spoken about Nate in a long while.

"I have a restraining order against him. If I move somewhere in the hopes of keeping my new address private from *Nate* in particular, I won't be able to. One of the provisions of the restraining order is that he has to know my home address just so he can stay away from me."

They all tense.

Thatcher's nose flares, his eyes pierced like he could murder Nate.

Farrow is not much better, and Maximoff is cracking his knuckles next to me. His glare just as hot and deadly.

My coffee has gone cold in my hands. I haven't even taken a sip. "To be frank…it feels more violating if Nate knows something that is *meant to be private*."

Like the location of a new home.

I would much rather protect what we have. Maintain control.

"We're not moving," Maximoff reiterates, and this time, both Thatcher and Farrow nod without a single hesitation.

The need to scrub the house and myself clean hasn't vanished. I set my mug on the coffee table. "Do you think you can check my room again?" I ask Thatcher.

Partly, I want him to ensure it's safe. But really, I want to share his company for longer tonight.

He's already headed to the staircase. "I can check now."

33

THATCHER MORETTI

I know Jane better than I've known past girlfriends. I know she always tries to push forward with a lighthearted stride. I know that I handle things a lot worse. I'm about as fucking walled-off and shut down as they come.

With most people.

For as much time as we've spent around one another, Jane and I— we've never dug deep into the past surrounding Nate. Never breached anything personal, anything emotional. We just touched on security facts: Nate only got a short stint in jail and a restraining order, not allowed near Maximoff or Jane.

And I promised Jane I'd protect her.

I still take fault for the past. I'm her bodyguard, and a serious target wasn't in my peripheral or even on my radar. And I'm not making that same mistake again.

It's why I'm dialed into comms chatter tonight, and I sweep her bedroom a fourth time for threats and hidden cameras while Jane takes a quick shower.

The team is concerned the suspect broke in to bug the house.

"You need to check the outlets," Akara tells me over comms. "Fake USB ports can double as cameras."

I click my mic at the collar of my black button-down. "Copy." I hike around the small room. Inspecting every outlet, and I pick up some of her blouses off the floor, folding them on her vanity stool.

I crouch and eye the electrical outlet behind her headboard, then I straighten up to a towering stance. Back on comms, I respond, "All clear." Right then, my phone rings.

I don't guess who it could be. Reaching the back pocket of my slacks, I pull out my cell. My gaze tightens on the screen.

Connor Cobalt is calling me.

I soften comms chatter in my ear. No hesitation. I have to talk to him.

He's considered the *king* of this American dynasty—and he's Jane's dad. Guys on the team say Connor Cobalt is all-knowing, all-seeing like the Wizard of fucking Oz and if you have the honor of protecting him, you'll come back with a higher IQ.

I can't know what he'd think of me because to him, I'm just a bodyguard and a pawn in a ploy to protect his daughter.

My mission is to maintain professionalism. And it's abnormal for him to be calling me while I'm not a lead.

I've never been the bodyguard to Connor Cobalt. Parents typically don't reach out directly to their child's 24/7 bodyguard. Not unless they've built some type of bond already with them. Like how Farrow was the bodyguard to Maximoff's mom.

Parents, instead, communicate with the three *leads*, who'll then pass intel to men on their respective force.

Connor should've called Akara. It's likely he already did.

My brows pull together. I'm not slow to answer. I put the phone to my ear on the second ring. "Sir."

"Akara knows I'm reaching out to you," Connor says calmly. "I'm assuming you already know I've talked to my daughter."

"Yes, sir." I fix the cord to my earpiece.

Earlier, Jane spoke to her mom and dad over the phone. They were concerned about the break-in, but Jane told me, *"My parents are brilliant at solving problems—but they know not to solve mine. And if I really need them, I recognize they are one call away from unlocking a cabinetry of battle armor and hell. But we have this covered."*

Maximoff and Jane like being self-reliant, and after the parents made a massive fuck-up at the Camp Away, not initially believing Jane about the incest rumor—they've tried to back off and not involve themselves.

"You've been a lead and a bodyguard for over six years. When it comes to the safety of my daughter, I value your opinion." His calm, smooth voice never changes shape. "So I'm asking, is the townhouse safe for Jane to sleep there tonight?"

"It is, sir," I say sternly.

She's with me. I'm staying alert so she can sleep peacefully. It's my job. *My duty.* I add, "We're posting more guards outside tonight to secure the perimeter."

"I heard. Do you think it's enough?"

I sweep the room while I talk. "Yes, sir. Farrow and I are prepared if anything were to happen. We're confident in our ability to defuse all targets."

We know this townhouse is safe. We just wish it could be safer.

Farrow wouldn't let Maximoff spend the night here if he believed the threats were critical. I wouldn't let Jane. We'd already pack their shit up and drive them to a hotel.

But it hasn't come to that.

Hopefully it never will.

"Thank you," Connor says. "I'll keep in touch." He hangs up. Brief. To have longer conversations with Connor Cobalt, you have to be important to him.

I pocket my phone. Floorboards creak.

I turn my head a few seconds before Jane appears. Already dressed in a long-sleeved, collared pajama top and matching pants. What some bodyguards and family call her *grannie jammies*—and this blue pair has images of kittens and yarn balls.

She's cute in them.

Jane twists a towel around her wet hair, and I watch as her blue eyes dart around the bedroom.

"It's safe," I assure.

"Thank you." She shuts the door behind her. "I know it's overkill to have you check again, but…I'm…" She lets out a tight breath and wafts her cotton top away from her chest. "Do you think it's hot in here?"

Unsaid serious things are cranking up the fucking temperature. I go to the middle of the room and tug the cord to her ceiling fan. It whirls and circulates some cool air.

"It's not overkill to check again," I tell her deeply. "I wanted to."

She starts to smile. "Do you think…could you check my closet, just once more while I'm here? I think seeing you do so…it makes me feel less apprehensive."

I'm already there. Opening the mirrored closet door, I push through some of her skirts, and I use my phone's flashlight to examine the darker spaces and clutter.

I sense Jane crawling onto the four-poster bed. Mattress squeaking. "Can I talk or will I distract you?" she questions.

"You won't." It's not the first time she's asked me this. I glance back at Jane. "I'd rather you talk." I'm trained to listen to comms chatter and my client and scope out a room all at the same time.

She's quiet for a full minute. Trying to figure out what question to ask or what to say first, and I squat and check the bottom of her closet.

"I've noticed that you mostly wear black and your brother is often in white. Is that a stylistic choice or so other people can tell you apart?"

I open some of her old shoeboxes. "Stylistic." I adjust my earpiece as someone on Alpha yells at another bodyguard. Nailing my eardrum. My jaw hardens, and I continue without much falter, "But when we were young, our mom dressed us in certain colors so she wouldn't confuse us."

I explain briefly how Banks was blue.

I was red.

Now it's harder to wear blue without feeling like I look like my brother. Same with white, which he gravitates towards as an adult. It's not like I never wear those colors. I have plenty of white button-downs, but most of my clothes are black and red.

"I see." Jane has a smile to her voice. "It's not for other people. It's for you."

My chest rises in a stronger breath, but I don't falter as I search her shoeboxes. My face is still stoic. Eyes still narrowed in focus. I like how

I never have to say much for her to understand, I recognize.

I nod in reply and stand up. Shutting the closet door, I turn to face her. "It's clear." I skim Jane, who rests against the headboard, elbow on her bent knee and chin perched on her fist. She's gorgeous. It'd be a sin to think she's anything short of that.

And I've captured most of her attention. More importantly, she's not as uneasy. *This is good.*

I let go of my radio. "Want me to check anything else?"

Her curious eyes brush over my biceps, carved against my black button-down, and then trace the gold horns against my chest. "The window, possibly?"

Her bed is tucked up against the only window. I come closer, and I watch her take a shallow breath. I cradle her gaze, then rest a knee on the pink comforter and stretch over to the window. Pushing aside the cheetah-print drapes and resetting the alarm.

I've done this before.

I've also been deep inside Jane every night on this bed.

But it's too early for that routine. This isn't the usual hour that I sneak into her room and fuck her senseless. We have to be careful with Farrow and Maximoff awake in this townhouse, and until I take off my radio, I'm still on-duty.

Her safety comes first.

I never forget that.

Jane relaxes more. "What was your favorite class in high school?"

"P.E."

"No hesitation," she notes like she's still constructing a PowerPoint about me. It's one of the cutest things she does. "You're scoring very high on the *jock* charts." She already knows I played football all four years at a Catholic high school. The church gave Banks and me financial assistance so we could afford tuition, and in return we had to do community service hours.

I catch her staring at my ripped biceps again, and then I push up on the window. Testing the latch.

Secure.

She keeps talking. "I have a hard time picturing you as a beat-your-chest, beer-crushing jock."

My mouth almost curves upward. "That's because I was more like a stiff-stone-wall, beer-drinking jock." I fix the drapes. Concealing the window, blinds already shut.

"So you were very similar to how you are now?"

"Probably close." I briefly mention how there'd be a good chance of me becoming that chest-thumping, beer-crushing jackass if I weren't an identical twin. Being that self-involved isn't an option when I'm being mistaken as my brother or seen as a *unit*.

I lean back and drop my boot on the ground. Standing strictly next to the wooden bedpost, I ask Jane, "Were you friends with the jocks at your school?"

She untwists the towel from her hair, wavy brown strands cascading over her shoulders. "Not particularly..." Her voice tapers off, and I zone in on the way her eyes glaze in a rare faraway expression.

Which strains the air and my muscles.

My gaze strengthens on her, and my nose flares.

Something happened. In the past. When she was younger.

I don't like getting into raw places with anyone, but I keep finding myself wanting to dig there with Jane.

How do I?

Pull the fucking trigger, Thatcher. "Did you have problems with guys on the football team?" I ask straight out.

"Hmm?" She seeks more solace in my hard gaze, her bedroom a million degrees in the silence. "Not football...I had some issues with the boy's lacrosse team at Dalton Academy." She pauses.

I make sure to never look away.

Her eyes glide over my strict features while she talks. "The boys were signing up for my after-school math tutoring sessions. But they had no real interest in learning derivatives."

This isn't public knowledge. Or security knowledge.

We share a deeper look knowing she's revealing something extremely personal and private.

"They'd spend the whole time asking rude questions," she tells me. *"Are you like your mom? Do you like to be held down and tied up?"*

I rake a tense hand across my jaw and mouth. My blood is boiling. They ragged on her like that because they knew her parents prefer BDSM and the public compares Jane to her mom every day.

And because they're immature shit-fucks. Who probably feel entitled to girls. To women. To her. Like they're toys to fuck with.

Jane continues. *"Is your leather collar in your backpack? How many times have you watched your parent's sex tape?* Zero—by the way," she says quickly. "Not even my morbid curiosity could tempt me." Her cheeks are reddened, more angered at the memory. "The questions weren't the worst, really."

My gaze narrows. "Did they touch you?"

"No, *no*. I always told them I had a fleet of bodyguards and police on speed-dial and they'd arrive in a minute flat if anyone laid a hand on me. I think my confidence sold the lie well enough."

Security protocol varies on school grounds. Depending on the client, a bodyguard might just be around for the drop-off and pick-up. I'm betting hers was in the school parking lot or nearby.

But not the whole team.

"Their snickering was always the worst," Jane clarifies, arms loose around her legs. "Between each question…they'd laugh like I didn't realize I was the butt of the joke. It was shrill and…ugly."

I'm clenching my jaw. "Fucking shitheads." I set my glare on the drapes because it's caustic as all hell. And I don't want to glare at Jane. "You shouldn't have had to deal with that." I push myself to add more and I try to soften my gaze.

I look back at her when I do. "I hope you know that you're a strong person, Jane. I don't think you hear it enough from people who aren't your family."

She has her knuckles to her lips, an overwhelmed smile forming. "I suppose I don't because that felt…really nice." She swallows hard, eyes reddening. "Can you stay a little longer?"

I check my watch. Nineteen hundred hours. Too early in the night.

I should go back to security's townhouse soon—*fuck it.*

"I can stay." With a stringent stride, I head to the door and lock it. Just so Farrow and Maximoff can't storm inside and catch me holding her.

Jane watches me yank off my boots. "When did you know you wanted to be in the military?"

I set my shoes near her nightstand. Closest to the bed in case I need to jam my feet into them and move out. "I was adamant that I'd enlist around twelve, thirteen. Banks, not so much."

"How come?" she wonders.

I explain how my brother wasn't sure he wanted to follow me. "We were going through a period where we felt like we had to have different interests in order for people to treat us like separate individuals."

Banks is the one who plays basketball.

Thatcher is the one who plays football.

Really, Banks hated basketball. Couldn't make a free throw if our grandma's life depended on it. He was good at football like me, and then in high school when we both joined the team, it became *who's better at football?*

I take off my holstered gun. "It just took him a while to accept that he wanted to enlist in the Marine Corps too, and that was okay." It doesn't make us the same person.

I place my weapon on the nightstand. I'm about to move closer, but Jane suddenly says something that I don't hear often from people outside my family.

"You have immensely different personalities to me."

I stare at her firmly. A breath stuck in my chest. Wanting to know more, and I don't have to ask. She's already telling me.

"You're logical. You take charge of situations, and you're very disciplined and regimented. I think that Banks has more of a creative-brain. He also seems more apt to go with the flow than shoulder what you carry. There's more, of course. I think people are dreadfully complex creatures."

I nod slowly, stunned. That was really accurate.

She tips her head in thought. "You remind me of Moffy—but that's *not* why I'm attracted to you." She speaks quickly, hands raised. "It's just an observation. You both share some of the same qualities. Like how you shoulder responsibility and your stoicism—" Jane cuts herself off when I climb onto the bed and take her hands in mine, holding her burning cheek.

"I know what you meant, honey." I think Maximoff Hale is a better man than I'll ever be. He's compassionate in ways that I struggle to outwardly show. But I love my country and I love my family and her family and *her*, and I've put my life on the line to protect all of them.

Her lips are a breath from mine, and my hand descends the length of her leg. I pull her further down the bed, our noses brushing while I stay close.

The air around us has a pulse. My blood pumping with each heavy beat, and our eyes dive deeper. Grasping something crucial, something critical that neither of us is saying yet.

A feeling.

An emotion, and I shouldn't touch it. Shouldn't near it.

Bearing my weight on my forearm, I hover over Jane. My large frame shielding her, our legs woven, our lips skimming like a hot breath over the surface of a steaming lake.

Her small hands roam my cut muscles, then linger on my ass.

I whisper against her lips, "My cock isn't going in your pussy yet, Jane."

Her breath shallows. "Yes...not yet." But our carnal eyes want deeper physically. I tuck her against my build, and I sink my shoulders back into the pink duvet. My head on the pillow.

She nestles into the crook of my arm while I hold her. Her warm freckled cheek on my chest, she eyes the radio on my waistband and the cord that runs to my earpiece.

Comms are still on. An SFA argument is still in my ear, regular background noise in my life. Just like camera clicking and paparazzi screaming are hers. "I can't turn off comms until I get word about Nate," I explain to Jane.

Her lips rise, but just for a moment. "Do you think of the night often…the one where Farrow caught…" She takes a measured breath and looks up at me, resting her chin on her arm. Which is across my chest. Her voice softens to a whisper. "Where he caught Nate destroying Moffy's room?"

Blood.

There was blood everywhere. I can still fucking see Farrow and Nate covered in it. *Animal blood.*

"Yeah. I think about it." My eyes sear, but I have trouble letting emotion through. "The worst nights of my life tend to stick around." I think she needs me to go first. I see this look in her eye like she's afraid.

But she wants to talk about Nate, and I'd rather crawl through barbed wire first and push it out of the way.

So I don't ask her anything yet. I keep my arms wrapped around her shoulders and lower back. Waiting for her next question.

She searches my gaze. "What was the worst part about it for you?"

"Having to leave with security once the house was secured. Not being able to be with you after." I breathe a constricted breath, my nose flaring, and I know she can feel my muscles clenching. "But I couldn't be with you like that."

She knows why.

Her eyes redden more. "Just knowing…" She swallows. "Knowing that you wanted to be next to me, that means a great deal."

I nod and brush her damp hair off her cheek, strands already frizzing.

"It's not what I thought you were going to say," she admits. "I thought the worst part would be confronting Nate."

"It's up there." I blink back the image. Blood. Farrow. Nate unconscious on the fucking floor. I train my focus on Jane, and I say what I'm thinking, "I should've ripped his head off his neck."

But that night was more complicated than my anger, her hurt or his hatred.

"What stopped you?" she murmurs.

I wish I could say *morality*. But outside of the civilian world, morality means something else and I have blood on my hands from war.

"Protocol," I answer. "The target was already neutralized." I pause. "But I'd be lying to say it didn't cross my mind. I was left alone in the attic with him."

I remember how Farrow and Maximoff went to go shower. To wash off the blood. And Farrow needed to leave the scene. He was shaking with adrenaline, and he knew it.

It was just me and an unresponsive Nate. "Quinn knocked on the door, and I wouldn't let him in." I hold her gaze. "I didn't want any of the men to see the scene until it was cleaned. That was my focus."

She opens her mouth, tentative to ask something else. "Is it so bad to say that I don't think I want to know exactly what it looked like?"

She never saw the room.

I wouldn't let her.

"No. I don't want to paint the picture for you," I tell her.

Jane exhales deeper, seeing that we're on the same page.

Police took photos, cuffed Nate, and I knew Jane wouldn't want more strangers walking through her house. Not that night. So no one called a cleaning company.

I scrubbed the floorboards while Moffy was with Jane. Farrow came in and helped me.

In dead silence we cleaned the attic room and threw out the shredded mattress. Hauled in a new one that Quinn went out and bought.

So it looked like nothing ever happened.

It was our responsibility, and we'd do it all over again. In a heartbeat.

Jane sits up to see me better, and I follow suit, my shoulders against the headboard. My arm stays around her waist.

"I think about that night often too." She rubs her lips together, her bloodshot eyes on me, and she's close enough where her fingers trace the gold chain around my neck.

I have to ask her. "What was the worst part?"

Her eyes immediately flood. "The feeling. So painfully invasive. The break-in tonight reminded me of it." She motions to her body. "My skin crawling and an eeriness lingering around me, and the only thing that seems to make me feel better are people I love."

She pauses on that.

And then speaks even faster. "And he wasn't just a stranger. He was someone I *trusted* with everything in me, and I let him in. *I let him in.*" Her face twists in pain, chin trembling—tears dripping down her cheeks.

Instantly, I hug her against my body. Strongly. Protecting this girl with everything inside of me, giving her all that I fucking have.

My hand on the back of her head, she cries into my chest, "I had sex with him." Her whole body shudders in a sob. "I never told anyone, the night where he came over—we had sex before he destroyed Moffy's room."

Something wrenches my stomach. Pain.

Rage.

Guilt.

And what I feel for her—it's suffocating. I press a kiss to her temple, and I whisper, "He's never going to hurt you again."

There is no way in hell I'll ever let him near her.

I finally unclip my radio. Just got word that Nate doesn't have a substantial alibi. I've been ordered to keep him on my radar. Regardless if he was a part of tonight's break-in or not, he'll always be in my line of sight.

Jane and I are quiet in the next hour. *We have to be.*

Wax-dripping candles lit on the vanity, firelight flickering. Our shadows dance along the walls while our hands travel. While we undress one another, while our lips skim, and I have her bare and soaked beneath me.

Coated in sweat, I support my weight on my forearm, my other hand between her legs—and I kiss her strongly, each one welding our bodies. Our tongues tangling, and I feel her explore my build like we're on day one.

All heat. All visceral desire torching us in the night.

My muscles tighten as she grinds up into me. Our movements are somehow slow and scorching but combustible and urgent. I pulse my fingers inside her tight warmth.

Pleasure tremors her limbs, and she tries to shelter a gasp. "Oh... *God.*"

"Softer," I whisper against her lips. My cock is begging to fill Jane. Throbbing. Blood blistering.

She bucks upward again.

Fuck. I stifle a guttural groan. Gritting down. My muscles tighten while her heat clenches. She's been riding more than one orgasm to shore, and I need in.

I break apart her legs even more. Spreading her open so I can thrust inside her pussy. Her head falls back in a whimper. "*Yes.*" She grips my hair with eager fingers.

I run my hand along the softness of her thigh, and we stare deeper, *deeper* and my mouth moves to her ear.

"Jane," I breathe. "I'm going to push into you. Tell me if you're not ready."

"I'm ready, please. *Please,*" she pants, squirming beneath me in want.

I grip my rock-hard erection, veins bulged with hot need. We keep our eyes on each other as I carefully slide into her heat. Watching her reaction.

Her lips break apart in a short gasp. She clutches my ass with two hands—and I begin to add friction. Rocking between her legs, the pressure around my cock is fucking heaven on Earth.

Involuntary high-pitched sounds erupt out of Jane—I muffle the noise with my hand, covering her mouth.

Her back is already arching.

She speaks against my large palm. I lift my hand just a bit to hear. "Thatcher. Deeper, *deeper.*" I cover her mouth again as she cries in ecstasy.

My nose flares, arousal pummeling me. I could watch her come for eternity.

I'm not all the way in yet. I hoist her leg higher, hooking my arm underneath her knee. And I shift slightly.

Deeper. I go deeper.

And deeper.

Christ. My muscles contract, my nerves lit, and I reach a place inside Jane that causes her back to bow, toes to curl. Eyes to roll. I split my fingers apart on her mouth, afraid she's not going to fucking breathe.

I hold her tighter and push into this spot in deep, slow strokes. Hitting this sensitive area in hypnotic succession. She's almost completely gone.

I'm hanging on to a throttling edge.

Sweat drips down my temples, and tendons pull taut in my neck. Thrusting, *thrusting,* bringing her further into a mind-altering, levitating climax.

And then cats scratch at the door. Wanting in her room. Meowing incessantly—and I hear footsteps and creaking stairs. All while I'm fucking Jane.

Goddammit.

I turn my head and hawk-eye the door. The footsteps stop on the second-floor landing. *Too early.* This is why I usually sneak here later in the night. When everyone is already asleep or in their rooms.

I distinguish Maximoff's voice. Hushed, his words inaudible. He must be speaking to her cats.

Right now, Jane is in another realm. Out of it, and I stop moving inside of her. But I don't pull out.

A fist lightly raps the door. "Janie," Maximoff calls, concern hardening his voice. "You want me to let them in your room? They're all here, except for Toodles."

I slide my hand off her mouth and cup her cheek. Her eyelids are fluttering, coming down from a fucking tidal wave. "Honey," I whisper against her ear. "*Jane.* You need to respond to him. Breathe, breathe."

She inhales a lung full, blinking repeatedly.

Almost there.

If Maximoff senses something's wrong, he'll smash down the door. Especially tonight when a break-in has already happened.

He knocks harder. "Janie, are you okay?"

She swallows a pant and turns her head. "Yuh…yes, *yes*."

"You want me to let them in?"

"I…" Confusion bunches her brows.

She didn't hear him ask. I mouth, *your cats.*

Realization bathes her face, but she's too late to reply. Maximoff is worried, and the knob jiggles as he tries to come in. "You locked your door? If you're scared, I can sleep in your room tonight."

"No." Her voice spikes, and she takes a breath to level the tone, then looks at the door while she speaks. "I'm fine, really. I'm actually having…personal time." Her eyes flit to me. "And I'd rather my cats not watch."

"Sorry," Maximoff says fast. "Text me if you're afraid later on." He speaks in French, and I think he's saying goodnight.

She replies back in the same language. Footsteps drift, and he manages to lead the cats away from the door.

Too close.

Other things are taking precedence than talking about that near-encounter. Jane stares down at my cock that's disappeared between her legs.

Her voice is a gentle whisper. "I love how you feel inside of me." Her hips arch against my pelvis.

I smother a grunt in my lungs, and I dip my head down more. To kiss her reddened lips and knead her breast, my thumb teasing her hardened nipple. Huskily, I say, "I love being inside of you." I rock again.

Quiet.

Careful not to let the bed squeak, and she hangs on to my back. Building her up to another peak after some minutes, and I find a spot that sends her over. Deep.

Deep.

Again.

She cries against my palm, sounds deadened, her thighs quaking, and I fist her pink sheets with my left hand. Doing everything in my power not to make a fucking noise as a mind-exploding, blistering sensation crashes into me and ignites me on fire.

Fuck.

Fuck.

Fuckfuckfuck. I come hard with Jane in total silence.

34

Light streams into my room, a sore feeling making me smile. It feels like he's still in me. I roll over…but to an empty bed.

Of course it's empty, Jane.

I made Thatcher leave at 3 a.m. exactly, and I didn't ask if he wanted to stay longer. We have structure for a reason. My bodyguard can't be caught sleeping with me, and I'm not going to put his job in jeopardy.

But there's no harm in just imagining mornings with him. Sometimes I wonder what it'd be like to wake up to Thatcher in my bedroom. And my mind whirls, recalling all the moments of yesterday. He made an eerie, cold night safe and warm and loving.

I stretch my arms out, and then rub my eyes. Focusing on Thatcher's side of the mattress. Made neatly already. Pink duvet pulled up, tucked in, and smoothed. On the pillow rests a yellow sticky note.

I prop myself on my elbow and read his legible handwriting.

THANKS FOR LAST NIGHT. SEE YOU IN THE DAY.

I feel my smile beneath my fingertips, and I notice a little arrow drawn underneath the word *day*. I flip the note over, more words on the back:

COFFEE IS DOWNSTAIRS.

He must've put a timer on the pot, so it'd brew around the time I normally wake.

No one has ever left a note for me. Not like this. My heart swells, and I stare longer at the note like it'll disappear in my fingertips.

This is a Cinderella dream that'll end, but I want to remember it all later. My favorite moments, these magical nights and days.

I scoot off the bed, slipping my arms into my robe, and I tie the belt around my waist. With the tug of my vanity drawer, I find a square tin and toss out the cotton swabs. Gently, I place the note inside and snap the tin closed.

Not letting this one fade.

35

JANE COBALT

"The condom broke," *I whisper to Thatcher,* the ripped latex in my hand. I'm sitting on my vanity, my legs spread wide open for him.

Our bodies glistening in sweat, pulsating, and we do our best not to breathe loudly. He's sheltered so many of my gasps just tonight. I think he's the only man I'd want to cover my mouth. Because I know he'd only do so for my safety.

Right now, he's buck-naked, incredibly masculine and confident, even as I said a phrase that would panic most.

Thatcher takes the condom out of my grasp. Inspecting it in the dim lighting. Only a candle lit on the nightstand. I hadn't even tried to sheath his long erection yet.

I glance down. Bulging veins spindle along his hard shaft. He stands intimidatingly like he's a man on guard in an ancient epic tale full of brawn and heroism.

I hold his round ass with two hands. "I must've torn it when I tore the wrapper." Thankfully it didn't rip while we were having sex. I wish I could say this is the first time I've failed at unwrapping a condom, but it's sadly not.

Thatcher nods, lowering his voice. "It's unusable." He cups my sensitive heat, soaked. My body aches for his length. For that fullness.

He steps back, bending down and closing my knees together.

I pulse and watch him place the ripped condom in the trash bin.

We're both trying to be painfully quiet. It's much easier for him. After Moffy was close to catching us in bed the other night, we know we need to be more careful.

Thatcher can't be in my bedroom that early ever again. And we're already running out of time tonight. It's 2 a.m.—one hour remaining.

"Where's the box?" I murmur.

"That was my last one." He doesn't seem alarmed. His experience cloaks me like a hot blanket, and I want to wrap it tighter around my body.

Thatcher rises to his feet and dips his head down to me. Listening as I speak. Because he knows I'm going to suggest something.

"There are alternatives," I whisper. "I could put you in my mouth." I brush my fingers along his cock. "And then you could put a toy in me."

His lips brush against my ear. "I could also go grab a condom so that I can thrust deep inside you."

My hips arch towards him, and my hands fall to the vanity surface beside me. "Yes...I agree." Really, I *want*.

He kisses my temple, and I ogle him as he walks buck-ass naked over to the rug. He bends down and picks up his boxer-briefs, and it hits me that I have no idea where he's going.

I stand off the vanity and quickly find a clean pair of panties on the floor. I step into them. "Where are the condoms?"

He lifts the elastic to his muscular waist. Walking towards me, he whispers, "My brother's room."

My eyes widen, and I snatch my pair of jeans off the vanity stool. "There's a higher probability you'll run into a bodyguard if you return to security's townhouse." I hop into my pants and snap on a bra.

"Jane, *Jane*." He catches my wrist, drawing me more against his chest. "Explain."

I fit my arms through the sleeves of my sequined blouse. "It'll be much easier for me to just grab condoms from Luna's room."

During the beginning stages of my sex hiatus, I gave all my condoms to Luna. I thought I'd have no use for them.

And Luna has recently begun to adopt the one-night stand tactic like her older brother used to.

"I know your size is in there," I whisper to Thatcher. "And Luna's bedroom is barely five steps from my door."

His brows harden. "She could ask questions. Like why you need a condom."

"So could Banks," I say quietly.

Our heads turn at a sudden noise. It sounds like paws pattering up the stairs.

Thatcher focuses on me. "Banks learning we're having sex has less consequences. My brother will keep his mouth shut."

"It's not like I'm asking my brothers, who would inquire unto my untimely death. It's Luna," I whisper. "If I tell her I need one just in case, she won't bat an eye."

He checks his watch.

"She might not even be in her room," I add. "You running in and out of security's townhouse has inherently more risk. You could bump into Akara or Quinn."

He's a natural leader. He makes calls and executes, and I'm a valuable asset in our mission to have intercourse.

He sees this. "Be careful."

"I will try." All dressed, I put my hand on the doorknob.

"Jane," Thatcher calls out under his breath, but I hear the firmness. "Your shirt."

I stop and look down.

Sure enough, my yellow sequined blouse is inside out.

"Merde." Heat bathes me as I remove my top. *Hurry, Jane.*

I spin around for him, arms outstretched. We inhale. We both stare at one another like we ache to be nearer. Me wrapped up in his arms. His cock inside of me.

Less than an hour left.

He mouths, *good to go.*

I slip out of my room.

Muffled voices come from downstairs. I tiptoe softer, wooden floorboards creaking, and I strain my ears. I had no clue people gathered downstairs.

They weren't here when Thatcher snuck over, and he's going to have a harder time sneaking out.

I hear a familiar voice, but I can't distinguish words.

My brother.

Beckett.

He must be stopping by to see Sulli, his best friend. He could have a rare night off from ballet rehearsals. It's not unheard of.

I catch a recognizable laugh and snort.

Sulli, most surely.

I smile and close my door gently. Carefully, I head over to Luna's bedroom. Directly across the landing. I knock. "Luna?" I whisper.

There's no answer. If she brought a one-night stand over, Quinn Oliveira would be outside her door on-duty. But so far, she hasn't hooked up with a stranger in this house.

She goes to their place or a hotel.

I don't believe she went out tonight. So I'm assuming she's with Beckett and Sulli downstairs.

Search the room.

Find the condoms.

I try the knob. The door is unlocked.

I easily step inside—I freeze. Luna is under the neon-green sheets on her bottom bunk, but her face is exposed. Her lips in an *O*. And by the other body shape and movement happening under the sheet, she's not alone.

A guy's head is definitely between her legs.

My feet don't move and my eyelids don't work properly when I need them to. She spots me quickly and also tenses.

"Shitshit," Luna curses.

I open my mouth, but the guy's head pops out of the sheet in a flash. He stares up at Luna with wide, concerned eyes.

324 KRISTA & BECCA RITCHIE

I know him.

Chestnut brown hair, tattoo sleeve, and cut muscles, trained in MMA—he's a twenty-seven-year-old Omega *bodyguard*.

Paul Donnelly.

"What's wrong?" he asks Luna, worried. He's already turning his head towards the entrance.

Towards me.

I'm frozen.

She's frozen.

Donnelly is like water on a hot summer's day. Thawed completely, he moves. Carefully slipping out of the bottom bunk while also keeping Luna covered with the sheet.

He's wearing black pants, but he grabs a tattered Van Halen tee off the floor.

Luna watches him, then looks to me, more wide-eyed.

My vocal cords loosen. "I'm *so* sorry, Luna."

Never did I imagine I'd walk in on my almost-nineteen-year-old cousin receiving oral sex. Let alone from a bodyguard. I haven't even accidentally walked in on Moffy having sex with *his* bodyguard.

I'm having sex with mine.

Oh my God.

This just became dreadfully more complicated.

"I'm going to come back later," I manage to add quickly. I head to the door, backing away from this.

"Waitwait!" Luna whisper-hisses. "Don't leave before I can explain."

Curiosity has me in a vice. I waver.

I cave beneath the pleading look in her eyes. I do as she instructs and come forward. She shimmies up the headboard and snaps on a bra.

I have many questions. Like why Beckett's bodyguard is in her room and going down on her.

I shut the door behind me. I'd love for Thatcher to be here, but he's not even supposed to be in my bedroom. So I can't call him in as a right-hand.

Donnelly fixes his safety pin that's functioning as a cartilage earring, and he sits down on an alien beanbag. He appears cool, calm, like I didn't just interrupt him.

Luna wiggles her shorts on underneath the sheet, and then she slides out of the bunk. Landing on her butt, rather than her feet.

She leans on the bedframe, hugging her legs. "So Donnelly was here to design my tattoo."

Donnelly nods, slipping a cigarette behind his ear.

I notice his sketchbook on the floor. "I see."

Luna points to the desk near him. "Donnelly, that's for you, by the way. Just as payment for the design. I have cash for the actual tattoo."

He's in arm's reach and stretches. Grabbing a burnt orange sweater, a green alien peace sign stitched in the middle. "Sick. Did you make this?"

"Yeah, I knitted it." Luna shrugs.

Donnelly pulls the sweater over his head. It stops well above his belly-button. He smirks and leans back on the beanbag. "Fits perfect."

Luna smiles, then to me she says, "Alrighty, so me and him—we're here for the tattoo design."

"I believe you, but that doesn't really explain what I saw."

She clarifies, "We were in my room going over the design, and I asked him if he could show me what good head feels like."

I've recently asked my bodyguard to put his cock in me, so...

I can relate to Luna, I suppose. On some level.

Recently, Luna has said she prefers one-night stands than having to muddle through the dynamics and complications of an actual relationship.

I've shared the same views, so I understand where she's coming from.

I'm just...

A little stunned that I'm not the only one secretly hooking up with a bodyguard at the current moment.

I steeple my fingers to my lips, thinking. "More facts," I say. "You and you." I point from Luna to Donnelly. "Hooked up just because you wanted to see what good head felt like?"

"I knew you'd get me," Luna says into a nod. "I just can't really tell the good sex from the bad ones. They all feel pretty good to me, so I came up with a scientific study. Have a baseline that everything is compared to."

Donnelly raises his hand. "I'm her baseline."

"I followed that." My brows crinkle at Luna. "You don't even like science."

"Exactly," Luna says. "Tom, Eliot and I have this theory that you can make anything fun, given the right circumstances. I'm making science fun. With sex."

I love her.

And we're both silly grinning right now. But I have to put on my best friend hat because my best friend happens to be her older, very protective brother.

"Maximoff—" I start.

"Can't know," Luna says adamantly. "I can't even imagine what his reaction would be if he knew Donnelly and I hooked up—for scientific purposes—but still." She looks to Donnelly. "Moffy goes three-fourths Loren Hale, and there is no universe you'd ever survive one-half of my dad if he found out."

She's right.

Uncle Lo would surely do damage.

But this is Maximoff. And I'm already keeping one giant secret from him. I can't imagine holstering another.

I take a sharper breath. To keep so much from him—it will break my heart. It hurts imagining him doing that to me.

Luna notices my wince. "Jane," she pleads. "It was just a *one-time* thing. He really doesn't need to know."

I glance to Donnelly. He holds up his hands like he doesn't want to be involved. "I'm cool with whatever she wants to do."

I can't imagine he'd be okay with Maximoff *or* Farrow knowing. But then again, I'm not that close to Donnelly. He could very well be that confident in his friendship with Farrow. Thinking they can weather this together.

Turning back to Luna, I realize my heart has been set this whole time. Her brother is my best friend. My brothers are hers. Given the opportunity, I would hope that Luna would keep a secret for me and not spill it to Eliot and Tom.

And I know Maximoff will understand. My mom taught me that there are some things mightier than friendship.

Sisterhood.

"Okay," I say to Luna. "I won't say anything to Moffy."

Luna charges forward and wraps her gangly arms around my neck, clinging in a tight hug. "If the Thebulan gods were real, they'd anoint you with glitter and a lifetime supply of great sex in thanks for keeping my great sex a secret."

I try not to blush. Little does she know, I've already been anointed with great sex. And I'm glad her "baseline" has fallen into that category, too.

We release and I look to Donnelly. "Don't you dare hurt her."

"I'd rather die." Seriousness coats his voice. This is also the same person who has *Cobalts Never Die* tattooed on his kneecap and is incredibly close to Beckett—my most honest brother. I think there's a reason for that.

I forgot the condom.

I return to my bedroom, wide-eyed and dazed. Like possibly I just imagined everything. I close the door behind me, and Thatcher is already on his feet.

Alert and vigilant, and as soon as he sees me, his concern bears down in a dark wave. "What happened?" He speaks hushed, nearing me. His hand slides along the small of my back, his arm wrapping around me. Pulling me closer to his chest.

He's wearing pants now. And a gray crew-neck.

I crane my head to look up at him, and I start with, "I don't have a condom."

"I don't fucking care about that."

It swells inside of me a little. Because I failed today, as I typically somehow seem to do, and he doesn't really care.

"Jane," he says seriously. "I can tell something happened."

I want to share this with him. More than I've ever wanted to tell someone anything.

I haven't had that feeling with anyone but Moffy before.

"No one suspected me and you," I whisper.

"You ran into someone?"

"Luna and another person." I tread carefully because Thatcher is a loyal bodyguard to the entire team. "I'm trusting that what I tell you stays between you and me. A bodyguard is involved."

His jaw sets sternly. "Did the bodyguard endanger your family?"

"No."

"Was the bodyguard endangered in some way?"

"No."

"I won't say anything," he promises.

I've never been good at brevity. I paint an uncomfortably *vivid* picture of what I stepped into and all the happenings thereafter.

Thatcher has a strict hand over his mouth. When I finish, he drops his palm to my hip. Holding me again. "No one can know," he reaffirms. "Alpha and Epsilon will have Omega by the ass. If they think more of our guys are fucking the clients, no one will be safe." He's lumping himself in with the "fucking" part.

Factually, it's accurate.

"She said it was a one-time occasion," I remind him. "So their risk of being caught again is zero."

We stare more knowingly into each other. Our risk is catastrophically high.

But it will go back to *zero* once our fake dating ploy ends. And everything will return to the way it was. No more late-night visits from Thatcher Moretti.

I ignore my sinking stomach.

36

 THATCHER MORETTI

We made a plan. One that will unfuck Jane's guilt.

The team recently approved her request for a double date. So we're doing it now. The Tri-Force even threw me a fucking bone and let me pick the double date location in my area of the city.

South Philly. I chose an old bingo hall—since she's never been to one before and she asked a million questions when I mentioned how Banks and I used to go as kids with my mom and grandma.

Bringing her to a place that I remember vividly from my *childhood*— it's surreal.

Jane shifts her metal chair nearer mine during intermission.

We're in the middle-left smoking area. I keep a vigilant eye on our surroundings and her, more than my bingo cards.

She leans close to whisper, "I know we agreed to be direct. But maybe we should be a bit *less* direct. Subtext could be better."

I follow her focus.

Which is on Maximoff and Farrow, who stand in a winding line several meters away from us. They're waiting to order hot dogs and nachos at the kitchen window.

Familiar.

Everything about this place takes me back.

The smell: like an old, stuffy wooden gym dipped in an ashtray.

And the people: disgruntled elderly patrons, who fill most of the long wooden tables and metal foldout chairs.

Most don't pay attention to us. Truth is, they're not interested in twenty-something celebrities. Everyone here is trying to win money. More than ever since Jane and Maximoff made an anonymous donation. They added an extra zero to the end of the winnings.

The jackpot is five grand.

They do that wherever they go like its second nature. How they were born and raised and meant to use their wealth.

My arm is draped around Jane's shoulders. "There won't be an easy way to tell them we're sleeping together."

"True." Jane takes a tense sip of glass-bottled root beer.

I was going to buy her an actual beer. But I'm on-duty. Farrow is on-duty, and Maximoff doesn't drink alcohol. Jane said she didn't want to be the only one drinking tonight. So she asked what I used to get as a kid.

I came back with two bottles of root beer.

Jane turns more into my shoulder as she speaks. "But maybe we should *ease* them in. Start with a simple, *we have something to tell you and it's not terrible. It could be wonderfully funny from certain viewpoints.*"

I don't know whose viewpoint would call me fucking Jane *wonderfully funny*—but it's definitely not mine. I have a lot of adjectives to describe sex with her and that's not even a fucking foot near my hundredth list.

"Direct is better," I tell Jane. "We don't want to lead this into a clusterfuck."

Ever since Jane swore to protect Luna's secret, she's been feeling terrible for keeping *two* secrets from Maximoff, and I've been feeling like shit for keeping one from Banks.

So we're unleashing this.

But looping them in means they have to keep our secret now. Putting a burden on them to relieve ours is selfish. And hard. I know. I already went through this once tonight with my brother.

I said point-blank, "I'm sleeping with Jane." Clear-cut. Nothing more, but I was on edge.

He just laughed and smacked my chest.

Told me he had a feeling.

Said he'd never tell a soul.

And that was that. My relationship with Banks is one of the purest forms of love, and I'm selfishly glad that I have him to confide in again. I'm already thinking about all the shit I want to talk about. Ask him for advice.

Lord fucking knows I needed his advice *weeks* ago.

"They're on their way back," Jane says aloud. Straightening up.

Farrow and Maximoff walk over to the table with four aluminum-wrapped hot dogs and nachos. Their voices audible as they approach.

"Taste this." Farrow grins and raises the tray of nachos to Maximoff. He glares. "No fucking way. You put jalapeños on it."

His lips stretch in a smile. "In the corner, wolf scout." He motions to the middle. "Pick a chip over here. Promise you won't die." They reach the table.

"You can't promise that, man." Maximoff pulls out two metal chairs. "I could choke on the chip and die."

Farrow tilts his head. "I'd give you the Heimlich. I'm your doctor." They both take their seats.

Maximoff blinks. "Sounds like you just want to touch me."

"I wouldn't need to be your doctor to touch you. I'm your *fiancé*," he says pointedly.

Maximoff grimaces, trying not to smile. "I'd rather Janie save me." He swings his head over to his best friend. His brows suddenly furrow. "You okay? You look super pale."

She's lost some color in her cheeks. "I'm okay. Perfect, actually."

Maximoff is more rigid. "You know...lately you've been acting seriously weird around me."

She gulps her root beer.

"Like that." He motions to Jane.

"Like what?" Her eyes grow.

He scoots forward and lowers his voice. "You know you can tell me anything. Right?" Both of them look *pained*.

And this just started. I can pull this pin for Jane—say what needs to be said in a few words, but I can't slip into her dynamic with Maximoff. Neither can Farrow.

"I know I can," Jane says wholeheartedly to him.

Farrow scrutinizes me until comms hit us. There's chatter about crowds amassing outside the bingo hall. We both glance at the extra security posted at the entrance.

Should be fine.

His tattooed fingers peel aluminum, and I pick up my bottle of root beer.

Jane folds her hands on the table. "There is something we've been wanting to share with you and Farrow—it's actually sort of funny…" Her eyes are huge; she didn't mean to say that, and then she slides me an apologetic look.

I can't believe I'm almost smiling. I take a swig of root beer. Keeping my arm around her.

"By *we*, you mean…" Maximoff's eyes drift from me to her. "Thatcher and you—"

"Take your seats!" the caller announces, a bingo ball just rolled out. "We're beginning with I-28! I-28!"

People suddenly shift. The sounds of asses hitting chairs, uncapping paint dabbers, and ripping bingo cards for the next game. And then the hall deadens in silence.

It's common courtesy. No one speaks loudly while everyone's listening to the caller.

Jane stretches more on the table to stay quiet. "Yes," she whispers. "Thatcher and I."

"G-50! G-50!"

None of us have started playing this round yet. Numbers light up on the board, and Maximoff puts a hand on the back of Farrow's neck. Leaning in close so his lips brush his ear. Talking quietly.

All the while, Farrow is staring at me. I wouldn't call it a glare.

Jane leans into my side, and I dip my head down so she can speak to me.

"I can't do brief, I've realized." Her breath is warm against my ear.

"I can," I remind her.

She nods. "Please."

"I'll do it," I confirm. I'd like to rip this off and push forward

Some people are shooting us looks to shut the fuck up.

Jane picks up a purple dabber and multitasks while we have to be silent for another minute. Catching up with the numbers.

She marks my sheets too. Trying to fill-in a postage stamp shape.

"I-20! I-20!"

I wait for Maximoff and Farrow to look back at us.

More numbers are being called, and excitement builds in the hall. People tensing, some smiling the closer they are to a *bingo*.

I hear double doors opening from commotion outside. My head turns, and I watch them slam shut. Late arrivals just came in.

No.

My eyes sear.

Jane must sense the strain in my muscles. Because she follows my narrowed gaze to Tony Ramella. He just walked in, his arm hooked around his grandma.

He's off-duty. Xander must be safe at home. But Tony has to know we're all here.

Seeing him almost instantly pisses me off, and I'm on-duty. *I'm on fucking duty.* I can't let my anger or past grievances distract me. My blood simmers, and I roll up my red flannel sleeves.

"B-5! B-5!"

Out of the corner of my eye, I see Tony shuffling slowly at Michelina's pace. Headed to the long table to buy booklets.

"N-42!"

"BINGO!" Two women shout at nearly the same time. Groans fill the hall and tears of paper.

We have time as the caller verifies the bingo and goes to the next round. Five to ten minutes. People already talk and stand to use the restroom and to grab chow.

Maximoff and Farrow finally turn their heads back to us.

I let it out. "Jane and I are having sex."

"No shit." Farrow pops a chip in his mouth.

"For real," Jane whispers, probably thinking *he* thinks we're playing into the fake dating op. "I love sex, and these past few weeks, Thatcher and I have found ourselves inexplicably tangled together. In bed, and more metaphorically, and because we love sex, which I already mentioned, and…say something, please." She's looking at Maximoff, who's stoic and harder to read.

He lifts his squared shoulders. "I don't know…Farrow kept telling me you two were banging, and I feel like a fucking idiot not believing the signs." He winces, holding her gaze. "But I just thought that you'd tell me, Janie. Nowhere in my mind did I think you wouldn't. And I know you're telling me now…I'm just confused why you wouldn't sooner. You felt like I'd be angry? I'm not, *I'm not.*" He tries to reassure her quickly.

"It's not that." She shakes her head repeatedly, blinking back tears. "I knew you'd be terribly happy if I'm happy, and I am."

Good to hear. Except that this has an ending. *You knew this couldn't last, Thatcher.*

Don't stop forgetting that.

I have to partially listen to comms. Farrow looks to his three o'clock. We're being given details on the crowds outside.

Growing hostile.

Jane touches her heart. "You and Farrow just found yourselves *free* of all secrets. You're the happiest I've seen you, and I didn't want you to have to skirt around the security team again. Especially while you're in pre-wedding bliss."

Farrow smiles teasingly at Maximoff.

He groans. "I'm in pre-wedding *nothing.* We haven't even figured out a wedding location, and if this is going to put distance between us, then you need to tell me what I can do to fix it. Because I want you to feel like you can come to me and share things with me *right* when you want to share them. Not because you feel like you can't."

Jane takes a strong breath and reaches out to touch his hand. "Can we make a promise? Don't shut me out of your wedding planning because you feel like my life takes precedence, and I'll share my life with you because I want to—and you truly have no idea just how unequivocally I am dying to."

They're both already standing and hugging across the table. They talk to each other more quietly.

I lower my voice and nod to Farrow who lights a cigarette. "Did you tell anyone else you thought me and her were having sex?"

"Fuck no," he says, blowing smoke off to the side. He slides me the pack.

It's a small peace offering that I don't deserve. But I take out a cigarette.

"Your family is getting harassed in South Philly." That's why he's treating me like a friend. Because he just went through this.

I nod once. Journalists keep knocking on my mom's door, and more recently, paparazzi have trailed her car. "My uncles are taking care of it." I light a cigarette, taking a short drag. Most guys on the team are recreational smokers. Some are habitual, or like my brother, trying to kick it.

On-duty and off.

It helps us stay awake.

I hawk-eye the entrance, and before the bingo caller starts the next round soon, I ask Farrow, "How'd you know about Jane and me?"

Jane and Maximoff sit back down. Hearing this.

"We've been careful," Jane whispers to us, "and we'll continue to be."

I'm not bringing up the end-date. Neither is she.

Farrow blows a line of smoke away from Maximoff. "I'm a bodyguard and I notice shit."

I grit down because that doesn't bode well for keeping this secret from the team. I glance at Jane, and she sends me an alarmed look.

She scoots forward toward Farrow. "You think the rest of security will find out?"

"No." He taps ash. "Because I'm the only bodyguard who lives in the same townhouse as you. See, you came downstairs every morning with a giddy as fuck smile like you just got laid. And not from a sex toy."

Jane downs the rest of her root beer, then tells me, "If I'd known I have a terrible post-sex poker-face, I would've practiced."

I wish I could've seen her those mornings.

Don't wish that. "It makes this easier," I tell Jane. She knows I'm referring to them already *slightly* knowing, but as far as Farrow and me... "You don't care that I'm sleeping with her?"

"I'm not your mom or your conscience, Moretti. But you are a fucking hypocrite."

I nod. Not disagreeing. "You need me to tattoo it on my ass?"

His brows spike. "Would you?"

I wouldn't care. "Why not?"

When he sees that I'm serious, because I always fucking am, he laughs into a smile. "This can definitely be arranged—"

"Can't you put a different word on his ass?" Jane asks, bartering for me.

I'm about to speak, Farrow is too. But we both go quiet. Noticing Tony approaching the table from my side.

I snuff out my cigarette. He has to come say hi or else Michelina will chew him out.

"Hey." Tony checks back on the bingo caller, still not ready for the next round, then looks to Jane. "How about them Eagles, huh?" He smiles and tries to perch his hands on the back of her chair.

I extend my arm, blocking him. "No."

If he thinks being on the team grants him access to flirt with the girls in these families—he's out of his fucking mind.

He's a bodyguard to a minor.

Not the over-eighteen girls, and their bodyguards will rip him the fuck apart. The only reason I'm not in his face right now is because I don't trust myself not to punch him.

Irritation cinches his brows. "I'm part of the team. Or did you forget that?"

I stare him dead in the eye. Loudly, I say, "She's my *girlfriend*, or did you fucking forget that?" People whisper and look over at us. Publicly, we're together.

A smile tugs her cheeks. It fades fast as Tony laughs under his breath. He stuffs his hands in his aviator jacket. "Right, right." He has a shit-eating grin, and only audible to me, he lowers his head and says, "I see you took your balls out of her purse."

I shake my head. "You're a fucking scustamad'." *You're a fucking stupid person.* I raise the volume of comms, more intel coming through about outside.

Farrow puts out his cigarette and pockets the pack. He whispers in Maximoff's ear.

Jane leans more into my side, and I wrap my arm around her waist. She tells Tony, "We're actually about to return to our cards. The game should start soon."

"Just stopping by to say hi." Tony cocks his head. "Moretti knows how it is." He glances over at Michelina, then to me. "You know whenever I think of this place, I always picture that time your brother got into a fistfight with Jay Amaro and knocked over the bingo balls. Gave an old woman a literal heart attack. Paramedics came." He lets out a laugh. "Fuck, that was a long time ago."

My ribs constrict, thinking about that memory. Knives cutting a single breath. Just one.

I exhale through my nose, and the weight is gone. Fifteen years in the past.

"Banks was in a fight?" Jane asks, like she can't picture him swinging first.

Tony shakes his head. "Not Banks. Their other brother, Skylar."

My eyes tighten.

Skylar.

Sky.

I've been trying to tell her about him, and I couldn't figure out when. I'm gearing my ass up for the middle of fucking hell.

I should've just let it out in the costume shop earlier. Before Charlie's phone call cut us off. Or in the car afterwards. It's on me.

A million times, I missed the chance. I fucked it, and now *Tony* dropped this before I could.

Jane tips her head, thinking rapidly. Her brows bunched. Maximoff and Farrow exchange confusion.

Mostly, I watch her. "Jane—"

"None of you knew about Skylar?" Tony realizes, looking between the three of them. He lets out a light laugh.

"That's funny?" I ask, voice strict.

He laughs more. "It's not *not* funny."

"Vaffangul'." *Fuck you.* I grip my knee to keep from standing. Do not harm another bodyguard. Do not fight while on-duty. Protect your client.

Protect her.

He motions to Jane. "She's your girlfriend and you didn't tell her about your own brother—"

I shoot to my feet. Towering over him. Staring down. Blood rushes in my ears. Rage annihilating my senses. Until I'm hyper-focused on this shitbag.

My anger.

His face.

He spreads his arms, goading me to hit him. "I just did you a fucking favor. It's not my fault you couldn't man-up and say what needs to be sa—"

I have Tony by the collar. I'm five seconds from slamming his entire body into the fucking ground. Farrow is quick.

He's already climbed over the table onto my side. He wedges himself between us and rotates to Tony. "Man, I'm sick of listening to you. Walk the fuck away."

I pull back and I get my mind right almost instantly. Sensing her close.

I turn.

She's standing. I assess her in one sweep. Chunky heels, a ruffled purple tutu, and a frilly blouse—she has her hand in her purse. Where her pepper spray and switchblade are contained, ready to defend me. She lets go when our eyes meet. "Thatcher."

Nothing else matters to me right now but this girl. "Jane," I say strongly. I come closer, my hand on her lower back. I soften my gaze on her. "You good?"

"Yes, are you?"

I nod. "Can you be Oscar Mike in five?" We need to move out.

I notice the bingo caller headed over to us. We've disturbed the whole event, and beyond that, Maximoff is a hothead and if Tony tries to fuck with Farrow, which I'm pretty positive he will try—Maximoff is going to throw a fist.

He's the client here.

His life. Her life.

That's what we're protecting.

Jane adjusts her purse over her shoulder. "I'm ready now."

Tony sizes Farrow up. "I've heard a lot about you from Epsilon—"

"Farrow," I call. "We're shoving off." I click my radio, not taking one of my hands off her. "Thatcher to security, Jane and Maximoff are Oscar Mike in five."

Farrow steps back over the table and drops down next to Maximoff, taking his hand.

I take hers.

Clearheaded.

Focused.

There is hell outside. Which we have to push through.

37

 THATCHER MORETTI

"Does it hurt badly?" Jane asks me after we've returned to the townhouse from the bingo hall.

We sit on a weight bench in the quiet garage. Pressed up against the brick wall and facing her parked Volkswagen.

I watch her eyes trace the deep, long cut along my bicep. Clean and stitched just moments ago. My bloodied flannel and T-shirt are balled up and trashed in a bin next to a red toolkit.

Jane turns more towards me. "I can see if we have stronger pain medication or ice, perhaps?"

I rest my shoulders on the brick. My gaze not leaving Jane, watching her concern travel across my body. "I'm good, honey." Farrow numbed the cut well. He just went back into the townhouse with his trauma bag. Maximoff beside him.

Calm after the storm.

The crowds were aggressive for no good reason. Something I've encountered countless times as a bodyguard, and I like the rush of it. The impending nature of this hellfire, the sudden blast and challenge as we confront it and try to diverge from it. How my senses snap into focus, and the stakes are always high.

We escorted Jane and Maximoff safely to their vehicles. They protested because they saw us being dragged back and tried to help. But

I literally picked Jane up, and I've never seen Farrow shove Maximoff that hard into the car.

Their lives come first.

I prefer that chaos a thousand leagues over my confrontation with Tony. I failed there. Lost my temper for a split-second, and that's all it takes.

One second and a bad night becomes the worst of your life.

Jane lifts her eyes up to me. "I can't believe you both got hurt."

I'm not that affected by it. "It's not bad. Minor injuries to security are normal."

She's only just now seeing them because she's gotten closer to the team. *To me.* It's impossible not to get knocked around on this job.

Especially when hostile crowds start breaking bottles. Some leather-jacket-wearing fuckbag tried to smash a beer bottle over Farrow's head, and I blocked the blow with my arm and restrained the threat.

Farrow got cut on the knee with glass. He was able to bandage his own wound in the car.

Jane gives her whole attention to me. "Do you feel like you're being targeted more, in terms of crowds? Now that you and Farrow are more publicly recognizable?"

I unclip my radio off my waistband. "It's hard to say." Hecklers will sometimes pick fights with security to get to the client. So I can't tell if they're coming at me because I'm publicly Jane's boyfriend or because I'm just the man in their way.

I describe this to Jane, and she nods in understanding. "Are you going off-duty?" She sees me taking out my earpiece.

"I am." I twist the cord around the radio. "Unless you want to go out—"

"No," she says quickly. "No, I'm staying in for the rest of the night." Her eyes light up in realization. "I forgot I have a bottle of Dalmore stashed away somewhere in here—though, don't feel pressured to drink whiskey with me." She raises her hands. "I was only thinking that, possibly, with your...cut, it'd help take the edge off." She clears her throat, soaking up my hard gaze.

I study her shallow breath, and I almost reach out and touch her hand that lies flat on the weight bench. Near mine. Heat washes over my chest. Like we're in a steaming sauna somewhere remote and alone.

We're in a fucking garage.

Where one door leads to security's townhouse, the other to hers. And Akara, Quinn, Sulli, and Luna are already home tonight.

I can't pretend that we're in her bedroom with a locked door. In privacy.

She wafts her blouse. "I'm not asking you to drink with me as a fake boyfriend and girlfriend…because clearly, we're not in public, you see."

My brows knit. What we are together in private, in public, in every other setting, is starting to confuse the hell out of me. And we have to be in agreement.

"You need to clarify," I say deeply. "What do you think you are to me right now?"

Jane tucks a piece of hair behind her ear, then motions to me. "This is just friendship…just two ole pals drinking whiskey. If you'd like to drink with me, that is."

Friendship.

I've been inside her pussy. She's not some platonic friend. My jaw hardens. "We're pals who fuck each other?"

"Precisely," she says like we're still on the same page.

But my chest tightens. She's used to friends-with-benefits, and that's where she's placed me. That's all she wants.

The fact that I'm sitting here and feeling like it's not just *that*—it's a fucking problem. I shouldn't be veering off course.

"Correct?" she asks, waiting for my confirmation.

I nod. "Affirmative."

"So what do you think?" She's referring to the whiskey.

I consider her offer in a short beat.

Drinking *alone* with a client and not in a group setting—it's a straight shot to buddy-guard territory. Something I normally don't fuck around with.

But I'm not looking forward to leaving for security's townhouse. I don't want to separate from her yet. And I love whiskey.

I set my radio aside on the weight bench. "If we drink, I can't touch you. It's too inappropriate if someone walks in and sees." I've one-hundred percent exhausted the "practicing for the op" excuse, and we need to be more careful.

"Oui." Jane sits straighter, hands flat on her thighs. "No touching, it's a necessary parameter."

"I'll get the liquor." I start to stand up.

Her curious blue eyes follow my movement. All six-foot-seven of me rising, and a small breath parts her lips.

I zero in on her knees that knock together. *Goddamn.* My cock strains against my slacks. "Jane," I say in my core.

She inhales. "Yes?"

I rub my mouth. "Where's the whiskey?"

"Oh, um." Jane shakes out her thoughts, then points to an old wooden cabinet. Where the team stores flashlights and extra batteries. "Top shelf, I think."

It's not far. Opening the creaky cabinet door, I find a bottle full of dark amber liquid in the back corner, third shelf. I brush off the dust and read the label on my way to Jane.

Taking a seat next to her, I wait to open it. "This is a thirty-year-old whiskey." *Expensive.* "You sure?"

"Positive. It's just been sitting there for years. It was a housewarming present from my brothers. I thought they would've all drunk it by now, but Beckett hid it so they wouldn't."

I open the bottle and pass it to her. The mention of her brothers reminds me of mine.

Tell her about Skylar.

She hasn't pressured me to explain more. Neither did Maximoff or Farrow in the car. They're good people. Compassionate, and I don't want to wake up tomorrow and regret not saying something.

I've compartmentalized so much of my fucking life in order to push through. Built walls that I can't even break down.

But I think compassion deserves compassion, and I want to be deserving of her.

Even if I can't have her in the end.

She puts the bottle to her lips. Taking a small sip, then inspecting the label. "Tastes like burnt chocolate and oranges. Though I'm more of a whiskey novice, so I wouldn't know if it's any good other than I think I like it."

I grab the bottle as she passes it. Our fingers accidentally touching. And lingering too long in the exchange.

Neither of us mentions it. The garage blisters, and I wipe sweat off my forehead with my bicep, the one without the numbed, stitched cut.

Tell her.

I'm looking at Jane more than the Dalmore. "I had an older brother growing up." My voice is even-keeled.

Her brows jump. "Skylar?"

I watch her eyes soften on me. "Yeah." I swallow a rock in my throat. "I've wanted to tell you about him. But it's not something I usually talk about." I swig from the bottle. Liquor sliding down smoothly, and my thumb brushes over the label, then I hand it back to Jane. "Skylar probably would've gotten a kick out of me drinking whiskey with a girl."

She swishes the liquid. "Did he like whiskey?"

I breathe deeper for a second. I recognize that I want her curiosity. And intrigue. Full-force.

It makes this easier for me.

"More than he should've," I answer. "He broke every rule my dad ever made." I watch her sip the whiskey. "Banks and I were the *good* sons. Obedient. But I looked up to Sky, asked him a lot."

She hands me the bottle, listening intently.

"I think he told me a lot of horseshit. But it was loving horseshit." I rest the bottle on my knee. Staring at the blue Beetle for a second.

If she looks at you a lot, it means she likes you. His advice. He'd ruffle my hair with his hand and grin. Teasing me, and I thought he was a badass. Some kind of invincible warrior.

I tell this to Jane. Succinctly. Probably too stoically. Some walls will never break down. I don't think I could ever cry about it, but I can at least try to share this, finally.

My gaze tightens, brows drawn together, and I take another swig. "It was a long time ago. We were kids, and then we weren't."

I tell her how Skylar was three years older. He died at fifteen. Banks and I were twelve at the time. "His death caused a lot of friction in my family."

I notice her lips slowly parting in realization. She's adding up pieces. "You were *twelve* when your parents divorced, weren't you?"

I nod.

Same age as my brother's passing.

More dawns on her. How I was around *twelve, thirteen* when I was adamant I'd join the military.

I've also told Jane that I'm not close to my dad. Not since the divorce. We only really talk about football.

I pass back the whiskey. "When my brother died, my dad said a lot of things. Things that he thought he could never take back. To my mom. To Banks. To me."

"To you?" She draws nearer, her knees almost knocking into my legs. "You were only twelve."

I'll never forget the blackout rage on my dad's face. "He probably would've lashed out at a fucking garden gnome that night."

Jane hugs the bottle to her chest. "Has he ever mentioned it? That night and what he said to you?"

"Hell no." I shake my head a couple times. "He's too ashamed."

Instead of making it right, he just withdrew. Became distant. He never showed me how to seek forgiveness, ask for it or accept it. Just to take fault for my mistakes.

To carry blame.

I'm good at that. But I'm not him. If I were, I would've never walked over to Jane on the beach in Greece and tried to right what I'd wronged.

"My mom wasn't doing well," I explain, a pit in my ribs. There's not a word to describe my mom around this time. Eviscerated seems too light. "But we were all lucky."

346 KRISTA & BECCA RITCHIE

She hands back the whiskey without taking a sip. "In what way?"

"We had my grandma." I tell Jane how Carol Piscitelli, my four-foot-eleven grandma, packed up our small, one-bedroom apartment and found us a row house to live in.

She moved in with us.

She got my mom back on her feet.

She made sure that we kept our heads up. "We didn't have a lot of things growing up," I tell Jane. "But we had family."

At a time where we were starved for anything but emptiness and grief, our grandma gave so much love.

"She sounds like a beautiful person," Jane tells me, her soft smile so genuine. "I'd love to meet her and your mom one day—if appropriate. I know it may not be possible for security reasons, but I just..." She takes a measured breath. "They seem quite lovely, is all."

My chest rises. "They'd like to meet you."

She smiles more. "They would?"

I nod and I put the rim of the bottle to my mouth. Taking another swig. I watch a thousand other questions rush through her eyes.

She smooths her lips repeatedly. Contemplating what to ask.

She's quiet for a while, and I almost move closer. I almost brush a strand of frizzed hair off her cheek. I almost pull her onto my lap.

Don't touch her.

My muscles tense, and I look her over. "What are you most curious about?"

She's wary. "That's an incredibly dangerous thing to ask, you realize."

"I'm good to go." I nod to her. "Shoot."

"What did your dad tell you that night?"

I figured this could've been on her mind. And I've never told this to anyone. Never repeated it. But I just let it out now. "He said I should've biked harder." Off her confusion, I explain the rest.

How my brother died.

He used to bike out to a quarry. He'd sneak a few beers to drink, throw rocks, and swim. Sometimes alone, sometime with friends. Always to let off steam.

Occasionally he'd let me and Banks tag along. One night, I heard him sneak out, and I knew he was probably headed there.

I asked my mom if I could go with Sky. She said yes. I followed on my bike.

I was slower up hills. I left probably fifteen minutes after him.

When I got there, I dropped my bike and ran straight in the water. Skylar had jumped off a common diving point. But it was dark. No moonlight. The water was too shallow, and he hit rock.

He ended up unconscious in the water around ten minutes before I showed up.

There wasn't anything I could do. But I tried.

I was strong for twelve.

I learned I was stronger than Sky, and I wished I'd seen how badly he coped with our strict dad. I wished he didn't go to that fucking quarry and horse around.

And I wished I could've taken the burden off him like I did Banks.

I dragged him out of the water, and my gold chain twisted on the gold chain around his neck. Our cornics stuck together.

Later, my grandma unknotted the chains and put both gold horns on one necklace. She said they were meant to be together.

"It's over fifteen years ago," I remind Jane. "It feels distant most days." I blink, my eyes burning. "It was a footnote in the news. Which is why it hasn't blown-up in the media yet."

Some local boy hit his head and drowned. There are too many deaths at that quarry every year.

Jane listens as I tell her the last part.

I set the whiskey bottle on the ground. "Skylar used to say to our dad, *I'm going to be a Marine one day*. To piss him off." My dad used to be die-hard Navy.

Until after my brother died, when I said, *"I'm going to be a Marine."* For Sky.

And then he said, *"Okay."*

Jane is closer to me. The empathy welled up in her blue eyes says everything. We drift even nearer on the weight bench. Our gazes trailing over one another in burning waves, and her fingers inch towards my thigh.

My hand hovers near her hip. *God*, I want to touch her.

Don't.

I want her in my arms.

Don't.

"Thatcher," she breathes like she's already in my embrace.

I dip my head down to hear her. Space shrinking between us. Everywhere.

"I want to tell you," Jane murmurs, swallowing hard, "just how much I admire you before it's too late."

My chest rises and falls heavily. I breathe the scorching air through my nose. *Don't touch her.*

Don't.

Our lips brush.

Don't.

I clasp her cheek—we crash into each other. Kissing strongly, all restraints wrapping us together. Like seatbelts I'm clicking in while she's welded against me.

I swiftly pull her onto my lap. Against my chest, my hand running up her thigh. Jane straddles me, gripping the back of my head with starved fingers. I clutch her ass and push her against me. A high-pitched noise catches in her throat.

My large build cocoons her, and she hangs on tight.

"Don't stop," she begs.

Every kiss is a resounding *stay.*

And a *touch me.*

Touch me.

Please, touch me.

I harden, and I rip her blouse with two hands, and she cries, "*Yes.*"

My pulse is hammering. I press my forehead to hers, kneading her breast, hidden behind a cotton bra. We kiss in raw, explosive hunger. She tugs my hair, and a grunt knots in my chest.

Muscles flexed, I stand up with Jane around my waist. My hand on her ass, her back. I walk further back into the garage. Behind her Beetle.

She runs her hand along my jaw, down my neck—to my gold chain.

We deepen the kiss, and something heady overtakes me. I cup the back of her neck.

And then I solidify at a noise.

She freezes. "Is that...?" We listen.

"Footsteps," I whisper, eagle-eyeing the door to security's townhouse. I hear Akara and Quinn's voice.

Quickly and carefully, I set her down.

I ripped her blouse. Without pause, I open her car door. She has a zebra-print sweater in the backseat, and I hand it to her.

"Thank you." She slips her arms through. I go grab my radio and hide the whiskey further beneath the weight bench.

The door is about to open.

We're both tense. We're both pent-up.

In her urgency, she buttons the sweater unevenly.

"You need to go, Jane." I nod to her townhouse. I hate saying that, but Akara and Quinn can't see her like this.

She nods in agreement, and she quickly heads to the other door. To her townhouse. She glances back. "À la prochaine." *Until next time.*

And she's gone.

It's like a fucking pumpkin is beginning to form and I can't stop it.

38

 THATCHER MORETTI

Akara came into the garage because I went off-duty. I shut off comms. And something else just happened outside the townhouse.

Something surrounding Jane.

We just finished taking care of the threat. My muscles can't unbind. My shoulders are locked, and I yank open the fridge in security's townhouse and grab a beer. Pop the cap, and I pass the bottle to Akara.

"Thanks, man." Akara swigs, leaning on the stove. It's been hectic tonight.

"You should have one, too," Banks tells me, eyeing the beer. My brother sits on the counter and sticks a toothpick between his teeth. His brows knot and his gaze narrows on the stitched cut along my bicep.

I shake my head and pass him a beer.

I've already been drinking whiskey. And I need to be more alert. "I should stay sober until these fucking targets die down."

"It could be months," Akara warns me. "The police still don't know who broke into the house, and now she has a habitual stalker jerking off outside her window."

I cross my arms over my taut chest. My nose flares.

Banks tips his beer to Akara. "It's good that you're the one who caught *Sneakers* getting his rocks off in his car. Thatcher would've killed him."

I stay unmoving but send a glare to my brother. The middle-aged man who dresses in baggy jeans, white *sneakers*, and carries around roses—he's been on my radar since the Cinderella ad. And Akara spotted him masturbating in his parked car before our around-the-clock security outside did.

Cops arrested Sneakers and will charge him with public indecency. Lewdness. The best security can do is a restraining order.

Target destroyed.

But his insistence to keep coming around—after so many bodyguards told him off—makes me think he'll be back. He'll violate his restraining order. Go to jail.

The cycle will continue, and I shouldn't be emotionally invested in this situation. I should be able to handle this without wanting blood. But I just keep thinking that this middle-aged fucker was in a car and rubbing his dick almost *in sight* of Jane.

Too close.

Too fucking close.

And this is the girl who I'm sleeping with. Who I'm protecting and have held while she's cried against my chest—so I'm not feeling fucking even-tempered. Not as much as I should be. As any bodyguard should be.

"My civic duty," Akara banters, "keep Thatcher from murdering targets."

Banks smiles. "Amen." They clink bottles and swig.

I uncross my arms, opening the fridge to grab a water.

"Did Jane text you?" Banks asks me.

I nod. "She heard the cop sirens and asked if everyone was safe." I start putting some leftover containers next to Banks. "I texted back that a minor threat was being detained. She didn't want more."

"Sulli is like that," Akara says, beer to his lips. "She doesn't ever want extra details."

"Who would?" Banks asks.

"Maximoff," Akara and I say at the same time. Though, my brother knows this too. His question was really rhetorical, but we just didn't give a shit.

I pop open the container of roasted goose and potatoes.

Banks sniffs the meat. "Smells like roadkill."

"No it doesn't." I stick a fork in the cold meat.

He steals the container and holds it to Akara.

Akara is texting, but he sniffs it anyway. He smiles. "Smells like a Cobalt Empire Wednesday Night Dinner. Three days old, still edible."

I grab the container from Banks.

Jane always brings her leftovers from every Wednesday family dinner. Usually for Maximoff. Sometimes she'll put a container in security's fridge.

Only Cobalts have ever attended. No Hales, no Meadows. Never bodyguards.

What goes on there is almost urban legend on the security team. No one really knows. Except that if you have a Cobalt client, they'll usually fight to make it back to their childhood house every Wednesday, every week.

Akara glares at his cellphone, then he takes off his baseball hat and pushes his black hair back.

"What's wrong?" I ask.

"You remember Will Rochester?" Akara throws his cell on the counter. "Apparently he's planning on throwing Sulli a *Hallow Friends Eve* party the day before Halloween." He shakes his head repeatedly. "I don't like where this is fucking going. He seems…"

"Like he's into her?" Banks finishes. "Because that's one-hundred percent certain—"

"I know that," Akara growls, heat flashing in his eyes. "That's not it."

He established a buddy-guard friendship with Sullivan Meadows, and he walks a blurry line like he was born on one. No sweat. Better than I could with my feet cemented to the thing.

But ever since last year, he's picked up that Sulli is starting to show real interest in *dating*. And his overprotectiveness and his level of care for his client has shot through the fucking roof.

"You're not jealous?" Banks wants confirmation.

Akara glares. "Shut the fuck up."

I don't make those comments about him and Sulli. He gets enough shit from the rest of SFO. But Banks eases up faster than the other guys would.

"Is it a sixth sense?" I ask Akara about Will. Wondering if his caution is based on gut or intel.

"Yeah, it's just a feeling. He's renting out a farm." Akara fists the neck of his beer and puts a container of Ripped Fuel on the counter. "He's taking an entire open field and putting together haunted houses from *scratch*."

"Rich guys can do that," Banks points out.

"I'm rich," Akara says, "and I can't do half of what he's planning." Akara had about the same wealth as Farrow growing up.

His dad was a big shot broker. But he died when Akara was seventeen. Akara used the life insurance money to open up Studio 9.

"The Rochesters are old money." I unscrew my water, pushing back my chow for a second.

Banks nods. "They can afford mega yachts."

Like Jane.

I sometimes forget she's that wealthy. She lives modestly in comparison to her parents. I look to Akara. "How many people will be at the farm?" Wherever the Hallow Friends Eve party takes place, I know Jane will be there, and I need the details.

"I don't know yet," Akara says. "But Will promised that every single guest would sign an NDA or they wouldn't be permitted on the grounds. It's their ticket into the party. Sul said it was really sweet of him." His hand slips on the Ripped Fuel container and pills spill out. "Shit." He cleans it up.

Banks nods to Akara. "So this Will guy lives around here. How deep is he?"

Akara tosses pills back into the jug. "Banks, I love you, man, but we talked about that phrase. No one but you and your brother use it, and all I picture is someone's cock deep between a set of thighs."

"You're welcome." Banks smiles with his toothpick between his teeth.

"How far away is he?" I rephrase *how deep is he?*

Akara explains that he lives in a gated neighborhood twenty minutes away. He's been background checked. "I have a feeling he's just buying her trust so he can fuck her, and Sul said she's not looking for a hookup, so what am I supposed to do?"

Let it happen.

Akara wouldn't direct Sulli away from Will if he thought she liked him. He's venting to us, and he knows there's nothing he can do about the situation.

That's going to be me, I realize.

Once this op ends soon, Jane could easily meet a rich prick. Could I help her fall in love with another man? Could I watch that fucking happen?

My stomach roils.

I'm stuck between a rock and another fucking rock.

39

JANE COBALT

Failure is a dear friend of mine. And it reared its ugly head again today. I'm trying my best not to visualize what happened, or else I'll feel a repeat wave of mortification and disappointment.

But it's hard not to think about.

Especially when it happened mere hours ago.

I showed up to the recording studio for my first session narrating *Wildfire Heart*. It lasted ten minutes before the producer paused and took a phone call. When he came back, he simply said, "I'm sorry Jane. I just got a call from the publisher. They want to go in a different direction."

It was so formal and direct. Like a swing of an axe, I was cut just like that.

Different direction is so vague. It could have been my fault—they didn't like my voice or didn't want my name attached to the audiobook—and they're just trying to be professional and diplomatic. Not wanting to burn bridges. Or it could have been something out of my control.

I don't know.

I suppose I never will. And that's the hardest part in all of this. When you don't know why you've truly failed, but you have. Eliot told me it's like that all the time in casting, and you just have to believe you're talented enough. It's just outside factors. And the truth—it doesn't matter in the end.

But I truly don't know if I'm talented enough at anything that could deem me worthy of my Cobalt name. Except math.

Tom says it's a curse. To have talent for something you don't love.

Lately it's felt that way.

Girls Night has never been more necessary. I'm in Luna and Sulli's room, and I need to forget about *Wildfire Heart.*

And I especially need to forget about the call I made to my little sister, breaking the news that I'd no longer be narrating one of her favorite books. Or any books.

She just stared at me through FaceTime, red hair framing her face. "Oh Jane," she said in her whimsical, velvety voice like she stepped out of the pages of a Jane Austen novel. "Please don't weep. Those publishers truly don't know what they lost. They should be the ones in tears."

Disappointing her is what hurts the most.

"Jane." Sulli tosses one of her squishy basketballs at my face. It bounces off my forehead. Sulli turns to Luna. "We've fucking lost her."

"To the aliens," Luna nods.

"I'm here," I say into a sigh and pick up the ball. I try and aim for the small hoop on the back of the door. Sulli and Luna's room is a combination of them both. Alien beanbags on a fuzzy rug, hand weights tucked under the bottom bunk, and posters taped over every inch of the wall.

I lob the ball. It doesn't even reach the net.

"That air ball must be a metaphor for my life," I muse aloud.

Sulli tosses me a bottle of avocado facemask. "You can't think everything is a sign. It'll drive you fucking crazy."

She's not wrong. I uncap the bottle.

Luna lounges on the bottom bunk. She squirts three bottles of the creamy green facemask in a large bowl. "I dunno," she says. "I kind of like thinking everything is a sign. It's a reminder that we're not alone." Luna also tells us that she's been taking online classes at Penn on extraterrestrial life in the universe.

Sulli adds, "All I'm saying is that we go with the hard-earned facts. And fact is everyone in this room is fucking awesome. Including you." She looks straight at me.

I slide on a cloth headband above my hairline to avoid avocado hair. "Thank you," I say. "I needed to hear that today." I look between them.

They're not much younger than me, but in a completely different place in their lives. They can figure things out. Take some time off. But I've already done that.

I'm heading into my mid-twenties and it feels like the clock has officially run down. That I should have my shit together by now. Thank God, I'm still on the Cobalt social media blackout. I can't look online at the tweets or comments on Instagram. I'm sure the majority of them are reaffirming what they already believed.

That I am a complete disappointment. And how could I be the eldest child of Rose and Connor Cobalt?

"Luna, what's your theory on body-snatching?" I ask.

Sulli gives me a look like *no fucking way have you been body-snatched.* Luna now squirts body glitter into her bowl. "Body-snatching is not impossible. I once thought I had this out-of-body experience one summer. But I think I was just huffing too much glue."

Sulli and I look at her.

"Please tell me my brothers didn't put you up to that," I say.

"All I'll say is that it was the summer of a lot of stupid shit, not all I would repeat, and Tom, Eliot, and I have officially dubbed it the Stoopid Summer. Stoopid with two O's."

They have a name for a summer. I shouldn't be surprised.

"And speaking of summer," Sulli says, a smile burgeoning on her face as she glances to Luna. Like they're in on something. Can't be surprised about that either. They do share a room together. They're practically college dormmates.

I rub the avocado cream on my face and pass the bottle to Sulli.

Luna sheds her shirt and pants, only in a pair of underwear and a bra. She starts lathering her avocado cream-glitter mixture all over her belly. "You know how Moffy will offhandedly mention that Farrow says he smells like summer? Like all the time."

Yes, Maximoff will do that frequently. Almost like he doesn't even know he's speaking out loud.

"Oui."

Sulli swipes two green stripes underneath her eyes like warpaint. "And then we overheard Thatcher saying you smell like spring. I wasn't fucking eavesdropping or anything—"

"I was." Luna raises a green glitter hand.

My heart thumps hard in my chest. *Please tell me they didn't hear anything else.*

"Your door was cracked open," Luna explains.

Thank God.

Relief washes over me. Thatcher and I most definitely always closed *and* locked the door when we had sex. Very little chance of being overheard.

Luna rubs the green glitter on her legs, about to completely cover herself in the avocado mask.

I try to follow their logic. "So Maximoff smells like summer. I smell like spring." Where is this going?

Sulli nods. "And Farrow has white fucking hair. And Thatcher always wears those plaid flannels like he's about to chop some wood in the forest."

Uh-oh.

Luna beams. "Farrow is winter. Thatcher is fall. Which makes the four of you the *Seasons*." She claps her hands accidently. "You have your own friendship name. We do our best." She pounds a fist with Sulli.

"The Seasons," I say with a smile.

"And the best part of it," Sulli says. "Is that the media doesn't know about it, so they can't ruin a good thing like they always do."

Luna and I share a look this time. Sulli blames the media for picking up the story about Beckett's texts so quickly.

It spread like wildfire and made it harder for security to remove them. And even with the girl breaking her NDA, all she did was pay a fine. Beckett shouldered most of the consequences. Now he doesn't text anyone. Not even me. He'll only call or FaceTime.

A knock suddenly raps on the door.

"Jane." Thatcher's deep voice is a bit muffled outside. "My mom wants to know if you prefer white or red pasta sauce."

I'm meeting his family in a couple days.

Security surprisingly approved the outing. Thatcher isn't sure why they would, and I know it's put him on edge.

I want to make a good impression with his family. I'm nervous that I'll fail at this too. I've never had to do this before, and I can't ask Moffy for advice.

Farrow doesn't have much of a family. So Moffy didn't really "meet the parents" in the traditional sense.

I speak to the door. "I like both sauces."

"Say again?" He can't hear me through the wood.

"You can come in!" Sulli calls out to him.

He cracks the door. Catching sight of my green face, he opens it wider. He steps in, and then spots Luna in her underwear—swiftly, he rotates. "Sorry." His eyes are on me, back to her. "I thought everyone was decent."

"We are very decent," Luna says. "I'm basically in a bikini. Plus... I'm posting it on Instagram anyway." I watch as she holds up the phone and snaps a picture. "Sulli." She hands the phone to her so she can help take a wide shot.

I don't want to be in the room when her dad sees that photo online. He might have a stroke.

Hopefully Aunt Lily is with him. She always knows what to say to calm Uncle Lo.

I focus on Thatcher and his earlier question. "I like both," I say. "Can you tell your mom that whatever she wants is perfect? I, um..." My tongue is caught because he's staring at me more intensely. "...you."

I shut my mouth, inhaling a deeper breath.

Thatcher nods and eyes my facemask, not looking below my neck. He casts a furtive glance at my cousins.

They can't know we're intimate.

Yet, how much time do we even have left?

"Heyhey, Thatcher," Luna says. "You should stay."

"Yeah," Sulli agrees. "Why don't you join the facemask party?"

Luna nods. "Yeah yeah, Insta Live it for the fake dating thing."

He can't see my cousins. But they are both grinning like they've discovered fairy dust and fountains of eternal youth. Between this and the Seasons name, I'm beginning to think Sul and Luna are like two impish pixies.

I'm all here for it. Sitting straighter, a smile tugging my cheeks. Seeing Thatcher in a green facemask is something I didn't know I needed until right now.

"Do you want to?" I ask Thatcher.

He stares at me and nods. But he still adds, "If you think it'll help with the fake dating op." It's a cursory statement. Like he knows he has to say it in front of my cousins. I do believe he'd want to do this with me regardless of the fake dating ruse.

Like drinking whiskey in the garage.

"It should help." I grab the bottle of facemask, and Thatcher sits down on an alien beanbag.

"I'll film," Luna says, using her phone and Instagram account since mine is still deactivated.

I straddle Thatcher's lap. It's easiest instead of bending down. His hands fall to my hips, easy and comfortable. Yet tension winds between us. Like we're both caging our breaths.

There are two factors at play.

One: our Instagram viewers think this is real.

Two: Sulli and Luna think this is all fake.

I know this is real. Every touch has been real since we had sex at the B&B. I'm certain of that. But as we get closer and closer to Halloween, the end is near. I wish I could just…push it out of my mind.

But it's there.

Present. Like the worst kind of ticking clock.

Silence blankets the room as I rub Thatcher's skin with a cleansing cloth. This could be the last time I touch him…

My stomach knots.

Enjoy it then.

I will.

I uncap the green cream. One dollop on my finger, I smear the green facemask down his nose like sunblock. My lips lift. "Mr. Moretti, I do say, you are quite handsome."

He doesn't reply, quiet as usual. But his palm slides underneath the hem of my shirt. His skin is warm against my skin, and his hand trails to the small of my back. Goosebumps prick my flesh. Cold and hot all at once.

I rub the mask on his cheekbones and forehead. My fingers trace every curve of his face, and it feels like one of the most intimate things we've ever done together.

His eyes fall into me like the video isn't live recording behind me. Like the world is so far, far away. I lean in. He leans in. Our lips meet briefly. Suddenly. Like they were drawn together from the start.

We break apart just as quick. Heat compiling, but we can't create a firestorm here.

I glance over my shoulder. Luna holds up a finger. "And—we're off live."

Sulli's brows are sky high. "Fuck, are you two going for an Emmy or something?"

Luna beams like she's witnessing something extraterrestrial. "Spring and fall are rising."

More accurately, those seasons can't rise together.

Fall rises when spring ends.

40

 THATCHER MORETTI

"Wait." Jane breathes against my neck. "Do you hear something?"

I stop thrusting up into her, my senses still sharp despite Jane sitting on my cock. Despite our skin slick with sweat, limbs rubbing and intertwined. She pauses grinding and moving up and down on me.

I'm leaning against the headboard of her four-poster bed. My hand lost in her brown hair, my other palm keeps her pressed against me protectively.

If need be, I'd be able to carry her out of her room in a swift second. No hesitation. No faltering.

My voice is a cavernous whisper. "Carpenter knocked a headband off the vanity."

She has her back to the calico cat, perched proudly on the surface. The *feline* audience is necessary. Or else they'll cry at her door.

I sense Jane focused on my eyes that sweep her room. Assessing. Landing on each cat.

Walrus is stalking a shadow from moonlight. Licorice is peeking out from the closet. Lady Macbeth sleeps like an old queen on the cushioned stool.

And Ophelia is at the *foot* of the bed. Curled up watching me fuck her owner. We've shooed her off the mattress four times already.

I focus directly on Jane. "All clear."

Desire wells up in her eyes. "Thatcher."

My pulse thumps. I cup her warm face, her pink lips unable to press together. In a permanent pant, and my cock throbs for friction while deep inside her tight heat.

In my peripheral, I catch the glint of light under the door.

Shadow passing by. A nearly inaudible *creak*.

Jane turns her head.

"It's Toodles," I whisper. The laziest cat sometimes camps out on the second-floor landing at night.

Jane eases, focusing on each other.

She holds my hard jaw in two delicate hands, our foreheads pressing. Looking into one another. Breath scorching my lungs. A power surge flames my nerve-endings.

I bring her closer on instinct. Our lips meshing, rampaging carnal needs, and I rock my hips up. She whimpers softly into the kiss.

My muscles contract. Every part of Jane feels fucking *amazing* against me. Hands. Thighs. Pussy.

She curls her arm around my neck. Rising higher to intensify the kiss, and my erection slides further out of her warmth.

I plunge my tongue between her lips. She trembles and searches my mouth with hers.

I flex up into Jane. Cock burying back into her.

She nestles her face in the crook of my shoulder. Smothering her gasps, but I feel them hot against my skin. Pressure fists me as I pump in slow waves—*fuuck*.

Fuck.

I brush her sweaty hair off her neck and suck her nape. Her hips bow forward. Grinding, her breasts smashed against my sculpted chest. As close as physically fucking possible.

She clenches around me.

Goddamn. My head spins. Oxygen ejecting, and I breathe hotter breath through my nose. Gritting down to keep from grunting.

Jane looks back, her eyes melting in pleasure while I thrust up and back down. Tonight has been one of the longest, most intense fucks of my life.

Slow and quiet. Passionate, exhausting in the best endurance-challenging way. I don't remember when we started. I can't tell when we're going to stop.

As I push back into her, she reaches down, and I watch her touch her swollen clit. "*Fuck*," I grunt under my breath.

She contracts around me again—and Jane lifts her glistening fingers, her shimmering eyes on me. I know what she wants.

I clutch her wrist, and I guide her hand closer to my mouth. She smiles, and as she slides her fingers between my lips, I taste her against my tongue.

Gripping her wrist tight, I suck her fingers.

She crumbles to pieces, her body shuddering in silent waves. Her head against my chest. I wrap a strong arm around her back. Tucking her in close to me. I take her fingers out of my mouth and thrust deeper.

I barely hear her muffled words.

"Right there," she moans. "*Don't stop. Please, please.*"

I quicken my pace. Sweat dripping down my temples.

Jane keeps moving her hips until she can't any longer. A prisoner to her own pleasure that ripples through her body. *Fuckfuckfuck.* I press my forehead on the top of her head. *Don't come.*

Don't come

Not fucking yet.

My cock screams at me for release. But I breathe harder through my nose, controlling myself. She comes down, stilling, and I lift her hips and gently pull out of Jane. We don't shift a lot. She's on my lap. But my rock-solid cock stands at attention against her belly.

Jane inhales at the sight.

I'm about to change positions. But her fingers graze my shaft, and my chest collapses, shoulders tensed against the headboard.

Our eyes flit to each other, then to our bodies.

"Can you…?" Jane whispers, breathless.

I grip and tug my cock. What she wants to see. My large hand stroking my need. I hold the back of her head.

Jane watches, open-mouthed, her arousal building back up. Her eyes glimmer and she toys with my balls—my breath knots.

Christ. We kiss deeper, more urgently, and I can't jack off anymore. Swiftly, I hoist her up, and she sinks back down on me.

Pressure overwhelming me again.

I thrust up. Careful with each pump, watching her reaction, and then I create more friction. *Faster.* More heat. *Deeper.* I shelter her high-pitched moans against my palm.

Quiet.

She kisses my palm and then licks it. A groan scratches my throat. Lights blink in my vision. I'm holding my breath.

My muscles stretch beyond fucking taut. Pulled into a raw visceral place. Our eyes embrace, clinging. I never turn away from Jane. Never look away, passion overgrown, and she cries out against my hand. Her body vibrating all over again.

God.

I push up. And erupt, releasing hard into an explosion of emotion. My chest rises and falls heavily.

We both come down, and as I pull out and we naturally shift to our sides under her pink sheets, I hold Jane and feel her heartbeat slow against my chest.

Her eyes flutter closed.

Exhaustion tries to sink me too. I'm almost there. *You can't spend the night.* I should leave now, but heaviness and the warmth of her body draws me in.

I don't want to disturb her. *Not yet.* She's sleeping peacefully. Safe and content.

I shut my eyes, and the world goes dark.

Radio static fills my ears. "Phantom Two One, this is Phantom Two Actual. Maintain speed."

"This is Phantom Two One. Roger that."

Humvees on gravel and dirt mix with the static. "Viper Two Two, cleared hot."

I wake.

Eyes snapped open. I'm covered in sweat. My head pounds.

Jane sleeps soundlessly next to me, her freckled cheek on my bicep. I check the clock. Zero four hundred hours. *Unholy shit.* I overslept.

I needed to leave an hour ago. I carefully shift my arm out from under Jane. Lifting the sheet and blankets higher on her bare, beautiful body.

I stand off the bed. Cats greeting me, all five rubbing up against my calves while I find my clothes, as quietly as I can.

I move in systematic order. Boxer-briefs on, black slacks on—I pull a black crewneck over my head, and then I grab my radio, holster my gun to my waistband.

And I find her sticky pad on the end table. About to jot down a quick note, but I notice her illegible handwriting. I trained myself to decipher it when I was a lead.

I read the words clearly.

Merci mille fois Pour tout.

xoxo *Jane*

She knows I can translate simple French phrases. She wrote: *Thank you a thousand times. For everything.*

My lungs expand. I tear her note off the pad. Pocketing it, and then I write on the top blank one.

ITS MY HONOR TO BE WITH YOU IN EVERYTHING.

I place the note on the pillow next to her. And I'm at the door in two strides. I look back. Checking on my client, she breathes contently.

I grip the doorknob. I fucking hate this part.

Leaving Jane after we had sex.

At the beginning, it was hard. Now it's excruciating. The reality is, I've never been a frat-bro and she's never been a quick meaningless fuck to me.

What happened last night deserves a morning. Where she wakes up in my arms.

But that's not part of the agreement.

I've already *accidentally* pushed a fucking hour. And right now, my head is killing me. I rub at my eyes, static still in my ear. But my radio isn't on.

Fuck me.

I slip out of the room. No lights on. Toodles, her sixth cat, lounges sluggishly by the bathroom.

With my long legs, I skip two stairs at a time. Bypassing ones that I know squeak. Silent as I descend.

I reach the living room. Dark—but soft light illuminates from the kitchen archway. I pick up sound in that direction.

Someone is awake.

I strain my ears…

And I hear Farrow. Contempt in his rough voice, and it takes a hell of a lot to push his buttons. *I would know.*

Concern drives me toward his location, and I listen to his angered whisper.

"I'm not bartering with you…" A pause is taken. "You worthless bastard… Is that a threat? Yeah?"

Instinct pushes me through the archway.

I see Farrow with a phone to his ear, elbows on the counter. Hunched forward in a lunge. He sees me, surprise flashing in his heated eyes. But he doesn't stiffen or move a muscle.

He cuts his gaze forward. "You're in prison, you motherfucker. This call is recorded."

Prison.

Donnelly's dad or mom could be on the line. His dad is supposed to be released from prison soon, and I only ever considered that intel in terms of *Donnelly's* wellbeing. But if he's threating Farrow from prison...

My brows pull together, and then a sharp ringing pierces my head—I touch my ear. My heart rate spikes.

Fuck this.

I walk tensely to the sink. Turn on the faucet and splash water on my face.

Farrow watches my movements. Still talking on the phone. "No. Never..." His jaw muscle tics, and then he hangs up.

I rub water off my eyes. "Was that Sean Donnelly?" I name Donnelly's dad.

"Yeah." Farrow leans his side casually on the counter. Just in drawstring pants, tattoos scatter his chest, ribs, arms, and neck. He's assessing me as much as I'm looking at him.

I grip the sink's ledge. "Is he going to be a problem?"

Farrow eyes me up and down. "I'll let you know when I know."

He's not sure yet. I nod once. And I splash more water on my face before shutting off the faucet. My heart rate is starting to slow. I dry off my forehead and jaw using the hem of my shirt.

Farrow goes to the fridge and tugs a water bottle out of the door. He extends the drink to me. Like I once tried to do for him in Greece.

I take the water and nod in thanks.

"What helps you?" Farrow asks me, vague. We've been vague about PTSD.

"Water on my face should be enough." I unscrew the bottle. "You said yours is triggered by rain?"

He kicks back against the closed fridge. "Yeah, but it's been better." He pauses. "Is yours frequent?"

"No." I swig the water, coolness rushing down my throat. "I haven't had a nightmare in a while."

"It kicked your ass awake?"

I meet his eyes. "Like a hammer to the skull."

He nods a few times.

We exchange this look that reaches into me. Acknowledgement. An *I understand you* and *I'm here.* Something that I've never shared with Farrow face-to-face.

SFO is a brotherhood. More than any other force.

After hurting him, I've wanted to be deserving of it. Can't say that I am, can't say that I'll ever be—but I won't retreat.

I hold his gaze. "I stuck a fucking thorn in your side."

"No, you were the thorn," he says matter-of-factly. "And being honest, I didn't know what Jane saw in you. I didn't think you'd *ever* break a rule to give her what she wants and needs, and the fact that you did—it makes you someone I don't mind hanging around."

I nod slowly, realizing this fucking whole time, he would've appreciated me *breaking* the "don't fuck your client" rule. For Jane.

I cap the water bottle, my eyes narrowed at the reality. With the looming breakup, it'll all reverse. Like I never broke the rule to begin with.

Farrow checks the oven clock. "And you broke her little 3 a.m. get-the-fuck-out rule."

"*Accidental.*" I set the water bottle on the counter. "Don't go buying me a fucking round."

"Man, you don't have to worry that I will." He pushes away from the fridge. "I only buy rounds for broken hearts."

I open my mouth to speak—a *crash* thunders from upstairs. Shaking the kitchen. Like a body just hit the ground. We don't wait for the vibrating to stop.

We bolt. As fast as our fucking feet can carry us. Concern detonating a strong force inside of me. Fear hyper-focuses me. Four souls upstairs. Jane, Sulli, Luna, Maximoff.

Jane.

Jane.

We don't call out to them.

In case someone broke in without setting off the alarms, we *can't* yell their fucking names and give our positions away. We're already risking being heard as we race up the old stairs. I'm out in front of Farrow.

Adrenaline pitching my pulse. Her name is a scream caged inside me.

Maximoff is running down the stairs from the attic. Towards the second-floor. Where the girls are.

We come up to the landing, just as Jane's door opens and she steps out, cautious. "Thatcher?" Her eyes widen, scared for her cousins.

I act fast. Clutching her waist, I pull Jane further out of the room. Behind my back, and Farrow goes straight to Luna and Sulli's door. He kicks it open.

"Whoa, *fuck*," Sulli curses from inside.

By her surprised tone, I can already tell this is a false alarm. But we need to check her room regardless.

Protocol: *Jane can't come in until it's all-clear*. Neither can Maximoff.

It's hard to leave her. My chest knots. "Wait here until I call you," I tell her strictly. *She's safe*.

"I will—"

Our heads turn as Sulli suddenly fills the doorway, yanking earbuds out, drenched in sweat. "Uh, guys…is this about the fucking *bang* because that was me. I'm so fucking sorry." She wipes her forehead with her toned bicep. "I was doing deadlifts and dropped the bar too hard. Luna slept through the noise, so I didn't think anything of it."

"It's okay," Maximoff says.

Jane lets out a deeper breath. "We're just glad you're safe." Her gaze pins back to me, and our eyes lock. Thoughts and feelings tumble between us. But we're quiet. Even with Maximoff and Farrow knowing our secret, Luna and Sulli are still in the dark. It's a reminder that we still have to be careful. Can't get too comfortable.

But she is right—at least everyone is safe.

Especially her.

41

JANE COBALT

I knew I'd be nervous when this day finally came. But I didn't know I'd have a swarm of caterpillars crawling around my stomach. So naturally, I called in reinforcements.

"Oooh, I like this one." Aunt Daisy playfully waves a cheetah print vest.

"Or this one." Aunt Lily scoots out from the bottom of my closet with a tulle mint-green skirt.

And ladies and gentlemen, behind me is a sword, a cannon blast, a shoulder to cry on, a stroke of hope—my mom.

In a form-fitting black dress, long matte black nails, and dark rouge lipstick, Rose Calloway Cobalt stands pin-straight, her posture stiff and rigid. And cold. But she wields such deep love for me in her piercing yellow-green eyes.

I watch her through my vanity mirror. She curls my hair. Methodical and slow, but she snaps the curling iron at her sisters. "Don't confuse her."

It is all very confusing.

I'm about to meet Thatcher's *entire* family. His mom, stepmom, cousins, uncles, and aunts. The only person missing in action will be his dad.

Pressure is a creature I know good and well, but I find myself caring about how his family perceives me, most of all.

I glance between the skirt and vest. "I like them both, really. They'd look perfectly un-matching together." Which is what I love best.

"Wow, we're like stylists," Daisy says, giving Lily a silly grin and wagging her brows.

Lily takes a sip from a can of Diet Fizz. "Must be why I'm wearing…" She has to look down to remember what she's dressed in today. "Leggings and…" She frowns as she inspects the Spider-Man T-shirt. "Uh, I think this is Lo's? Everything gets mixed up in the wash."

"So true." Daisy plucks a cat-ear headband off my mirror and places it atop her head. Blonde hair chopped bluntly a little below her shoulders. She smiles at me, radiant like the sun.

My cheeks always hurt when I'm around all of them. But I've smiled far less today. Pressure keeps sinking my stomach.

My mom finishes my hair. "You're done, gremlin."

All three women turn to look at me as I stand and approach my closet door's full-length mirror.

Brown waves cascade on my collarbones, frizz successfully combatted. More presentable for a meet-the-parents dinner. This is my best foot forward.

I untie my cotton robe, a little hot all of a sudden. "What if I'm so awfully verbose and I annoy them?"

My mom snaps a glare at me through the mirror. "You're not too verbose. Your words are an asset." She speaks like it's written in stone and blood and all indelible things. "And if they don't like you, then that says more about them than you."

I love that she doesn't tell me they *will* love me and give me a false sense of confidence. She lays battle armor on my shoulders.

Sometimes I feel as though I'm the daughter of Joan of Arc. Ready for war.

I try to take a breath. Another insecurity rises. "What if they hate me?" A good portion of the world does, and I catch all three sisters glancing cautiously at each other.

I spin on my heels. "I recognize that I'm only fake dating Thatcher— it's not serious between us." *Do I sound defensive?*

My eyes bug.

I keep going. "We will break up soon. *We will.* It is in the stars." My collarbones protrude, my eyes burn. "But his family is special to him, and he's my bodyguard. I'd rather them *not* hate me."

"If they judge you that harshly after *one* meal, you don't want to be loved by them," my mom retorts.

Lily nods repeatedly. "What Rose said."

Daisy looks at my mom. "Didn't you throw *wine* on your mother-in-law's blouse when you first met her?"

My lips rise, remembering this story.

My mom sighs at the memory, then flips her hair off her shoulder. "And I prevailed."

"See," Daisy smiles at me. "You could throw wine on someone, and all could end miraculously."

I breathe in their encouragements the best I can.

"How are you doing with the fake dating thing?" Lily asks. All of them thought the ploy was a good idea.

I remember the notes he's been leaving me, and I smile. "It's worked rather well."

My mom crosses her arms. "Security told me it's dispelled some potential stalkers."

"It has."

Only a handful remain. Thatcher and the rest of security are taking care of them.

"So it was worth it then?" Daisy asks, adjusting the cat ears. "Fake dating your bodyguard?"

I picture all the nights we've spent together. "Yes, I'd say so." I sound more morose than I intend.

Lily frowns deeply. "You know, you don't have to go meet his family. If it'd be easier, you could just come up with an excuse."

"Like a cold or 24-hour flu," Daisy offers.

That thought sends a wave of knives into my stomach. "Why would that be easier?" I take the skirt and vest from their hands.

"Because," my mom says icily, "you're going to be lying to them. All of them."

I'm going to be lying to his family.

To their faces. None of them think this is a *fake* relationship. His family believes we're really together.

I understand now. My aunts and my mom are concerned about me. They want to protect me from this deception. In truth, I haven't felt like I was going over there to lie or fabricate some story.

I haven't been nervous about that.

I'm just nervous they won't like me.

And I'm already lying to the people in front of me. The ones I love most. Who have no idea that I've been intimate with my bodyguard.

But I'm not alone in this. Thatcher and I are ensnared, and that has a comfort all its own.

I force out the words, "I want to go. Even if it's hard."

42

 THATCHER MORETTI

"*Ah, you buncha loud mouths. Statazitt! I'm* tryin' to make a toast here." One of my uncles raises his brash voice above the other fucking brash voices.

Songs by Lou Monte play right on top of that. "Hey Gumbaree" blaring at the current moment.

It's all an Italian earful. And it's home.

Sunday family dinner is a weekly gathering at my Uncle Joe's row house. Braggiol' already eaten, dishes cleared—after the meal, the women stay clustered around the table drinking coffee and eating cream pie.

Jane is in sight while I hang around the kitchen with Banks and the other men. More wine bottles being uncorked and poured. But my gaze is gripped on *her*.

How she laughs with the women, talks breezily and bows toward every person at the dining table. Making all of them feel like they're her sole focus.

Those women are deserving of her gaze.

And Jane doesn't realize just how much she can make people feel *loved* in a single glance. My mom has a hand on Jane's arm while they talk into brighter laughter.

My grandma's rosy cheeks are in a perpetual smile, and Nicola, my stepmom, sees me watching and mouths, *we love her.*

I thought she'd fit in, but seeing it happen is something else. *Surreal.* Overwhelming. Conflicting—because I shouldn't be emotionally invested in this picture.

It's supposed to only happen one time. *One fucking time.*

That's all we get.

My mom catches my gaze and shoos me with the swat of her hand. Her words are inaudible from the ear-splitting commotion around me. But I read her lips: *Go, go.*

I rotate. Just slightly. Standing near the coffee pot, Banks and I still tower but not as much here. Most men are tall and in occupations that require us to stay fit. Bodies built.

Multiple conversations are happening at once, and I tune into the closest one. Talking about car trackers. They think paparazzi bugged my mom's vehicle.

"How else could they've known she'd be at the bank?"

Guilt tries to ride me like a fucking buck-toothed hitchhiker. *Don't let it.* I knew the risks of going public.

I cut in, "Paparazzi probably followed her from the shop. Her job is public information." My mom used to be a bookkeeper at an auto mechanic shop. Until they finally let her, a woman, work as a mechanic.

"Are we sure?" Uncle Joe asks.

Banks fists a beer. "I already checked her vehicle. I didn't find anything."

The louder voices overtake our talk. We turn our heads.

"Youse been making toasts all fuckin' night."

"I don't see you making any."

"Because youse been doin' 'em all!"

"Statazitt'!" many guys yell, telling them to *shut up.*

The corners of my mouth almost rise. My phone buzzes in my back pocket. I uncross my arms and grab my cell.

One of my uncles squeezes through and clamps a hand on my shoulder. "Why aren't youse drinking? Your girl brought over an expensive bottle of wine." *Plus flowers for my mom, stepmom, and grandma.*

My grandma pinched Jane's cheeks and hugged her for a full minute, and I'm sure it'll be longer when we leave.

Banks answers, "He doesn't want to drink for a while."

"For the job," I add. *For her protection.* I unlock my phone and read a text from the Alpha lead—my stern demeanor darkens. Eyes narrowing like barrels of a gun.

> We have an official breakup date. Op ends the day after Halloween. The reason will be she didn't get along with your family. Leave the dinner in separate vehicles. Farrow is picking her up. — Price

They want me to put my family on fucking blast in the media. To be a fucking *scapegoat* in order to end the fake dating op.

No.

Hell no.

I rake my hand across my hardened jaw. Hardly blinking. Just cussing a hundred times over in my head. Until my brain is fucking overloaded with *fucks* and goddammits and mannaggias.

I text back: using my family as the reason for the breakup will endanger them.

He responds fast.

> We've discussed this with a publicist. They said it's minimal blowback. Your family will be safe. — Price

I'm yelling at the top of my lungs internally. But really I'm stoic. Painfully still. Silent. Veins bulge in my tensed neck.

Banks comes close, ripping my phone out of my fist.

He reads the text.

I lower my voice so only he can hear. "They fucked me." My nose flares. "Or maybe I fucked me." I'm the one who made the request to bring Jane to meet my family. Full well knowing it'd be for the op.

A public ploy. Paparazzi asked Jane where she was going before we left. She said, "To meet my boyfriend's family."

I just never imagined security would push further and use this for the breakup.

I have to tell Jane.

This is going to hurt her—and I don't want to follow through with this fucking order. For too many reasons.

Banks is pissed. Less pissed than me, but still fucking pissed. "They couldn't have told us at the last meeting before you brought her here?"

It feels like Price and Sinclair are punishing me. Akara couldn't have known. He warned me that he had a bad feeling and that those two were leaving him out of some discussions.

My family here can sense that I'm upset. The men start looking over in concern, and Uncle Joe is the one who approaches.

Banks slips my phone in my pocket and backs up. Uncle Joe puts an arm around my strict shoulders. He's the only one as tall as us.

His hoarse voice is consoling as he says, "Whadda you so angry about, huh?"

Losing her. This way. I shake my head, the movement stiff and short.

He cups the side of my face. "Fuhgeddabout it. Come have a drink."

I take a shot with my uncles, and after many pats on my shoulder, I push out of the kitchen and into the dining room.

I hang in the archway, not interrupting my rosy-cheeked grandma who's in the middle of a story for Jane. One about how her mom immigrated to America alone at twelve-years-old.

"...she sewed jewelry into her panties so no one would steal 'em, and she had to wear the same pair from Italy all the way to Ellis Island." Italy sounds like *it-ly*.

All the women smile and laugh. Jane has her chin on her knuckles, enrapt. As soon as she sees my hardened expression, her face begins to fall and her arm drops to the table.

My mom frowns at me. "What's wrong?"

"We need to leave soon," I announce, and I come around to Jane's chair next to my mom.

I bend down behind Jane, curving my arm over her collarbones, and I whisper against her ear, "Farrow is going to pick you up and take you home."

"What?" Her voice pitches.

Staying behind her, I cup my phone in front of Jane. Letting her read the text. Careful not to angle the screen. Only Jane can see.

I press my lips to the top of her head in a kiss. She reads quickly. I feel her breastbone collapse beneath my forearm.

"Confirm," I whisper, pocketing my phone.

She tilts her head back to meet my eyes. I clasp her soft cheek, my large hand almost engulfing her. Jane blinks back pained emotion, inhaling a breath in preparation for what needs to be done. "Yes," she whispers. "I understand."

We've been pretending that she's an ordinary girl coming to break bread with my family. But she's an American princess who is internationally recognizable.

I'm her bodyguard.

That hasn't changed. It can't change.

Her safety comes first.

But for Jane, I'm positive she's agreeing to this order just to protect my career.

I straighten to a stance, my hands on her shoulders, and Jane looks forward again.

My mom places a hand on Jane's. "Everything alright with your family?"

"You can't ask her that," an aunt snaps. "The Cobalts are *celebrities*, Gloria."

"You think I'm dumb? I know whatta celebrity is." My mom clutches Jane's arm. "This is my son's girlfriend." My mom smiles up at me, almost teasingly.

Mustering cheerfulness, Jane manages to say, "My family is well. I'm just sad I have to go so soon."

My mom nods. "Come back around. We'll take you to Sunday mass before the next dinner." We all go to an LGBT-friendly Catholic church and consider ourselves cafeteria Catholics: practicing, but we dissent from less progressive teachings.

I cut in, "We're busy next Sunday, ma, and you haven't gone to mass since Easter."

Everyone laughs.

My mom makes a face at me, a smile creeping. "Busy with what—?" Her voice is cut off as loud commotion comes from the front door.

A target.

I'm about to move toward the noise. But I hear the boastful laugh of Tony Ramella—and there's no chance in any fucking hell that I'm leaving Jane's side.

I can't be surprised that Tony is here. Three surnames dominate the house: Moretti, Piscitelli—sometimes changed to Fish, depending on whose ancestors had to Americanize their name to get jobs—and lastly, *Ramella*.

My grandma reaches out to Jane, clasping her hand. "Youse already met my cumare?"

Jane wracks her brain for *cumare*. I can't remember if I mentioned that Italian word. It means a friend who's a girl.

I'm about to help Jane, but realization strikes her fast. "Michelina? Yes, we've met; she's quite wonderful." Jane goes on, talking more, and my grandma is beaming the whole time. She smiles from me to Jane, back to me.

We need to leave. I can't stand here and do this much longer. Not in front of these women, and Jane is having a harder time too.

I'm about to excuse us, but then Michelina shuffles into the dining room with Tony. *Goddammit.*

My aunts, cousins, and moms stand up to hug and kiss them.

Jane rises to her feet too, and I wrap a protective arm around her hips. I watch Tony snatch a bottle of whiskey off the table. Everyone had been drinking whiskey with black coffee.

He spreads his arms out to me. "Aren't you going to give your uncle a hug?"

I want to give him a right hook to the jaw. My glare intensifies. We're both twenty-eight, and un-*fucking*-fortunately, he is actually my uncle.

On paper. Not by blood.

His older sister is Nicola Ramella, my stepmom who has a heart of gold. Tony and Nicola have a large age gap for siblings.

I already told Jane my relation to him, and how my mom and Nicola were in the same grade at Saint Joseph's. They used to date before my mom got with my dad. And they reconnected at a high school reunion, fell back in love, and married.

Tony drops his arms. "No?" This fucking tool winks at Jane. "What about you, sweetheart?"

I step out in front of Jane, my eyes lethal, and all the women yell at the men to come separate us.

"Antonio!" Uncle Joe calls to Tony. "Get your ass in here."

I'm being told to go talk to my grandma before I leave. I check back on Jane before I do. "You good?"

"Yes. You?"

I nod. "Has Farrow texted you?"

She softens her voice. "He has. He's with Moffy. They'll be here in five minutes."

I kiss her temple before I draw away, our hands stay clasped until the very last second that our fingers have to pull apart.

I approach my grandma at the table. Short gray hair, petite, wrinkles and age spots blemishing her frail skin—her eyes already fill with tears seeing that I'm about to go.

I take a knee in front of her chair and kiss her cheek. Whispering, "I wish we could stay longer with you."

My grandma places a loving hand against my jaw, cradling my face. "You put too much on yourself, you hear? There's only one thing you need to remember. Just one." She brings my face closer to hers. "Be happy."

43

JANE COBALT

My dad is practically a lie detector.

It has made every Wednesday night family dinner tense. For me.
The one who is holstering a giant secret. There are only so many times
a girl can pretend she *isn't* sleeping with her bodyguard before all the
beans are spilled. And there will be no spilling of any beans.

Which is why I've come prepared tonight.

To conceal my facial expressions, I wear a silver Venetian mask,
cheap and plastic. I even haphazardly hot-glued feathers to the edge.
Costumes are typical, so it won't draw suspicion.

Dinner will formally begin when my parents arrive. Two velveteen
chairs wait for them.

All six of my siblings are already seated at the elegant, ornately-carved
dining table, the surface stuffed for a feast. Roasted goose emits a familiar
and savory aroma, surrounded by platters of cranberries, green beans,
and potatoes. A vegan roast made from seitan sits at Ben's end.

The menu never changes. When I was little, I'd grow sick of the
meal. But now, I crave it.

"Jane, wearing a mask to dinner," Eliot says, a wry smile playing at
his lips. He's dressed in an English vintage suit: black-fitted tailcoat and
white chin-high dress shirt with a blood-red cravat tied at the neck. As
fashionably theatric as he is.

I notice how all my brothers and sister fixate on my mask now.

My back is painfully straight. And I wait for Eliot to say something else.

But he's stopped speaking and lights his pipe. We all have the pleasure of watching him blow smoke rings in the air.

I take an encouraging breath. I'm not a toothless lion, even when it comes to my younger brothers who love to tease me mercilessly.

"Is that all?" I ask Eliot. "You're just making a stray observation? Did you notice how Charlie is shirtless then?"

Charlie tilts his head at me, a cigarette burning between two fingers. He wears nothing more than thousand-dollar suit pants and a chic black-diamond-encrusted harness hooked around his shoulders.

He always comes to dinner as he pleases. A grin lifts his lip. "I am who I am, and that is not you."

Pithy and pointed.

My cheeks pull in a smile. "I wouldn't want you to be me, nor I you."

Charlie raises his goblet in cheers, but he seems to stare through my mask. My lips slowly fall. He acts like he can see far into me and my deceits and intentions.

I sweat beneath my armpits. *It's just a trick of the mind, Jane.* A chess move. Charlie can't know anything at all.

"Well, I think Jane's mask is positively lovely," Audrey says beside me, her voice extra whimsical on Wednesday night. We all somehow become our most dramatic selves during this dinner.

"Thank you, Audrey." I clink my goblet to hers. Just water in mine. I'm too nervous to drink. I must stay sharp.

Tom grins, more devilish with half his face painted like a skeleton. He wraps an arm around Eliot's chair. "I think it's hands-down the *ugliest* thing I've ever seen."

We all laugh.

Eliot passes Tom the pipe, and Ben refills his glass with water, wearing a blue-gray shirt with simple font that says *because there is no planet B.*

He's only sixteen, and it's strange to think how Ben and Audrey have had more empty dinners than the rest of us. I can't remember the last time we were all under one roof on a Wednesday night.

Now that some of us are older and moved out, it's more difficult to get together. Even when we all can't make it, those two are here, still at home. The youngest of the brood.

But we do make it a point to try our hardest to be back these nights. No one wishes to miss a Wednesday dinner.

Beckett has graced this table the least. Usually, he has rehearsals or a show. Right now, he reaches for a goblet of wine, his honest eyes pinned to me. "Will you try to narrate another audiobook, sis?"

"No." I fold my hands on my lap. "After my failure, I believe it's not where I should be."

"Fate decrees it so," Audrey says, fixing a bonnet atop her carrot-orange hair. Fresh flowers tucked to the hat with blush ribbon.

"Precisely. Fate says I should find work elsewhere." I ramble on. "And with my life so upside down and sideways with the fake dating ruse, I've given myself a new deadline. I will find a suitable career after the holidays."

Eliot is about to respond, but the familiar sound of heels clicking on floor breaks our attention.

Our heads swerve nearly in unison at the doorway.

Poised and unflappable, our mom and dad push inside with purpose and determination. Each in their finest formal outfits. Black dress and tailored suit, respectively.

Our dad takes one head of the table.

"I apologize, my beautiful gremlins," my mom says, reaching the head nearest me. "For being five minutes late you all may—" She stops short, finally noticing the table. Her eyes go wide and her red lips part in shock.

No one told her that Beckett would be here tonight. And I know she's mentally counting each chair. How they're all filled with each of her children.

She fights tears, eyes reddened, and her hands brace the top of the chair, still standing. "What are you doing here?" she asks Beckett. "I thought you had a performance."

"Power outage at the theatre," Beckett says. "Tonight's was cancelled." Wearing a simple leather jacket and white T-shirt, he pushes back his chair and stands to hug her.

She's notorious for iron-stiff, but loving, hugs. When they break apart, she touches a tear in the crease of her eye.

Beckett gives our dad a hug before returning to his seat.

My mom shoots my dad a deadly look. "Did you know, Richard?" She often uses his first name in battle: *Richard* Connor Cobalt.

His grin burgeons. All-knowing. And his blue eyes flit to me, just briefly.

Enough to toss my stomach.

My dad cocks his head to my mom. "The power outage was in the news, darling."

She rolls her eyes, trying not to smile at him, and then she looks to all of us. "What a wonderful surprise, and I will excuse all of your chicanery this once." To our dad, she says, "Yours, *never*. You trick me, Richard, and I will roast your heart on an open fire."

His grin only grows. "My heart is yours to do with as you please."

"Stab it." She picks up a steak knife. "Roast it. *Eat* it."

My siblings explode in applause, drumming their feet to the floor. Palms to the table, the room beginning to rumble.

I pat my thighs, a peculiar feeling sinking inside me as I watch and look around at my dramatic family.

My smile flickers in and out.

And I wonder...

What would it feel like for Thatcher to be at the table next to me? There's never been harm in just imagining, but the more I do, the more my stomach descends and my head droops.

He's my bodyguard.

That's all he'll be soon—no fake boyfriend, no late-night sex—and I have no need for security when I'm at my childhood home in a gated neighborhood.

No need for him.

It hurts to think.

So I won't think it. I won't feel it.

"To eat my heart," my dad says smoothly, "is to have me with you always."

Thunderous noise escalates.

"Incorrect." She zeroes in on him. "It is cannibalism. It is murder."

"You love me," he declares, his eyes fixed to hers in victory and affection.

Usually, she'll deny. Tonight, my mom lifts her chin and restrains a smile.

She turns to the rest of us and taps her goblet with the knife. "As with every Wednesday, it is what you make it."

"And someone will win," my dad adds.

Someone will win. Most faces teem with some sort of excitement. I hope mine appears the same, but if not, the mask should do.

Every Wednesday night…it's not just a dinner. The second half is a trivia game. Sometimes, depending on the night, we'll even have different rules. Once only French was allowed at the dinner table, no one speaking a single word of English. Another Wednesday night, all cursing was banned and if someone slipped, they had to put money in a goblet—which would later be delivered to Uncle Ryke.

Tonight, as far as I know, is more of a traditional Wednesday night dinner. No new rules.

"Opening remarks have commenced," my mom announces, lowering in unison with my dad onto the velveteen chairs.

This time is occupied for us to share our lives. Or not. It's up to each person.

I intake a breath. Ignoring the sinking pit.

Eliot grabs the moment first. He almost always does. Rising to his feet, climbing onto his chair—and like an orchestrated play, we all reach for our goblets. Eliot pounds his boot to the lip of the table.

Rattling the dishes.

He bows forward, elbow to his knee. "I'd like to talk of deception."

I frown behind my mask. My heart quickening. Eliot will most often quote a play and use up his time with someone else's words.

His intense gaze sweeps the table. "To be able to deceive…" He looks directly at me for an extended beat. Emotion bleeding through his eyes. "You need to know where the lie is at all times. So as not to deceive yourself."

I sip my water, hand frozen on my goblet.

"Was that *Macbeth*?" Ben asks.

"No," everyone says.

Eliot stands up further onto the table, the surface quaking. "It was an Eliot Alice Cobalt original. This is Macbeth." He takes a puff from the pipe. "'Away!'" His blue eyes pulse with raw feeling. "'False face must hide what the false heart doth know.'"

Breath traps in my lungs as those words pool into me.

Tom snaps his fingers.

Possibly, his speech was all coincidence and I'm suffering from severe paranoia.

Eliot takes a single step backward, not even looking. His boot lands on the cushion of his seat and he sits down on the top frame.

All the while, Tom grips the chair so it won't tip over.

Eliot has broken many chairs throughout our childhood. He's a six-four strong-built nineteen-year-old. And right now, he roots his gaze on me.

I don't turn away. "Do you wish to ask me something?"

"No, dear sister." He looks to Tom. "Dear brother."

"Dear brother." Tom quickly rises and stands triumphantly on a chair. He often talks of music and issues in his band. I'm waiting for him to mention a recent dilemma. How his drummer has quit, right before The Carraways were recording an EP.

Tom hoists his goblet of liquor. "Fear."

I breathe harder. They can't be speaking to me.

He scans the table like Eliot had done. "The feeling that lets you know you're alive." He puts the goblet to his lips just as Eliot slings open a Zippo lighter. Flame in his hand.

Tom blows liquor at the fire, and I feel the heat of the amassed blaze, sputtering out as quickly as it came.

One dinner in the past, Eliot lit the entire tablecloth on fire, purposefully. Their show tonight is entirely normal.

Except for the fact that Tom pins his eyes to mine.

My lips part, confusion and some other sentiment ascending. I try to understand.

Part of me is afraid to.

Tom remains standing on his chair, and I wait for slingshot banter. For another person to comment on *fear* or their theatrics, but there is silence. And movement down the table.

Beckett shifts his plate, lining the silverware. He often spends his opening remarks catching us up on his life. Moments we may've missed. He stays seated nearly every time.

Powerfully, Beckett rises. Graceful like water, he puts a foot on the cushion to stand, and that's when I'm certain—this is for me.

He turns. Eyes on mine. "Sacrifice."

It crashes against my body, and I stare at him, my brother who understands that word most deeply.

"The act of surrendering something to gain something else. Your greatest desire isn't without sacrifice."

I swallow hard. I picture Thatcher. But his career is not mine to sacrifice. I will never; I could never.

He's needed as my bodyguard.

Yes. That's what we agreed on.

Beckett stays standing on his chair too, and then Charlie snuffs his cigarette on a dish. His opening remark almost never changes.

He will say, *I invoke the right to pass.*

Careened back on his chair, he kicks his feet up on his plate. Clattering silverware and cranberries. And loudly, he says, "Love."

I freeze, eyes burning.

I can't.

Charlie tilts his head to me. "To love is to reach true fulfillment."

I can't.

There is no scenario, no possibility, where Thatcher and I can be together beyond the ruse. I can't love him.

I can be fulfilled without him.

I have to be.

Dropping his feet off the table, Charlie stands on his chair. Staring strikingly down at me.

"Courage," Ben says as he steps onto his cushion. Towering over everyone as the tallest here. Warmth in his gaze. "Meaningful change takes great acts of courage. Confront what scares you the most."

Tears prick me, and my sister rises elegantly. "Heartache. What comes with love." She stares earnestly onto me. "What can be necessary."

This is a riddle I've just solved. My family loves riddles, I love riddles, and this one was meant to rip down my defenses. To be open to love, even if it hurts.

I pull off my mask, and I brush my fingers under my watery eyes.

My parents rise together, not to join my siblings. They value the bond between me and my brothers and sister, and they want us to work together.

Always.

They begin to walk out, my mom staring fiercely at me. Her hand glides across my shoulders in comfort before she leaves.

My dad passes my chair. He pauses, his calming hand on my arm. "Ne fais pas mes erreurs, mon coeur," he whispers. *Don't make my mistakes, my heart.*

He wouldn't accept how much he loved my mom.

I breathe in.

Once my dad exits with her, I'm left with my siblings. All standing on their chairs. Eyes all on me.

They all know this will end miserably, don't they? *Of course they do, Jane.* There is no realm where a bodyguard could be with me.

They believe Thatcher is strictly professional and I have a crush from the fake dating ruse—and soon, we'll break up.

I'm on a one-way street of love, and I'm afraid to drive down alone. But I must in order to *feel* something.

Is that it?

I repeat all of this, and they say *yes*. They can't know that I'm sleeping with my bodyguard, none would've held back from mentioning it. But I suppose it doesn't change the feelings that I'm fighting.

I wipe my splotchy cheeks. A pain in my heart, my stomach still sinking, and I reach out and clasp my little sister's hand.

I stand up on my chair next to her. "Whose idea was this tonight?" I ask curiously.

Everyone looks to Eliot.

It worked well.

Because my chest floods, and I hold on to the possibility that I might be hopelessly in…

"It's alright, Jane Eleanor." Tom tilts his head and gives the room a sweep with his gaze. "Thatcher wouldn't fit in here anyway."

All of my siblings nod in concrete agreement.

I feel like I can't even give Thatcher the chance to try.

44

 THATCHER MORETTI

I'm at one of the most elaborate, private Halloween parties I've ever seen. Mostly, it's a challenge for the team.

Fog rolls along a dark, sprawling farm. Three-hundred pre-vetted guests in costumes run around screaming and shrieking. A massive graveyard sits on a steep, muddy hill. Where a DJ plays remixes of classic Halloween songs, adding to the cacophony.

The real threat so far tonight is a heeled leather boot.

"I doubt it's broken," Jane winces, eyes on her foot. *If I could, I'd take a fucking bat to every smoke machine here.* She didn't even stumble. The heel of her boot just sunk into wet mud that neither of us could see.

She's seated on a hay bale around the carnival games. In my peripheral, a cluster of costumed fairies bob for apples and ogle us, interested in my relationship with Jane.

I'm squatting and cupping her ankle in my large hand. With my right, I quickly but carefully unlace her leather boot. "Could be a sprain," I say.

Farrow hasn't checked it yet, but I've already radioed him. He's grabbing ice with Maximoff before they return to this side of the farm.

"That's most likely." She holds on to her witch hat that tries to take flight in a gust of wind.

Our gazes brushing as I look up, constantly checking on Jane. Green paint coats her face, hiding her freckles, but she's flat-out the cutest witch I've ever seen.

After Jane, Sulli, and Luna posted a picture from their facemask night on Instagram, fans started affectionately referring to them as the *Witches of Philadelphia*, and they embraced the name for Hallow Friends Eve.

All three are witches. Green faces, black dresses, black hat, and black leather fucking boots. Which I'm still unlacing.

Jane watches, and I notice how her eyes skim the whistle around my neck and my red trunks. An October chill tries to nip my bare chest. I gave Banks my windbreaker since he forgot to bring his, and I can withstand the cold.

To boost morale, the Tri-Force let the whole team decide on a group costume. We're lifeguards, but I didn't really care what was chosen.

Other actual concerns bear on my chest. Like how this is my *last* public outing with Jane as boyfriend and girlfriend.

The end. We've reached it. And I hate it.

Jane keeps two hands on her hat. Still eyeing my costume, she says in thought, "I realize we weren't ever given the chance to wear couple costumes, so at the time, I hadn't considered what you and I would be." She pauses. "But now I think I know what I would've loved…"

Our gazes latch for a strong beat.

Very softly, she says, "You would've been my Tarzan, and I would've been your Jane."

It slams into me. The *would've been*. And the feeling that she might be open to more. Is that my role in her fucking life—I just prepared her heart for some other man?

I nod a few times. A pit in my ribs. "I wanted that too."

"Bien," she says, wiping the crease of her eye.

It's killing me. "Jane," I say deeply.

"I'm fine, really. Don't worry about me."

Not possible. "I'm your bodyguard, honey." I gently pull off her boot, and I see heartache filling her eyes. She clutches my muscular shoulder for support.

"I'm not trying to make this harder for you," she whispers, wide-eyed. "It's not my intention. I know there's no way we can have everything, and I don't want to be unfair to you."

I clutch her green-painted cheek. "You're not, Jane." I suddenly sense movement coming in on my three o'clock, and I drop my hand off her face.

My expression hardens as I watch actors in masks wield chainsaws and chase two zombie girls in our direction.

My head is so wrapped up in my emotions, I need to keep checking myself.

Get your mind right.

Protect her. Protect her—that's my sole duty.

The girls shriek bloody murder, running towards us, and I shoot a death glare at one of the actors who hawk-eyes Jane.

No.

If he comes over here and tries to wave a weapon at her—unchained or not—he's on the ground. It's too easy for a masked actor to harass a famous one under the guise of *Halloween*. A clown has been trying to "poke" Luna all night, and we posted most of the extra security on her detail with Quinn.

Security Rules: SFO aren't supposed to work events like tonight's. It's been a stipulation in the past, after Omega gained fame. Farrow and I are even higher on that fucking shit list for being more publicly recognizable now. But we need more eyes tonight, so the Tri-Force allowed us to go on-duty. We just had to bring twice as many temp guards along.

If I weren't the one protecting Jane here, I'd be going out of my fucking mind.

The actor sees me and lifts up his growling chainsaw, high-tailing his ass toward the crate of floating apples. He scares off the cluster of fairies.

Focusing back on her ankle, I gently slip off her untied boot. Her ankle is swollen. I study the wince in her bunched brows. Her jaw sets like she bites down pain.

I just want to comfort her in any way I can. "Tell me if I'm hurting you." The words come out, and my chest knots. Whatever hard call I make soon, I feel like I'm hurting Jane. She loses a bodyguard or she loses a boyfriend.

I can't be both to her anymore, and even now, it's only halfway. Rules and red tape and 3 a.m. closing hours.

"You're not," she says quickly, exactly what I just said to her. *You're not being unfair to me, Jane. You're not hurting me, Thatcher.*

But this is unfair to us and it is hurting us, and I rake a hand through my hair. "If you can't walk, I'm going to carry you." I peel a flyaway, frizzed strand of hair off her lips.

She smiles, but it fades in a thought. "Are you allowed to carry me? Didn't security tell you that we're supposed to appear distant for the breakup?"

Alpha and Epsilon gave me clear instructions:

Don't be too physical with her.

No kissing.

Treat her more like she's just a client.

In this situation, I'd carry my client, but also, fuck them for these fucking orders. It's unnecessary. "Yeah, I'm allowed—"

"Janie!" Maximoff calls from the distance, jogging over like she's in mortal danger. He's dressed as Captain America. Farrow smiles over at his fiancé, more at ease but keeping pace. I notice a baggie of ice in his hand, trauma bag strapped across his chest.

Farrow could've been a lifeguard like the rest of the team. But he had a choice, and he made the right call.

He's the Winter Soldier, but with his regular dyed, bleach-white hair. SFO has been talking about how Farrow and Maximoff broke the internet when they stepped outside together.

It's taken a spotlight off the public hating that I didn't dress up with Jane.

My brother is also in tow. He's been attached to Maximoff tonight since Farrow has had to make med calls.

Banks stares deeply into me like *it's going to be alright.* He's been giving me that look all day.

I asked him what I should do, and he said, *"I'm not the one who makes the calls. You are."* I almost rolled my eyes, but he gave me advice.

He said, *"I think she's afraid, and you're afraid."*

Yeah. I think he's right, and this is going to be the hardest trigger I have to pull. In either direction. It's still tearing me up.

Indecision is hell to me.

"I'm okay," Jane says to her best friend. Maximoff takes a seat on the hay bale and hugs her shoulders.

I stand up, and Farrow replaces me to check her ankle. He presses around her foot, and I scan the perimeter and her.

Banks is beside me, and comms are active, constant chatter in my ear. I tune in.

"Sulli is going into Hell 2," Akara says, using the code for one of the haunted houses. He's required to go into those areas with his client. He's just updating the team of their location change.

Banks clicks his mic. "With or without the Rooster?" *Rooster* is code for Will Rochester.

"With," Akara says heatedly.

Jane was hanging out with Luna and Sulli earlier tonight. Before the ankle injury. So I saw Akara on-duty, and at first, he was trying to do what I would've done in his situation.

Do not watch her and him. He can survey Sulli's surroundings. His eyes don't have to be on her laughter while a shitbag is flirting with intent to fuck.

But he has a real friendship with Sulli, and they began teasing each other. He stole her witch hat, and she took his whistle. From the outside, it would've been hard to decipher who she was actually on a date with: Akara or Will.

It reminds me that if the Alpha and Epsilon lead find out I've slept with Jane, they'd start really worrying about other bodyguards on SFO fucking their clients. Especially Akara, who has one of the closest relationships to a client you can have without crossing that line.

"No fractures," Farrow says, adjusting the ice on her ankle. "Just a sprain. You need to ice for twenty minutes—"

"Ben?!" Maximoff calls, voice firm, and all of our heads swing towards Jane's youngest brother.

Ben Cobalt is ten meters away and turns to look at Maximoff. He wipes wet hair out of his face, his *climate-change-is-real* shirt drenched after he just bobbed for apples. Twenty-three of his high school friends surround him, most dressed as baseball players—he got them on the guest list.

He's allowed to be here, but I already know why Maximoff is concerned. *Xander.*

Banks and I share a hard look, and I lift my mic to my mouth. "Thatcher to Tony, what's your client's AO?"

Ben jogs over to the hay bale. "Hey, Moffy...Jane?" Concern floods his eyes when he sees his older sister icing her ankle.

"I'm okay," Jane assures with a soft smile, meeting my gaze for the shortest second.

My muscles tighten.

Maximoff stands up. "Ben, I thought my brother was with you? You said you were looking out for him tonight."

Ben puts an earnest hand to his chest. "Xander told me he wanted to be alone. He was adamant, and I didn't want to hassle him—and he seemed okay, like happy. I would've called you if I thought he wasn't."

Maximoff nods. "I'll check on my brother. Just have fun."

Ben clasps his hand, they hug, and then he speaks in French to Jane.

I'm still waiting for Tony to reply to comms. *He's not rogering up.* Blood starting to boil, I try again. "What's your AO, Tony?"

Banks shakes his head, pissed. He scouts our six and whispers, "And Epsilon thinks he's the Messiah of their force. Yeah right. And I'm the Virgin Mary."

SFE hates Farrow so much that they're desperate to tote an Epsilon bodyguard who's better. But praising Tony is like waving around a gold-foiled candy bar believing it's solid gold.

I start to think Tony isn't rogering up because of personal grievances. *Fucking shitbag.* "If he's not responding just to fuck with me, I'm going to break his itty-bitty dick in half."

Banks nods. "Amen."

Farrow uses comms. "Farrow to security, anyone seen Xander?"

While I listen to comms, I head back to Jane. Seeing that she's about to rise off the hay, I clasp her hand. Helping her to her feet, and she grips my waist, bracing herself to me.

"Thank you," she whispers, our eyes meeting more than once.

"Can you put weight on it?" I wrap my arm around her hips.

She tries, and intakes a sharp breath. *Negative.* Jane looks up at me. "I have a feeling we're going to need to go on a search for Xander. Maybe I should wait alone and find a crutch so I don't hold the group back?" She turns her head, noticing Banks grabbing her boot and ice. "Thatcher—"

I already pull her in my arms.

"Oh my God," she gasps under her breath while I easily cradle her against my chest. Her cheeks flushed, holding on to her black hat. She's almost panting, and it takes me too long to stop looking at her.

This is where she's meant to be. In my arms.

In *my* arms.

But as a bodyguard or a boyfriend? *Can't have both.*

I narrow my searing eyes on the perimeter. Doing a quick scan for nearby threats. And for a red Power Ranger. Xander's costume.

"He's not answering my calls," Maximoff says, phone to his ear again.

"We'll find him," Jane assures, her arm hooked around my neck. She's careful not to pull out my earpiece.

Farrow tosses Banks a bandage from the trauma bag, and while I'm cradling Jane, my brother places the ice on her ankle and secures it with the wrap.

Still no word from security.

Maximoff slips his phone in the belt of his Captain America costume. He throws the red and blue shield aside in case he has to run. Ready to be with his brother. *We have to find Xander.*

I stay rooted to the present moment. To the mission. "Let's push out," I say.

"Together," Jane adds. "I don't think we should split apart."

Maximoff nods in agreement, and Farrow clutches the back of his neck in comfort.

As we all head away from the carnival area, concern finally infiltrates me. *Don't think it.* But I already am—I'm thinking about how Xander reminds me of the brother I lost.

He always has, and I've always tried to let that raw thought go.

But Xander is fifteen now. He's the same age that Skylar died. And I can't lose that kid like I lost my brother. He was *mine* to protect.

They both were.

We finally get word from temp security.

Xander is at the graveyard on the hill. Where the DJ is stationed, and we move out in that direction. To ensure he's okay.

The farm is massive. Over a hundred acres, and a four-wheeler passes with a giggling group of college-aged kids dressed as ghouls.

We pass the back of Hell 4: a rickety barn transformed into a haunted house, and sitting against the red chipped wood, Charlie Cobalt smokes a blunt and reads a book.

No guests approach him, per the rules of the party: *no autographs, no pictures, no hassling the famous ones.*

Oscar Oliveira is standing next to him. Scoping the area. So his gaze lands on me first, curly pieces of his hair falling over a rolled bandana. Looking the most Baywatch-ready with aviators on.

"Charlie," Oscar says, alerting his client.

Charlie sees us, folding his book. He stands up, not bothering to dust dirt off his three-piece suit, and he joins our group.

Maximoff texted Charlie earlier to see if he wanted to come along and help find Xander. Charlie replied, "You'll pass me."

That was it.

And now he's on the trek with us.

Jane smiles in my arms, seeing her brother and best friend work closer together.

Charlie sucks on a blunt and scrutinizes me holding Jane. Saying nothing about his sister in my arms. He's been nice towards me specifically. And Banks too.

I didn't know why until I asked Jane. She said Charlie told her, *"Thatcher chose his twin, knowing it'd be harder to be seen as an individual."*

I chose to be around Banks instead of distance myself. We both chose that. A harder path, but the only one we've known. And apparently, Charlie values that.

That's good. Considering Charlie is Jane's brother. And I don't know which one of her brothers would be the hardest to gain trust or respect from—she has five.

My jaw tics. *Why would I need to gain anything from them?* She'll just be my client soon. I can still feel myself vacillating in two directions—I hate it.

I look down at Jane. She ditched her witch hat, and she rests her temple on my shoulder, comfortable against me.

She needs a bodyguard who she trusts. *Stability.* It's vital to Jane, and I can't abandon her detail.

"Stay frosty," Banks says as we approach the muddy hill. Orange strobe lights swaying up towards the star-blanketed sky.

I focus. Tuning into my instincts, my senses. I hear yelling and cheering that accompanies competitions. Fervent. Loud.

Aggressive.

And that's when I see the red Power Ranger, and adrenaline fuels my brain and blood. At the peak of the hill, Xander is in a full-blown fistfight with a white ranger.

No helmets to their costumes. I spot his shaggy brown hair, his gangly body, and pretty boy face: one-hundred percent him. And an audience is howling and goading them to hit harder.

I taught Xander to fight, but not so he could lay punches in at a fucking Halloween party. Guilt barrels into my chest, and Farrow's jaw muscle twitches. He helped teach Xander to box with me. So did Banks, who inhales a strained breath.

Where is Tony? His bodyguard should've broken this up. I look to Banks. "Tell the temp guards to break up the fight." I see three just watching.

Banks switches radio frequencies and speaks to them in comms.

Maximoff starts to run up the slick, muddy hill, and Farrow drops his trauma bag. Catching up to his fiancé's side. It's not an easy climb. They slide.

When the white ranger slams a left hook into Xander's jaw, Maximoff digs in harder and yells, "XANDER!"

Banks goes to help.

My muscles flex, and Jane can feel my shoulders contracting as she holds on to them.

I'm not planning to join. Neither is Charlie or Oscar. Our clients are here. We stay here. We stand near, but far enough from the foot of the hill that our view of Xander isn't obstructed.

"Put me down," Jane says instantly, hurriedly. "Go, *go*—I'll stay with Charlie."

"No. I'm not leaving your side." My voice is concrete. In my head, there is no other option. And even if there were, this is what I want. Her detail.

Her.

I trust my brother. I trust Farrow and even Maximoff to get the job done.

Suddenly, part of the audience breaks off, mostly drunk frat-bro-looking shitbags dressed as *Vikings,* and they slide down the hill. Grinning, aiming for Farrow and Maximoff, the Winter Soldier and Captain America.

Being a bodyguard for so long, I sense what's about to happen. The Vikings want to push our men down. Just to prolong the entertainment at the top of the hill.

Oscar and I exchange a severe look. They're not making it to Xander. And the temps aren't moving a muscle, which means the extra guards are listening to another order.

Tony, I'm guessing.

I'm about to tell Oscar to go and I'll watch Charlie. But he beats me to speak. "You go, Moretti. You're taller." Oscar is over six feet, but I assume he thinks my longer limbs will help me climb up the fucking hill faster.

Probably because Banks was high up, almost to the top. But he changes course to protect Maximoff and Farrow.

Jane looks panicked at the scene. "Go, *go*." She taps my shoulder.

"Listen to my sister," Charlie says, shooting me a harsher look.

I glance at Oscar, and he nods to me, "I have her." *I trust him.* Instantly. I move into action. Carefully setting Jane onto her feet, and she hangs on to Charlie's arm.

Fear strikes her eyes. She pushes me towards the hill. "Thatcher." Her empathy for her best friend takes over.

A Viking charges Maximoff, about to shove him, and Farrow intervenes fast. He cold-cocks the Viking hard. Lights out instantly, and the rest erupt on both of them.

I run.

Maximoff is brawling his way through these shitbags, and Farrow is swifter, more trained. Nailing one with an uppercut to the jaw. Banks keeps about three from storming in on them, putting a guy in a headlock, and I ascend another part of the hill.

Clear of Viking targets.

I'm not able to check back on Jane. I place all my trust in Oscar. Sounds of cheering escalate the higher I climb, my boots muddying.

I've been in harsher terrain. Under harsher conditions. But I wouldn't call this a cakewalk by any fucking means.

My pulse pounds in my temple. The DJ plays "I Put a Spell On You" on full blast, the bass shaking the ground.

I dig my foot into mud, and with one last shove up, I reach the graveyard. Seeing over every head, I have an eye on Xander.

He almost trips backwards into a fake headstone, dodging a jab to the nose. Blood already gushes down his mouth and chin.

I don't waste a second. "Break up!" I yell, storming toward the fistfight in the center of the graveyard. No one tries to restrain me here. They see my imposing height and build, domineering stance, and lethal glare—and they part instantly.

Making a clear path for me to go through. But they *boo*. Pissed that I'm about to end their party.

My boots crunch red Solo cups while I charge ahead. Unblinking, reflexes humming. Not far.

And then the white ranger lands a hard blow into Xander's face. Blood gushes out of his nose.

And he crumples on a headstone in a heap. *I'm here.* One second too late, but I wrench the white ranger back by the collar.

Someone yells, "Holy shit! Baywatch-Thor is coming out of nowhere!"

The white ranger flails at me. "Heymangetoffme."

I throw him to the side with extreme force. His chest thuds on a mound of dirt. Quickly, I crouch to Xander, who groans and cups his nose.

Lanky at six-foot-two, he's pretty scrawny for fifteen—and without pause, I lift him in my arms.

He tucks his head into my chest with some type of familiarity, seeking safety in my clutch. As though he knows exactly who I am without checking.

I'm almost whiplashed with how many years I've spent protecting him, and as I carry Xander down the hill, I feel like he's nine-years-old again.

He's safe.

Probably broke his nose, but he's safe. Hell, he'll be joining the broken nose club. Many bodyguards are in it, and so is Maximoff.

I swat a plastic cup that someone tries to throw at me. *Booing* intensified. I don't give a rat's ass.

Finding some foot traction, I reach the bottom of the hill without slipping. And right as I lock eyes with Jane—Tony motherfucking Ramella cuts into my path.

I glower. Wanting to choke him with his lifeguard whistle.

He looks just as murderous. "What the fuck do you think you're doing, Moretti?"

"I'm holding your bloodied client and you're asking *me* that? You shouldn't have even let Xander swing—"

"He *wanted* to fight," Tony sneers, his blue eyes pulsating with rage that I feel. "It was a boxing match."

"Where's the fucking *ring*?" I growl.

Tony points at me. "See, that's your goddamn problem. You can't hover over your client. You gotta let him live his life."

"He's fifteen!"

"He's a fuckin' teenager! You did worse at his age—"

"Vaffangul'," I growl. *Fuck you.*

He spits the same Italian curse at me.

If Xander weren't in my clutch right now, hiding in the crook of my arm, I wouldn't be able to control my hot-blooded urge to deck Tony in the fucking face.

It's the only reason I walk away from him now.

He shouts at my back, "You're gonna regret this, Moretti!"

We'll see.

45

JANE COBALT

Everything changes today. The first day of November.

I'm home. I lean back against the brick wall, right beside the adjoining door that leads to security's townhouse. It's so strange to think that just on the other side, Thatcher is meeting with the three leads to discover exactly *how* we have to announce our breakup for tonight.

Press release.

Instagram post.

Rocket flare.

I can't imagine a suitable way to do it because there's no part of me that wants to wake up tomorrow and be someone less to Thatcher than what I've been. To rewind and be nothing more than his client again...

Ophelia nudges my hand for pets, and I stroke her white fur.

"Janie," Maximoff whispers, his voice tough but incredibly consoling. He has an arm around my shoulders, and I lean my weight into my best friend.

His black eye isn't so swollen anymore, but a yellowish bruise blemishes his cheek, the aftermath of the fight on the hill. Farrow only has a split lip, and Banks strained a muscle in his shoulder. I'm just thankful no one was more severely injured. Including Xander, who's recuperating from a minor nose fracture.

I glance over at the kitchen archway. Seeing a portion of Donnelly's outstretched legs. He's sitting on the floor against the cupboards.

Farrow is next to him, the same way that Moffy is beside me. I walked past this morning and saw Donnelly pinching his watery eyes.

He was called here earlier to talk to the Tri-Force. They're transferring him off Beckett's detail. It wasn't such a shock, really. Beckett learned about Donnelly's deep-seated family history with drugs, and he didn't want his bodyguard around cocaine. So he requested a transfer.

Everyone is trying to protect Donnelly, it seems. Oscar and Farrow were the ones to tell Beckett.

I take a breath in the quiet. Ophelia turns to Moffy, bumping her nose into his wrist. He scratches her, but looks at me. Deep empathy coursing through his green eyes.

He's known longer than anyone that I've liked Thatcher. That I've been attracted to him. That I've slept with him, and he's seen from the start where this could lead. And he's been afraid for me. One-way roads. Not together. Different directions.

My lips are chapped and I lick the cuts forming on my bottom one. "I've been telling him that I don't want him to quit security for me," I whisper to Moffy. "And I don't...but...at the same time, I do." Tears well up in my eyes. "And I hate that part of me. That'd wish him to sacrifice *anything* to be with me."

I rub at my eyes.

Moffy hugs me closer. "Sacrifice is a part of being in a relationship with people like us," he says softly.

Sacrifice.

I hear Beckett's voice.

Ophelia darts off at the sound of birds chirping outside. I rest my cheek to his shoulder. Tears spilling down my face.

Moffy looks pained, but he hugs tighter.

I rub snot on the sleeve of my blouse. "I'm just thinking about how he's going to come back through those doors and everything will be different. I won't even be able to touch his hand..." I take a sharp breath. "Or run my fingers through his hair." My sleeve is sufficiently wet. "He has really good hair."

I try to smile.

Moffy tries too. "I know. He's got great hair."

We both laugh. Me through my tears. Him through his reddened eyes.

In all of this, I'm glad I have him. And just as deeply, I'm so very glad Thatcher has Banks. We both won't be alone. No matter what.

And yet...

My heart is still breaking.

46

 THATCHER MORETTI

I've got my head on right. It's what I know when I take a seat across from the Tri-Force. Price, Sinclair and Akara all lounge on security's leather couch. Price has a tablet on his knee, Sinclair a notebook, and Akara, his phone.

I've pulled up a chair. Only the coffee table separating us.

Not long ago, I would've been sitting on the other side as a lead. I was their equal. I'm not intimidated by them. I'm not cowering or shrinking back.

But I understand that Price cuts the checks. All three of the leads have the same power, but make no mistake, this is *his* company. He built Triple Shield Services, the legal name for the security team as a whole, which everyone sees on their 1099. Keeping in good graces with Price was always a priority.

Each lead examines their notes. About to discuss further details concerning the breakup announcement. One of which is to use my family as a *reason* for fake animosity between me and Jane.

Banks told me, *"A few headlines isn't going to knock our family down. We've survived worse."*

I know we have.

My stringent posture stretches my muscles taut. Obedient, patient, and I sense more rules. More boundaries being reconstructed in solid brick.

All the walls I smashed down, that she smashed down, are being cemented back together. Right in front of me.

But there's one thing I've realized in all of this:

I couldn't compartmentalize Jane.

Not very well in the past, not at all in the present, and there's no fucking way I'll be able to in the future.

I've given up a lead position. I've lost my privacy. I've risked the safety of my family. All for her—and at the end of the fucking line, I can't shove her in one box and walk away. I couldn't then; I can't now.

She is everywhere inside of me. And that's where I *want* her to be.

I can see my grandma. Feel her loving hand on my face. Hear her soft, aching voice. Wishing with her whole soul for me to just be happy.

I inhale strongly.

"Before you all start," I tell them. "I'd like to say something."

Sinclair gives me a quick once-over. We've been on good terms, despite his grievances with a couple men on Omega. That's about to change. He nods. "Go ahead."

Sitting forward, I cup my hands. "I don't want to waste your time," I say as a professional courtesy. "So I'm not going to beat around this."

Akara slips me a confused look, his brows crossing.

I expel a breath through my nose, and I address all three. "I'm not breaking up with Jane."

Price frowns. "Pardon?"

"We want to be together, sir, and I understand that there may be a conflict of interest with me working for security. If that's going to be a problem, I'm willing to give you my formal resignation today."

They're all stunned silent. Whiplashed. This is probably the last thing they expected to hear.

Akara keeps shaking his head. Shock and heat building in his gaze. *I'm sorry.*

Fucking him over is one of the worst things I have to do. But I couldn't warn him because he needs to wipe his hands clean of me. And even hate me. Maybe then he can try to maintain trust with Price and Sinclair.

"You both want to be together?" Sinclair repeats, like it doesn't make sense.

"Yes, sir." I'm more on edge, waiting to see where the shrapnel lands.

Price locks eyes with me. His fingers clenching his tablet tighter. But he's not about to jump the table. They're all leads for a reason. A cool, controlled temperament is a hallmark to being a good bodyguard.

"I'm going to ask you one question," Price says, his voice even, despite the bite in his eyes. "And you better be fucking honest with me."

I nod.

"Did you sleep with her?"

"Yes, sir."

Sinclair lets out an aggravated laugh. Price shoots to his feet. I stand at the same time as Akara, who slashes his hurt, angered gaze at me.

"You and me, Thatcher," he says harshly. "You and me—*we've* protected our men for years. That's the way it's been."

Covering asses, cleaning messes. Good cop, bad cop. Him and me.

I nod.

"And you should've known better," Akara says between gritted teeth. "*You knew*, more than anyone, what you'd fucking destroy." His nose flares, pained.

SFO.

His men.

His responsibility.

Nothing I say will make a difference. But he deserves an apology. "I'm sorry," I say from my core.

Akara shakes his head more, still fuming, still in disbelief.

Sinclair glowers. "This fake dating op wasn't a gateway for you to stick your dick in her."

I rake a hand across my mouth, acid in my throat, shifting tensely on my feet. *Don't charge.* But I fucking hate how he's talking about Jane.

"You took advantage of my trust in you," Price states like a leader disappointed in his men. "And I should fire you right now. I honestly can't stand to even look at your *fucking* face."

That one cuts.

Only because I think of Banks.

How much shit is he going to get for this?

My jaw clenches, muscles flexed. Staying quiet. Opening my mouth isn't going to help, and I can't disagree with them. I did take advantage of the op. And of their trust in me to stay professional.

I screwed them.

Price runs two angered hands over his head. He blows out a breath and looks at Sinclair. "He needs to go."

"He can't," Sinclair states. "We have that problem."

My brows knit in confusion.

Price turns to Akara and asks him, "What are the chances that if we fire Thatcher, Banks will quit security?"

"One-hundred percent," Akara says, still glaring at me.

That's not really true. And Akara knows this. My brother would want to stay and protect these families. And I'd want him to keep them safe. Especially if I'm dating Jane.

But I keep my mouth shut.

I trust Akara, who knows a hell of a lot more than I do right now.

Price lets out a long breath and narrows his gaze on me. "I won't accept your resignation."

What the fuck is going on?

I look between all three of them. Not interrupting.

Price continues, "After the fight on Halloween, Lily and Loren Hale have requested that you or Banks return to Xander's 24/7 detail." *Their son.*

The Tri-Force only needs one of us on the team. But Akara just saved me with a package-deal lie.

My chest rises, a surge of emotion rushing through me. I'm going to keep my job as a bodyguard.

They're not taking my radio or my gun—but where the hell am I going?

Jane.

Let me stay with Jane.

Breath imprisons my lungs.

Price picks up the tablet he'd thrown down. "We were planning on putting Banks with Xander."

I nod stiffly.

Sensing the hammer about to drop.

"But you're not staying on Jane's detail after this. You sealed your own fate."

My mind is reeling. They're punishing me. Because they couldn't fire me.

I try to exhale, reminding myself that I'm being given more than I thought I'd receive coming in here. And I knew there'd be consequences to my decision.

"You want me on Xander's detail, sir?" My voice is professional. Stern. *Like always.*

"Correct. Your post will start soon."

I nod. "Thank you, sir."

He nods to me, hurt still in his brow. Hurt in all of them.

Price became a bodyguard at twenty-two for the long-haul, same age that I did, and I think he saw his longevity and leadership in me.

Sinclair is the one who relates to the military in me. I'm supposed to be like one of him.

And Akara. *Him and me.* He has the most reason to be upset.

I'm concerned about Jane. More than anything. Because if I'm not on her detail, then it's wide open for the taking. "Will you put Banks with Jane, sir?" I ask.

"You'd love that," Price snaps. "No, it won't be your twin."

Donnelly is up for transfer.

Donnelly, then. I'm praying.

"Her new bodyguard is going to be Tony Ramella."

I solidify.

The man I wouldn't trust with a fucking goldfish—and I'm supposed to let him protect her? I would die for Jane. All of SFO would die for Jane. And I can't say that Tony would.

And that's the level of dedication she *needs* if I can't protect her.

"He's the best man for the job," Price continues. "He has the highest skillset and experience from security services in LA. It'll benefit Jane."

No. I breathe coarse breath, trying to control my temper. "Respectfully, sir," I say, pausing so I don't growl out a *fuck no.* "He got his own client beat up."

"No," Price refutes. "Xander Hale asked to be in the fight. He was abiding by his client's wishes. He followed protocol."

My eyes tighten. "Xander is a minor."

"Tony spent years protecting one of the most internationally recognized boy bands, *teenagers* close to Xander's age. He's experienced and understands the nuances of this job."

We're talking about the same guy who slept with my high school girlfriend.

I try again. "Jane doesn't trust Tony, sir. In my *professional* opinion, they're not suited for each other."

Sinclair cocks his head. "You sure you aren't just jealous, Moretti? This sounds like personal crap-in-a-bag to me."

"Sir, you can talk to Jane," I say sternly. "She'll tell you."

Price retorts, "We can't have your personal feelings towards a bodyguard affecting Jane's view of him. Tony is one of the best guards. *The end.* If she's feeling uneasy because of your grievances, you can help her learn to trust him."

I hear, *help her learn to fuck him.*

Goddammit.

But I can't lose what they've just given me. *My job.* It's the best way I can protect her. Even if I'm not on her detail.

"You don't have a voice in this, Moretti," Sinclair snaps. "Stand down."

I'm not a lead. Seniority. Hierarchy. Everything that I cherish and honor and respect.

Akara pockets his phone and speaks to Price and Sinclair. "As formality, we should take a vote."

Akara should vote with them. To gain favor.

I watch and listen as the Tri-Force do a quick vote for both transfers. Me to Xander. Tony to Jane.

Both votes are 2-1.

Akara opposed. He's die-hard SFO, and by still vouching for me, he just made it known to the Alpha and Epsilon leads.

I rub my tensed jaw. "Are we done?" I ask. I just want to see her. Hug her. Tell her myself. Take the good and put away the bad for now.

And Jane—she's everything good to me.

"One more question," Price says. "And this stays here. We won't tell anyone. But we need to know so that we can see the warning signs when we hire new guys."

I stiffen, having no clue what's coming.

Price says, "Was it for the fame or the sex?"

"Neither," I say, not even hesitating. "It was just her."

It was always just *her.*

47

JANE COBALT

I'm frozen, hands cupped over my parted lips. Tears filling my eyes, the kind stirred from a skipping heart and stolen breath.

I stand on the foot of the staircase. Staring at the closed adjoining door that Thatcher left through. I could hear everything when their voices grew louder.

He was willing to quit for me. So we could be together.

He's sacrificed so much of what he loves. All for me. And I've never had someone make so many endless declarations. I feel them swelling up inside me.

He's still a bodyguard. I didn't take that from him. He kept something, and that breathes sunlight into my lungs.

The door blows open.

Thatcher instantly lays his eyes on me, and we take sharp breaths. "Jane," he says huskily, soaking in my overcome expression. "You heard?"

I drop my hands off my mouth. My heart racing, nearly floating out of me. "I heard," I confirm.

He comes straight for me.

And I can't shut up.

"I heard...all of what you said, and I... I think you're... I find you..." I watch his unwavering stride—not faltering, not hesitating— his strong eyes already clutching me before his hands do.

Swiftly, Thatcher lifts me against his chest, a gasp breaking apart my lips. My legs instinctively wrap around his waist while he holds me. While I clasp his hard, scruffy jaw between two palms. Staring deep into his yearning and affection.

His mouth brushes mine, longing in the air between our lips, and we kiss with unraveling passion.

He carries me up the narrow stairs, and when we get to my room, he kicks the door closed. Our lips haven't parted. Each kiss like a blazing promise—this will happen again tomorrow. And the day after that. And after that.

No one is telling us this has to end.

We only break apart when my back hits the bedpost. Lips swollen and red, breathing heavy, and heartbeat sputtering a mile a minute.

Cats dart past his heels, and my animal-print drapes blow in a gentle breeze. Window cracked, blinds open and light shining through.

I speak, words tumbling out of my mouth at rapid pace. "I'm feeling so many things at once… and it's so overwhelming." Our eyes graze each other, and I just think aloud, "Will you stay with me here in my room?"

"Right now?" He brushes a piece of hair off my lips.

Heat flushes my cheeks. "I meant longer. You won't be able to live in security's townhouse if you're not my bodyguard. But you can stay in mine, here with me—you can say no. I just thought it'd be easier and with the suspect not caught, the one who broke-in…" I trail off because he's already nodding. He's been nodding for a while.

Maybe since I first explained.

"I want to live with you," he says strongly against my lips.

I dizzy. "And you want to be my boyfriend," I say out loud, my lips lifting into an overwhelmed smile. "My real boyfriend."

"You want to have a boyfriend." He says what is true. I'm no longer closed off from the idea of a relationship. My heart is open for him to hold.

And to protect.

Breathless, I whisper, "Only if that boyfriend is you."

His hand encases my cheek. "I love you, Jane."

My lungs swell with deeper emotions.

He cradles my gaze. "You don't have to say it back. I know it may take time for you because of your feelings about love—"

"I'm falling so terribly in love with you," I say, my heart speaking for me. It feels good and right and perfect. "I think I've been falling for you for some time now."

He inhales, his forehead pressing to mine. I thread my fingers through his soft hair.

We kiss again. This one sensual and tender, and as our lips pull back in a breath, we turn our heads, sensing something outside the window.

Snow flutters softly down. I watch the wind carry the white flakes in whirling arcs.

"It's early," I say to him. "One of the earliest snowfalls, if I remember correctly."

"First snow of November," Thatcher breathes, but his eyes have already returned to me. Hands still holding me. Protecting me.

He may not be *my* bodyguard anymore, but he doesn't have to be for me to feel unequivocally safe in his arms.

And the road ahead may be filled with more potholes and storms, but I'm not driving down a one-way street. We're together.

Whatever we have to face, that's all that matters to me.

We're together in love.

Oral Assistance

 THATCHER MORETTI

Midnight on a tour bus. Kansas is full of empty roads, and I'm the one driving down them tonight. Hands tight on the steering wheel, I ignore the commotion from the crowded lounge, so that I can focus on my brother's voice.

"You're the only person I know who intentionally cock-block themselves. Like your brain is one big cock-block blocking you from good pussy."

I almost roll my eyes. Banks is back home in Philly, and luckily, his words come through an earbud. My phone is hooked up to headphones for privacy. One earbud in, the other dangling down so that I can hear if anyone calls me from the front lounge.

"I'm not cock-blocking myself," I grumble to my brother, keeping my voice low and strict.

"Akara says the guys are landing lays left and right. Except you. What else do you call that?"

"Doing my job. I'm a lead and Jane's a new client—"

"So it's because of Jane," he interrupts, humor lacing his words.

"Banks," I warn.

He lets out a low laugh. "Thatcher," he replies. "I'm just saying that if I were you, I'd be taking full advantage of the easy access." I can't tell if he means easy access to quick hookups at the tour stops or...easy access to Jane. My muscles tense just thinking the latter. He's definitely *not* insinuating that.

For one, Banks wouldn't refer to any of the clients as "easy access." And he knows I'd shut that shit so far down with Jane, it'd make its way into the Earth's crust.

She shouldn't be on my mind like that. It's without a doubt un-fucking-professional. Stepping onto this bus is starting to feel like boarding the Blurred Lines Train. Everything we do here creates messy, fogged boundaries, and navigating them shouldn't be this conflicting.

I know what's right.

I know what's wrong.

My jaw sets. "Well, I'm not you," I tell him. I can't just turn *it* off for a moment. My duty. My responsibility.

It's to Jane.

And this FanCon puts us in unnatural situations that hoist my guards. While they're sky-high, there is no room for hotel quickies in a bathroom with a nameless stranger. Sexually frustrated, yes. Will I survive, *fuck yes.*

I'm not a teenage boy. My dick doesn't need something wet to get by.

Point-blank: she's worth more than taking my eyes off the road for a fucking blow job.

"You're definitely not me," Banks agrees and pauses for a second. "I just wish one of us was getting laid."

A ghost of a smile flutters across my lips. "Maybe you should try harder."

He snorts. "Not for lack of trying. I just don't have the damn time."

We haven't spoken much about what happened with Xander. How he had locked himself in the bathroom not that long ago, and I hate that I wasn't there. If I could split myself down the middle and be two places at the same time, I would. In a heartbeat. And most people might assume having Banks in Philly is basically the same thing.

But like he said, he's not me. I'm not him.

I don't have his memories. When we're apart, I won't ever be able to see what he sees.

That's his life. His reality.

Mine's on this bus, driving down the dark Kansas roads. I take in a strained breath. "How is he?" I don't have to say Xander's name. We're on the same page. It's just like that.

"Alright. Better, I think," Banks says. "His parents made him add an extra day of therapy, so he's going to that. It's helping a little."

"That's goo—" The bus jerks to a halt, the momentum pushing my chest against the seatbelt. A mechanical screech fills the air. "*Fuck.*"

"What is it?" Banks' worry shoots adrenaline in my nerves.

"Bus problems," I tell him and then crane my head over my shoulder. "Everyone okay?!" I yell to the lounge.

Half-hearted *yeahs* are thrown back at me.

"Hey, I'll let you go," Banks says. "Don't break it even more."

I wish you were here, I want to tell him. Like fuck do I know about cars and mechanics. My brother could fix this in a snap. So could our mom. I try the ignition again, but the bus doesn't start up. Yeah…I fucked it somehow.

"I'm calling you if I can't fix it," I tell him gruffly. "Keep your cell on."

"Roger that. Stay frosty."

We hang up, and I rip the earbud from my ear just as Maximoff enters the lounge, his phone tight in his fist. "What's going on?"

"The bus broke down." Quickly, I unsnap my seatbelt and rise to my feet. I have to duck a little, since I'm too tall for parts of this bus. Walking through the narrow aisle, my gaze drifts to one of the gray couches in the first lounge. Jane is curled up in a fuzzy purple blanket. Her big blue eyes land on me. Curiosities pulsing in them.

I want to ask if she's alright. Clearly, she is. But I'd prefer a verbal response.

Banks is suddenly in my head, telling me that I just want to hear her voice.

He'd be wrong.

I'm being *vigilant*. Covering all my bases. That means making sure she's squared away. I shake off his annoying voice in my head and stop by the couch. I bend a little and splay a hand on the back cushion, near her shoulder. "You good, Jane?" I ask, my voice set like stone.

She tucks a frizzed piece of hair behind her ear. "Yes, quite." She looks me up and down. "Are you?"

I nod strictly. My blood simmers just hearing the light, airy cadence to her voice. Fuck, I shouldn't be into that. *I'm not.* Pack that shit away. Ship it off.

I *un*plant my hand from the couch and push past her. Down the aisle towards the second lounge in the back. My eyes latch with the man I need to see. Akara's already shrugging on a light jacket. "Outside," I tell him.

"Right behind you," he says.

We both bypass the bunks and the noisy first lounge. Everyone's here now. All the famous ones on the tour: Maximoff, Jane, Sulli, Charlie, and Beckett. Plus, their bodyguards and Jack Highland.

It's a full crowd, and when questions start flying towards me about the status of the bus, I ignore them to swing open the door and head to the back of the bus.

"It was driving fine up until the last ten seconds before it let out that noise. Now it won't start up," I tell Akara and pop the back panel where the engine is located. It's dark outside, and we both stare at the mishmash of mechanical parts. Heat radiates and small gusts of smoke emit from fuck-knows-where.

Akara makes a face. "No offense, but I wish you were Banks right now."

"Believe me, I have that same feeling." I slip out my cell. "I'm calling him."

Akara slides his thumb over his own phone. "In the meantime, I'm going to see if I can get a hold of a local mechanic." He walks off, and I FaceTime my brother.

"Hey, I need a grease monkey," I tell Banks and rotate the camera to the engine.

He whistles. "Fuck me, how old is your phone, man?"

I roll my eyes. "It's not the phone. There's shit lighting out here. Stand by." I try adjusting the settings and turn on the flashlight.

"I can't see shit with the smoke. I'd need to get my hands in her."

If he directs me to fix things without a good set of eyes, I might make the problem worse. I rotate the camera back to me. We both share a look, knowing it's useless. He's out there. I'm here.

"Akara making calls?" Banks asks what he already knows. Akara can be predictable like that, or maybe we both just know him too well.

I nod. "We're going to get a mechanic out here. Hopefully he can do as good of a job as you would."

He smiles. "You're definitely not that lucky."

I almost share his smile. "Probably not."

Akara's walking back, so I say a quick goodbye to my brother. I notice everyone piling out of the bus and sidling to the curb.

"Oh fuck, is that smoke?" Sulli asks, eyes wide.

"Yeah," Akara nods to her. "Sul, stay back."

"All of you stay back," I add. "We have it under control."

Akara signals to me with a nod, and we move out of earshot and view of the famous ones, towards the other side of the bus.

And then he lets out an annoyed sigh. "Mechanic shops are closed. No one's picking up. I can keep calling around, but even if I get ahold of someone, they'll most likely wait until morning."

"Fuck," I curse, and glance back at the bus. The smoke isn't too thick, but it's a steady stream. "It might have just overheated."

Akara looks hopeful. "That's what Banks said?"

Shit. I thread my arms over my firm chest. "No, he couldn't see anything," I say. "It's what I said."

Akara laughs. "Well, you're all I have, so it's better than nothing." He snaps his fingers to his palm. "Alright, let's make the call. We keep everyone on the bus until morning."

I nod in agreement. "Everyone should rack out. Get some sleep." I don't like the idea of Jane staying awake needlessly.

"Yeah. Plus, I don't want them on the roads this late," Akara explains.

"Last thing we need are some locals spotting them and starting shit. We'll take rotations to keep an eye on the engine."

At that, we return to the curb where everyone is sitting on the pavement. Wheat fields sprawl behind the street.

"You all should get back on the bus," I tell everyone.

Maximoff frowns deeply. "You want my family and SFO to get on the thing that's smoking and may catch on fire? That's a hard no."

I'm not really surprised Maximoff is the one to push back. He's always wanted to be in control of things he can't control on security. It won't even matter to him that SFO would be keeping an eye on the engine to make sure it *doesn't* catch on fire.

For Maximoff, he'd want the front row seat to the engine. All night. So I don't surface this point, just in case he offers himself for the task.

Akara puts his baseball cap on. "It's late. No one is coming until morning."

My focus remains on Maximoff. He's the one that I'll have to convince, and by his stubborn, firm expression, I'm positive he's not about to budge.

"Okay," I say. "We'll stay outside."

Silence blankets the darkness. The only noise comes from distant frogs croaking and crickets chirping.

I nod to Akara. Change of plans means we need to talk again. We return to the back of the bus and discuss logistics. Midway through our conversation, we overhear the famous ones and SFO discussing horror movie tropes.

"Virgins raise their hands," Oscar says.

I shake my head. Omega has become way too comfortable with the famous ones. I guess I have, too. In the name of camaraderie and morale, I've done my fair share of crossing lines. Being off-duty on this bus has put us all in different positions. It's why I don't say anything now. Don't shut this shit down.

Akara sidesteps to take a quick peek at the group.

I'm positive the only person raising their hand is Sulli.

"What? Really? I'm the only fucking one?" Sulli asks.

Akara stiffens a little, and I recognize that look. The one in his heated eye that says he's just *waiting* for the shitbag who's about to make fun of her.

"We love you most," Jane tells her. "But not because you're a virgin. That's just a coincidence."

Laughter fills the air and Akara's shoulders slacken.

I almost feel my lips rise at hearing Jane.

Lifting my eyes, I focus on Akara. I'd say he has feelings for Sulli, but he's just protective of her like a bodyguard should be.

Like I am with Jane.

That's it.

I zone out the rest of the conversation to take another look at the engine. A couple quick searches on the internet tell me that if I even *attempt* to fix this shit myself, I'll 100% nuke it.

Waiting. I don't love it.

I pocket my phone just as I hear *her* voice.

"Maybe we should put some distance between ourselves and the bus," Jane suggests. I quickly curve around the tail end of the bus, watching as she hops to her feet and doesn't even so much as pause before taking off down the dark, pitch-black road.

Maximoff follows her in a flash, but he has to jog to catch up.

As I join the others, Oscar passes me a flashlight, and the entire group trails behind those two.

But at a much slower pace.

Akara and I hang near the back, far enough away where we can process the situation together. "There's not much at the end of the street," Akara tells me, his eyes on his cell.

I'm looking at the maps on mine, but my focus is split.

Up ahead, I spot Jane. She's using her phone's flashlight to guide her, while Maximoff has some sort of small light clipped to a carabiner.

She's fine.

She's fine.

But I'm nowhere near her and we're on a deserted road in the fucking dark. I feel like I'm doing half my job.

"And we have a destination," Akara says, drawing my attention. "There's a small town. Mile out. Maybe something's open? We can grab a bite at least. Worst case scenario, it's a scenic tour of some random place."

He hands me his phone, so that I can see the spot on the map. It's tiny. Barely there. I search for any reviews or information about what's in the town. *No intel.* Everything is blank.

"Okay," I say. "It's better than doing nothing."

"Truth," Akara says, pocketing his phone after I pass it back.

My gaze travels to Jane. Only her back in view. She's set a good pace with Maximoff, so it shouldn't take long to reach the town. I keep my eyes on the back of her head for a long beat. It's different in the dark with random flashlights from SFO skimming her frame. Illuminating different parts of Jane at different intervals.

Her shoulders. Her hips. Her round…

Shouldn't be thinking that.

Shouldn't be looking there.

I'm not. I'm just fucking walking. My muscles tense. I don't like walking behind her right now. "I'm going to tell Jane the plan," I say to Akara. She should know the destination since she's leading the pack.

He nods to me, his focus split too. But I don't check to see what he's looking at. I make my way ahead, passing Charlie and Beckett and Sulli. Passing Donnelly, Oscar, and Farrow.

Jane and Maximoff are so far out front that I have to pick up my pace to an almost-jog. I only slow when I near.

A couple feet behind Jane, I can finally hear her voice.

"Oh yes, in your life, bodyguard duties include giving head," she says to Maximoff. "God, could you even imagine? What would I say? *Hello Mr. Moretti, I'm in need of some oral assistance. Would you be so kind to spread my knees?*"

My pulse flatlines.

She didn't just say that.

I force my eyes not to widen in raw shock.

Before this goes more sideways, I should alert them that I'm right fucking here.

I clear my throat. "Maximoff," I say. *Don't even fucking think about what she just said. Don't fucking do it.*

Maximoff and Jane freeze in place. Their backs still to me.

In their silence, her words are running over and over through my brain. *Would you be so kind to spread my knees?* My muscles are taut rubber bands. Breath imprisoned in my lungs. Eyes not shifting. Features not changing.

But I'm thinking things I shouldn't.

She wants me to go down on her?

She'd ask me to?

I slam those questions in drawers. *Ship them off.*

I'm trying.

My pulse thumps in my neck. My cock almost twitches.

I've done a damn good job of not daydreaming about my head between her thighs. There are other vivid imaginations I've conjured, but that one, that one is new and it's going to send me to hell. One-way ticket. No return.

Jane curses in French before spinning on her heels to face me. Maximoff follows suit.

"Yeah?" Maximoff asks. His gaze wanders past me, probably to see just how far back everyone else is.

I keep my attention on him. *Don't look at her.* It'll make this exponentially worse. For both of us.

These past months on the tour bus have been sexually frustrating for Jane *and* me. She hasn't had her…friend-with-benefits around to satisfy her—not that I'm complaining. I'm selfishly glad I don't have to stand outside the door while they fuck in a hotel room.

But without a sexual release, we're both riding a thin line. Not now—I'm not even glancing her way—but over the course of this tour, I keep drifting to her. Her gaze has lingered on me. I'd like to think it's out of camaraderie. We're the horniest people on this damn bus, so we keep looking at each other knowingly. Solidarity. That shit.

But hearing her say what she just said about *me* and *her* together—it's a new level.

Still, I don't look at her now. I just don't want to embarrass her further.

Maybe she won't ever know I heard what she said.

I tell Maximoff, "There's a small town a mile up. We're all heading that way."

"Alright, sounds good."

"Thatcher," Jane greets. She barely pauses. "I'm just going to come out and ask. Did you hear what we were talking about?"

Hello Mr. Moretti, I'm in need of some oral assistance. Would you be so kind to spread my knees?

Yeah…I'm never forgetting that one.

My face sets to stone. I finally glance down to her, and I focus on two words. Just two. That's all I need to say. "I did."

She crosses her arms, not breaking eye contact. Confidence fuels every cell in her body, and I'm cementing my feet into the ground. I can't move towards her, even if every part of me wants to fill this need for her.

"And?" she asks me. I love how she's not backing down from this, even though her cheeks are flushed from embarrassed heat.

A similar warmth spreads through me.

Even as the wind rolls through, I'm hot as all hell. I unroll the sleeve to my red flannel shirt.

And? Her question blisters in the air.

And?

And…I want to tell her I'll bring her to safety and fulfill all her sexual requests. Better than any other man would. I'll drop to my knees right now. I'll roll down her panties and press my mouth between her legs. I'll spread her open.

I'll lick her.

I'll eat her out until her thighs are trembling in my grip and she's crying for more.

But I can't say any of that.

Because it's wildly fucking *inappropriate*.

Words form in my head—words I don't mean but I have to say. "And if you need any kind of oral assistance," I tell her while my ribs contract around my lungs, "then I can call someone for you. Nate or—"

"I can make my own phone calls, thank you," she says breezily. "That's all." She rotates on the tip of her toes, facing forward, away from me.

I feel winded. What in the fuck? I offered to call Nate for her. So that *he* could give her head. I hate that those words were even in my vocabulary, and yet, I'd do just about anything to please her. Even if it can't be me.

And it definitely can't.

I glance to Maximoff. "You good?"

He nods. "Yeah."

I hesitate for a beat, thinking maybe I should say something else to her. Make sure she's okay. But I've fucked it too much tonight. Let's not test the fates anymore.

So I leave.

Every step away from her, I keep thinking about what she said.

What I said.

What was left unsaid.

I know I did the right thing by offering to call someone else to fuck her, but this is one of those times where being right feels like complete, utter shit.

WANT MORE BONUS SCENES LIKE ORAL ASSISTANCE?

Join Krista & Becca's Patreon at www.patreon.com/kbritchie

Joining Krista & Becca's Patreon will give you access to all previously posted bonus scenes. Plus new content and extras release every month! Patreon is a great place for readers who love behind-the-scenes posts and all the extra goodies.

CONNECT WITH KRISTA & BECCA
www.kbritchie.com
www.facebook.com/KBRitchie
www.instagram.com/kbmritchie

ACKNOWLEDGMENTS

Usually, our acknowledgments are filled with a list of people we need to thank and all the outpouring of gratitude to the people who made this book possible. Writing Tangled Like Us was different, and so this section is also going to be a little different, too.

Each of our books has a piece of ourselves in them. Personal, always. Even if we don't come out and publicly say what specific part came from our lives, it's there. Tangled Like Us has so much of ourselves in it. But the most important—it has our family. Our big, loud and loving Italian-American family.

It has our grandma.

Her spirit and love exists inside of Thatcher's grandma. When we were writing Tangled Like Us, we talked with our Grandma Lou about her childhood and the Italian she grew up with in her home. Our long conversations discussing how to pronounce words like *gabbadost'* and *cumare*, and how her mom traveled to America alone at twelve-years-old with jewelry sewn into her panties will be some of the things we cherish most about writing this book.

We didn't expect her passing. It came suddenly and unexpectedly while we were finishing the last part of Tangled, and it rocked our world to its core. One of our last conversations with her was talking about the cornic' and how it would play an important role in the story.

Her excitement and enthusiasm over this book, which she never read but knew would exist, was such a fuel for us. She would say, "*my* Italian will be in the book, right?" Yes. Your Italian, Grandma, is in this book. She never believed that the way she spoke was "correct" because it was a broken Italian that those in Italy wouldn't understand. But the Italian-American immigrant language is so very special and close to our hearts. It's what we heard growing up, and since we didn't know any other Italians in the area, it felt like only our families understood the words.

Our grandma was a light in the world. Now she's a spirit in the sky, but she has impacted so many people with her love and generosity. And when our mom needed her when we were born, she packed up her bags and traveled hundreds of miles to be with our mom. Without hesitation.

So this is our very long-winded but necessary way to express our gratitude and thanks to our grandma for being a part of this novel. A part of our lives. For providing us so much love and wisdom and laughter, and for teaching us so much about the world and our Italian culture.

This was one of the most difficult books we had to finish—we weren't sure if we would make it—but we did. For her. And we love you, Grandma, so tremendously. Thank you from the bottom of our hearts.

The other person that needs a special thanks is our mom.

Mom – Thank you for reading and editing this book under our intense deadline and during a time where it couldn't be an easy read. We will forever be grateful for all you do for us. We are so lucky to be raised by such a remarkable woman, and every day we're blessed you're in our life. We always refer to you as our very own Rose Calloway. But you are that and more.

Thank you for packing up your bags and running to us when we needed you most. Without hesitation.

Thank you.

MORE THANKS

To Marie – Thank you for the wonderful French translations. You are incredible and talented beyond belief and we're so very lucky to have your touch on this book.

To Jenn and Lanie – Thank you for your continued friendship that we cherish so dearly and all the work you both put into the Fizzle Force FB Group. You two are magical gems.

To our agent, Kimberly – Thank you for everything you do and for finding this book a home in audio. We know all the audiobook lovers thank you, too.

To the Fizzle Force – Thank you for being a bright light and for your loving support. We're awed at your love for ours books and our words.

To the patrons from our Patreon – Thank you for changing our lives and wanting more content from this world. Our creative process has never been more full of love and life, and that's all thanks to all of you.

To our loving family – Thank you for your input and suggestions on all things Italian-American. For your unwavering love and support. For our aunts, who will undoubtedly be reading this, we hope we did you proud.

PRONUNCIATION GLOSSARY

The Italian used in this book is an Italian-American language developed by Italian immigrants. It is an incomplete language and uses Italian, English, or both. Different Italians speak different dialects in certain areas, and what is used in the Like Us series is prominent on the East Coast. Words may vary in pronunciation and spelling in different communities.

agita: pronounced AA-jih-tuh (Origin: acidità)

braggiol': pronounced BRAAJH-oel (Origin: bracciole)

cornic': pronounced kor-neek (Origin: cornicello)

cumare: pronounced KOO-mar (Origin: comare)

gabbadost': pronounced gaa-baa-dahst (Origin: capa dura/capa tosta)

gomesegiam'?: pronounced go-maa-say-GYAM
(Origin: come si chiama?)

ma che bell': pronounced maa-KAY-bell (Origin: ma che bella)

maliocch': pronounced maal-YOAK (Origin: malocchio)

mannaggia: pronounced MAA-NAA-juh
(Origin: male ne aggia/ male ne abbia)

mapeen: pronounced maa-PEEN (Origin: moppina)

menzamenz: pronounced mehnz-AA-mehnz (Origin: mezza mezza)

scustamad': pronounced skoo-stoo-MAAD (Origin: scostumato)

statazitt'!: pronounced stah-tuh-ZEET (Origin: stai zitto)

vaffangul': pronounced VAA-faan-GOOL (Origin: vai a fare in culo)

veni qua: pronounced veh-nee-kwaa (Origin: vieni qui)